A DANGEROUS BUSINESS

I was born to do this, Matti thought. I want to do this forever.

"Optronics have acquired the targets … targets positively identified," Jaska said, "and designated. Ready to engage."

"Roger," Matti said. "Weapons free."

"Weapons free," Jaska responded. "Cannons to auto, threat plot is green, no hostile activity. Dumb bastards have shut down."

Dumb is right, Matti murmured under his breath, the adrenaline beginning to pump. *They won't know we're here until it's too late.*

Bitsa closed in, the ground-attack lander moving so fast that the appalling noise from its two main engines was unable to keep up. Matti spotted the two orbital shuttles he and Jaska had come so far to destroy: two squat black shapes off to the left-hand side of the airstrip, rock steady in the lander's holocam. An instant later, *Bitsa's* quadruple 30-millimeter cannons opened up; the lander shuddered as hypervelocity shells ripped into the targets, the ground around them torn and blasted into clouds of dust and pulverized rock. Then they were past. Matti chopped the power and lifted the nose sharply to aerobrake *Bitsa*, stressing the foamalloy wings up into sharp curves as the lander's speed bled off, wingtips stabbing back and up into a sky of palest blue. He banked the craft and let the speed decay to give the cannons time to finish the job, holding the turn until the two shuttles reappeared on the nose before steadying *Bitsa* for its second pass.

Cannon shells tore at the shuttles. Belatedly, one returned fire, but *Bitsa*'s armored hull shrugged off the pulsed lasers. Just as Matti began to wonder how much more damage the shuttles could absorb, first one and then the second erupted in brutal explosions that punched massive balls of pure energy into the air as their fusion plants lost containment, the shock waves tossing *Bitsa* into a violent, plunging roll to starboard that had Matti fighting for control.

"Shiiiiit," he hissed as he fought *Bitsa*'s massive bulk back to level, trying to forget the awful sight of a wingtip screwing vortices of dust out of the ground. *There you have it*, he thought as *Bitsa* steadied. *Sometimes the difference between life and death is only a couple of meters.*

VENDETTA

Books 1 to 4 of the Helfort's War series are published in the United States by Del Rey Books, an imprint of the Random House Publishing Group, a division of Random House Inc., New York.

THE GUILD WAR BOOK 1: VENDETTA is a work of fiction.

Names, characters, places, incidents, and persons are the products of the
author's imagination or are used fictitiously. Any resemblance to actual
names, characters, places, incidents, or persons alive or dead
is entirely coincidental.

Cover Art Copyright © Chris McGrath 2012
Cover Design Copyright © Alessio De Vecchi 2012
E-Book production by 52 Novels

ISBN: 978-0-9872613-3-5

VENDETTA

The Guild War
Book One

Graham Sharp Paul

For Vicki

Acknowledgments

My thanks to Tara Wynne and Liz Scheier for their support, encouragement and advice.

PROLOGUE

"No, don't!" the woman screamed. "Please don't."

The man's fist was huge, a tightly packed mass of bone, muscle, and sinew. For a moment it hung, poised over the woman; she stared up at it, shocked, disbelieving.

"No, don't!" she screamed again. "Stop! I'm sorry. I won't—"

"Shut your mouth, you lying whore," the man snarled, and his fist exploded toward the woman's face, a lethal weapon powered by rage and fear and self-loathing. Eyes wide in terror, the woman flinched as death drove into her face, her head turning aside a fraction, just enough to turn the killer punch into a blow that shattered her cheek and jaw before skidding off her temple to smash into the wall, its awful force exhausted in a mass of broken bones and ripped sinews.

Agony exploded up the man's arm; the room filled with his tormented shrieks. Ruined fist cradled to his chest, he reeled back, the anger drowned by waves of agony that forced him to his knees, head down, as he fought to regain control.

When the pain finally eased, he lifted his head to look at the woman.

"What have I done?" he whispered, staring at her crumpled body. His head dropped again. "What have I done?"

1

Out on the street, the music was loud. Its heavy bass beat promised a night rich with opportunity. The excited crush milling around the door to the Warehouse Club was pulsating in anticipation.

"It's going to be great, Samira, just so great," Nat Qaaliba squealed as the mobibot pulled up. "I told Jezza and Kolo to expect the best night of their short, sad lives. And you know what? They believed me!"

"Nat!" Samira Anders protested, following her out of the mobibot and into the crowd. "You might think Jezza's the guy for you, and maybe he is," she said, "but Kolo is not for me. He is such a loser, and I don't like him anyway. I'm only doing this because you asked me to."

"And so you should, 'cause that's what best friends are for," Nat declared, dismissing Samira's objections with an airy wave of her hand. "I'd do the same for you, and you know it. Look, when I've hooked up with Jezza, you can ditch Kolo. Then you can find someone better or you can try the Cave. It'll still be kicking."

"Gee, thanks, Nat." Samira sighed. "It's so good to know you care. What a great evening I'm in for: fighting off Kolo while I watch you slobber all over Jezza. Ecchh!"

"Hey!"

"Yeah, yeah. More to the point, have you got the stim-tabs? Thanks to Judge Tamsin Tightbuttocks, I'm going to be scanned on the way in."

"Yeah, I've got some. But are you sure you want them? You've been clean for weeks now."

"Do I want them? Are you kidding? Shit, yes, I want them. I'm in the mood to party, and no judge with a stick up her ass is going to stop me."

Nat shook her head. "It's your call, even if it's a really dumb one. If the police nail you …"

"They won't, and you're getting boring, so shut it. Hey! How're my tats?"

Nat glanced at Samira's nanocrystal tattoos, a dusting of tiny lights splashed across her cheekbones, a coruscating smear that danced up and down the spectrum in sync with her mood. "Great," she sniffed. "They look just great."

"So they should," Samira said, ignoring the sniff. Her tattoos were a sore point with Nat. "They cost me a fortune, every cent of which I earned, Natalie Qaaliba."

"Whatever."

"Thank you so much, Nat. Come on, move your ass. I need a stimtab and a shot—like now."

Black hair thrashing, Samira Anders threw her head back; piercing blue eyes staring and mouth open wide, she howled out an ululating scream that pulsed in time to the waves of raw energy beating down from overhead flatspeakers. Around her a mob of heaving humanity packed shoulder to shoulder followed suit, goaded into a stimtab-fueled frenzy by the hard-pounding music.

Nat and Jezza were long gone—Samira had no idea where to, not that she cared—and the hapless Kolo had been told to bug off, leaving her lost in a world of her own, her body driven on and on and on by an unstoppable sense of power. Her head went back again. "Don't try and stop me, you baaaaastaaards," she screamed. "Don't try and stop me, because Samira … Anders … is … un … fucking … stoppable!"

Trooper Djamani stretched in a futile attempt to ease the knots out of her back. It had been a long, slow shift, and—not for the first time—she wondered why she'd ever agreed to leave Old Earth to come to Klimath with that asshole of a husband of hers.

Talk about mistakes, she thought. *They don't come much bigger.*

Klimath, the man had said, eyes sparkling with excitement, was the place for them: one of the Rogue Planets and a place blessed with a light-handed government, a place groaning with opportunities, a place to grow rich and live well.

She'd believed him, lovelorn idiot that she was, only to find when she arrived that Klimath was a wreck struggling to get back on its feet after a short but brutal civil war.

Six months later, she'd woken up to find the son of a bitch gone; the last she'd heard, he had taken off for Karleon-IV, an even bigger shithole than Klimath, taking with him some slut he'd met at the gym and every last cent in their joint account.

Cop or not, if she ever caught up with the man, she was going to rip his smooth-talking tongue out and jam it up his ass.

She lifted her head to look up at the night sky, wondering if she'd ever save up enough money to return home. She sighed. She knew the answer to that question: never, not on a police trooper's pay. Old Earth was more than two thousand light-years away, and the starship fares were ruinously expensive, more than fifty times the migrant fare she and the asshole had paid to get to Klimath.

So, while the rest of the human race was living in the twenty-third century, where was she? Marooned on a planet doomed never to break out of the twenty-first, or so it seemed to her jaundiced eye.

The radio dragged her back to reality. "67-Bravo, Control. Reports of a disturbance outside the Warehouse, corner Merrick and Christakos. Can you take it?"

Trooper Djamani swore under her breath; better a long, slow night than dealing with the Warehouse and its brain-fried patrons. Aggravation was all the Bellingen police department ever got from the bloody place. "Show me responding," she replied, trying not to sound too grumpy.

She swore some more as she sent her cruiser on its way. Merrick and Christakos were at the heart of Bellingen's club district, and that always meant trouble of the worst sort at closing time: kids, lots of them, all fired up on alcohol and stimtabs. *The little bastards*, she thought moodily, *all seething hormones and not one speck of common sense.*

Cruiser 67-Bravo turned onto Merrick. "Oh, shit," she murmured as she scanned the scene. The wave of people who had been pushed out when the Warehouse closed had spilled onto the street, the brawl at its heart escalating as new fighters joined in, goaded on by the mob.

When her repeated warnings to disperse or be arrested were ignored, Trooper Djamani's patience ran out. Punching buttons, she deployed 67-Bravo's squad of crowdbots. Squat and ugly, the bots fanned out into a wedge before plowing through the crowd to head directly for the fight, loudspeakers bellowing instructions to step aside, any laggards shoved aside with mindless efficiency, hyperslip skins frustrating those dumb enough to try to push the bots away. In only a matter of seconds, the wedge had punched through to the mob's heart. Trooper Djamani's fingers danced across her control console as she designated the priority targets for her bots; one by one, they pulled fighters out of the melee with mindless efficiency, then plasticuffed them and dropped them to the ground before moving on to the next, any resistance crushed by a short, sharp burst from a neural stunner.

As finger and thumb snuff out a candle, so Djamani's bots snuffed out the brawl; it was over before many in the crowd realized what was happening. Leaving the trussed bodies to writhe and scream out their frustration and anger, Djamani's bots moved the crowd on, herding it away down the street, harassing the mob until it disintegrated into a melee fleeing into the night.

Now that's how it's done, Djamani said to herself, nodding her satisfaction as she keyed her mike. "Control, 67-Bravo. Disturbance is under control. I have, let me see … sixteen in custody. Request bodybot."

"Sixteen in custody, understood. Bodybot is on its way, 67-Bravo."

"Roger that. Thanks."

Djamani climbed out of the air-conditioned comfort of her cruiser, cursing the night air as it enveloped her in a thick, damp blanket that started the sweat trickling down her face and neck. She was from the far north of Old Earth and had always hated Bellingen's unremittingly hot, muggy climate.

She walked over to where her crowdbots waited in a protective circle around trussed bodies. "Right," she shouted. "Hands up anyone who thinks they've been wrongly arrested. Anybody … no?"

Djamani laughed at her own joke—she always did, even if the joke was old and tired—and got to work. Ignoring the invective, she made sure none of the kids was going to die on her, then checked their identities, made the formal arrests, and read them their rights.

The bodybot arrived as she was uploading the arrest files back to base. "Evening, Jacqui," the trooper in charge called out, climbing down from the cab.

"Well, well, well, if it isn't Trooper Nikolai Bertoni," Djamani called. "Sorry I had to get your big fat ass out of bed."

"The hell you are!" Bertoni said, looking around at the carnage. "Only sixteen tonight?" he went on, waving a hand across the bodies. "You taking it easy or what?"

"Shit, no," Djamani said, shaking her head, "I'm just ruthlessly efficient. Come on, give me a hand."

Together, the troopers manhandled bodies into the bodybot, Djamani swearing sotto voce throughout as the sweat started to trickle down her back in earnest. She swore some more as she pushed the last of them—Samira Anders, according to her ID, and barely eighteen, her face dominated by intense blue eyes that burned with rage—into the cage, feet flailing in a vain attempt to delay the inevitable.

"I hope they send you down, sugar," Djamani said, "because this is the second time I've arrested you, and that's twice too often. Not that those useless bastard judges will; they never bloody well do."

7

"Right, Nik, that's it," she said, scanning the area to make sure they had everyone. "Off you go. I'm going to talk to the scumbags who run the Warehouse Club … again."

Bertoni shook his head. "You're wasting your time, girlie."

"I know; nothing's ever their damn fault."

"No, it's not. See ya, Jacqui."

"Not tonight, I hope."

"Get out!"

"Take me home, Dad," Samira Anders said, her voice slurred by the residual effects of too many stimtabs and too much alcohol. "I don't want to—"

"I don't care what you want," Matti Anders said, his face red with anger. "When you moved out, I told you there was no coming back. It was your decision to live in a rat hole with your shithead friends, so that's exactly what you're going to do."

"But I don't feel so good."

"I'm not interested. Now get out before I kick you out."

"You'd like that, wouldn't you?" Samira snarled. "You'd like to kick me out. Why do you think I left home? Because I was sick of the way you kept beating the crap out of me all the time. You're damn lucky I didn't press charges the last time you put me in hospital, you bastard."

"Get out, now!" Matti Anders shouted.

"Screw you," Samira mumbled as she opened the mobibot's door and staggered out.

"Don't push me, Samira, or I'll make you wish you hadn't."

"Whatever."

"I'll be back at nine to pick you up, so be ready. Now is not the time to piss the police off by turning up late for the judge."

"Late for the judge?" Samira snorted dismissively. "Screw her too."

"Listen to me, Samira! You're out of chances. You're damn lucky they only charged you with public drunkenness and creating a disturbance. Throwing that punch at Sergeant Paulescu wasn't smart."

"I barely touched her."

"Doesn't matter. You could have been charged with assault."

"Yeah, yeah. Like I give a shit."

"You should. The cops won't cut you any slack the next time you step out of line. Nine o'clock, Samira, and don't be late or I will kick your useless butt," Matti called as Samira slammed the door in his face.

"Asshole," Samira screamed as the mobibot pulled away.

"Bloody judges," Matti said, banging the door open and pushing Samira inside. "That's all I need, having you back home."

"If it makes you feel any better," Samira said, "I'm not happy about it either."

"I'm warning you," Matti snapped. "You put one foot wrong and I'm throwing you back to the police. Do you understand what that means?"

"Piss off, Dad. I know what my bail conditions are."

Matti stepped back, his face mottled red with anger. "Get out of my sight," he hissed. "I don't want to see you again today. I've had all I can take from you."

"Don't worry, the feeling's mutual," Samira shouted as she headed for the kitchen, all too aware of the risks she ran every time she pushed her father too hard. "By the way, Dad," she called over her shoulder when she was safely out of his reach, "I want to talk about the business tomorrow."

Samira slammed the kitchen door on Matti Anders, leaving him speechless with rage, fists clenching and unclenching as he fought to keep control.

2

"Don't walk away from me, Samira. I haven't finished yet!"

"Go fuck yourself."

"And watch your language, young lady!" Matti Anders shouted.

"Don't you 'young lady' me!" Samira Anders spit, spinning on her heel so fast that her shoulder-length black hair fanned out away from a face flushed red with anger. Piercing blue eyes narrowed, she stamped her frustration into the dust. "All I get from you is the same old bullshit. You never give me a proper answer. Never!"

"Yes, I do," Matti snapped. "A hundred times, and my answer's the same: No! You're only eighteen. You're too inexperienced, you're too damn mouthy to go on operations, and that's the end of it."

"Crap! You were a year younger than me when Granddad took you on your first mission, and you hadn't even joined the military. A full year younger!"

"That was different."

"Oh, really? Come on, Dad. The age thing won't wash, and you know it. I've finished school, and I don't want to do anything else; you know that. As for being too inexperienced, how am I ever going to get the experience sitting on my butt?

Besides, I'm a better systems operator than Uncle Jaska. Every time we go head to head in the simulator, I whip his ass. He won't take me on anymore. And my command pilot rating is almost as good as yours," she added, flashing a smug, self-satisfied grin.

"I wish I'd never agreed to you getting your lander license," Matti said. "That was the worst damn mistake I ever made … that and letting you fly *Bitsa* solo." He shook his head. "What the hell was I thinking?"

"I got my command pilot's qualification first time, Dad, remember? I wanted that license, and I made sure I got it. I didn't let you down, did I?"

"No, no, you didn't," Matti said with a grudging nod, "but a license is just a bit of fancy paper to hang on the wall. It doesn't count for shit when people start firing cannon shells at you. Besides, after what happened last night, how the hell can I trust you?"

"Dad! I've said sorry. I didn't mean to get into that fight; it just happened."

"Oh, really? And the alcohol and stimtabs had nothing to do with it, then? Why the judge hasn't kept you locked up, I do not know. I would have."

"Gee, thanks, Dad. Good to know I can count on you."

"Watch it, Samira." Matti paused to take a deep breath. "Like I say, the fact that you ended up in a fight at all proves I can't trust you."

"That's just another of your piss-weak excuses," Samira said. "You don't get it, do you?"

"What?" Matti demanded. "What don't I get?"

"I'm bored shitless, Dad. I know exactly what I want to do with my life; why can't you see that? It's time for me to join the business. You know I can do the job. How many more sims do I have to do to prove that?"

"There's more to this business than being good in the simulator, one hell of a lot more. And I don't care how smart you are; you cannot take Jaska's place on this or any other mission and you never will. If you really want to be a lander pilot, go join the KDF; they'll—"

"Join the Klimath Defense Force?" Samira snorted. "You've got to be joking! They're a bunch of clowns. Marching around, saluting, fancy uniforms, yes sir, no sir, and all the rest of that military bullshit? Forget it. Anyway, when did they last do anything? They haven't seen combat since the civil war."

"Combat?" Matti said, his voice rising to a half shout. "Is that what you want? Combat? You have no idea what you're talking about, Samira, none at all."

"You've got that right," she said, her face soured by a sullen scowl. "How could I know? You won't let me fly missions."

"Listen to me, Samira. Simulators teach you nothing about the real world, about death, how it feels to kill someone, to be so terrified you can barely breathe, the fear so bad all you want to do is run away and hide. Combat is a bloody business. It still frightens me, and I've been doing it a long time. Kill or be killed, Samira; that's what combat is about. You ready for that? No, how can you be? Everything you know comes from time in the simulator. Please," he continued, his voice softening, "please … give me a break. We're due to fly out tonight, and I've a lot to do before we go."

"Dad, I—"

"Enough, Samira!" Matti Anders turned and started to walk away. "No more, please."

"I wish Mom was still alive." Samira yelled. "She'd say it was okay; I know she would."

Matti spun around, his right hand coming up, balling into a fist. Samira flinched, instinctively stepping back, her hands going up to ward her father off; it had been many years since he had last hurt her, but she had never forgotten the pain and humiliation.

"You have no idea what she'd—" Matti stopped. His hand opened, and a finger stabbed out, puncturing the air with each word. "Don't bring your mother into this, you hear me!" he shouted. "Never, or I'll kick your ass. You got that?"

"Yes, Dad," Samira replied with a scowl, puzzled as always by her father's explosive reaction to any mention of her mother. She wished she knew why; she had made the mistake of asking once. She had never asked again; she could still feel the stinging pain from his open palm slamming across her face and shoulders again and again and again, his face red with fury.

"I hope so," Matti growled. "Now piss off and leave me alone. I've got work to do even if you don't."

You are a complete asshole, Samira murmured under her breath. She glared after her father as he stamped his way up the ladder into a battered ground-attack lander, a brutally ugly slab-sided machine that towered a good fifteen meters over her, heat from the morning sun rising off its scarred ceramsteel armor in shimmers of twisting air blown away on the wind.

The family had christened it *Bitsa* because of the way pieces kept dropping off its overworked frame—how the damn thing stayed airborne was a complete mystery to her—and Samira loved every dent and scratch.

The cargo-bay access door slammed shut behind Matti Anders, as if to emphasize his unshakeable determination not to let her take her rightful place onboard.

"Why?" she shouted at the lander's brooding mass. "Why won't you let me do my bit? Stubborn cantankerous miserable old bastard!"

A sudden rage flared, hot and explosive. Samira booted a rock into *Bitsa*'s side armor, a vicious full-bodied kick that bounced the stone off timeworn ceramsteel with a metallic *plink* before it dropped uselessly into the dust. *Just like arguing with her father*, Samira thought, her anger gone as quickly as it had come, *a complete waste of time*. She should talk to Uncle Jaska. At least he understood her, and he didn't think she was too young to be *Bitsa*'s systems operator. Any time you want my seat, you can have it, he would say before adding—as he always did—that he was too old and too tired to enjoy being shot at by the Rogue Worlds' criminal classes.

Honestly, she thought, *why was talking to Uncle Jaska so easy and talking to her father so difficult?*

She'd re-run the sim of the most dangerous mission her father had ever done, she decided. It was a doozy, a mission she had never been able to complete without having *Bitsa* blown out from under her. *If you can use an antiquated attack lander to blast a Lassarian privateer out of low earth orbit*, she said to herself, *then so can I.*

And when I do, she added, *maybe then you'll give me my chance.*

With newfound determination, she set off for the simulator.

Jaska Anders had watched the confrontation from *Bitsa*'s maintenance shop, a hardened ceramcrete shelter arching high enough to hold two heavy landers, where he and Buqisi Karua had been working on a recalcitrant hydraulic pump. He straightened up, wincing as his back protested the hours spent hunched over broken equipment.

The fights between Matti and Samira were weekly events, and it was always a relief to see them end without Matti losing it. The thought that the man might do to Samira what he had done to so many others haunted Jaska's every waking moment.

"Hey, Jaska! Stop daydreaming; this damn pump's not going to fix itself." Buqisi's protest snapped Jaska back to reality.

"Sorry, Buq," he said. "Just watching the latest bust-up. I wish Matti would cut Samira a bit more slack."

"You worry too much. Samira will be fine."

"I'm not sure about that. And anyway, why shouldn't I worry? That girl's the closest thing I'll ever have to a daughter."

"I know she is," Buqisi said, walking over, "but you still worry too much,"

"She pushes Matti pretty hard. I'm afraid that one day he'll …" Jaska's voice trailed away.

"Yeah. And you're right. She needs to be careful."

"She does." Jaska nodded. "She knows how to punch his buttons. I worry she's going to push too hard, tip him over the edge."

"We all know what Matti's capable of, but somehow I don't think he would lose it with Samira, not after what he did—"

"Don't!" Jaska snapped. "Don't say it; don't even think it."

"Sorry, Jaska," Buqisi said. "You know what?" she said, breaking the long silence that followed.

"What?"

"As long as I live, I'll never understand that girl."

"Nor me," Jaska said, "but I do know where she's going in such a hurry."

"Ah, let me guess," Buq said, tapping her lips with a forefinger. "It's Friday afternoon, so that means … yes, self-defense class, then two hours with Nat Qaaliba planning the weekend's fun and games, another two hours getting dressed to go out, and then on to one of those crappy clubs in town. Right?"

"You are." Jaska laughed. "That girl's nothing if not predictable."

"She is. I just hope she doesn't get herself arrested again."

"Now, that is something to worry about," Jaska said. "Her social life is getting less social and more criminal by the day."

"It is. But she'll learn. We did."

"Took us a while, though," Jaska said with a rueful smile.

"Kids are kids, Jaska. We can talk until we're blue in the face, and Samira won't hear a damn word. The way she's going, it's going to take a miracle to keep her out of jail, and that may be just the lesson she needs."

"I wish Matti understood that. And I wish he understood how badly she wants to be part of the business."

"He doesn't, and he never will."

"No," Jaska said, shaking his head. "Not that Samira has any idea of what it's like being a gun for hire."

"Did you, Jaska?" Buqisi demanded. "No, you damn well didn't. Give the girl a break. She's an adult now; she has the right to make her own decisions. She's known what she's wanted to do for years. If she wants in, let her in. It's the only way to find out whether it's what she really wants."

"I know, I know. And you can't blame her. Her whole life has revolved around Matti, and his life has revolved around the business. I don't think they ever talked about much else. Guess what she told me once."

"What?"

"That she lies awake nights when her dad's away on a mission, wondering how things are going, hoping he gets back okay, wishing she could be with him to make sure things go well."

"Let me guess," Buqisi said. "Matti has no idea?"

"No, none. A rock has more empathy. I asked him once if he worried about leaving Samira. He said no, why would he when she had the housekeeper to talk to?"

"The housekeeper? How many of those have there been over the years?"

"Too many; more than I can remember."

"That damn temper of his."

"Yeah. But I think she'll be okay. Might take a while, but she'll turn out good. She's got her mother's smarts and toughness."

"Her mother was a good woman; I think Samira is too."

"She is. We're lucky she didn't inherit Matti's temper."

Buqisi grinned. "One's enough, eh?"

"Oh, yes," Jaska said.

"Right, enough of that," Buqisi said, all business. "Time to get back to that pump."

"Yeah, yeah. Who made you the boss?"

"Jaska! In my workshop I'm the boss, and you know it."

"Sadly, Buq," Jaska said with a sigh, "that is the truth, and I do know it."

"I would hope so. Come on, then; Matti's going to kick my ass if the bloody thing isn't back in *Bitsa* soon."

"Pity you can't fix my back while you're at it," Jaska grumbled as he followed Buq back into the workshop, trying in vain to stretch the kinks out of a back damaged by a single fragment from a 40-millimeter cannon shell, the injury not helped by too many hours spent jammed into a combat spacesuit.

"Yup, I think that's it," Buqisi said, stepping back, her eyes scanning *Bitsa*'s hull to make sure everything was buttoned up. "I've got no idea how, but the old girl is ready."

"I was beginning to wonder if we'd be able to get away," Jaska said as the pair walked back to the workshop, the evening sun bathing the maintenance shop in a golden yellow light that made the timeworn ceramcrete structure look almost new. "That damn pump was a bitch."

"I'll order a replacement. We can't go on stripping it out after every mission, and anyway, it's pretty much had it."

"Matti won't like that. Pumps are expensive."

"When it comes to spare parts for a lander as old as that one—" Buqisi waved a dismissive hand in *Bitsa*'s direction. "—everything's expensive. I'll go down and talk to old man Kaitana, see what I can do."

"That old crook? Good luck."

"Good luck?" Buqisi smiled to reveal teeth startlingly white against skin so dark that it was almost black. "Don't need good luck. That old crook owes me."

"He still screws us, though."

"Yeah, he does, just not as badly as he could. You want a beer, Jaska?" she asked, reaching into a battered fridge.

"Nah. Too close to takeoff."

"Come on! You can always slap on a detox patch."

"No thanks."

"Suit yourself," Buqisi said, ripping open the can and draining the contents in one swallow. Tossing the empty over her shoulder in the general direction of the recycling bin, she reached back into the fridge to pull out a second. "You always were one for the rules."

"Kept me alive all these years, Buq, so I'm not going to change things now. I intend to live long enough to enjoy my retirement."

"Which won't happen unless you stop flying missions."

"I will."

"Yeah, yeah. So you say, Jaska. You never do, though."

A long silence followed, the only sound a soft creaking as the ceramcrete overhead started to give up the day's heat, cooled by the evening air.

"No, I don't," Jaska whispered softly. "No, I don't."

And he wouldn't, not until Matti allowed Samira to take over from him. Samira might be young and out of control, but from the moment she'd taken *Bitsa*'s controls for the first time, she had known what she wanted to do with her life. If he quit, Matti would find himself another systems operator, and that would spell the end of Samira's ambitions.

He might only be Samira's great-uncle, but she was like a daughter to him, and what she wanted from life mattered. If he quit, he would be betraying her, and that he would never do.

3

A pink smear announced the new day, faint and uncertain at first, then strengthening through red, then gold, then yellow as the rising sun scoured night from the eastern sky. The extravagant display did not impress Konrad Onuku; every dawn on Kapsos-VII was the same, and he had seen too many of them.

Onuku cursed under his breath and spit into the dust. A cloudless sky promised another hot day, the latest in an unending succession of hot days. One week; that was all this operation was supposed to take: one week. And here they were, into the third week with no end in sight. Onuku spit again; he scanned the ground in front of his position for the umpteenth time. He saw nothing except a rock-strewn expanse of dirt that dropped away from the old mining base down to a dry creek bed. It looked the same as it did the day they brought the girl here; he wondered why he stood watch.

Nobody in his right mind would come anywhere near the place. Kapsos-VII was a long-forgotten world: dry and dusty, a planet rich with broken promises, misspent money, lost years, a planet that crushed hope as easily as boots crushed bugs. The last prospectors had given up almost a century ago, leaving the ball of rock and wind-driven sand to its own devices, a worthless speck, one of millions in the immensity of space, a monument to failure and forgotten all the sooner because of it.

Onuku had hated Kapsos-VII the minute the down-shuttle had dumped him dirtside.

Rubbing the dust from his eyes, he shifted his optronics down into infrared and then up to ultraviolet and back again; it made no difference. He had seen everything there was to see a thousand times. It never changed.

A soft scuffing from behind him broke what little concentration he had left; he did not bother to turn around. Why would he? It was 05:55, and for all the man's faults—and they were many—Clem Bartels was always punctual. With a muffled curse, Onuku's relief eased his way under the chromaflaged canopy over the observation post and slid into position amid a cloud of dust.

"Hey, shithead," Bartels whispered, "anything to tell me?"

"Not a damn thing," Onuku replied. "I'm out of here. See ya, pencil dick."

"Yeah."

Onuku grabbed his assault rifle and backpack, turned, stopped. "Oh," he mumbled. He lifted his hand to scratch away a sudden pricking on the back of his neck. His hand got only halfway before he crumpled facedown into the dirt, the tiny stinger invisible against his ebony-black skin, a swinging arm slapping Bartels across the shoulders as he fell.

"Hey!" Bartels snapped, turning. He reared back from the body. "What the—" he said before he toppled forward onto Onuku, the pair slumped across the ground in one last grotesque embrace.

For a moment, all was still. Then a shape—manlike, but only if you knew it was there—shimmered its way across the ground and into the observation post. The man pushed his chromaflage cape off his face before sliding his way across the bodies of Onuku and Bartels. He eased his assault rifle into position to cover the path back to the old mining base, a battered collection of sandblasted buildings sprawled across a rock promontory with a commanding view of the valley and its airstrip. A pair of shuttles were parked on the apron under crude chromaflage nets in front of a small storage hut.

"Alfa, Boxcar Six. Position Kilo secure," he whispered. "Hostiles India 2, India 7 are down. No movement visible."

"Alfa, roger. Assault team and snatch squad moving in now. Out."

His part in one of humankind's less important dramas all but over, the man settled down to wait, and before long the long-planned operation began to unfold in earnest.

"Watchdog One, this is Alfa. Execute; I say again execute."

Finally, Matti Anders said to himself. "Alfa, Watchdog One. Execute, roger. Airborne in two minutes. Watchdog One, out … Okay, Jaska, we're on," he called out. He flicked a glance across the flight deck at the man hunched over the systems operator's workstation.

"About time, too," Jaska Anders replied, eyes locked on the holovids that curtained his station, the three-dimensional screens alive with icons tracking every element of the operation. "I've been ready for bloody hours."

Matti only grunted in reply; with practiced efficiency, he ordered the lander's AI to power up the massive ground-attack lander before finalizing the preflight checklist. *Bitsa's* twin fusion plants came on line with the subdued rumble of high-pressure cooling pumps, and Matti took a deep breath to steady himself. An operation might promise to be easy or difficult; it made no difference. He always felt nervous, and with good reason: He had seen too many supposedly simple operations go wrong.

"Ready?"

"Ready," Jaska replied. "All systems nominal."

With maddening slowness, the fusion plants that powered *Bitsa*'s main engines came up to full power. "Alfa, this is Watchdog One," Matti said. "Launching now."

"Alfa, roger. Confirm time on target."

"Watchdog One, roger. Stand by time on target. Out."

Matti fed power to the lander's belly thrusters. Slow to respond, the lander lifted into the air and balanced for a moment on twin pillars of incandescent fire that blasted huge rolling clouds of dust and sand across the dirt and into the sky; then he eased the lander's nose down to begin the transition into forward flight. A rush of pure excitement flushed his nerves away. Matti was a simple man; even though the lander's AI could fly the mission on its own, he loved the challenge of doing things the old-fashioned way: by hand.

Matti shifted power back to the main engines, and now the lander accelerated hard; foamalloy wings flexed upward as they bit into the air. He kept the lander close to the ground and let the speed build up, then eased it around in a shallow climbing turn until the old mining base lay right on the nose at thirty kilometers.

"Alfa, Watchdog One," he said. "Time on target four minutes. I say again, four minutes."

"Alfa, four minutes, roger, out."

For an instant, time stood still, an endless moment of sheer joy as the desert raced past underneath *Bitsa* in a blur of browns, grays, and blacks. The ground-attack lander was smooth and responsive under his left hand in the calm morning air, the flying easy.

I was born to do this, Matti thought. *I want to do this forever.*

"Optronics have acquired the targets … targets positively identified," Jaska said, "and designated. Ready to engage."

"Roger," Matti said. "Weapons free."

"Weapons free," Jaska responded. "Cannons to auto, threat plot is green, no hostile activity. Dumb bastards have shut down."

Dumb is right, Matti murmured under his breath, the adrenaline beginning to pump. *They won't know we're here until it's too late.*

Bitsa closed in, moving so fast that the appalling noise from its two main engines was unable to keep up. Matti spotted the two orbital shuttles he and Jaska had come so far to destroy: two squat black shapes off to the left-hand side of the airstrip, rock steady in the lander's holocam. An instant later, *Bitsa*'s quadruple 30-millimeter cannons opened up; the lander shuddered as hypervelocity shells ripped into the targets, the ground around them torn and blasted into clouds of dust and pulverized rock. Then they were past. Matti chopped the power and lifted the nose sharply to aerobrake *Bitsa*, stressing the foamalloy wings up into sharp curves as the lander's speed bled off, wingtips stabbing back and up into a sky of palest blue. He banked the craft and let the speed decay to give the cannons time to finish the job, holding the turn until the two shuttles reappeared on the nose before steadying *Bitsa* for its second pass.

Cannon shells tore at the shuttles. Belatedly, one returned fire, but *Bitsa*'s armored hull shrugged off the pulsed lasers. Just as Matti began to wonder how much more damage the shuttles could absorb, first one and then the second erupted in brutal explosions that punched massive balls of pure energy into the air as their fusion plants lost containment, the shock waves tossing *Bitsa* into a violent, plunging roll to starboard that had Matti fighting for control.

"Shiiiiit," he hissed as he fought *Bitsa*'s massive bulk back to level, trying to forget the awful sight of a wingtip screwing vortices of dust out of the ground. *There you have it*, he thought as *Bitsa* steadied. *Sometimes the difference between life and death is only a couple of meters.*

"Targets destroyed," Jaska said, voice calm, apparently untroubled by the fact that death had come so dangerously close.

"Roger that," Matti said. He fed power to the engines and eased *Bitsa* into a shallow climb away from the pillars of smoke climbing skyward from the carnage. He checked the systems status boards, relieved to see that the old lady had not suffered any damage.

"Watchdog One, Alfa. Hold station overhead until we call you in."

"Watchdog One, roger," Matti replied. He turned to Jaska. "Another successful mission for Klimath Security Services. Well done."

"Yeah," Jaska grunted. "KSS, the employer of choice for clapped-out old systems operators like me."

Matti said nothing.

• • •

Bitsa bobbed on its undercarriage as Matti stamped hard on the brakes. "Shut her down, Jaska, while I go and talk to the man paying the bills."

"Better you than me," Jaska replied, fingers flying across the control panels arrayed around his station. "I wouldn't piss on the Armatos or their people. Slimeballs, every last one of them."

"That's as may be," Matti said as he struggled out of his cramped seat and started to shed his combat spacesuit, "but their money's good. You don't have to like them."

Jaska's hand shot out to take Matti by the arm. "We came close again," Jaska said, "real close."

"Yeah, we did. Occupational hazard."

"Too close, and it's not the first time, Matti. I can't do this much longer. You do know that, don't you?"

"Yes, I do. And like I've said, when it's time for you to call it quits, you just say so. Okay?"

"I will, and soon, Matti. Soon."

Matti nodded. "It's up to you, Jaska; you know that."

Finally free of his suit, Matti squeezed his way aft from the flight deck, dropped down the ladder to the cargo bay, and made his way down the ramp, happy to breathe fresh morning air instead of the recycled muck produced by *Bitsa*'s obsolete and overworked environmental control units. The man he knew only as Kevlakis was walking over from a commercial shuttle now parked close to the still-blazing hulks of the two shuttles, its flanks emblazoned with the blue starburst of Armato Industries.

"Nice job, Captain Anders," Kevlakis said, his eyes hidden behind mirrored sunglasses. Matti had no idea what those eyes looked like. In all the times they had met, Kevlakis had never taken the glasses off. "Quick, clean, and efficient, just as you promised. I've already sent instructions to the bank. The balance of the contract sum will be in your account before the end of the day."

"Thank you, Mr. Kevlakis. Anything else we can do?"

"No. That's it. You can go."

"Thanks. But tell me—the operation. You got the girl back okay?"

"Silla Armato is safe and well. Her father will be very pleased, which is more than I can say for the kidnappers."

Matti thought that was an understatement. None of them would be going home. Whoever had organized the kidnapping would be pissed, not to mention badly out of pocket. An operation this big would have cost millions to mount, an investment justified only by the payoff. Rumor had it that the kidnappers had demanded a quarter of a billion dollars for Silla Armato's safe return.

"I'm sure," Matti said. "Anyway, we'll be off as soon as we've refilled our mass bunkers. Any time you need us, just call."

"I do not think that will be necessary," Kevlakis replied with a bleak, wintry smile before he turned to walk away.

A shiver caressed Matti's spine as he watched the man make his way back to the shuttle. Whoever had planned and executed the kidnapping of Karlos Armato's only child must have been deranged to take on Armato and his people, people like Kevlakis, unless they were even bigger and uglier than Armato. Was that possible? he wondered. Armato's brutality and ruthlessness were legendary, his wealth and power unimaginable, his political base on Jalmaniya unassailable. Whoever the kidnappers were, he would not want to be in their shoes when Armato caught up with them.

And he would; Matti Anders was sure of it.

An hour later, *Bitsa* roared down the airstrip and into the air. Accelerating hard in a gentle climb, Matti let the lander's speed increase, the aged airframe creaking and groaning as the aerodynamic stresses started to build. Passing through Mach 5 and thirty thousand meters, he retracted the wings and lifted the nose for the climb into orbit, twin plumes of incandescent driver mass from the main engines blazing *Bitsa*'s path back into space.

4

Fury erupted out of nowhere with a ferocity that threatened to engulf Matti Anders. All he wanted to do was reach into the holovid and tear the grin off the face of the young woman in front of him.

Breathe, he urged himself, dragging air deep into his lungs before letting it out slowly over and over until the rage subsided and he was able to concentrate on what his daughter was saying.

"… and so things y' know got … got like a bit …" Samira was burbling, her voice slurred, sweat-matted hair dropping across her eyes. "What was I saying … Oh, yeah; Cosmo hacked a bot, but he couldn't drive 'cause he was so wasted, so I did. Problem was I was a bit wasted too, and … and things got a bit out of hand when I crashed it and then the pigs turned up. They got all shitty with me and Nat, so I told them to back off … They didn't like that, and then I think I might have hit one of them with my shoe … Ah, hell, what does it matter? You'd better come down and get me out of here. This damn place stinks … Oh, shit, I think I'm going to be sick."

Before Matti Anders could respond, Samira toppled out of the holocam's field of view, the sound of retching filling the air as Matti chopped the holovid off.

"You stupid, stupid bitch!" he swore as he climbed out of bed, a foot lashing out in a destructive scything kick that catapulted a small table into the wall, all traces of sleep flushed out of his body by a violent rush of adrenaline that got his heart pumping hard.

The police station doors swished open; Matti forced himself to walk into reception even though he was tempted to turn around and leave Samira to get herself out of trouble.

The room was bleak, harshly lit, and dominated by a long counter protected by scarred plasglass behind which a single officer in dark blue police fatigues sat. Matti's heart sank; the man, Trooper T'chenitz, according to a frayed yellow-on-blue name patch, had been on duty the last time he'd come to collect Samira.

"Ah, Mr. Anders," T'chenitz said, looking up. "Can't say it's a pleasure to see you … again."

"What can I say?" Matti's hands went up in an attempt to placate the man. "I don't like this any more than you do."

"Really?" T'chenitz muttered. "You don't say."

"So, can we get this over with? Give me the delinquency notice, I'll pay for the damages, and then I'll get her out of here."

"Delinquency notice? Damages?" The trooper shook his head. "No, I don't think so; not this time, Mr. Anders. The watch commander wants to see you. Through that door, then second office on the right. I'll tell her you're on your way."

"No delinquency notice?" Matti said with a puzzled frown.

"No." T'chenitz's voice was flat, devoid of any emotion. "She's eighteen now, Mr. Anders."

"I know that, but wh—"

"Through that door, then second office on the right."

"Right, sorry."

Matti did as he was told and found himself sitting across from a woman, also dressed in police combat fatigues, a look Matti hated; if they wanted to look like soldiers, they should join the damn military. She looked as pissed as any human being could look and glared at him for what seemed like a lifetime before speaking.

"I'm Lieutenant Adabae," she said, "and I'm the poor bastard with the bad luck to be the on-duty watch commander when your daughter and her shithead friends decided to cut loose … again."

"Look, Lieut—"

"Spare me, Mr. Anders. Just have a look at our statement of facts," she said, waving a hand at the wall-mounted holovid screen. "There are a couple of loose ends we want to tidy up, but there's no doubt about what happened."

When the holovid ended, Matti sat back with a sigh. Adabae was right; after he'd seen the police account, Samira's part in the night's stupidity was impossible to deny.

"Oh, shit," was all he could say.

"And your daughter's right in it, up to her pretty little neck. Now, let me just explain things in a way that even you can understand. Samira Anders is a problem we're not willing to tolerate anymore, Mr. Anders, and we won't. Oh, wait … let me just check here … Yes, that's what we said to you the last time she acted like a total idiot."

Matti's head bobbed; he felt ashamed, embarrassed, and angry. He forced himself to stay calm. "Yes, you did."

"And you promised us it wouldn't happen again, am I right?"

"Yes, I did."

"Well, I must say she has outdone herself this time."

"Look," Matti said, "I know she's a problem, but this is just stupid teenager stuff. We all did it when—"

"No!" Adabae's voice slashed through Matti's protestations. "No, we did not all do it, Mr. Anders. A bit too much alcohol, maybe. A few stimtabs over the legal limit, fine, no big deal. We have better things to worry about than minor breaches of the recreational drug limits. But even the dumbest teenager knows not to mix alcohol and stimtabs ... which makes your daughter what?"

Adabae shook her head, then continued. "In any case, she's eighteen now; that means she's an adult, and she's had all the chances we were going to give her. So," she continued, "we have formally arrested her. We have filed charges of theft, criminal damage, assaulting a police officer, and resisting arrest. I will send you a copy of the charges, but by law I need to give you a hard copy—" She slid a single sheet of paper across the desk. "—so here it is. Her arraignment will be at Bellingen magistrates' court this afternoon. I suggest you be there. Until then, she'll remain in police custody."

"Oh," Matti said, too shocked to say more.

"And get a lawyer, Mr. Anders, a good one."

5

"… so Ms. Anders … look at me, please. Are you listening?"

"Yes … yes, I am, Your Honor," Samira replied softly, the tremor in her voice clearly audible.

You look like shit, Matti thought as he watched her keep her head up with an effort: Samira's skin—normally a lustrous olive—had been washed out to dirty gray by fatigue and drugs, her eyes dull and rimmed red, hair a matted mess, the faded blue prison jumpsuit too big for her.

"I hope so," the judge said. "Things changed when you got to be eighteen, Ms. Anders, even if that fact seems to have escaped your notice. Now, the only good thing I can say is that you had the good sense to plead guilty to the charges laid against you, not that there was any doubt at all that you committed those offenses. So let's not waste any more time. I want you back here in one week's time to hear presentencing submissions; until then you're released on your own recognizance provided you live in your father's house. And stay out of trouble if you can: no dance clubs, no alcohol, no stimtabs. Understood?"

"Yes … yes, I understand, Your Honor."

"I'm so pleased to hear it," the judge said with studied irony, "so pleased. Next case."

• • •

Barely minutes from home, Samira broke the frozen silence that had prevailed from the moment she had been handed back to her father.

"Sorry, Dad." Her voice was so soft that Matti had to strain to hear her. "That's the last time I'm going to put you through this."

Matti took a deep breath, choking off a savage response before it could pass his lips. "It won't wash, Samira," he responded after a long pause. "That's exactly what you said last time."

"I know, but I mean it."

"You said that last time as well."

"But I do, Dad; really, I do mean it."

"And that too."

"Dad!"

"Pull over and stop," Matti barked to the mobibot before turning to Samira. "Words, words, words," he said. "They're just words, and your words don't mean a damn thing. They never do. Listen, it's up to you, Samira," he added, his voice softening. "I know I cannot stop you from disappearing off into the night to do whatever crazy stuff you and your friends want to do. But the next time it all goes wrong, I won't be there for you. You do understand that, don't you?"

"I do." Samira nodded. "But you know what?"

"What?"

"I have said all that stuff before, and you're right: I didn't mean any of it, but you need—"

"Samira!" Matti's voice crackled with anger.

"Hear me out, Dad. Just for once, hear what I'm saying and try, try real hard to understand me, because if you don't, then …" Samira's voice trailed away into silence, her eyes filling with tears.

"Okay, okay. I will."

Samira took a long deep breath and let it out in a soft hiss. Matti tried not to flinch as the inside of the mobibot filled with the sour smell of an abused body struggling to regain its equilibrium; he failed, not that Samira seemed to notice.

"Look, Dad," she said. "I don't want what you want for me, and I never will. Biomechanical engineering's not for me, Dad. Sorry. I know I said that's what I wanted to do, but I don't. I said yes only to shut you up. And that leaves only one option."

"If that's taking over from Uncle Jaska, then you can forg—"

"Why are you fighting me on this? I can do the damn job, and you know it. Yes, there are a million things I don't know, things that the sims will never teach me, so you teach me. You teach me, Dad! Uncle Jaska's had enough, and I'm ready. Do you think I want to waste my time with losers? Do you think I want to go to jail? No way! Just say yes, Dad, and then I can promise you there'll be no more bullshit, and this time I mean it."

After a long silence, Matti sighed, shaking his head. "You're blackmailing me," he said. "That's what you're doing. Shit! Blackmailed by my own daughter!" He shook his head again. "Now there's a first."

"No, Dad! I'm not blackmailing you."

"Yes, you are, Samira, and I won't buy it. My answer's the same as it's always been, and if you don't like it, you can go to jail for all I care. It won't change my decision."

"And what would? I'll tell you what would. Being a boy, not a girl, that's what would. It's because I'm not the son you always wanted, isn't it?"

"Drive on," was Matti's only response, the words forced out past clenched teeth. Unable even to look at Samira, he turned his head away to stare out of the window while the mobibot accelerated away.

6

"Come on, Samira, cheer up. It could have been a lot worse."

"I know, Dad, but it's not easy. I know I'm up for parole after three months, but who's to say I'll get it?"

"By proving to them that you have the self-control to be a different person, that's how. How's the behavioral therapy going?"

"It's only been a week, so it's a bit early to say. So far, it's been very tough; the counselors always seem to know when you're bullshitting, but I think I'm doing okay. They won't tell me how I've done until the end of eight weeks, but I will make it, Dad. I will."

"You know what, Samira?"

"What?"

"I think you will too."

"Maybe."

"What are the rest of the ... you know, the rest of ..." Matti's voice trailed off into an awkward silence.

"Oh, for heaven's sake, Dad. Prisoners: That's what they are, and that's what I am. Prisoner KP-433452, to be precise."

"Sorry. So what are they like?"

"All sorts. Low-security places like this don't get the hard cases, though there are still people best avoided. So far, I've only been in one fight—" Matti now understood where the faded bruise on Samira's left cheek had come from. "—and I think I did okay. Seems I haven't been wasting my time in those self-defense classes."

Matti shook his head; he was lost for words. What could he say to this girl—no, not a girl anymore—to this woman that he had not already said?

The voice of one of the guards broke into his thoughts. "Anders, your time's up," the woman said.

"Okay. I've got to go, Dad. See you next week?'

"Yup. And make this work … please?"

"Doing my best," she said, getting up to kiss him on the cheek. "Bye, Dad. See you."

"Yeah."

Matti watched her as she made her way out of the visitors' center, a bleak space filled with metal tables bolted to the floor and plasfiber seats. The net effect was a soulless place, precisely the effect prison managers seemed to work so hard to achieve.

And I should know, Matti thought. *I've seen the inside of a few prisons over the years.*

With a sigh that came from the very core of his being, he stood up and left.

"You know what I hate most of all?" Jenna Ward, Samira's cellmate, said. It was two hours after they had been locked up for the night, and still neither was asleep.

"Let me guess. The dogs?"

"Much as I hate those scumsucking guards, no."

"What, then?"

"It's that damn light. It burns day and night, and there's not a thing we can do about it. I hate that light."

Samira lay on her bunk, staring at the ceiling light safe behind its recessed plasglass. "I think the dogs keep it on for a reason," she said. "It's how the bastards who run this shithole make sure we don't forget that they are the ones in control."

"I reckon you're right."

"How do you do it, Jenna? Put up with all the crap, I mean."

"Not a lot of choice. I won't get parole for another three years at least, more if I screw things up, so I just take it one day at a time. What else can you do? I can't change anything, so I don't waste my time trying."

"Doesn't stop you from hating the place, though."

"No. I tried all that Zen bullshit, you know, accept what you can't change, life's a journey not a destination, and so on, but I couldn't make any of it work. I still hate this place; I just hate it one day at a time."

"I couldn't do three years in this place," Samira said. "Twelve months is bad enough."

"You could if you had to," Jenna said. "Anyway, you won't do the full stretch. First-timers like you always get parole pretty quickly.'

"I hope so."

"You will; trust me. Just take it day by day and stay clear of that bitch Chou."

"I will," Samira said, running her fingers across her bruised cheek. "I've already met her."

"I heard. I mean it, Samira. Stay away from her; she's bad news. And don't expect the guards to look out for you. Chou's got them in her pocket."

"How the hell can she do that? What does she have to offer?"

"That's a good question."

"So how?" Samira demanded. "Come on, tell me."

"Not my business. Just make sure you don't find out the hard way. Just keep well clear of her."

"Haven't been able to so far. Everywhere I go, I seem to run into her."

"Do it anyway," Jenna said.

"Gee, thanks."

"Okay, wake me up at six with a cup of coffee and a biscuit."

Samira smiled; the woman said the same thing every night when she was through talking. "Night, Jenna," she said.

Samira lay staring at the raw ceramcrete ceiling of the cell, wondering as she did every night what was she going to do with her life.

Take over from Jaska? Not a chance.

Join the KDF? Even if she wanted to, she couldn't, not with a criminal record.

Become a biomechanical engineer the way her dad wanted? What a joke. She hated cyborgs.

A life of crime? The money appealed to her, the risk and the excitement even more so. And she was smart, she was surrounded by criminals who could teach her what she needed to know, she was tough, she'd seen enough of the police not to be frightened of them anymore, and maybe prison time was just one of those things you had to put up with along the way.

She thought about that for a while. "Who are you trying to kid?" she whispered. She laughed softly, a bitter laugh of self-disgust. "Prison, you stupid bitch," she said. "Years and years of prison; that's where that life will lead you."

And there has to be something better than that, she thought, *there has to be.*

7

Head back and eyes closed, Samira luxuriated in the flood of hot water, running her hands through her hair to rinse the last traces of shampoo away.

A voice, harsh and demanding, dragged her back to reality. "Hey, Anders," it barked. "I need to talk to you."

"What?" Samira wiped the water out her eyes. "Oh, it's you," she said.

"Yes, it is me," Wendy Chou said.

Samira's heart sank when she realized she and Chou were alone. "I'm busy, Chou, so piss off."

"I don't think so. In fact, I think you've finished. Why don't you step out like a good girl?"

After a moment's indecision, Samira did as she was told, grabbing her towel in an attempt to recover some of her dignity. "What the hell do you want? Are you ... you know?"

"As it happens, I am, so thanks for asking. But you're not my type, Anders. You're not fat exactly, but you do carry too much weight for my taste."

"Piss off, Chou, you scrawny dyke."

"Yes, I am a scrawny dyke," Chou said, her voice calm and untroubled, "and proud of it."

"Get out of my way."

Samira did not wait for Chou's response. She hurled her towel into Chou's face and threw herself to one side in a desperate bid to get away. She did not get even a meter. Swatting the towel away with one hand, Chou swayed aside to let her pass, then turned and grabbed her hair, jerking back so hard that Samira's feet skidded on the wet tiles; back she went, arms flailing, the air driven out her lungs with an "*ooof*" as first her back and then her head hit the floor with a soft thud.

"Oh, shit, that hurt," she groaned, unable to move, struggling to recover her breath.

Chou leaned over her, a thin smile on her face. "You're a smart girl, Anders. That's why I think you'll agree with me that I am not to be fucked with."

"What the hell do you want, Chou?" Samira said.

"Me? What makes you think I want anything?"

"Fine. I'll be on my way then," Samira said, levering herself up.

Chou's foot stopped her; planted firmly on her shoulder, it pushed her down. "Not so fast, Anders. As it happens, I don't want anything, but a friend of mine, a very good friend, does. And unless you want your time in here to be a living hell, I strongly suggest you do what my friend asks."

Samira's eyes narrowed in suspicion. "What friend?"

"Oh, didn't I say? Sergeant Castillo; he might be one of the dogs, but he's a very, very good friend of mine. Unlike me, he likes his women … shall we say a bit more on the comfortable side? Just like you, in fact, Samira Anders."

Samira stared up at Chou. "I don't believe this."

"You'd better, because it's all true." Chou stepped back. "Charlie! Charlie, get your fat ass in here."

43

Samira's heart sank as Castillo stepped into view, his gut straining against his blue stab-resistant fatigues to hang out over his equipment belt. Nervous, his eyes scanned left and right, his stun gun out.

"Put that thing away, Charlie," Chou snapped. "The silly bitch is not going to attack you. Anyway, I'm done. She's all yours. Just don't mark her, okay?"

"I owe you, Chou." Castillo nodded, hungry eyes staring at Samira's naked body.

"Yes, you damn well do."

"Just make sure we're not disturbed. I want to take my time with this one."

"Sure." And with that Chou was gone, leaving Samira to stare up at Castillo, unable to accept what was about to happen. She was no innocent, but this was like nothing she had ever experienced. This had nothing to do with doing what came naturally; it had everything to do with power, the exercise of raw, brutal power for its own sake, for the fun of it, because the bastard could, and there was nothing she could do to stop him. And they both knew it.

Holstering his stun gun, Castillo paused, a smile of excitement and anticipation on his face. "Brace yourself, bitch," he said softly.

"Go screw yourself, Castillo. You think you're going to get away with this? Think again, asshole."

"Now, now. Be nice," Castillo said. "And just so as you know, yes, I will get away with this. The medical officer is a particularly good friend of mine, so don't waste your time complaining. She'll swear that you're as untouched as fresh snow."

"You piece of crap!"

44

Castillo scowled. "I told you once, and I won't tell you again. Be nice and we'll both enjoy this. Fight me and I'll make you pay, girlie." He stepped forward to stand over her.

Without thinking, Samira reacted. Her right foot exploded off the floor up into Castillo's groin; an instant later, her left followed, driving her heel up hard into the fold of his gut as he doubled over, forcing him back with a soft, sobbing moan, hands clasped firmly to his crotch. Hitting the wall, he slid slowly down to the floor, his face a twisted mask of pain, hands still clamped to his groin. "You little bitch," he gasped, hate-filled eyes swimming with tears. "You'll pay for that."

She scrambled to her feet. "Maybe so, you fat pig," she said softly, "but you'll never have me." She stepped up to him. "Never," she said as she drove her foot into his stomach a second time, forcing his lungs to empty in an explosive *whoof.* "Never. I'd rather die than have you touch me, you slimy bastard."

"I'll get you, Anders," he said, his voice a pain-wracked croak.

"Screw you, Castillo," she hissed.

"Ah, you're awake," the hospital orderly said. "How do you feel?"

"Sore," Samira croaked. And she was; after the beating she had received at the hands of Chou and her friends, her body was a twisted mess of agony.

"I'll up the painkillers."

"What's the damage?"

"Nothing serious. Whoever did this knew how to hurt you without doing too much damage, so you should count yourself lucky. They could have killed you if they wanted to."

"Yeah, but they didn't."

"I know the people you pissed off," the orderly said, "so I wouldn't do it again. You might not be so lucky next time."

"There won't be a next time," Samira whispered as the orderly left. Despite the pain, she still managed a smile as she drifted into sleep.

8

Matti Anders tried to suppress his excitement. Finally, some good news. It was long overdue. He threw a sideways glance at Piotr Mikoyan, his Mendozan lawyer.

"Come on, Piotr," he said, "talk to me. Have I missed anything?"

Piotr sighed. "No, Matti," he said, "you haven't. This is just what you need. It's a straightforward operation. The risks are manageable, the money's good, *Bitsa*'s up to the job, and best of all, you'll be away from Samira's bitching, about which you've done nothing but complain ever since you got dirtside."

Matti laughed despite himself. Piotr was right; from the moment the down-shuttle had dumped him at the city's spaceport, he had given Samira more airtime than she deserved.

The rest of the ride passed in silence until finally the mobibot drew up in front of a tired low-rise office block in Karavic, one of Mendoza City's industrial suburbs. As they climbed out into the muggy heat, a woman appeared.

"Captain Anders?" she said.

"That's me," Matti replied. He shook the woman's outstretched hand. "My lawyer, Piotr Mikoyan."

"Good to meet you both. I'm Sabine Shacar. Come this way, please."

Shacar lead the way into the building, long disused judging by the thick layer of dust that coated untidy piles of broken furniture. Matti suppressed a rush of unease. The mission brief sent to him by Mikoyan had described the client as an established Mendozan businessman; he had expected something more impressive than this.

"Here we are," Shacar said, waving them in ahead of her. "Please."

Matti followed Piotr into the room. It was empty save for two huge cyborgs, one male, one female—Matti's heart flipped at the sight of their heavily muscled frames—flanking a man: tall, running to fat, heavy jowls, olive-skinned face, wiry black hair cropped short, tired blue-gray eyes set deep over black bags, a beard trimmed into the neat goatee style favored by Mendozan men. His thickset frame was draped in an immaculately tailored high-collared black suit that screamed money and power.

"What's this?" Matti demanded, spinning around. But Shacar had gone, closing the door behind her without a sound.

"What the hell is going on?" Matti said turning back to the tall man in the center of the room. "And who the hell are you? You're not the man in the mission brief. You're not the man we came to meet."

"No, I'm not. But don't you recognize me anyway?" the man replied, his voice deep and rough, like gravel being crushed. "You should. We've met before."

"We have?" Matti stared at the man, eyes wide open in confusion, then turned to Mikoyan. "Piotr! Who the hell is this?"

Fear and uncertainty flickered across the lawyer's face. "I don't know, Matti. All I know is he's not the man we came to meet."

"Shit!" Matti said softly; he was sure he had never met the man even though something deep down inside insisted he had. But where and when? The man did look familiar, just not in any way he could even begin to describe. His heart pounded, kicked up a gear by a terrible certainty that something bad was about to happen.

"No," Matti declared, his voice steady with a confidence he did not feel, "I don't think we have met, sorry. And I've had enough of this; I don't do business with people who play games. Piotr, come on. We're out of here."

"Don't try to leave, Matti," the man in black said. "Don't waste your time. The door's locked."

Matti ignored him. He turned and tried the door. It refused to budge. He spun around and pushed Piotr behind him.

The man in black sighed, a theatrical sigh of pained resignation, overloud, forced. "Matti, Matti, Matti. You never were one to take advice, were you?"

"What are you going on about?" Matti demanded. "Either you want to use my services or you don't. If you do, we'll talk terms. If you don't, then open the door and we'll leave."

"Oh, we'll talk business, Matti. My business, though, not yours."

"What is this about? And who are you?"

"The Armato kidnapping, Matti. That's what this is about. And who am I? I'm sorry you don't recognize me. Not that you should, not living on that pissant dump of a planet you call home."

"Oh, shit," Matti hissed, his stomach filling with a sick dread. "Now I know who you are. You organized the kidnapping."

"No, I can't take the credit for that fiasco." The man waved his hand as if to dismiss the very idea. "Well, not personally, anyway. It was the people I work for, the only people with the balls to take on that son of a bitch Armato."

"So why am I here?"

"Because with your help, Armato kicked our asses, cost us a fortune, embarrassed us, and that we cannot tolerate."

"Maybe so, but what's that got to with me?" Matti demanded. "I run a lander-for-hire business; you must know that. I just did the job I was asked to do, that's all."

"Funny, that."

"What?"

"That's what that piece of shit Kevlakis said just before I blew his brains out."

With a sudden, awful certainty that turned his bowels to water, Matti knew he would not leave this place alive. "Look," he said, his voice trembling with fear. "This is not Piotr's business. He's just my lawyer. Let him go. You can do what you like to me. I don't care. Just let him go. Please."

"Oh, no. I don't think so. Why would I do that, anyway? He might have worked out who I am by now. He'd just run to the police, and I'd have no end of trouble persuading them to back off. That'd cost us a fortune. My boss prefers the cheaper option, and I must say, so do I."

"Fuck you!" Piotr shouted. Pushing Matti aside with a brutal shove in the small of his back, Piotr leaped right at the man in a desperate lunging dive, his hands reaching out for the throat. He never came close; one of the cyborgs, moving faster than Matti had seen any human move, stepped into Piotr's path, a single massive blow from his huge fist to the back of the neck clubbing Piotr to the floor.

"Amateurs," the goon growled, and stepped back from Piotr's unconscious body, running his hand across hair cut down to blond stubble.

"You bastards," Matti whispered, shocked by the cyborg's clinical brutality. "Let him go. He had nothing to do with the Armato operation. For pity's sake, let him go."

"For pity's sake?" The man in black shook his head. "Pity's not a word people use much when they talk about me, so no. I know he had nothing to do with it, but let's be honest here. He's in the wrong place at the wrong time, which is his problem, not mine. So sorry. Now, Matti, get down! On your knees, where you belong. It's time you learned what happens to people who screw with us."

"Okay, but not Piotr," Matti said, doing as he was told, his voice thick, half choked in defeat. "Let him go."

"I'm getting bored with this little charade." The man took a step forward and pulled out a small laser pistol, an ugly little weapon designed for close-range killing and nothing else. He lifted the pistol to Matti's temple and bent forward. "People who screw with us, Matti Anders, only screw with us once. And you want to know why that is?"

Matti could not speak, his mouth ash-dry, his throat choked shut by fear. He shook his head, nearly paralyzed by a raw, surging terror that turned his bowels to water.

"I'll tell you anyway. It's because, Matti Anders, we always catch up with them and make sure they can't screw with us again. It's time for you to go, so say goodbye to Piotr."

"Goodbye, Piotr," Matti croaked, "I'm so sorry—"

With a sharp snap the pistol fired, and the laser pulse, barely thicker than a human hair, cut him short as searing pain lanced a path of devastation through his brain. For an instant Matti stayed upright before his eyes rolled back up into his head and he crumpled to the floor.

So this is what it's like to die, he thought, the floor cold against his cheek, marveling at how quickly the fear had disappeared, replaced by a calm that swept through his body on a wave of pure cool, his mouth inexplicably filled with the icy taste of fresh mint. *Dying is not as bad as I thought it'd be; I hope Samira will be okay without …*

Slowly, slower than the fall of night, he slipped away, his mind's eye filling with soft, shimmering sheets of white shot through with searing flashes of crimson and gold that faded into gray and then into black as unconsciousness enveloped him, an unstoppable tide rising to engulf the last precious fragments of awareness.

Matti Anders was gone.

The man in black stepped back from the body. "Finish this one off," he ordered, pointing to Piotr, "then leave them. The boss likes people to know he means it when he tells people not to mess with us."

9

Samira pulled on a surgical glove and eased the shiv—a thin piece of metal torn off one of the hospital medibots and filed down to a needle-sharp point—out of her sock and fell in behind a line of prisoners heading for the showers. Her eyes were locked on Chou as she walked on, flanked by her lackeys, her walk a swaggering mix of arrogance and power. I am queen here, her gait said, so stand back.

The instant Samira was in the changing room and clear of the surveillance holocams, she moved fast, barging prisoners aside to get to Chou.

Chou's minders were slow to react; before anyone knew what was happening, Samira had wrapped an arm around Chou's neck, slipped the shiv through her prison overalls and into her side—not far enough to kill but far enough to make her stop struggling—and dragged her clear of the rest into a corner of the changing room.

"Get back," she barked as Chou's lackeys surged to her aid, "or I'll kill her, and then I'll kill you. Tell them, Chou, tell them."

"Get back," Chou said, her voice a strangled croak as Samira tightened the throat lock. "Get back."

"That's better."

"What the hell do you want from me, Anders?"

"Nothing, you bitch," Samira hissed into Chou's ear. "It's payback time."

Despite Samira's choke hold, Chou managed a strangled laugh. "Maybe, Anders," she said, "but you don't have the balls to slip that thing in any farther, so when you let me go—and you will—I'm going to kill you."

"Oh, you are so wrong." And then Samira pushed the shiv—not hard, she did not need to, it was that sharp—into Chou's side, not far, barely a centimeter, the shiv sliding effortlessly between Chou's ribs.

"Ahhh," Chou cried, her body trembling under Samira's arm. "Stop! Please stop!"

"How's that, Chou? You want some more?"

"No! Please, Anders, no more."

"Frightened now, are we? Know what?"

"What?"

"Your liver's about, oh, I don't know, I'm no anatomy expert—get back, you fucker," she shouted as one of Chou's people started toward her, "or I will kill her here and now! That's better," she said as the woman stepped away. "Now, where was I?"

"What do you want?" Chou said. "Tell me!"

"Hey, wait up. I was just explaining that the tip of my knife is just touching your liver, so if I push it in a bit more, you're going to be very sick. And if I push it all the way and mash it around a bit, you're going to be very dead by the time the dogs finally get here. So we're going to do a deal, Chou."

"Fine, whatever you want," Chou panted. "Just get that damn thing out of me."

"I will. Just promise me that you'll leave me alone, okay?"

"Yes, yes. I will."

"And your people too?"

"Yes, yes. We won't touch you, I promise."

"What a surprise. I thought you'd agree, Chou, but then again, I haven't exactly given you much choice. So here's my problem: I don't believe you, Chou, and I never will."

"Believe me, please. We won't touch you; I promise."

Samira put her mouth to Chou's ear. "You are a lying piece of shit," she whispered as she slid the shiv farther into Chou's body.

"Noooo," Chou sobbed, "please, no."

"Stop sniveling," Samira said, pulling the shiv out and letting Chou fall to the floor, a whimpering, crumpled heap. "You're not going to die. Now," she said, looking at the shocked faces arrayed around her, "any of you gutless assholes want a piece of me … no? Thought not. You!" she snapped to the nearest prisoner. "Get this sack of crap out of here, and if anyone asks, she fell over and that's all you know. You got that?"

"Whatever you say, Anders," the prisoner said, refusing to look her in the eye.

"Good, 'cause if you do open your big mouth, I'll get to you," she said, slashing the shiv so fast across the woman's neck that it had drawn blood before she had time to move, "and that's a promise."

"Okay, okay," the woman cried. "She fell over, she fell over. Got it."

"Well, get her out of here, then. She needs medical attention. Go!"

Samira waited as Chou was dragged away; distracted, nobody noticed her tuck the shiv under one of the benches.

Then, as if nothing had happened, she stripped off the glove, rinsed it clean of any incriminating forensics, tossed into the recycling bin, and walked out.

Ignoring the guards huddled around Chou, Samira had barely made it back to her cell before her stomach rebelled, forcing her to drop to her knees, her body wracked by spasm after spasm as she threw up into the toilet over and over. When there was nothing more, she sat back on her heels, wiping her mouth. "Damn," she whispered, her heart still pounding.

"You okay?" a voice behind her asked.

"Hi, Jenna," Samira said, turning. "Yeah, I'm fine." She was lying; she was far from fine. Her body trembled uncontrollably; she tried not to think about the appalling risk she had just taken. "Fine, I'm fine." Shaking, she pulled herself up to her bunk and collapsed. "I'm fine."

"I heard what happened," Jenna said.

"Already?" Samira shook her head. "It doesn't take long for word to get around."

"Why are you surprised?" Jenna said. "You think you're the only one Chou's handed over to Castillo? You're not, and I would know."

"You're kidding me," Samira said, staring open-eyed at Jenna. "You? Castillo?"

"Yes. Chou told me she would beat the living crap out of me if I didn't do whatever Castillo wanted. I believed her, so I did. I'm not strong like you. I've felt dirty ever since."

"Your poor thing," Samira said. "So what happens now?"

"Chou gets transferred; you won't see her again. The dogs hate problems, and Chou's a problem now, so she'll go for sure, and good riddance. Bitch!"

"What about Castillo?"

"Chou was his procurer, so his supply of women dries up. But he'll be back; he'll find another Chou." Jenna laughed. "He'll ask you, you know."

"You're kidding!"

"No, no I'm not. You've done us all a favor by taking Chou out, but nature abhors a vacuum, so there'll be another Chou along. There always is, not that I care. Castillo's already had me every which way to Christmas," Jenna added, her voice trembling.

"Maybe I should fix Castillo. Can't be hard to shiv the fat pig."

"Don't even think about it," Jenna hissed, putting a hand on Samira's arm. "Chou's one of us; nobody really cares what happens to her. The dogs sure as hell don't. But attack one of their own?" She shook her head. "They'll never stop until they find the person responsible, never! Promise me you'll leave him alone."

"Okay, okay, just a thought. Anyway, I'd best keep a low profile. My first parole hearing comes up soon, and I'd rather not screw it up."

10

"Sorry to interrupt, Marty," one of the prison guards said, sticking her head around the door, "but I need Anders."

Samira's heart started to pound. Were the dogs on to her? Had they been told about Chou? Had they intercepted the glove before it was recycled? Had they found the knife?

"No problems," Samira's counselor said. "We're almost done here."

"Come on," the guard said, beckoning Samira to follow.

"What's up?' Samira asked as she followed the woman through a succession of security doors, more than a bit concerned. Her parole hearing was due any day now; if the board found out about Chou, not only would she not get parole, she would be facing new charges, charges serious enough to see her locked up for years. That thought made her feel sick.

"Shut your damn mouth, Anders," the guard snarled. "You'll find out soon enough."

"Asshole," Samira murmured just loudly enough for the woman to hear her but not loudly enough for her to be sure of what was said.

The guard led her to one of the interview rooms; there, two police officers waited behind a desk.

"Thanks. I'll take it from here," one said. The older of the pair, he had sergeant's chevrons on the shoulders of his uniform. "Take a seat, Ms, Anders. I'm Sergeant Chen, and this is Trooper Perez, Bellingen police."

"Okay," Samira replied with a puzzled frown, wondering what the cops wanted. They were the last people she expected to see unless they were there to talk about Chou.

"Good. Look, there's no easy way for me to do this, so I'll be direct if that's okay."

"What on earth are you talking about?"

"It's your father, Ms. Anders. He went to Mendoza?"

"That's what he said: to Mendoza City on business. He's due back … let me see, yes, tomorrow."

"That fits." The sergeant paused for an instant, exchanging a glance with his partner. "We've just had a pinchcomm message from the police on Mendoza. I'm sorry to have to have to inform you that your father was found dead earlier today. Mendozan police believe his death was not accidental, but we don't have any details yet. We'll know more by tomorrow."

Samira stared at the policeman, eyes wide open in shock and disbelief. "No." She shook her head. "No, it can't be him. It must be a mistake."

"I'm sorry, Ms. Anders, but it's not a mistake. The Mendozans have confirmed his identity with a deep DNA scan. It was him."

"No," Samira whispered, "no, please no. No, tell me they're wrong. Tell me …" Her voice trailed away and her head went down as the thought of how life would be without her father started to sink in. "Oh, shit," she said, lifting her head to look right at Sergeant Chen, tears streaming down her cheeks. "There's no mistake, is there?" she whispered.

"No, none."

Samira sat silent for what seemed like a lifetime. "What happens now?" she said eventually.

"We should call someone for you. You can't handle this on your own. Family? Friend?"

"My great-uncle, Jaska Anders. He'll know what to do. Admin will have his details."

Sergeant Chen nodded to Perez; the pair left without another word. Numb with grief, Samira could only sit there unmoving. What came next, she had absolutely no idea, and the thought of being alone absolutely terrified her.

11

The chairman of the parole board waited until Samira resumed her seat before speaking.

"Well, Ms. Anders," she said, "your counselor says you have been making good progress through the behavioral therapy program and certainly doing well enough to be considered for parole. Ordinarily, we would have waited another month or two to be sure, but under the circumstances, we think you deserve the opportunity to make a new start. We believe that the tragic loss of your father will do more to persuade you to rethink your life than anything this institution can ever do. Therefore, your release on parole is approved, effective a week from today."

"But," the woman continued, cutting Samira off before she could say anything, "you must understand that your release is subject to very strict conditions, which the discharge office will explain to you. Breach just one of those conditions, Ms. Anders, just one, and you will be back here, most likely to serve out the rest of your sentence. Is that understood?"

"Yes, yes, it is."

"Good. That's all. You can go."

12

To Samira's dismay, the throng of well-meaning relatives, friends, and neighbors that had descended on her once word of her release on parole had gotten out showed no signs of thinning out.

If anything, there seemed to be even more people in the house than had turned up for her father's funeral, though in contrast to that somber affair, everyone seemed determined to celebrate an event she'd rather forget; the air was spiked with laughter and underscored by the buzz of cheerful conversation. Still unable to accept what had happened to her father, Samira had struggled to stay in control in the face of the endless stream of platitudes washing over her, all full of worthy statements about new beginnings, the words muddied into an incomprehensible chatter by grief, the faces all too often blurred into anonymity by tears, her only response a fleeting half smile and a nod of the head.

To her relief, she found herself in a corner and left alone for once. Sadly, the moment did not last as Jaska spotted her from across the room and made his way over. "How are you doing?" he said.

"Not too well, Uncle Jaska. I can't do this much longer. Dad's funeral was bad enough, but at least it was over and done with quickly. This is ten times worse. I have to get away."

"Okay," he said. "We'll go."

"Just me, Uncle, just me," Samira said, putting her hand on his arm. "I need to be on my own. I need to think—" She could not help smiling as Jaska managed to look concerned and hurt at the same time. "—and I can't do that if somebody's talking to me."

"Oh," was all Jaska said, looking indignant.

"Even you," Samira whispered as she threw her arms around him and squeezed hard. "Even you." She pushed back to look him in the face. "Just let me do things my way, Uncle. Please?"

"All right. Where can I find you?"

"In *Bitsa*."

"Oh, shit." Jaska reached up to take her arms from around his neck. "Are you thinking of taking her up?" he asked.

"Er … probably."

"And let me guess: Nothing I say will make any difference?"

"No, none. I'm going to take *Bitsa* for a flight, and before you suggest it, no, I don't need you in the systems operator's seat. I'm command pilot–qualified, I have an unrestricted lander license, and my parole officer says she doesn't care what I do as long as it's legal and I show up in her office once a week, so I don't think there's any problem," she added a touch curtly.

"Goddamn it," Jaska breathed out, the air hissing past pursed lips. "Fine, you do what you want, but be careful and remember everything your dad taught you."

"You knucklehead," Samira said, throwing her arms around Jaska again. "Why do you think I want to take the old girl out?"

"Ah, right. Come on, then. Let me drag Buq away so we can do the preflight with you, okay?"

"Okay," Samira said.

Samira turned *Bitsa* onto the threshold and lined up for takeoff. She throttled the main engines back and eased the massive lander to a stop, its nose bobbing down and then up as she applied the brakes. The runway, a ceramcrete strip shimmering in the heat of the late morning sun, disappeared into the distant haze; far away, the Merkati Ranges reared up out of the murk, the peaks sharp points of gray rock floating in the air, seemingly unsupported.

She took a deep breath, the air rich with *Bitsa*'s familiar smell: a mix of electrical equipment, hydraulic fluid, an environmental control system long past its prime, burned cannon propellant, heat-seared ceramsteel armor, and crew and passengers long forgotten. In an instant, the years were stripped away and she was a child again, sitting alongside her father for her maiden ride in *Bitsa*, the ride that had taken her into orbit for the first time in her life, the ride that had sown the seeds of an ambition that still burned strong and hot.

"Come on, focus," she said out loud, the words bouncing off the worn interior of the crew capsule, fingers and eyes working their way methodically across the lander's status boards. "Get this right, girl, because today is not the day to screw things up."

With the before-takeoff checklist complete, Samira wriggled her body down into her combat spacesuit in a futile attempt to make its stiff, awkward mass more comfortable. "Right," she said. "Let's do it."

Flicking her radio over to the company's admin channel, she called Jaska. "KSS, *Bitsa*. I'm all set, Uncle," she said. "All systems nominal, all checklists complete, flight plan's approved, I have orbital authorization from Nearspace Control, and Bellingen Air Traffic has cleared me for takeoff."

"Roger that, Samira. Buq confirms that the telemetry looks good, so *Bitsa* is all yours. Just … just bring her back in one piece, please."

Jaska's voice was strangely thick. He's worried, Samira realized. Something told her that he and Buq would be sitting in Klimath Security Services' makeshift control room watching the data feeds from *Bitsa* and would keep doing so until she returned.

"Will do. *Bitsa*, out." And don't worry, she added silently; I haven't spent thousands of hours flying this old lander for nothing. Ignoring a sudden rush of nerves, she ran her eyes one last time around the cramped space with its holovid screens, status boards, switches, and selectors.

All was as it should be: *Bitsa* was ready.

"Let's go," she said. "Bellingen Air Traffic, this is lander Golf Whiskey Lima 455, over," Samira said, her nerves easing as the long-practiced routines took over.

"455, Bellingen. Go ahead."

"Bellingen, 455. Ready to launch, flight plan Orange 56 Bravo. Over."

"Roger, 455, copy … stand by. Flight plan Orange 56 Bravo is approved. You are clear to launch."

"Roger, Bellingen … 455 is rolling. Out."

Holding the lander on the brakes, Samira eased the throttles forward, and *Bitsa* began to shudder as the thrust from its fusion-fed main engines ripped the air apart. Still she held the lander on the brakes, eyes scanning the status boards to make sure *Bitsa* was as ready to go as she felt.

"Go, you good thing," she said, releasing the brakes. "Go!"

Bitsa hesitated, but only for an instant, and then the lander started to roll, accelerating hard, the ceramcrete runway blurring under the nose, the speed building fast.

"V1," called the lander's master AI, "rotate."

"Rotating," Samira called out even though there was only the data logger and the AI to hear her as she eased the side-stick controller back to lift the lander's nose. For a moment *Bitsa* paused as if testing the air, and then the wings bit into the airflow in earnest, the massive slabs of foamalloy arcing sharply up into the air as they absorbed the lander's mass and lifted it up into a fast-darkening sky.

"Positive climb, V2 … gear up … flaps up."

"Gear up," Samira replied, slapping the handles up to retract *Bitsa*'s undercarriage, the ride smoothing out noticeably as the lander's massive wheel assemblies folded away into the wheel wells, "and flaps up. After-takeoff checklist."

While the AI ran through the list, Samira settled back, content for the first time since that terrible moment when she was told of her father's death.

This, she thought, scanning the blue-black sky as *Bitsa* rocketed through five thousand meters, still accelerating, *is where I belong*.

But content or not, she was going to have to talk to Uncle Jaska once she landed. There was something she had to do, and the sooner she told him, the better.

• • •

Jaska and Buqisi had watched the takeoff in silence, the center holovid screen taking its feed from the holocam mounted above and behind the command pilot's station, the screens on either side filled with schematics that reported the status of every one of the lander's flight-critical systems.

"She's good," Buqisi said as *Bitsa* headed into low-earth orbit. "Very good, just like her dad. She has lovely soft hands."

"So she should be after all those hours in the simulator." Jaska shook his head. "Why couldn't she be just an ordinary teenager?"

"Our Samira an ordinary teenager? Not a chance."

"I'm afraid you're right. Nothing ordinary about that girl."

"No, there's not," Buqisi said. "Anyway, something tells me Samira's past worrying about all that. Her time in jail might have been short, but it hit her pretty hard. And it's taught her there's always someone bigger and uglier."

Jaska nodded; he had visited Samira in the prison hospital the day after some thug had worked her over. She had not been a pretty sight. "Never seen anyone grow up so fast, that's for sure," he said.

"That's what happens when the real world collides with teenage illusion. Which is why she's going to want to take over the business, to keep it going. You do know that, don't you?"

Jaska grimaced. "No," he said. "She hasn't said anything."

"Well, brace yourself, because she will, and what will you do when she does?"

"For crying out loud, Buq," Jaska snapped, "we've only just buried Matti. Can we leave what happens next until another day?"

"Sure," Buqisi replied, unconcerned, "but you wait. She will. You'll see."

"Piss off, Buq. I'm not in the mood to talk about this."

"How was it?"

"Magic, Uncle Jaska," Samira said, patting *Bitsa*, the hull still hot from reentry. "Everything's so clean, so simple up there in orbit. Not like down here."

"I know."

"It gave me a chance to think things through."

"And?"

"I've made two promises."

'Oh?" Jaska's eyes narrowed. "I'm not sure I like the sound of this. Two promises?"

"Two promises, and I intend to keep them."

Jaska sighed. "Go on, then," he said with a frown of resignation, "I'm listening."

"First of all,' Samira said, her voice strong and firm, the voice of woman who would brook no argument, "I'm going to keep the business going. KSS was Dad's life, and it's going to be mine too."

"Oh, shit!" Jaska said, dropping his head into his hands. "Fine, you do that," he shot back, looking up. "You can do that, you can keep the business going, but not with me as *Bitsa*'s systems operator. I'm not young anymore, Samira. I know you're young enough and stupid enough and stubborn enough to do whatever the hell you want to. So keep the business going by all means, but I'm sorry, I won't be there."

"Tell me something new, Uncle. I can manage without you, though I'd rather not."

"Really? Do you know how much work you'd have to do? I'm not being rude, Samira, but what do you know about running a business? What they taught you in high school—all of that will be as much use as tits on a bull."

"Maybe," Samira replied with a touch of defiance, "but I can learn, especially if you help me."

"We'll see," Jaska said with a marked lack of enthusiasm. "What's the second promise?"

"I'm going to find Dad's killers."

"Samira!" Jaska snapped, a look of horror on his face. "No, leave that to the police, please."

"The Mendozan police?" Samira shot back, glaring at Jaska. "Didn't you say you wouldn't trust them as far as you could spit."

"Well, yes, I did," Jaska conceded, "but you should still let them do their job."

"Oh, I'll let them do their job, Uncle, but am I going to trust them to do it properly? Let me see now; how much progress have they made so far?"

"Not a lot, but it is early days yet."

"Bullshit, Uncle Jaska. They've had plenty of time."

"Please, Samira, let—"

"Listen to me," Samira said, the steel in her voice unmistakable. "With or without the Mendozan police's help, I'm going to everything I can to find the people who killed Dad, and when I do, I'm going to nail their scum-sucking hides to the fucking wall."

"Oh, no," Jaska said, putting his head in his hands.

13

"I never knew a business as small as KSS could be so damn complicated." Samira said. She looked up from the holovid screen and stretched. "And I've been thinking, Uncle Jaska."

"I hate it when you say that." Jaska sighed. "What now?"

"I'm going to Mendoza."

"Mendoza? What the hell for?"

"To talk to the asshole leading the police investigation."

"The asshole leading the police investigation? Yup, that'll work."

"Come on, Uncle," Samira protested. "I'll be polite. Look, I think it's worth a shot."

"I don't think your parole officer will be too happy."

"I've spoken to her, and she's okayed it, so I'm going, Uncle Jaska, and that's all there is to it."

"Samira, please. Leave the investigation to the Mendozans. If they come up with anything, they'll tell us."

"So you've told me a hundred times," Samira said, disdain written large all across her face, "and all they've been able to come up with so far is 'killed unlawfully by person or persons unknown.' And you think that's okay? Give me a break."

Jaska frowned, a mix of frustration and concern. "Samira, please. Listen to me. I know the Mendozans are as corrupt as they come, but you have to trust them. Going over to Mendoza to harangue them won't achieve anything. All you'll do is piss them off."

"Screw them," Samira snapped back. "This is not the Middle Ages. If they're not making progress, it's because they don't want to. I want to look the sons of bitches in the face while they try to explain why."

Jaska sat back, his hands in the air in resignation. "Doesn't matter what I say, does it?"

"No, Uncle. It doesn't."

"Got to say, you are your father's daughter. He was one stubborn bastard too. Sorry, Samira. I didn't mean … you know."

"Don't sweat it, Uncle Jaska," Samira said, smiling through the sudden tears flooding her eyes. "Yes, he was a stubborn bastard, and so am I, no doubt about it. So let me go, let me see what those useless Mendozan fucksticks have to say, I'll come home, and then we'll see what we do with the business."

"Oh, Samira," Jaska sighed, a long, drawn-out sigh of frustration. He shook his head. "Why am I not surprised? Fine, I won't argue with you. Go to Mendoza, talk to the cops. Just don't piss them off. But don't be away too long. There's a lot we need to do."

"I know," Samira said, "so wish me luck." Without another word, she got to her feet and, pausing only to kiss Jaska on the cheek, was out the door and gone.

14

"Welcome back," Jaska Anders said, pushing his way through the flood of passengers pouring off the down-shuttle to fold Samira into a bear hug. "I'm glad you're home. I don't trust Mendozans in general and their so-called police in particular."

"Why would you?" Samira replied, fighting her way out of the embrace to pick up her bag. "They are a pack of no-hopers … well, except for a detective called Takahashi. He was the only one who seemed to give a shit."

"I did warn you."

"Yes, you did. But I needed to see for myself. I owed Dad that much."

"So what happened?" Jaska asked as the mobibot pulled away from the spaceport terminal.

"The Mendozan police made a huge fuss over me. I met the area commander and the chief of his homicide squad, Lieutenant Okoro. They gave me a personal briefing and all the time I needed to ask questions, not that I got any answers. They took me to the crime scene. I met the forensics guys. I met the brass a second time just in case I had any more questions. Then they laid on a police mobibot to take me to my up-shuttle."

"That doesn't sound so bad."

"It wasn't, except it was all fluff and bullshit. Takahashi was the odd one out; I kept getting the feeling he wanted to say more. Pity he never got the chance. Anyway, it was a virtuoso performance from the Mendoza City Police Department. Why would they do that, Jaska? I'm a nobody from a nothing system, a system the average Mendozan wouldn't piss on; that's why."

Jaska had to smile; he felt much the same way about Mendoza.

"It took me a while to work it out, but I think I did. The whole point was to convince me how hard they were working, to trust them, to leave the case in their hands, to go away and leave them be because even though it might take time, they would find Dad's killers in the end.

"But I'll tell you this, Jaska. In the end, the dumb bastards were too smart by half. I didn't get the message they wanted me to get; I got the real message. Either they can't, or they don't want to, or they have been told not to. Not that it matters, but the Mendozan police will never find out who killed Dad."

"Oh, no," Jaska groaned out loud. "What now?"

"If the Mendozans won't do the job, then it's up to me to find out who killed Dad."

"Ah."

Not another word was said until the mobibot pulled up outside the modest house Samira and her father had called home. As they climbed out, Jaska broke the silence. "You going to be okay on your own? I can come in if you want."

"I'll be fine, Uncle, and anyway I won't be on my own. I've called Nat. She's on her way over."

"Is she okay ... you know?'

"With me being an ex-con? Yeah, she is. She's going to stay with me until … until …" Samira's voice cracked, and she stopped, the tears streaming down her face.

"Oh, Samira! You don't have to do this on our own, you know."

"I do, you know," she said, wiping the tears away, her voice fierce with determination. "I'm an adult now, and you won't be around forever—"

"Thanks, Samira."

"Sorry, but you know what I mean, Uncle."

"It's okay," Jaska said softly. "I do."

"I've got to make my own way. The Rogue Worlds are a tough place, so if I'm to survive, I need to stand on my own two feet, starting now."

"You sure?"

"Never been so sure of anything in all my life."

"That's my girl. All you need to know is that I'm here for you and I always will be. If you need me, all you have to do is ask. Right, I'm off. I'll see you at the lawyers."

"What a waste of time and money that'll be," Samira said with a dismissive flick of the wrist. "I already know Dad's left everything to me."

"I know he has, Samira, but you have to be there anyway, so don't be late."

"I won't. See you tomorrow."

15

Coffee in hand, Jaska leaned forward. He looked concerned. "Are you okay?" he asked.

"Yeah. Dad always said there was more to the business than flying *Bitsa*. He was right, and he did it all on his own. Why the hell didn't he use an AI to manage KSS?"

"The business was his life, Samira, so why would he? He had the time, good business AIs don't come cheap, and as you're going to find out, cash—or lack of it to be more precise—is always a problem."

"Tell me. I might know next to nothing about business, but I can understand a bank statement."

"That's my girl. You need learn the first and most important thing about running a business, and fast. Cash is king."

"Lesson one: Cash is king. Got it."

"Speaking of cash, I have some good news. We might have our first job. I've been talking—"

Samira's hand went up, stopping him dead. "Hold on, Jaska! First job? How can we talk about our first job when I don't have a systems operator? *Bitsa* needs one, and we haven't even started looking."

Jaska's head dropped for a moment, one foot scuffing out his embarrassment on the ceramcrete sidewalk. "Ah yes, you're right," he said. "That is a problem."

"Jaska!" Samira snapped, her frustration obvious.

"Sorry. Look, I'll stay on as your sys ops. Not forever, though; just until we find a replacement."

Samira looked Jaska full in the face for a moment, then shook her head. "No, I can't ask you to do that, Jaska. I always knew Dad made it hard for you to walk away, but I won't. You said you'd had enough, so let's call it a day. You've earned your time in the sun."

"You make me sound half dead." Jaska chuckled. "I might feel that way sometimes, but I'm not. Look, don't sweat it, Samira. We'll start looking for my replacement. A couple more missions won't kill me, and I can tell you this: You'll make a great command pilot, but you still have a lot to learn, and the only person who can teach you is me. I can't walk away, not yet."

"Thanks, Jaska. That means a lot. Now, what's the job?"

"We've got two prospects. First is Morgenstenner Engineering. They're closing down their operations on Kalutura-23B but haven't been able to get their people or equipment out thanks to a bunch of criminal hardasses who've taken control of the mine. They need us to help persuade them to stand aside."

"Sounds straightforward."

"Only if you believe that's all there is to the job." Jaska snorted derisively. "There are always things they don't tell us, always."

"Uh, okay. And that's lesson number two, am I right?"

"You're right. Clients make a habit of being economical with the truth, and it's up to us to fill in the gaps. Poor intelligence is the best way to screw up a mission, and don't you forget it."

"I won't."

"The second prospect is what your dad and I call a drop and pickup."

"Drop and pickup?"

"Yep. Some guy wants to be dropped off on Calloway and picked up a week later. Why, I have no idea, and I doubt we'll ever be told."

"That'll be straightforward," Samira said with a breezy smile.

"It will?"

"Of course. A drop and pickup; how hard can that be?"

"In which case, let me refer you to lesson number two."

"Ah, right. Noted." Samira thought for a moment. "I've got two questions," she said. "First, when do we meet the prospects? Second, how do we find out what the jobs we're being offered are really all about?"

"We have a holovid conference to talk about the Calloway job Monday morning. We'll do that from the office. The Morgenstenner people will be calling us tomorrow; we'll know more then. As to your second question—" Jaska consulted the old-fashioned wristwatch he had worn for as long as Samira could remember. "—that will be answered in fifteen minutes when we call on Arturo Brazzi; his office is two blocks from here."

"I know the name. What does he do?"

"He's the closest thing KSS has to an intelligence officer."

"Ah, right, and thanks for telling me about the meeting," Samira said in a voice that was all acid. "Lucky I hadn't made plans to drop a few stimtabs with my shithead friends then."

"Yeah, sorry about that," Jaska said, sounding anything but apologetic. "I just forgot. Though I know you wouldn't touch a stimtab," he added, opening his eyes wide in innocent inquiry, "because that would be a breach of your parole conditions."

"Yeah, yeah, smartass."

"Anyway, I'm trying to keep things simple. You know, one step at a time."

"We'll see. Come on, let's go. And you can pay for the coffees."

"Just like your father," Jaska sighed. "He was a cheapskate too."

Samira followed Jaska into the mobibot. "That Brazzi's one creepy guy," she said as the vehicle pulled away. "No wonder Dad never let me near him."

"Arturo Brazzi's not a man I'd ever go drinking with, I have to say, but he's the best intelligence asset we've got." Jaska chuckled softly. "Hell, what am I saying? He's the only intel asset we've got."

"Should I be worried?"

"No, you shouldn't," Jaska said. "He's expensive, but he's worth every cent. I've lost count of the missions where Brazzi's intelligence has been the only thing that's gotten us home. He's got a network that's better than most planetary intelligence services, so don't be tempted to cut costs by stopping his retainer."

"Lesson two, Uncle."

"Precisely."

"Think he'll come up with anything on the Morgenstenner and Calloway jobs?"

"I hope so. That brings me to lesson three: The more the client knows that we don't, the more likely we are to get screwed: on duration, on costs, on risk, on what we can charge. So pray that Brazzi comes up with something useful. We need those jobs."

"I wish we had more time."

"We don't, and most of the time we don't, so get used to it. Which brings me to lesson four: Our best chance of getting a job is when the client is in a hurry. Problem is—"

"That doesn't give Mr. Brazzi much time to find out whether the job's one we should take."

"Exactly right."

"This business sucks." Samira scowled. "Is there anything easy about it?"

"No, not really."

There was a prolonged silence. "Which is why we're going to miss Dad," she said at last. "Am I right?"

"Yes. He was very good, and that's why he was so reluctant to let you into the business. You always thought it was about the missions, the flying, getting shot at, all that sort of thing. That was part of it, true, but not all. Your dad knew a hundred ways to get screwed in this business—a hundred that he knew of, that is, a hundred that he'd learned to deal with along the way. What bothered him was the hundred other ways he didn't know about."

"The infamous unknown unknowns," muttered Samira.

"Never were smarter words said. This business is like life: It's what you don't know you don't know that kills you."

"Had Dad had enough to want out?"

"I don't know. I did wonder sometimes, but he would never talk about it. You know what he was like. If he didn't want to discuss something, it wasn't discussed."

"Well," Samira said, "it's all academic now. He's gone, the business is mine as of this morning, I'm determined to keep it going, and that's all there is to it."

"So I gather," Jaska said with a wry smile. "I hate the idea of you running the business without me, and I wish you wouldn't. But I know I'm only wasting my time trying to convince you of that, so I won't. We'll find someone good to take over from me and hope for the best."

"Sounds like a plan. Now," Samira said with a studied cheerfulness that belied the leaden feeling in her stomach, a feeling of self-doubt, of fear, of uncertainty, of all those damned unknown unknowns waiting out there to kill her, "what's next?"

"The bloodsuckers that supply most of our spare parts," Jaska said, a sour smile on his face, "Kaitana Aerospace. They are not my problem, thankfully, so Buq said she'll meet you there."

"Friends of ours, are they?"

"Hell, no. Biggest crooks this side of Old Earth."

"So why do we deal with them?"

"They're the only ones who can supply spares for *Bitsa*. They're going to try and tighten the screws on us now that your dad's gone, but let Buq deal with that. Kaitana's kids run the business now, but the old man and Buq go back a long way, and she knows him rather better than he realizes. So sit back, say nothing, and do less. Just let Buq handle it. Got it?"

"Yes, boss."

"Good. Off you go. I'll meet you at the ministry at four. Kamarov is a complete prick, so make sure you have all your ducks in a row."

"Oh, don't worry, I will."

"Good. We need him to approve that license."

"Ah. Ms. Anders. Welcome. Everyone here at the Ministry of Interstellar Affairs was sorry to hear about your father."

"Thank you, Mr. Kamarov; appreciated. You know Jaska, of course."

"I do," the man said with a bob of the head at Jaska.

"Gerry. It's been a while," Jaska said, his tone of voice making it obvious that it had not been long enough. "Can we make this quick, please? We have a lot to do, as I'm sure you appreciate."

"Yes, yes, certainly, Jaska. Now," he said, studying his desktop holovid screen, "this all seems in order, Samira—may I call you Samira?"

"Of course, Mr. Kamarov, please."

"Gerry," Kamarov said with a leer that made Samira's skin crawl. "Call me Gerry. Now, let me see. Yes, your application for a Class 602 licence authorizing Klimath Security Services to conduct mercenary operations under the Klimathian flag following its change of ownership looks fine."

"Good," Samira said, wanting nothing more than to be somewhere, anywhere, else; Kamarov was giving her the creeps. "In that case, we won't take up any more of your valuable time," she added, starting to her feet.

"Sir down, Ms. Anders," Kamarov said, his voice hardening. "It's not that simple, not that simple at all."

"How can that be?" Samira demanded, sitting back down. "Our application's fine, you said so yourself, and I meet all the criteria for a license. I know; we've checked."

"I'm sure you have. But as I say, it's not that simple."

"Why?"

"Because, Ms. Anders," Kamarov said portentously, slowly, as if speaking to a child, "under the regulations, the Ministry of Interstellar Affairs has the discretion to withhold a Class 602 license if we think the applicant might act in a way that might reflect badly on the Klimathian government. All we need is reasonable grounds. Now," he continued even more slowly, "in this context, 'reasonable grounds' means—"

"Mr. Kamarov," Samira said, choking off a sudden urge to climb across the desk to smack the man in the head, "I paid attention during my high school law studies, and I know what 'reasonable grounds' means. So please don't lecture me; just tell me what your grounds are."

"Ah, okay." Kamarov blinked, taken aback, the bluff and bluster gone all of a sudden. "Yes, let me see now … We believe that a Klimath Security Services with you as owner will commit an act or acts that will bring discredit on the Klimathian government," he said. Recovering some of his composure, he sat back, a small smile on his face.

"That's it?" Samira demanded, anger flooding through her system. "Those are your reasonable grounds?"

"Steady, Samira," Jaska whispered.

Samira ignored him. "And why do you think that, Mr. Kamarov?" she said.

"Your age, your inexperience, and your criminal record, Ms. Anders," Kamarov said, smug now. "It's inevitable; you will make a mistake. Now, we don't care if you kill yourself, but we do care about the good name of Klimath."

Samira snorted. True, Klimath was a very long way from being the most corrupt of the Rogue Worlds, but it was hardly a shining example of good governance.

"Age, inexperience, criminal record," she said, taking care to keep her voice level, businesslike. "Those are your reasons?"

"Those are our reasons, and here—" Kamarov pushed a single sheet of paper across the desk at her. "—is formal notification that your application has been rejected."

"I see," Samira said, scanning the document. She looked up. "So you printed this before the meeting?"

"I did."

"Big mistake. That denies me my right to due process, Mr. Kamarov, which makes this—" She pushed the paper forcefully back at Kamarov. "—null and void."

"Don't tell me how to do my job, Ms. Anders."

"Somebody should." She shot a glance at Jaska, who nodded. "Jaska, perhaps you would like to take over."

"I think I will, Samira," Jaska said. He looked right at Kamarov. "You're a damn fool, Gerry. Long as I've known you, you've been a damn fool, a bully too, but you're going to have to find somebody else to take your inadequacies out on. I had a feeling you couldn't help sticking it to Samira—she's only a young girl, after all—and I was right. So here—" He reached down into his briefcase to pull out a document, which he pushed across the desk at Kamarov. "—is our bit of paper."

"And what's this?" Kamarov said, poking at the paper with a finger.

"One you should read, but to save you the trouble, it's a legal opinion from our lawyers. It says there are no grounds for you to refuse our application, none at all. Not age, not experience, not criminal record. No surprises there: The Ministry of Interstellar Affairs last refused a Class 602 license application six decades ago, and that was only because the man in question was a court-certified psychopath. You guys do not refuse these applications, you never have, and now is not the time to start. So withdraw your rejection, give us the approval we want, and we'll forget this meeting ever happened."

Kamarov glared at Jaska through slitted eyes. "I can't do that."

"I think you can, unless of course you'd prefer me to go to your minister for a ruling. He and I were both in the 145th Spaceborne, by the way. He goes to the 145th's reunions, so I'm sure he'd be interested to hear about the bullshit you get up to when you're allowed out on your own."

Saying nothing, Kamarov kept staring at Jaska, who returned the look, unblinking. The standoff lasted a good minute; then the man's head dropped to read Jaska's document. "Well," he said finally, "in light of this new opinion—" Samira snorted, contemptuous. "—I agree I should reconsider the rejection."

"You're too kind, Mr. Kamarov," Samira said, her face illuminated by the sweetest smile she could muster. "We'll wait if you don't mind."

"Didn't know you and the minister were old buddies," Samira said as they left the Ministry of Interstellar Affairs, heading for the mobibot rank, a hard copy of the precious license tucked safely away in a folder under her arm.

"Me and the minister? Jaska laughed. "I never said we were, and we're not, by the way."

"You're kidding me!"

"No," Jaska said, shaking his head. "No, I'm not. I've only met him once. Yes, we both served in the 145th Spaceborne, just not at the same time. But Kamarov is too dumb to work that out, and even if he did, he's too piss-weak to call my bluff. Come on, I've had enough for one day. Let's get you home."

16

Samira hoped she did not look as worried as she felt. Wiping suddenly damp hands across the front of her pilot's jumpsuit, she sat down in front of the holocam.

"Don't look so nervous," Jaska said.

"I'm trying," Samira said.

"We'll be fine."

"I wish I shared your confidence, Uncle. Losing the Morgenstenner job was a blow. That would have been a good mission for us."

"It would have been, but don't tell me you were surprised."

"No," Samira said, shaking her head, "I wasn't. Even the dumbest client was going to notice the difference between a lander commanded by a combat-proven pilot and one commanded by an eighteen-year-old with no successful missions under her belt. Like that asshole Kamarov said: I'm too young and too inexperienced. So no, I wasn't surprised."

"The first mission will be the hardest to get, so have faith. And this client is in a hurry, so he doesn't have the luxury of picking and choosing. He wants this job done yesterday, and we're the only ones who can do it. Go with us or don't go; those are his only options."

Samira frowned. "It's not quite that easy, Uncle Jaska. Why would he retain us if he thinks I'm too inexperienced to be trusted?"

"Well, the mission brief says this is a straightforward drop and pickup, Brazzi hasn't uncovered any nasties, so maybe the client isn't that fussed."

"I wish Brazzi had been able to work out who the client is. It'd make me a whole lot happier."

"Me too. Okay, here we go. Ready?"

"Ready," Samira said, taking a deep breath in an attempt to slow her pounding heart.

The status light on the holocam shifted from blinking amber to a steady red; as it did, the holovid screen blossomed into life to reveal the avatar of a middle-aged man. From somewhere deep inside Samira, a tiny alarm bell began to ring.

If this client is kosher, she thought, *then why is he using an avatar? Why can't we see him in person?*

She flicked a glance at Jaska; if it bothered him, he was not letting it show.

"Good afternoon, Mr. Anders," the avatar said. "I'm Daalit Hagen."

"Mr. Hagen," Jaska said with a nod. "Call me Jaska, please."

"And you must be Samira Anders," the Hagen avatar said. "Good to meet you."

"Good afternoon, Mr. Hagen," Samira replied.

If he's Daalit Hagen, she thought, *then I'm the tooth fairy.* And the avatar software was the worst she had seen in a long time, the three-dimensional image grainy and unstable, the product of cut-price software engineering.

"I was sorry to hear about the loss of your father, Samira. He was a fine man, good at his job. Very solid, very reliable."

"Yes, he was. I will miss him."

"I'm sure you will. He will be a very hard man to replace."

Samira resisted an urge to groan. Okay, okay, I got the message, she wanted to say as Hagen reinforced his point with a theatrical shake of the head. Dad was experienced and I'm not. So what? You want this job done or not?

"Mr. Hagen," Jaska said, "you've had time to study our proposal?"

"Yes, I have."

"Along with our sims of the mission?"

"Yes."

"And those sims prove that our new command pilot is more than capable of flying this mission successfully. So can we move on to talk—"

"Hold on, Jaska," Hagen said. "Hold on. Yes, the client thought the sims were most impressive, but a simulation is just that, a simulation. There's no danger, no stress. And if you make a mistake—" Hagen shrugged his shoulders. "—it doesn't matter. You learn the lesson and start again."

"Mr. Hagen," Jaska said, his voice firm. "The mission brief—*your* mission brief—tells us this is a straightforward mission. We drop the client on Calloway, come back a week later, pick him up, and take him to Gennafax-43. Calloway is a nothing planet populated only by a handful of survey teams. A simple mission, so I'm not sure what lessons we stand to learn. Or have we missed something?"

"No, Jaska, you haven't missed anything. Just as you say, it is a very straightforward mission. But … but …"

"But what, Mr. Hagen?" Samira said, with an effort keeping her voice steady while ignoring Jaska's frantic hand signal to back off. "We can do this mission, we can do it when you want, we can do it how you want it done. I don't see the problem. Unless there's more to it, of course, in which case we'd have no choice but to rethink our involvement." She turned to Jaska. "Wouldn't we?"

Please, please, please back me up here, Uncle, Samira thought while Jaska took his time, as if weighing the issue.

Jaska nodded. "Samira's absolutely right, Mr. Hagen. If you were asking us to punch a hole in, say, Mendoza's planetary defenses, you'd certainly have a point. But that's not what you're asking us to do so, and so, with all due respect, we don't think you have a point."

To Samira's surprise, Hagen's head went back and he roared with laughter. "What the hell?" she mouthed to Jaska.

"Just wait," he mouthed back.

"Oh, please forgive me. You two are a class act," Hagen said when he recovered himself. "I have to give you that. Okay, okay. I get the point. You can do the job. Now, can we move on?"

"Please," Samira said, allowing herself to breathe out, waving Jaska to take over again.

"Okay," Hagen said. "Now, first let's have a look at …"

"Well, Samira, Jaska, I think we have a deal."

"I think we do, Mr. Hagen," Samira said.

"I'll send you an executed copy of the contract with those changes. The mobilization fee will be in your account by close of business. Is there anything more to talk about?"

Samira glanced at Jaska, wincing when she saw the anger in his face. *Oh, shit*, she thought. *He's going to kill me.* "Jaska?"

"No," he said, voice tight. "We'll see your client here at 06:00 Monday. We take off at 07:00. Please tell him not to be late and make sure he brings a full personal survival kit and has valid ID. We won't take him if there are any warrants out for his arrest, and we will be checking."

"06:00 Monday, survival kit, and ID, got it. Thank you both. Goodbye."

The silence that followed was profound. Samira waited until the strain was more than she could bear before speaking. "Oh, Uncle Jaska," she said, "I'm sorry, I really am. Please forgive me, please."

"Why?" Jaska demanded. "I should kick your ass from here to breakfast time, Samira. Didn't I tell you to leave the negotiations to me? Didn't we agree to that?"

"We did."

"Yes, we did agree to that. So why the hell did you open your big mouth and give away half the mobilization fee? We need that money; it covers our costs if the client walks away."

"But why would a client walk away?"

"How the hell would I know?" Jaska said, his voice rising to a half shout. "Clients do that sort of shit from time to time. Trust the client by all means, Samira, but only after getting as much money up front as possible." Jaska took a deep breath, running his hands across his buzz-cut hair. "Lesson one, remember? Cash is king?"

"Sorry, Uncle."

"Sorry is not enough. Look, Samira. There's one thing you have to learn right now. And if you can't, then I'm going to walk out the door and KSS is finished. You understand that?"

"Yes, I do," Samira said softly, embarrassed by her stupidity. "Tell me."

"If you say you're going to do something, I have to be able to trust you with my life, and right now I can't. This is not a game, Samira. This is not like going out with Nat on a

Saturday night. This stuff matters, because if we get it wrong, we die."

"Oh."

"So here's the deal, and it's nonnegotiable. You look me in the eye and tell me that when we agree to something, it stays agreed. You promise me that, but before you do, make sure you mean it. And if you can't, then have the guts to say so."

Samira swallowed hard, the steel in Jaska's voice making it all too clear that this was not the time to brush him off. The way he looked at her, she felt he was looking right into her soul; his eyes were like washed-out blue pebbles: hard and unyielding. She realized that she was getting a glimpse of the real Jaska Anders for the first time; this was not warm, cuddly, friendly Great-Uncle Jaska anymore. This was a man she did not even begin to understand.

But one thing she did understand: If she lied to Jaska, he would know, and then it would all be over. She took a huge breath in, letting it out in a rush to steady herself, and then another.

"I was wrong, and I apologize," she said. "From here on out, what we agree to stays agreed. What I just did will not happen again—ever. You have my word on it."

Jaska leaned forward to look right at Samira so long and so hard that the sweat started to bead on her forehead.

"You know what," he said at last, sitting back at last, a half smile on his face, "I actually think you mean it this time. I hope so; it's about time."

"Oh, Uncle," Samira said, hurling herself into his arms, "sorry."

"Hey, hey, hey!" Jaska said after a long pause, easing her away. "Enough of the emotional stuff. Want to know something?"

"What?"

"You did pretty well under the circumstances."

Samira shot backward, throwing off Jaska's arms. "You bastard!" she said. "So what was all that 'giving away half the mobilization fee' business?"

"Oh, I meant that bit." Jaska grinned. "But hell, Hagen was right. We are an unknown quantity, so we were always going to have to make concessions. The only difference is that I would have taken time out, talked it through with you before agreeing. Better to negotiate that way. It gives the decision more gravitas, makes it harder for the client to push us back. Anyway, what's done is done, so let's not waste any more time on it."

"Agreed," she said, and they both laughed. "But I have a question … well, more of an observation, really," she added.

"Oh?"

"Yes. I think the man behind the avatar wasn't the agent; was he our passenger? I think he might be."

"Wondered if you'd picked it, and, yes, I agree. I'll pass that on to Brazzi. The crappy avatar software and the call routing will give him something to work with. Maybe he can find out who our mystery passenger is."

"Never occurred to me to do that." Samira was reminded for the umpteenth time how little she knew.

"Don't hold your breath; it's not much to go on. Now, I want you back in the simulator while I have another go at that damn hydraulic pump."

"Okay," Samira said, the word catching in her throat as she realized what had just happened.

She was going on her first mission as command pilot of *Bitsa*.

17

Samira watched the mobibot make its way onto the apron. "Client's here," she shouted across to Jaska, who had his head inside one of Bitsa's landing gear nacelles.

"You handle him. There's a small leak I need to fix."

"Okay."

The mobibot drew up in front of her, on time to the second. After a short pause, the passenger door hissed open, and out stepped a woman. Tall, rangy, dark-skinned with an open face dominated by high, angular cheekbones under an unruly mop of jet-black hair, she was dressed in a dark green jumpsuit and carrying a bulky backpack, her large brown eyes looking right at Samira with penetrating intensity. For a moment, Samira could only stand there and gape. Recovering her equilibrium, she stepped forward.

"Here," she said, reaching for the backpack, "let me take that for you."

"No, I'm fine," the woman said. "I can manage. I suppose I should call you Captain Anders even if you look like you belong in school."

"Samira will do," Samira said, not sure whether she should feel pleased or patronized. "I'm sorry, but what do we call you?"

"I'm Melzita Kohl. Please call me Mel."

Kohl's not a local, Samira thought, *not with that accent.*

The woman was not from any of the Rogue Worlds. She spoke like someone in the trashvids Buq liked so much; that meant she was from Old Earth.

You're a long way from home, Melzita Kohl, Samira thought.

"Welcome to Klimath Security Services, Mel," she said. "Leave your kit by the door and follow me. We need to confirm your ID, and then we're ready to go."

"Sure."

Samira led the way into the office, a cramped space barely big enough to contain a desk and a couple of chairs. "Take a seat," she said.

"Cozy," Kohl said.

"Does the job," Samira said, wondering if she was going to like the woman. "Now, comm me your identity certificate and then put your finger in the DNA scanner, please."

Kohl did as she was told, and Samira waited while some antiquated AI somewhere deep in the bowels of the Klimath Department of Records got to work. Her patience was finally rewarded by a terse message confirming that yes, Kohl was who she said she was and she was clean: no outstanding warrants.

"That's all fine, Mel. One last thing. Any personal weapons in your kit?"

Kohl looked surprised. "Er, yes. A machine pistol. Is that a problem? Nobody said it would be."

"It's no problem," Samira said. "We just need to stow it in the small arms rack until we start our approach to Calloway. Any ammunition?"

"Of course," Kohl said with a disgruntled look, "and five microgrenade magazines."

"They'll need to go in the magazine as well."

"Is that strictly necessary?"

"Yes, Ms. Kohl, it is. It's for safety reasons. I'm sure you understand," Samira added, flashing Kohl her best "I'm the captain and you can trust me" smile.

Kohl still looked unimpressed. "Okay," she conceded with a reluctant bob of the head.

"Fine, now unless you want some of Jaska's foul coffee, I suggest we get you and your gear onboard. Once you're settled, we'll do the safety brief, get you fitted with a emergency skinsuit, and then we'll be off."

"Lead on, Captain Anders, lead on."

"So what do you think?"

"Don't know, Uncle," Samira said with a frown. "Part of me likes her, wants to trust her. Part of me says … oh, I don't know … be careful?"

"Careful is best, though I do wonder why she needs a JZK-44 machine pistol. That's a serious piece of ordnance. Expensive too."

"Well, that's her problem. We ready to go?"

"When you are, Captain Anders."

"Oh, please, Uncle, cut it out."

"Hell, no. I'm having too much fun. But seriously, while you're still learning, let's keep it by the book."

"Fine. You call me Captain, I'll call you … Uncle Jaska. Now, let me get suited up, and then we'll start the preflight checklist."

"Ms. Kohl, this is the captain."

"Go ahead."

"We're ready to go up here. Please confirm you're suited up, faceplate down, your suit's showing all greens, and you are strapped in."

"Stand by … all confirmed."

"Roger that. We'll be taking off shortly."

Samira looked across at Jaska. "Ready?"

"Ready. All systems nominal. Still want to do this on manual?"

"On manual, confirmed. Bellingen Air Traffic, this is lander Golf Whiskey Lima 455, over," Samira said, her nerves easing as the long-practiced routines took over.

"455, Bellingen. Go ahead."

"Bellingen, 455. We're ready to launch and will be following flight plan Blue 66 Zulu. Over."

"Roger, 455, copy that … Stand by, flight plan Blue 66 Zulu is approved. You are clear to launch."

"Bellingen, 455, roger. Rolling now, 455 out … Okay, folks, we're off."

Four hours later, *Bitsa* jumped into pinchspace en route for Calloway.

18

"Right, Mel. You have any more questions?" Samira said.

Kohl shook her head. "No, I think you've covered everything. And thanks for the offer of a backup beacon. I have no intention of missing the pickup, but you never know."

"Just be there when we come back, please. Okay, we're going to do this fast like we planned, so go strap yourself in. Jaska's put your ammunition and microgrenades beside your seat; your gun is racked by the hatch; just don't forget it on your way out."

"Oh, don't worry. I won't."

"Glad to hear it. And when I say go, go. No hanging around."

"Got it, Captain Anders," Mel said, flicking Samira a half salute.

"Good luck. See you at the pickup."

Samira made her way back to the flight deck and started to suit up. "What a pain," she said. "I never had to do that in the sims."

"What? Talk to customers?"

"Exactly."

"Well," Jaska said, "your dad did say the sims aren't like the real thing, and there's one reason why."

"If that's the only difference, I'll be happy. Right, how're we looking?"

"All good. *Bitsa*'s behaving, and all systems are nominal. We're due to start reentry on schedule, and then it's up to you get us in and out. Just do it fast, faster if you can. Never pays to hang around."

"We've simmed it often enough, so hopefully we'll be fine," Samira said, squeezing her space-suited bulk into the command pilot's chair. "Right, let's do it."

After an intense burst of savage deceleration under full power, Samira had turned *Bitsa* end for end. Now the lander dropped nose first in a parabolic fall toward the planetary surface, a turbulent mass of searingly white cloud slashed open here and there to reveal the greens and browns of Calloway's largest continent far below.

"All stations, coming up on reentry. We good to go, Jaska?"

"Affirmative; we are nominal for reentry."

"Roger."

Samira pushed the nose even farther forward until *Bitsa* plunged straight down, holding it steady until the hull began to feel the first wisps of Calloway's atmosphere. Easing the nose up, she held the lander at an angle to the airflow; despite the best efforts of the artificial gravity, the fast-thickening atmosphere was now buffeting *Bitsa* in earnest, shaking the airframe hard in a series of random jerks that bounced Samira's head off the well-worn headrest of her seat.

"All stations, stand by aerobrake. Hold on, folks; this could get rough."

It did; Samira pushed the lander's nose up to put its belly flat against the onrushing air. *Bitsa*'s hull screeched and twanged in protest as it struggled to absorb the enormous stresses loaded on it as the lander dumped huge quantities of kinetic energy into the air ripping past, the artificial gravity fighting to absorb the g forces.

Bitsa lost speed quickly enough to allow Samira to turn the lander from a barely controlled lump of armored ceramsteel into an aircraft. Extending the wings meter by cautious meter, she eased the nose back down until *Bitsa* was in airborne flight for the first time in days. Then she allowed herself to relax a tiny fraction.

"On vector," Jaska said, his voice devoid of any emotion. "Drop zone on the nose, time to run ten minutes."

"Roger that. Threat board?"

"Is green. Orbital traffic, no change: still only one survey ship in low-earth orbit."

"Roger, threat board is green," Samira said. "Mel, this is the captain."

"Go ahead," Kohl said shakily.

"You okay?"

"Just about. That was a bit rough."

"Sorry about that. Necessary evil, I'm afraid. We did warn you."

"Yeah, you did."

"Right, the good news is that our threat board is green, which means the chances of anybody shooting at us are remote. We are tracking a survey ship, but it's on the far side of Calloway; it won't even know we're here. All being well, we'll be at the drop zone in less than ten minutes. So unstrap, get your gear, go stand by the hatch, and hang on. As soon as the hatch opens, debark and keep going. And remember to get well clear; otherwise we're going to fry you when we lift off. Got all that?"

"Yup."

"Okay. Good luck. See you in a week."

"Thanks. Oh, I almost forgot. I've approved your progress payment; check with the bank on Kyalawi to make sure it's gone through okay."

"We will when we remass. Thanks, Mel."

"Don't thank me. Just make sure you get me down in one piece."

Riding twin pillars of blazing driver mass, *Bitsa* skimmed across the treetops and slowed to a halt over a large clearing. For a moment, the lander's enormous bulk hung in the air before Samira backed off the throttles a fraction and dropped *Bitsa* to the ground, the air around the landing site erupting in a giant steaming cloud of incinerated soil, water, and vegetation before Samira shut down the main engines to drop the ship's full weight onto the undercarriage.

"Contact … three greens, we're down. Go!"

Jaska was not wasting any time, already slapping the hatch switch to open. When the clouds cleared, Samira was relieved to see the external holocams tracking Kohl's figure as she fled into the forest fringe.

"We're clear," Jaska said the moment Kohl vanished.

"Roger," Samira said, powering up *Bitsa*'s main engines and lifting off.

Long hours later, Samira threw off her straps and climbed out of her seat, her body a mass of stress-induced aches, to start the tedious process of unsuiting. "Don't know about you, Uncle Jaska, but I think that'll do for today."

"I agree," Jaska said. "Those Kyalawi bastards know how to charge for driver mass, that's for damn sure."

"We're still making good money on this job, Uncle. And talking of money, did the bank confirm the transfer?"

"They did. Always a good feeling when a client pays us what they owe."

"It sure is."

"Right, I'm done here," Jaska said, forcing himself out of his seat, the effort obvious.

"You okay?"

"Oh, yeah. But this is not an old man's business, Samira."

"I can see that, Uncle. Soon as we get back, we'll find a replacement for you. I promise."

"That'd be good. Come on. Captain's perks mean you shower first, and trust me, you need to. I can smell you from here."

"Hey!"

"You're wasting time. While you shower, I'll see if I can find something worth eating, and if you're lucky, I might even have something decent to drink."

"Sounds damn good, Uncle Jaska."

The meal over, Samira and Jaska sat in *Bitsa*'s cramped crew room, nursing the last of a very good bottle of white wine.

"Going to be one hell of a boring week, Uncle."

"Won't be for me. I need a break."

"I wonder what Kohl's doing down there," Samira said, hooking a thumb at the crew-room holovid screen. Calloway was a distant blue-white dot almost lost against the star-littered black of space.

"Who knows? Something to do with mining leases is all I can think of, though what good she's going to do all on her own is anyone's guess."

"Well, as long as it doesn't get us shot at, I don't give a damn."

"Here's hoping, Samira. But remember this: A mission can kill you with only seconds left to run."

"Now there's a cheery thought. Thought this was supposed to be a milk run."

"It is, but you never know."

Samira took a deep breath. "Uncle?"

"Yeah?"

"I know things have gone well so far …"

"Yeah." Jaska nodded. "They have."

"But I can't help feeling that Dad was right."

"About what?"

"I don't have what it takes to do this."

"Hey, Samira!"

"No, no. Hear me out, Uncle. He said there was more, much more to this business than flying *Bitsa*, and he was right. I see that now. What scares me is how little I really know, how much more I have to learn before I can come even close to being as good as he was."

"What are you saying?"

"I thought I could do this, and I can't. Worst of all, I think all I really wanted to do was prove Dad wrong. I don't want to be here anymore, Uncle. What the hell was I thinking of? The whole thing's a surefire recipe for disaster. So we're going to finish this damn mission, go home, and then I'm closing

KSS down. You can retire, and I'll go find something better to do. And I'm sorry I made those stupid promises. I should have known better."

"You finished?" Jaska asked softly.

"Er, yes. I guess I am."

"My turn. I think you're half right. You did underestimate things, but do I think that's a recipe for disaster? No, I don't. Not if we're smart. We've all got to start somewhere, and here is where you start. Everyone has a first mission, and first missions are never easy, trust me. But we'll do it together, Samira, because I know what you don't, and before I quit, I'll make you know it all."

Samira frowned. "I'm not sure."

"Well, I am. Anyway, you sleep on it. We'll talk again tomorrow."

"Okay."

"Right, I'm off. Don't wake me up when you turn in."

"I won't. Night."

Samira sat back as Jaska left the crew room. Never had she felt so alone, so unsure, so vulnerable, and she hated it.

19

Samira had been so wrong.

The week had been anything but boring, thanks to Jaska. He had kept her in the sims, running every threat that might be waiting for them when they returned to pick up the mysterious Melzita Kohl, She thought he'd overdone things, though, having Kohl burst out of cover with an enormous Tyrannosaurus rex in hot pursuit. She smiled at the memory; that sim had ended with the dinosaur mincemeat, Kohl safely onboard, and the pair of them in hysterical laughter.

Samira wasn't laughing now. She was so nervous, she hadn't slept or eaten in two days. She took a deep breath to steady herself. "Surveillance drone seeing anything?" she asked.

Jaska shook his head. "Nothing," he said. "The landing zone is clear. Threat board remains green, and that survey ship is still doing a lot of nothing. The radio intercepts we picked up earlier are now at Red 35. Nothing to be concerned about; they're commercial transmitters, digital voice, and datalinks with low-level encryption."

"Still think it's a survey party?"

"Yes. We're seeing the same mix of ground and airborne transmitters, but slow-moving. I've taken running fixes on their position, and they are closer to the landing zone than I would like, so we'll need to watch them."

"They spotted us?" Samira said with an anxious frown.

"By now? Almost certainly. Weather's perfect: no cloud, very little wind. They'd have to be blind not to have seen a lander doing a high-g reentry and deaf not to have heard us. But so far there's been no change to their position or activity levels, which tells me they're not interested in us."

"Roger that," Samira said, suppressing a faint feeling of unease. If the transmitters were coming from a survey party, where had they been last week? Time to act as if there were a serious threat out there, she decided, even if it was only a hunch. "Right, Jaska. Screw this. If they know we're here, there's no point in gagging our search radar. Time to go active?"

"I think so. Going active on search, stand by … No airborne or surface contacts inside missile engagement zone, threat board remains green."

"Roger that," Samira said, feeling somewhat foolish even though Jaska had been quick to agree.

"On vector," he said, voice devoid of any emotion. "Landing zone on the nose. Drone confirms LZ is clear."

"Okay, Jaska. Change of plan. Put all weapons to auto, then I want you to lose the suit and get down at the access hatch in case you have to give Kohl a hand getting onboard. And keep talking to me. I've got a bad feeling about this."

"Funny, that," Jaska said, throwing off his straps to start the tedious process of desuiting. "So have I."

"Oh, shit," Samira whispered; if Jaska was worried …

She forced herself to concentrate, losing altitude until *Bitsa* was skimming only meters above the forest canopy ripping past below in a blurred palette of every imaginable shade of green. This was not the time to lose the bubble. All she had to do was get *Bitsa* down in the center of the landing zone; if Kohl was there, well and good. If not, *Bitsa* wasn't waiting one second longer than the two minutes specified in the contract.

Jaska had finally fought his way free of his suit. "Wish me luck," he said as he disappeared down the ladder.

"Good luck," Samira shouted over her shoulder as she lifted *Bitsa*'s nose, "and hang on!" Ramming the throttles onto the stops, she shifted power to the lander's belly thrusters, the artificial gravity rippling and twitching as the savage deceleration stripped off *Bitsa*'s speed.

"LZ on the nose at a thousand meters," she called out. "500 ... 200 ... 100 ... at the LZ."

Rather harder than she intended, Samira dropped the lander, its landing gear screaming in protest as shock absorbers soaked up the impact, white-hot efflux from the belly thrusters driving clouds of steam and dirt boiling up into the sky.

"Stand by, Jaska ... Okay, main engines are shut down, clear to open the hatch."

"Opening ... hatch open."

"Clock's running," she said. "Any sign of her?" she asked, wishing she'd overruled Jaska's and Kohl's insistence on maintaining radio silence. It would have been good to know the woman was actually out there, somewhere close, preferably.

"Give me a break, Samira. All I can see is steam."

"Goddamnit," Samira said, scanning the feed from the drone's holocam. As the air cleared, there was nothing to see except the short, matted grass of the landing zone and beyond it patches of broken scrub and then the rain forest proper. "One minute and then we're gone, Jaska," she said.

"How's the threat board?"

"Still green."

"Suggest we hold on. If the board changes, we go."

"Okay," Samira said, not at all sure that was what they should do.

The seconds dragged and the pressure built until Samira, her eyes flicking back and forth between holovid screens and the threat board, could take it no more. "Jaska, we can't wait any longer. We're a sitting du—"

"There she is!" Jaska shouted. "Port side, inbound. Stand by to lift off."

Relief flooded through Samira as she spotted a figure running hard for the lander. "Roger that," she said. "Just tell me when."

Her relief was short-lived, blown away by the electronic warfare AI. "Green 15, two radar intercepts, Kravak search radars, classified hostile," it said in a flat voice overlaid by the intercept alarm. "Stand by range estimate."

"Oh, shit!" she said. The Kravak ground-attack flier might be only one-twentieth the size of *Bitsa*, but it was a nasty piece of work. For the first time in her life, Samira felt death reaching out for her, the thought sending unalloyed terror ripping through her. The fear lasted only a millisecond before an icy determination to survive took over, and the hours Samira had spent in the sims kicked in.

Acting on instinct, her mind raced through the options. Stay and fight, she decided: It was too late to lift off, the client was too close to abandon, and—best reason of all—she liked her chances. *Bitsa* was well armored, and she outgunned even a pair of Kravaks by a huge margin.

"Jaska! We're staying. Get that bloody woman onboard while I keep the Kravaks off our back."

"Roger," Jaska said calmly. "She's struggling, so we'll need a few minutes."

"Okay."

Samira put Kohl out of mind—either she made it or she didn't—and focused her attention on the threat plot, which was now scarred by two virulent scarlet lines marking the Kravak radar intercepts. "Give me a vector on those Kravaks," she barked at the AI running the threat plot. "I need one now!"

"Stand by," the AI said in a voice so flat, so calm that Samira wanted to reach behind the threat board to strangle the life out of it. "Stand by ... estimated range six kilometers, speed 750 kph."

They'll be on us in less than thirty seconds, Samira said to herself just as the drone's holocams finally picked up the incoming Kravaks, two small black shapes flying scarcely meters above the jungle canopy.

"Weapons free," she said to the AI. "Engage at will."

The two Kravaks, traveling fast, burst into clear air over the landing zone, and *Bitsa*'s lasers opened up. A moment later, the Kravaks too opened up, Samira flinching instinctively as their cannon shells chewed a path of destruction across the LZ toward her before slamming into *Bitsa*, the flight deck resonating with the vicious metallic cracking of cannon shells spalling fragments of ceramsteel armor off the hull.

Then the Kravaks were past, accelerating away and banking hard to keep *Bitsa*'s lasers away from their vulnerable sterns. *Minutes*, Samira thought, *that's all we have before the Kravaks turned and lined up for another run. Where the hell is Kohl?*

"Sitrep, Jaska!"

"Didn't want to bother you," Jaska replied, breathing heavily, "but Kohl's been hit. She's down, alive or dead I don't know. I'm on my way to bring her in."

"Are you mad, Jaska?" Samira took a deep breath. Jaska did not need her going off at him. "Sorry. We've got less than two minutes before the Kravaks hit us again. Can you get her back by then?"

"Yup. I'm with her now. She's a mess but still breathing. Hold on. I've got her, and I'm on my way back. Start powering up."

A quick glance at the port after holovid confirmed Jaska's report. Bent almost double under Kohl's weight, he was staggering back toward *Bitsa*. How the hell does he do that? Samira wondered.

"Go, go, go!" Jaska said as he heaved Kohl bodily through the hatch and dived in after her.

Samira did not bother with the niceties. As she slammed the throttles to emergency power, *Bitsa* leaped into the air; there it hung for a second before she slewed the lander around to face the incoming Kravaks, dropped the nose, and started to accelerate.

Tracked by the surveillance drone, the Kravaks never had a chance. With the lander clear of the ground, *Bitsa*'s belly-mounted ground-attack cannons could join the fight, their hypervelocity 30-mm rounds smashing into the fliers the instant they appeared, shredding them into hundreds of flaming fragments that hung in the air for a moment before arcing downward, trailing thin white lines of dirty gray-black smoke.

A fierce elation mixed with raw terror filled Samira as *Bitsa* punched through the turbulence left by one of the doomed Kravaks. "That's the way to do it," she said, easing back on the throttles once she'd confirmed that the Kravaks were history. "Jaska, threat board's green and we're on our way. How's Kohl?"

"Busy; call you back."

"Roger."

That doesn't sound too good, Samira thought, turning her attention back to the task of getting *Bitsa* as far away from Calloway as possible.

"What a mess," Samira said, trying to keep control of her stomach.

Melzita Kohl was indeed a mess, the blood-soaked wreck that was her body festooned with IV tubes and monitor leads, her face pale and drawn behind an oxygen mask, everywhere splotches and streaks of lurid green woundfoam.

"She is," Jaska said, "but she's alive, she's stable, and the medical AI says she'll stay that way until we get her to the base hospital on Kyalawi. She's one lucky woman. I watched her run through those cannon shells, and I have no idea how she made it without being chopped to pieces. Still, one cannon shell is all it takes, and she was lucky that it hit her in the shoulder. Down a bit and to the right and her heart would have been mincemeat. And I saved her damned backpack."

"Her bag?"

"Her bag. She refused to let it go; I had no choice."

"I wonder what's in it that's so damned important. We should have a look."

"You know what, Samira?" Jaska said as he covered Kohl with a blanket and sat back on his haunches, running bloody hands over his face without thinking.

"What?"

"We don't need to know. If her life was worth risking two Kravaks for, then whatever is in that pack is bigger than both of us. Better we let her keep her secrets."

"Hell, no, Jaska, I don't agree. Knowledge is power and all that. Anyway, how will she know?"

Without a word, Jaska hefted the pack up and held it in front of Samira's face.

"Jaska! What the hell are you doing?"

"See anything?"

"No."

"Look harder," Jaska said, finger stabbing down. "Here."

"Oh," Samira said, blushing with embarrassment at being reminded yet again of how little she knew. "Those thin blue threads? Jeez, you can hardly see them."

"That's because you're not meant to. If we open this, she'll know. We have a rule: Assume everyone we carry has telltales on their gear, so leave it alone. Scanning a bag is one thing; ferreting around inside it is another. That's the sort of thing that gets people like us killed, okay?"

"Sorry."

"Don't be. Just learn the lesson. Now, I need a shower."

"Go on. I'll keep an eye on her."

"Thanks. Oh, and by the way, you did a damn good job today, Samira. Damn good."

20

"Ms. Kohl?" the man at reception said, checking a screen. "Hold on … Yes, she's in regen on this level, Bay 13. Straight ahead for twenty meters, then take the first corridor on your left."

"Thanks," Samira said. "Come on, cheer up," she said to Jaska as they set off. "We need to talk to the woman, if only to get her to authorize our final payment."

"I know, I know."

"Why so glum, then?"

"The add-on costs," Jaska said with a scowl as they set off down the corridor, a laser-cut rock tunnel far below the surface of Kyalawi-44D. "They're always a problem."

"Think that'll be a problem?"

"We shot off a truckload of cannon shells, Samira, and getting clients to pay for stuff like that is always a problem, especially when the mission is over. She can tell us to go screw ourselves, and that's probably what we'd have to do. We don't have any leverage; a Klimathian contract is not enforceable on Kyalawi-44D, and I'd bet my life that Ms. Kohl is not who she says she is."

"But the money's in escrow. It's paid already."

Jaska stopped dead, his head snapping around. "I told you to read the contract, every last word of it. Did you?"

"Yeah, I did ... well, the important bits, obviously."

Jaska shook his head. "Goddamn it, Samira. When I say every word, I mean every word. Did you read every word?"

"Er ... no," Samira said, shamefaced.

"Samira!"

"Sorry, Jaska. What've I missed?'

"If the bank does not receive authorization from the client within six months of the contract date, all funds held in escrow are returned. That means we have to go to court to enforce payment, which, given the fact that a reasonable percentage of our clients are criminals in one jurisdiction or another, is not something they like to do. So they usually just bugger off, and we lose our money."

"Oh!"

"Which is why the mobilization fee is so important. And don't tell me it's not fair if clients do bugger off; it's just the business we're in, okay?"

Jaska did not wait for a reply; turning on his heel, he stormed off down the corridor, leaving Samira scrambling to catch up.

"Sorry, Jaska," she said when she did.

"You're going to have to stop saying that, my girl. Now, where the hell's Bay 13 ... right, here we are."

Bay 13 was an alcove laser-cut out of the rock. Fronted by a counter and brilliantly lit, it was home to a row of regeneration modules: plasfiber caskets hung with wires, cables, and pipes, all topped off with status screens tracking the life of the patients inside.

"We're here to see Ms. Kohl," Samira said to the technician behind the counter.

"Ms. Kohl? Let me see … Yes, she's talking, but only via a neuronal interface. It'll be another two weeks before she's out of regen if you want to talk to her in person."

"That'll be fine," Samira said.

"Follow me. Here we are." The technician scanned the status board for a moment. "And you're in luck; she's awake. Put these headsets on and just start talking. But not too long, please. She's very tired."

"Thanks. Ms. Kohl? It's Samira."

"Ah … hi, Samira," Kohl said in a harsh, metallic voice that made her sound like a cheap AI.

"How are you feeling?"

"I'm not feeling anything, Samira, but thanks for asking."

"The medical tech says you should be out in two weeks. The shoulder going to be okay?"

"They say it will. Be a long time, though. They say I'm very lucky to be alive, so I'm not complaining."

"We're glad you made it. You had us worried for a while."

"I bet, though I don't remember much. Last thing was those fliers. After that, it's all a bit blank."

"We've put together a complete log of the mission, Ms. Kohl. It'll be waiting for you when you come out. That should fill in any gaps."

"Good. Thanks."

"And we're going to see if we can identify those fliers. I'm sure you'd like to know who—"

"No! Don't do that!" Kohl rasped, the force of her words obvious even through the interface. "Don't even think about it."

Samira glanced at Jaska. "Let it go," he mouthed to her.

"Sure, Ms. Kohl," Samira said. "Whatever you want. We'll leave that to you. Not a problem."

"It's better that way, trust me."

"Okay."

There was an awkward silence, which was broken only when Samira worked out that Jaska was not going to come to her rescue. *You are a bastard*, she thought, scowling at him.

"Umm, Ms. Kohl," Samira said. "Can we talk business? You up to that?"

"Business?" the metallic voice grated. "You mean money, don't you?"

Samira couldn't help smiling. "Er, yes. The final payment; the consumables bill will be quite high. What do we do about that?"

"Thought you'd ask. Go see Gerard Singh at Kowalski & Kowalski. They're our lawyers back on Klimath. He has a copy of the contract. Give him the mission log and your final account. I've sent him a comm telling him to make sure you get paid. There'll be no dicking around. Promise."

"Okay," Samira said, frowning.

"I know what you're thinking, Samira, but don't worry. You guys took a big risk to save my life; that much I can remember. I'm not going to screw you over now."

"Didn't think you would, Ms. Kohl."

"Liar! But don't worry about it. Go home, talk to Singh. He'll fix you up."

Samira glanced at Jaska again. He shrugged his shoulders. "Have to do it," he whispered.

"Thanks, Ms. Kohl," Samira said. "Come see us next time you're on Klimath."

"Will do, and thanks again for saving my ass. You did very well. Forgive me, guys, but I'm too tired to talk anymore. I'll try to catch up with you sometime."

Kohl cut the link. Samira took off her headset and, with a quick word of thanks to the tech, followed Jaska out of the bay.

"You happy with that?" she asked him.

"I've been in this business a long time, Samira, and let me tell you this. Next to getting a cash card pressed into your sweaty little hand, that's as good as it gets. Come on. I've had enough. I want to go home."

"Me too," Samira said, and she meant it.

Refreshed by a shower that put a serious dent in *Bitsa*'s supply of fresh water, Samira made her way back to the crew room. "Don't care what that damn foodbot's churned out this time," she said. "Just serve it up. I'm starving."

"Not just yet," Jaska said, putting a bottle with an unreadable label and two balloon glasses on the table. "There's a small ritual me and your dad always went through after a mission."

Guilt stabbed Samira hard. She hadn't thought of her father for days. *It just shows*, she thought, *how quickly life moves on*. Surreptitiously wiping the tears from her eyes, Samira slid into her seat, hoping that Jaska had not noticed.

"Ritual? What ritual?" she asked.

"Neither of us was superstitious," Jaska continued, pouring two shots of a clear gold liquid into the glasses, "but ... well, we liked to think that a small toast to our survival was one of the things that kept us lucky. Silly, I know, but it became a habit."

"Silly maybe, but if that's what you and Dad did, that's what we're going to do."

Jaska raised his glass. "The toast is 'We made it back alive,'" he said, and knocked the contents back in one shot.

Samira lifted hers. "We made it back alive," she said, and followed suit.

A second later, she wished she hadn't. "Faaaackkk!" she spluttered as molten fire engulfed her mouth and throat, tears of pain springing into her eyes. "Aarghh! That hurts. Bloody hell, Jaska," she croaked. "You could have warned me."

"Yes, I could," he said, "but why spoil the fun?"

"What is that shit?" Samira said, wiping the tears from her eyes.

"That, my dear, was one shot of something that even the richest man in humanspace would have trouble buying because your father and I reckoned we had the last cases left, and we agreed we'd never sell them. It's Hennessey from Old Earth. The real thing, Samira, the real thing: cognac, 135 years old."

"Hundred-and-thirty-five-year-old cognac? Dare I ask where the hell it came from?"

"You may. Looted … er, taken in lieu of back pay from the cellars of the president of Mooral by your grandfather. He had some time on his hands while he was stealing *Bitsa*, the place was an absolute shambles, so he thought why not."

"Good to know I come from such enterprising criminal stock."

"You do, Samira, you do. Now, we'll have one more, I think, this time to toast your dad." Carefully, Jaska poured the two shots.

"To Dad," Samira said, flinching, her eyes flooding as she drained her glass.

"To Matti Anders, the best damn command pilot I ever flew with," Jaska said, taking his time to savor the cognac, "and I've flown with a few."

"Oh, that stuff's awful," Samira said, struggling to breathe, "but something tells me I'm stuck with drinking it. It might be the rarest drink in humanspace, and it might be as old as you are—"

"Hey," Jaska growled, "respect your elders."

"—but it sucks. It's horrible!"

"You are an ignorant peasant, Samira."

"And proud of it."

"Right, let's eat," Jaska said, carefully replacing the cap on the bottle and stowing it away. "The foodbot says we're getting a Goan fish curry, but I have my doubts."

"Doesn't matter what it is; I wouldn't know. That cognac has destroyed my taste buds."

Good or bad, the food did not last long.

"I think I'm done," Jaska said with a soft belch. He pushed his plate away.

"Me too," Samira said.

"How do you feel now?"

"A lot better, thanks."

"A successful mission always does that," Jaska said, rubbing his eyes. Samira was struck by how tired he looked.

"You okay, Jaska?"

"Yeah, I'm fine."

Samira looked at Jaska. "No, you're not, are you?"

Jaska took his time before answering. "No," he said softly, "I don't think I am. I'm old, Samira, and I'm getting older."

"You don't want to do this anymore, do you?"

Jaska shook his head. "No," was all he said, and that only after a long pause. "No, I don't."

"I'm sorry," Samira said.

"What the hell for?"

"For dragging you into this, this … this madness."

"Samira!"

"Hear me out, Uncle. It's taken me a while, but I know what I've done, and I'm not proud of it."

"What the hell are you talking about?"

"You. I'm talking about what I've done to you."

"You're still not making any sense, Samira."

"I made promises I couldn't keep … well, not without your help. Talk about emotional blackmail. Dad had just been murdered, I was out on parole wondering what the hell I was going to do with my life, the business I'd always wanted to be part of was finished, and what was I doing? I was promising to avenge Dad and keep the business going. How were you ever going to say no to me? You weren't and you didn't."

"No, I didn't, but not because you were blackmailing me."

"Which I was."

"Which you were," Jaska went on with a fleeting smile, "but because you were the daughter I never had and I loved you. How could I ever say no to you?"

"Oh, Uncle Jaska," Samira whispered, her eyes filling with tears, "I'm so sorry."

"Don't be. I'm big boy. Nobody put a gun to my head."

"Maybe, but it's over, Jaska. You've just flown your last mission. When we get back, we start looking for your replacement. We're not flying any more missions until we've found someone to take over. Okay?"

"Okay."

"Good, that's that, then. One question, though. Did you mean what you said, you know, that I'd done a good job back on Calloway?"

"Yes, I did. And you knew you had, so don't pretend you didn't."

Samira laughed. "When those Kravaks turned up, I never felt so alive, Uncle, never in my whole life. True, I was shitting myself, but I still felt good, better than I have in a very long time."

"You should have felt good. Your dad couldn't have handled those Kravaks any better. Now, that's enough, Samira," Jaska said. "I think I'm done. We'll do a full analysis of the mission tomorrow. Not everything was as good as it should have been."

"Sure," Samira said, too tired to press Jaska to explain. "You turn in. I'll clean up."

Jaska nodded; without another word, he slid out from behind the table and with obvious effort got to his feet and was gone.

21

Blinking in the blinding midday sun as she emerged from the offices of Kowalski & Kowalski, Samira put a call through to Jaska.

"Hi, Samira," Jaska said. "How'd it go?"

"Kohl meant what she said. Singh didn't argue. I've already checked, and the full amount owing has been transferred."

"Pleased to hear it."

"You don't sound very happy. What's up?"

"*Bitsa*'s cannons. Checked them out this morning; they need new barrels."

"Damn. That sounds expensive."

"It will be. Buq's talked to that old crook Kaitana, and she's put the order in already. We'll have them early next week."

"Fine; so why the long face?"

"I'll tell you when you get back."

"So what's up, Jaska?" Samira said, throwing herself into a chair.

"We've only had one applicant for the job of *Bitsa*'s systems operator. Ashok Samarth is his name."

"Only one? Jeez, I know we're a fringe operator—"

"You can say that again."

"—but we're not that dodgy." There was a very long silence. "Any good?" Samira said finally.

"That depends. Technically? Yes, the man is first-rate: ex–Klimath Defense Force with exceptional sim scores. There wouldn't be many systems operators as good. He's had no combat experience, though."

Samira snorted. "Nobody in the KDF has, Jaska," she said. "He's just what we need, a damn good sys ops."

"He has a criminal record."

"Oh, great!" Samira sighed. "Only one applicant, and he's a crook."

Jaska scowled. "That makes two of you; you should get along well."

"Gee, thanks. How the hell did you find him?"

"It turns out I know Ashok's grandfather, Charlie, Charlie Samarth. We served together in the KDF way back when; we became good friends during the Malakula and Berrath campaigns. I saved his ass, and he saved mine more than once. I don't see much of him these days, but we still talk now and again. He called me up, told me I was a silly old fart and much too old to be flying, said he'd heard we were looking for a new sys ops and he knew the right man to take over if I was prepared to overlook a small transgression."

"So what do we do?"

"Forget the criminal record. We know he can do the job, so you need to meet him to see if you can work with him."

"Okay," Samira said with a frown, not at all sure it was that simple, "but I need to know what he's done."

"Knocked off some gear from the KDF. Cost him his commission and earned him a slab of jail time and a dishonorable discharge."

"Theft?" Samira thought about that for a moment. "Maybe I can live with that," she continued. "I need to think about it some more, though. But let's meet him."

"I'll set up a time for you to meet. But on one condition, Samira."

"What?"

"I'm too young to go sit on my ass somewhere talking shit to a bunch of oldies waiting to die. I want to stay in the business. I'll help Buq run things dirtside while you're out on missions. I can help drum up new jobs, and we never have enough repairbots. Poor old Buq spends more time trying to fix them than she does working on *Bitsa*."

Samira's eyebrow shot up. She had assumed that Jaska would want to go off fishing or, even more depressing, take up golf. "That's the best news I've had in a long time, Jaska. If that's what you want, that's what I want. But one condition."

Jaska's eyes narrowed. "One condition?"

"Yup. I want you to be the boss."

"The boss? Me?" Jasla shook his head. "No, that's your job. It's your business."

"Legally, yes. But you've been half of this business for a long time."

"Buq too."

"I love Buq to death, but she's an engineer. A damn good one, it's true, but you've been at the sharp end. You know all there is to know about what we do and how. Buq doesn't. Listen, Jaska. I know some people won't take me seriously, and until they do, I need you to front the business."

"Ah, shit. Fine, if that's what you want. I'll be the boss, but we still have to agree on everything. Like before."

"Of course. And if you say no, then it's no."

"Deal. Right, enough of this. Let me get back to Mr. Samarth."

"Yes, boss," Samira said.

"Go away, little girl," Jaska growled.

22

Samira was finalizing the list of lessons learned from her first mission—a depressingly long list—when Jaska stuck his head through the doorway. "Mr. Samarth's here."

"Ah, good."

When Samarth appeared, he was not all what Samira expected; too much time watching crappy holovids of all-action KDF heroes was probably to blame. In his late twenties, well on the skinny side, medium height, coffee-skinned, and with brown eyes under an unruly mop of fine black hair, Ashok Samarth looked more like the class nerd than one of the KDF's finest. No, make that one of the KDF's former finest, she reminded herself. As his arm went out to shake hands, she could not help noticing his fine-boned hands and long, slender fingers.

"Ashok, welcome. I'm Samira Anders, owner of KSS and the command pilot of our lander. Take a seat. Coffee?"

"No, I'm fine."

"Okay, then, let's get on with it, shall we?"

"Let's."

No matter how often she reminded herself that this was not the time for her to be making emotional decisions, Samira found herself warming to the man as they talked. It was time, she decided after an hour had passed, to put the man on the rack.

"Okay, all of that's good," she said, looking directly at Samarth, "but I need to know why you did what you did: stealing stuff from the KDF, I mean."

"Do we really have to talk about that?"

"What the hell do you think, Ashok?"

For the first time, the man looked uncomfortable, eyes scanning the office, hands locking and unlocking, the tip of his tongue darting out to wet his lips. "Er, okay. Sorry, of course we do. It's just that it's not something I'm very proud of."

Samira leaned forward to look right at Samarth. "Let me tell you something, Ashok. I don't care what you've done. I'm not even worried that you might do it again; if you ever stole anything from KSS, you wouldn't spend time inside. Jaska would cut your balls off and shove them down your throat instead."

Samarth flinched.

"And I've done time too."

"Yeah, I heard."

"It's no secret. So are you going to answer the damn question?"

Samarth sat, his mouth sagging half open, clearly disconcerted by Samira's directness. "Right … I removed the AIs from a batch of landers—fire control and electronic warfare; they're the most valuable—and sold them. The KDF is upgrading its fleet, so they were state of the art. They were very easy to steal. KDF security is a joke; I just took them out when the landers were taken out of service to have new fusion plants and main engines fitted. I needed the money." He shrugged his shoulders. "Anyway, I got caught when someone decided to poke around and found the AIs missing. KDF internal security put surveillance holocams into a pair of landers and caught me in the act. Pity; those landers would not have been returned to service for months, and they would never have suspected me. The rest you know."

"I see," Samira said. "Interesting."

"Not really. Stupid, more like. Never did get to enjoy the money. Why else would I be out looking for a job?" he added, his voice bitter.

"Oh, but it is interesting, Ashok, just not in the way you think."

"Oh? How?"

"What's interesting is what you've left out: why you stole and who for. I've read the transcripts of your trial. You never explained why you needed the money, you didn't come clean on who you sold the gear to, and for some reason the prosecution seemed strangely uninterested in getting the answers to those questions, just like they made no effort to recover the stolen AIs.

"And there were two more things that don't sit right. The jail term! What a joke. Five years with a two-year non-parole period, and guess what? You got parole right away. All a bit lenient, wouldn't you say?"

"Your second point?" Samarth said, stony-faced.

"You didn't make much out of it even though those AIs must have been worth millions. Let me see … Yes, your cut was only 5 percent, Ashok. Awfully small cut considering the risks you took, don't you think?"

Ashok looked away. "It's a tough market," he said.

"I'll say. But the problem is this, Ashok. I'm not the Klimath Prosecution Service, Ashok, and I do care about the answers to all those questions. I have to trust the person who sits in my lander's right-hand seat, trust him with my life, and I can't do that unless I know why you would do something that seems so out of character."

"I understand all that, but I can't help you. I'm sorry."

"What do you mean you can't help me? No can't about it. You won't help me."

"Does it matter?"

Acutely aware that the man sitting across the desk from her was the only candidate for Jaska's job and that KSS was finished without him, Samira choked back her frustration. "Yes, it matters," she went on, "but we'll come back to that. I have one more question. Why do you want to work for KSS?"

Samarth smiled, obviously relieved by Samira's change of tack. "That's easy. I joined the KDF to be a lander pilot. Sadly, my brain's not wired the right way, so I became the next best thing: systems operator. The KDF won't have me anymore, and you might, so here I am. It's the only way I can keep flying."

"You know what we do?"

"It's no secret, Samira. Talk to the right people, they know, and my grandfather and your great-uncle are old friends. Oh, and by the way, I was sorry to hear about your dad. You must miss him."

"I do." Samira nodded. "But let's stick to the point, shall we?"

"Sorry."

"The fact that we are a one-ship operation flying a superannuated lander doesn't concern you?"

"No," Samarth said, shaking his head, "not one bit. All I want to do is fly, and as a disgraced ex-KDF officer, I'm not exactly swamped by job offers. Nobody else will touch me."

"I think that answers my question. So back to the ones you haven't answered: why you stole and who you stole for."

"Who says I stole for anyone in particular?" Samarth snarled, eyes narrowing with sudden anger. "You cannot know that."

"No, I cannot know that, but the longer we talk, the more certain I am that you did. Call it female intuition. Come on, Ashok. Tell me! Somebody asked you, didn't they?"

To Samira's surprise, all of a sudden the fight drained out of Samarth, leaving him slumped in his seat, head down, face slack, mouth half open, and for the first time she knew she was looking at the real man.

"Damn," Samarth said softly, "what a mess." He lifted his head. "Would you believe me if I said I did it for the money?"

"No," she said, "I wouldn't, and you know why. You need to tell me the real reason."

"Maybe I do, if only to get the job," Samarth said with a crooked half smile. "But if I do, then the secret's out and I really am screwed, along with some other people I really care about—and terminally, if you know what I mean."

"I need to know with whom I'm flying, so tell me."

"No," Samarth said, shaking his head. "I can't. Pity; I really wanted the job, and I think flying alongside you would be cool. But if I have to tell you the full story to get the job, then I'm sorry. I have to decline." He got to his feet. "Good to talk to you, Samira. See you around."

Samarth stood for a moment, as if deciding whether to say more. But he did not; without another word, he turned and was gone.

"Was I wrong to push him, Uncle?"

"No, you weren't. And I think you're right about someone forcing him to knock off those AIs. I spoke to his grandfather, and he agrees. He says the Ashok he knows would never have done something like that—never."

"So he has no idea why?"

"None. The family's baffled, and Ashok refuses to say anything. No, I'm sure of it. He was pressured into stealing those AIs, no doubt about it."

"Damn. The problem is this: If it can happen once, it can happen again."

"That's what bothers me, Samira. Only the next time you might be at risk. This business is dangerous enough without having a sys ops vulnerable to blackmail."

"But surely whoever put him up to it the last time won't be interested in him anymore. He doesn't have access to KDF hardware, and I don't think anyone would want anything out of *Bitsa*."

"Sad but true," Jaska said with a chuckle. "I don't know. Maybe we shouldn't be too worried."

"Maybe. He still the only candidate we have?"

"He is."

"Shit!" Samira scowled. "If we insist he talks and he won't, we're stuffed."

"And even if he does talk, how would we know he was telling us the truth? We might still be stuffed."

"Terrific." Samira put her head in her hands. "So what now?"

"Let me talk to his grandfather again. And I'll get Brazzi to dig a bit deeper. I know he's had no luck so far, but he might come up with something."

"Okay."

"By the way, Buq tells me the replacement cannon barrels have just arrived. She thinks it'd be a good idea if you started prepping them for installation."

"Me?" Samira said with a puzzled frown. "Why me? I wouldn't know where to start."

"That's why you're going to do the job, Samira. It's time you learned there's more to this business than running around being some sort of action hero. Put the ordnance bot into instructional mode; it'll talk you through what needs to be done. And if you really screw it up, Buq will be happy to put you straight."

"Oh, great," Samira whispered.

Goaded by the ordnance bot and harassed by Buq, Samira was well into the tedious and messy task of cleaning preservative grease off *Bitsa*'s new cannon barrels when a soft beep announced the arrival of a message. *Well, well, well,* she thought when she opened the vidmail. *I never expected to hear from you again.*

"Hi, Samira," the man said. "Remember me? I'm Jonah Takahashi, the detective in charge of your dad's case. I'm here on Klimath to give evidence in an extradition hearing. We should meet, but it has to be tonight. Sorry to rush you, but I'm booked back to Mendoza tomorrow, and I can't miss my shuttle. I'm staying at the Foundation City Hotel in Morgannen. Six this evening would be best. Let me know if you can make it."

You just try and stop me, she thought. Her reply was short and to the point. "Six, lobby. See you then."

Rather more forcefully than was necessary, Samira slapped the switch on the ordnance bot to put it back into autonomous maintenance mode. "You can clean those damn barrels yourself," she said to the inanimate mass. "I'm off to meet a man. Enjoy yourself. Hey, Buq!"

"Yes?"

"Got to go; something's come up. Sorry about that."

"Bloody hell," Buqisi grumbled, wiping grease from her hands. "Pilots! Prima donnas, every last one."

It had been a scramble, and to be sure Jaska wasn't happy—she had a string of very terse vidmails to prove it—but Samira had made the maglev to Morgannen in time for her meeting with Takahashi. He was waiting for her in the lobby of the Foundation City Hotel, a slight, unremarkable man dressed in a gray suit, the sort of man who faded into the background unless you knew to look for him.

"Ms. Anders," he said. "Good to see you."

"I hope to be able to say the same, Detective Takahashi."

"Please, call me Jonah. The bar here is quiet. That okay?"

"As long as you haven't dragged me all this way just to try and chat me up."

"No, Ms. Anders," Takahashi said with a tired smile. "Drink?"

"Beer, please."

Nothing more was said until the drinks had been ordered and served. Then the Mendozan detective started to talk so softly that Samira was forced the lean forward to hear him. "You know that what we put you through when you visited us was a charade," he was saying.

"Yup," Samira said, "it was."

"I apologize, but it wasn't my decision."

"Okay, I'll buy that. So what can you tell me?"

"Nothing formal, and that's because I have not been allowed to make any progress. Officially, our position has not changed."

Samira sat back, her face marred by a sour scowl. "Killed unlawfully by person or persons unknown," she said. "I already knew that. Now, listen to me, Detective; I've got a shitload on my plate at the moment, so either come to the point or I'm leaving."

"Take it easy, Ms. Anders. I'm taking a big risk talking to you, and I wouldn't be doing that just to enjoy the pleasure of your company."

"Okay, okay, I'm sorry. What can you tell me?"

"I can tell you my strictly unofficial position, and please do not discuss this with anyone. If people back on Mendoza find out it was me that told you, then I'm in serious trouble, terminal trouble."

"I won't," Samira said, troubled by an uneasy feeling she was getting herself into something she did not understand, something dangerous. Takahashi was the second person that day to talk about problems of a terminal kind, and she had trouble thinking it was a coincidence.

"That said, I've been a detective long enough," Takahashi continued, "to know that you will talk, but so be it. If you have to, then only to people you trust with your life, and don't mention my name—ever."

"I promise."

"Right," Takahashi said with a slight shrug of his shoulders, as if dismissing Samira's promise as worthless. "We know your father was set up. The obvious question is why, and we need to know that, because motive connects a crime to its perpetrator. This was no crime of opportunity, so we have to look to what your father was doing that might have upset someone so badly that he had to die, and there's only one thing that stands out: the job he did on Kapsos-VII, helping to free Silla Armato.

"Whoever killed your father did so because they lost big-time when Silla Armato was freed. Now, I tried to establish who that might be, but that's when the shutters came down, and I got my ass kicked. My boss told me to leave the Armato case to the Jalmaniyan police, and if I didn't, I could start looking for another job."

"My father's part in rescuing Armato's daughter? That's the motive?"

"That's the motive. I can't prove it, but I'm sure that's where you'll find the answers you're looking for."

"So if we find out who kidnapped Silla Armato, we find my dad's killers?"

"That's my theory. Would be good to have some evidence to support what I'm saying; sadly, I don't. But it's the only thing that works for me."

"The business we're in, we piss off a lot of people. How can you be sure?"

"I can't. But the Klimathian police sent me a summary of the missions KSS has carried out over the last three years, and two things stand out. The Armato job is the only one that cost the losers really big money, not to mention the enormous ransom they didn't collect. So there's your motive: payback. Second, the Armato kidnapping was very professionally done. Took a large organization with huge resources and plenty of cash."

"Can't be too many of those. Any ideas?"

Takahashi sighed. "There's the rub. There are what? Two hundred settled planets in the Rogue Worlds?"

"Yeah, something like that."

"And of those, at least a fifth—including Mendoza, I'm sorry to say—harbor what we call criminal corporations. They are run like proper businesses, with shareholders, a board, a chief executive, and managers; they even have customers. The only difference is the projects they invest in. Some are legal, but most are not, like kidnapping, not to mention every other criminal activity known to humankind."

"Shit! So that means your suspect list is, let me see ... at least forty strong?"

"I'd say double that, maybe even more, since each planet can have more than one criminal corporation and usually does. With a bit of work, we could narrow that down to maybe four or five, one of which would have to be Mendoza's biggest criminal corporation, the Guild. In fact, if I had to name my prime suspect, it's them."

"Why them? Jalmaniya's a long way from Mendoza."

"It is, but your dad was killed in Mendoza City, and the police here are being pressured not to solve the crime. Not the best of reasons, I know, but I'm old enough to take coincidences with a very large pinch of salt. The Guild has to be a suspect."

"That's it?" Samira said, frowning.

Takahashi sighed. "Yeah," he said. "I wish I had more, but my gut tells me it's them."

"And this Guild. They're big enough?"

"Oh, yeah. They're smaller than Armato's outfit but still plenty big enough."

"And let me guess: Armato Industries is another one of these criminal corporations."

"Arguably the biggest in all of the Rogue Worlds. Karlos Armato is its chairman and largest shareholder, and they are based on Jalmaniya though they operate across most of the systems in the Rogue Worlds. They are a very bad bunch. They hate the Guild, and the Guild hates them. We have some unconfirmed intelligence reports that suggest Armato is planning to move in on the Guild's operations."

Samira looked skeptical. "He can do that? Jalmaniya's a long way away, surely."

"Yes, it is. But the Guild has operations on ten systems within fifty light-years of Jalmaniya. Places like Welland, JuSen, Mercier. Small but very profitable, and Karlos knows it. So that's where Armato Industries would start."

"And why would Armato use an outfit like KSS? We're a minor player, surely."

"That's exactly why KSS got the job. Armato has enough clout to use the Jalmaniyan navy if he wanted to, but that would have meant too many people in the loop, too much publicity, massive loss of face, not to mention serious overkill. And besides, KSS has a good reputation. It always delivers, it keeps its mouth shut, and Klimath is a long way from Jalmaniya."

"Right ... oh, sorry. We've wandered off the point. Can you send me that list? It's a start."

"I can, plus as much background on the Guild as I can."

"That'd be great."

"Wish I could have done more."

"It all helps, so thanks. I appreciate it. I've got two last questions if that's okay."

"Make it quick; I really should go. I'm meeting the lawyers for dinner."

"I'll be quick. Know anything about a man called Ashok Samarth?"

"Ashok Samarth?" Takahashi thought for a moment, then shook his head. "No, can't say I do. Should I?"

"No, probably not. He was a KDF officer busted for stealing AIs a few years back. We might be doing business with him. I just wondered if there was a Mendozan connection, that's all. It's a long shot," Samira added, wondering what had made her ask the question.

"I'll have a look. If I find anything, I'll get it to you."

"Thanks. Last question. Why are you doing this?"

"Now, that *is* a good question; I wondered if you'd ask me. It's simple, really. Working for a police force that picks and chooses which crimes to investigate for reasons nobody can explain is not why I became a cop. It sucks, I hate it, and if I can do anything to change things, preferably without getting myself killed in the process, I will."

"Forgive me, Jonah, but you're an honest cop in a corrupt police force? Sounds like the plot for a trashvid to me. I can't say it's terribly convincing."

Takahashi's face tightened. "Maybe not, but that's all you're going to get. What I do and why is my business, Samira, not yours. All you need to know is that I have my reasons, very good reasons, for doing this, the same as you do. You're not the only one who's … Look! Just be grateful that I'm even here at all. Now, I'm sorry, but I really must go."

"Okay, and thanks."

"Don't mention it. Good luck, Samira."

I'm going to need all the luck I can get, Samira thought as she watched the man leave. If Jaska's scowling face was any guide, she was in for a rough ride when she got back.

• • •

"Look, Uncle Jaska, I've said I'm sorry, but I didn't have time to talk to you. I needed to go; I needed to hear what the man had to say. Come on! I didn't just piss off because I felt like it. I had my reasons."

"Not good ones," Jaska growled. "We're supposed to be a team, Samira: all the time, not just when it suits you. We're in a dangerous business; we have our enemies."

"And what?" Samira snapped, eyes brimming with tears. "After what happened to my dad, I don't know that?"

"Oh, Samira … Look, I'm sorry. Let's put it down to experience and move on. We've got enough to worry about."

Samira nodded, drying her cheeks with the backs of her hands. "That's the understatement of the decade, Uncle Jaska." She took a deep breath. "Right," she said with a forced briskness she did not feel, "let's talk business. Two issues we have to talk about: Samarth and Takahashi. You decide which we deal with first."

"Takahashi."

"Fine. What do you think?"

Jaska took a moment to think before responding. "I hate not knowing what his motives are," he said. "He's taking huge risks, but why?"

"I think he gave us a clue."

"I've been through your neuronics recording, Samira, and I didn't spot anything."

"Neither did I, not at the time. But I had another look, and I think he let something slip, something significant. Just before he left, he said, 'I wasn't the only who's …,' and then he stopped."

"I missed that." Jaska frowned. "That could mean anything, surely."

"Of course it could, but I think he was about to say that the Guild had done something to hurt him in some way.'

"That's one hell of a stretch, Samira."

"I know. Now, don't kick my head in, Uncle Jaska, but I've asked Brazzi to see if anyone close to Takahashi was hurt or killed in the last few years. If there is somebody, then I think we might have our answer."

"Why would I kick your head in?" Jaska said. "That is very smart, Samira."

"Thank you, Uncle Jaska."

"Don't let it go to your head. Now, what about what Takahashi said? Think he's right about the Guild being behind your dad's murder?"

"Yes, I do."

"So do I. Problem is I'm not sure it gets us anywhere. What good is a list of ... what did Takahashi call them?"

"Criminal corporations."

"Yeah, them. What good would a list of criminal corporations do us?"

"Not much, I suspect. But why don't we wait and see what he sends me and take it from there?"

"I think that's all we can do, though I have a feeling that the Guild is where the answer lies."

"Me too. Right, that was easy," Samira said, "whereas deciding what to do about Samarth is not. What did his grandfather say?"

"In a nutshell, Charlie said we could ... He said we should trust him with our lives."

"And you agree with that?"

"Most of me does. The problem is we don't know how big a risk he poses. Charlie doesn't either."

"But without him, the business is stone-cold dead. We need him, Jaska. I don't fancy becoming a trash hauler."

"I know. I hate the idea that there'd be no more KSS after all these years."

"Me too. It doesn't seem right." Samira stopped to think, a frown on her face. "I don't understand," she went on, "why Samarth is the only person in all of Klimath interested in working for us. I know Dad's death won't have helped our reputation, but surely we're not that bad a business."

"No, we're not."

Samira glanced at Jaska; he looked back at her, but only for a second, his eyes sliding away. "Jaska!" she said. "You are so bloody obvious, you know that? Come on, spit it out."

Jaska sighed. "You're just like your dad," he said. "He always knew when I wasn't telling him everything." Samira just glared at him. "Okay, okay," Jaska muttered, putting his hands up. "Kamarov is the reason."

Samira's eyebrows arched in surprise. "Kamarov? What's he got to do anything?"

"Because we operate under a Class 602 license, we have to submit the names of all applicants for operational jobs to the Ministry of Interstellar Affairs. That's why I had to submit your name, remember?"

"Ah, yes. Some bureaucratic bullshit about security, you said."

"I did, and it was all bullshit, because even if they don't like the people we hire, they won't pull our license. But what they can do, what Kamarov has done, is tell everyone who applied that they'd never get a job with a reputable operation if they came to work for KSS. His words, Samira, not mine," Jaska said in response to the thunderous look on Samira's face.

"What a crock," she muttered in reply.

"It's payback, I'm afraid. Kamarov couldn't resist the opportunity to jam one up us."

"Which he has."

"Well, yes, but not if we go with Samarth. He told Kamarov he'd never get a job with a reputable operation with his record, so the Ministry of Interstellar Affairs could go screw itself."

"I think I'm going to like Mr. Samarth. It's him or nobody, isn't it?"

"I'm afraid so."

"I've got an idea," Samira continued after a very long silence. "Why don't we just accept that he can't tell us who screwed him over—"

"Like we have a choice?" Jaska shook his head. "I think he made that pretty clear."

"Let me finish. He can't tell us, we say fine, that's okay, and he comes onboard but on one condition."

"Which is?"

"If whoever screwed him over the last time tries it again, he has to tell us so we know what we're up against."

"That's your solution?" Jaska frowned and shook his head. "How does that help?"

"It means we know what's going on. It means we don't get dragged into something without knowing about it. It means—"

"Absolutely nothing, Samira; it means absolutely nothing. He might tell us, but he might not. Come on, Samira! Don't be so naive. He won't tell us what happened the first time around, so why would he the next? Surely you can see that."

"Yes, I can, and it's a risk, I agree. But it's risk worth taking given what we lose if we just walk away. Do you trust Charlie Samarth?"

"I do, and I have. With my life."

"So trust his grandson with mine."

"Easy to say, hard to do."

"You have to. It's time to let go, time to walk away. I know I'm just a babe in the woods, but I'll never find out what I'm really capable of unless you let go. So let go, and let's say yes to Ashok."

Jaska sighed and raised his hands in surrender. "Go on, then."

"Yes! KSS lives to fight another day," Samira said, jumping to her feet and folding Jaska into a bear hug.

"Yes, it does," Jaska Anders said with a frown, "and that's what worries me."

23

"Hi, Samira."

"Hi, Nat. Sorry I'm late," Samira said, sliding into a seat.

"Coffee?"

"Please."

"I really need this," Samira said when the coffee arrived. "Things have been a bit frantic."

"I can tell. You look tired. And you've lost weight."

"There's always so much to do, Nat. It's never-ending, and finding a replacement for Jaska has been a nightmare."

"The new guy; he's signed on?"

"He has. He starts next week."

"Bet Jaska's pleased."

"Oh, yeah."

"Thanks for the holopic of the guy. Got to say your Mr. Samarth is cute."

"Oh, pleeeease," Samira groaned. "He is cute, very cute in fact, but before you ask, Natalie Qaaliba, he's not my type."

"Oh?" Nat murmured, arching a skeptical eyebrow. "Mmm, that's funny. I don't remember you ever having a type."

"Watch it," Samira growled; she glared at Nat before bursting out laughing. "Bitch!"

"You think he'll be okay?"

"Think so. He looks very good, so we're hoping." Samira took a deep breath. "He's got to work out," she said. "Otherwise there'll be no more business."

"I still think you're mad. I don't know how you do it, Samira. Flying that museum piece, getting shot at." She shivered her shoulders. "Not my thing."

"It's not so bad, Nat."

"Then why do you look the way you do?"

"It has been pretty tough," Samira said. "After we went to Calloway the first time, I thought … No, I knew it was all too much for me, but … but now I think it'll be okay."

"You sure?"

"No, Nat," Samira said softly. "No, I'm not. Dammit," she continued, wiping eyes brimming with sudden tears, "why did everything have to change? Why can't things have stayed the way they were?"

"They can't," Nat said, her voice gentle, reaching out to take Samira's hand in hers. "They just can't."

"I know, I know. But it's just so wrong what's happened."

"Let it go, Samira; please let it go. What's happened has happened, and nothing will ever change that. Things are looking up at last, your business has a future, it's what you want to do, Jaska's where he wants to be, Samarth looks like he's the right guy at the right time."

Samira squeezed Nat's hand. "Yes, it is time I moved on, I know that, but I can't forget what's happened."

"I'm not saying you should forget anything. Just don't let it rule your life, that's all."

"I'm trying not to, but … but I'm still going to find whoever killed my dad."

"That's what really bothers me. So you find them, kill them, and then what? These things have a habit of getting out of hand. Just read your history; vendettas are easy to start and hard to stop."

"They are, but if the Mendozans won't do anything, then somebody has to. Besides, I've spent a lot of time getting not very far, so maybe it's academic. Look, can we leave it? You think I'm wrong, and maybe I am, but that's me."

"Sure." Nat nodded. "And even though I think you are wrong, I'm still your friend, and if you need me to help, you just ask, okay?"

"Thanks, Nat. Can we change the subject?"

"Sure."

"How's the new job?"

"Great. Klimath Network News pays well, and the team is nice."

Samira shook her head. "Who'd have thought it? Natalie Qaaliba, party queen of Bellingen, earning an honest living as a researcher for KNN."

"Doing that journalism elective was a smart move," Nat said. "It seems high school wasn't a complete waste of time after all. But don't get too excited; in the news business, 'researcher' is just a fancy title for 'gofer,' and oh boy, I do a lot of gofering. The money might be good, but they work you hard."

"*Is* it fun?"

"Most of the time, and I'm learning heaps."

"What, gofering?"

"Hey, Ms. Smartass! I don't just get the coffee, okay?"

"All right, all right. So what then?"

146

"We've got a big project on. Can't say too much, but I tell you what: I had no idea what really goes on around Klimath, and some of it's scary."

"Oh, come on, Nat. Is that all you're going to tell me?"

"Pretty much. You can wait for the program like everybody else."

"That just won't do," Samira said, glaring at Nat, "and you know it. I thought we were best friends."

"We are, so I'll give you a hint, but you must promise me you'll never tell anyone. Deal?"

"Deal."

"The project's about Mendozan organized crime and its connections here on Klimath. Right, that's all I'm going to say."

Well, I'll be damned, Samira thought. *If KNN was looking at Mendozan organized crime, it would also be looking at the Guild.* "Sounds interesting," she said, careful not to react. "I'll look out for it."

"Make sure you do, because the producer says my name will appear in the credits."

24

Samira clapped a hand on Ashok Samarth's shoulder. "You ready to go?" she asked.

"As I'll ever be," he said, his face creased into an unhappy frown.

"Hey! Cheer up. I know *Bitsa* looks like she belongs in a museum—"

"Which it does," Ashok muttered.

"—but trust me, she's got what it takes. Come on, let's do it."

The pair walked across the ceramcrete apron to where the lander waited, a massive, brooding black shape cut out of the predawn sky.

"Oh, yes," Samira said, stopping to look the lander over. "*Bitsa* might be old, but she can do the biz."

"I hope so," Ashok replied, looking no happier.

Samira eased *Bitsa* into a shallow dive. "Ready?" she said, glancing across at the combat-space-suited figure to her right.

"As I'll ever be given the fact that I'm actually flying in something older than my father and wearing a suit dating back to the dawn of manned spaceflight."

"Focus," Samira snapped.

"Sorry. All systems nominal. Threat board is green. Passing through 25,000 meters; landing zone is on the nose at one-eighty klicks."

"Roger." Samira's fingers danced across a keypad, and all of a sudden the screens around the sys ops station erupted as one after another, *Bitsa* was lit up by hostile radars, intercept alarms screeching briefly before Ashok slapped them into silence.

Come on, come on, Samira thought. *We haven't got all—*

"Break right, break right," Ashok barked. "Go dirtside fast! Antiradiation missiles selected … ARMs away."

Doing as she was told, Samira fired *Bitsa*'s maneuvering thrusters, rolling its enormous bulk over onto its back and pushing the nose down hard. "Not fast enough for you? Suck this, then, flyboy," she whispered as she blipped the main engines, the brief burst of thrust driving the lander into a nearly vertical plunge to the ground before she eased the dive, rolling *Bitsa* back into a hard turn to starboard.

"Lock up," he said, silencing an alarm, "Snapper missile fire control radar. Expect missile launch from Red 45, continue turn hard right … infrared flares to auto, stand by lander decoys."

"No decoys," Samira said. "Can't afford them."

"Roger that," Ashok said calmly. "No decoys. Continue turn. All we can do is try to outrun the bast—"

"Negative. Coming back hard left."

"What?"

"Watch and learn," Samira said, mashing the throttles onto the stops.

"Roger … missile launch, flares away," Ashok said over the wailing of the missile alarms. "Four Snapper SAMs inbound on the nose. Time to impact thirty seconds. We're screwed."

"Maybe. Weapons free. Take them if you can."

"Roger … twenty-five seconds … twenty …"

In one fluid action, Samira rammed *Bitsa*'s nose high into the air and, leaving the throttles at full power, shifted all power to the lander's belly thrusters, twin pillars of quickly expanding incandescent gas lancing out to fill the rapidly closing gap between the missiles and their target.

And one after another, the missiles died, incinerated by the hellish efflux from *Bitsa*'s thrusters.

"Time to reload?" she snapped.

"Next salvo away in … twenty seconds."

"Which gives us just enough time to get clear," Samira said, shifting power back to the main engines and rolling *Bitsa* over into a rapidly accelerating dive away from the missile launcher and toward the protection of a convenient slab-sided canyon.

"Stand by … ARMs have lock, target position confirmed … on target … now! Snapper fire control radar destroyed; threat board is now green. Come hard left to 050; landing zone is at fifty klicks."

"Okay, Ashok. End of exercise. That'll do for today. Let's go home."

"Roger," he croaked as Samira steadied *Bitsa* down.

There was a very long silence before Ashok spoke again, and when he did, his voice was unsteady. "I don't think any of that's in the Klimath Defense Force's tactical handbook," he said slowly.

"Probably not. But then again, the KDF can afford decoys, and we can't. And by the way, when it comes to the real thing, please go easy on the ARMs. Antiradiation missiles are very expensive, and clients hate paying for them. As for lander decoys, forget them; wickedly expensive doesn't even begin to describe them. KSS has never had a client willing to pay what they cost."

"Ah! I must say that cost has never been something I've had to worry about until now."

"As us poor taxpayers can attest. What was the KDF's budget last fiscal year?"

"Huge," Ashok said with a grin.

"You're telling me. Jaska worked out once that the KDF needs fifteen times more money to operate one of their landers than we do to operate *Bitsa*. Bunch of overpaid jerk-offs ... Sorry, Ashok."

Wisely, he said nothing.

"Okay, eyes down," Samira continued. "Prelanding checklist."

"Welcome back, Samira," Jaska said. "How did our new man do?"

"Good," Samira said, flopping into a chair. "Steady under pressure. Scared the crap out of him."

"And me too. I was keeping an eye on the telemetry. You've got to watch your main and belly-thruster nozzle temperatures. You were redlining them. And go easy on those high-speed nose-up maneuvers, Samira. *Bitsa*'s wings are strong, but they are not indestructible."

"The load peaked at, let me see now ... yes, 11.4 g, am I right?"

Jaska nodded.

"And the limit is 12 g?"

"Okay, okay," Jaska conceded, "you were paying attention. But trust me when I say it's easy to lose the bubble, and the next thing you know the damn AI steps in to stop you from ripping the wings off. If some bastard is trying to kill you at the time, things can get difficult. Push *Bitsa* to her limits, but only when you have to. She's good, but she's old."

"Point taken. Hold on," Samira said. "Let me see who this vidmail is from … Well, well, well. Guess what?"

"What?"

"Our tame Mendozan detective has been in touch. Let me see … yes, with a list of criminal corporations plus what looks like very detailed background and … I'll be damned. Remember I asked him if he had anything on our new sys ops?"

"Yes?"

"He does. There's an entry in their crimint knowledge base. He was seen with a couple of known Klimathian criminals, Morris Peng and Futchwe N'dabele, on Mendoza. Apparently, Peng and N'dabele are lowlife scumbags known to do odd jobs for the Mendozan Guild, freelance thugs basically operating on the fringe. Why Samarth met them, the Mendozans have no idea, though I think we might. Interesting, eh?"

Jaska nodded. "Sure is. I think a chat with our Mr. Samarth is in order, don't you?"

"Yes, but let him put *Bitsa* to bed. And why don't we get the debrief out of the way first and then see what he has to say?"

"Fine." Jaska got up and stuck his head out the door. "Hey, Ashok," he shouted. "Office for the debrief when you're done."

"I'll be there," Ashok shouted back.

"I'm going to get cleaned up, Uncle. I'll see you at the debrief. Oh, by the way, anything back from Brazzi about Takahashi?"

"Ah, shit, I forgot. I heard from him while you were airborne."

"Jeez, Uncle!" Samira protested. "You should have told me."

"I know, I know. I was just a bit distracted, that's all."

"Wondering if I was going to crash *Bitsa*?"

"Maybe."

"Oh, for … So what's Brazzi have to say?"

"Two things. Takahashi has—had a sister. She was a senior policy adviser to the Mendozan defense minister and married to a Ben Kechwe, some finance hotshot with a reputation for cutting corners and doing deals with the wrong people. They had three kids, a nice house, and all the trappings. The whole family was killed in a mobibot accident five years ago. The bot ran off the road, went over a cliff, and blew up, all for no apparent reason; the road was dry, and there were no other vehicles involved. I'd say the mobibot's AI was hacked."

"And let me guess," Samira said. "Even though the circumstances were suspicious, the Mendozan police were never able to find the people responsible."

"Hah!" Jaska snorted derisively. "Of course not."

"The Guild," Samira whispered. "It has to be."

"Certainly looks that way," Jaska said. "Now, have a look at this."

Samira looked at the holopic of two men, their arms on each other's shoulders, heads back, laughing. "Who are these guys?" she asked.

"This was taken ten years ago. The man on the left is Ben Kechwe. The man on the right was a nasty piece of work called

Jack Ampad. He was the Guild's chief executive until he had his head blown off."

"By someone the Mendozan police never found?"

"Need you ask? I'd say Kechwe upset the Guild somehow, and they made him pay for his mistake. Anyway, there's your Guild connection."

"I think this says we can trust Takahashi," Samira said. "He's not a saint. He's a man on a mission."

"That's right. It's all circumstantial, but it does hang together."

"It does. I think we're in for an interesting chat with Mr. Samarth, don't you?"

"Oh, yes."

"So that's about it. Any final thoughts, Ashok?"

Ashok thought for a moment, then shook his head. "No, don't think so, Samira. I get the point about cost. That's really the only major difference between what we do and what I did in the KDF. Well, that and the age of our equipment."

"The age of our equipment?" Samira said. "Bloody nerve!"

"But true, sadly," Jaska said. "You'll find, Ashok, that defects are a big problem. *Bitsa* needs more than her fair share of loving care."

"Understood."

"Okay, moving on," Samira said briskly. "Ashok, Jaska's set up the sims of every major mission KSS has done. We'd like you to work your way through them as fast as you can. The old girl has her idiosyncrasies, and you need to know what they are."

"Will do."

"Good. Last item. Jaska. New business?"

"Maybe; I got an inquiry this morning from the Zaiyati Freedom Movement. Not much detail yet, but I'll follow them up and keep you posted. The mission's escorting ZFM resupply ships past what's left of the Zaiyat government."

"Zaiyat?" Samira frowned. "Isn't that some shithole out past New China?"

"Yes, a giant one cursed with one of humanspace's longest-running civil wars," Jaska said, "which, of course, makes Zaiyat our sort of place."

"Is that good or bad?" she asked.

"Both. Good for business. Your dad and I did lots of missions to Zaiyat; we made some serious money. But it's a dangerous place, so the missions are risky, which is why the money's good. If we take the job, we'll need to plan it properly, make sure we know what we're getting into."

"What's the next step, Jaska?" Ashok asked.

"Our contact in the ZFM is a woman called Pina Ricco. She's promised to get us the statement of mission requirements as soon as she can. When she does, I'll get Brazzi started on the intelligence brief. Until then, there's nothing more we can do."

"So are we done here?" Ashok said.

Samira glanced at Jaska; he nodded almost imperceptibly. "Yeah, we are," she said, "but there's just one last thing."

"Oh?" Ashok said, already halfway to his feet. "What?"

"Morris Peng and Futchwe N'dabele: mean anything to you?"

"Morris Peng and Futchwe N'dabele?" Ashok said, slumping back down, eyes narrowing. "Let me see … no," he said, shaking his head. "No, I don't think so."

"Ashok!" Samira barked. "Don't mess me around! We know they work for the Guild, and we also know you met them. We have contacts on Mendoza, and that's what they told us. Now, we had a deal. We trust you, and you trust us. We're pretty sure there's a link between my dad's murder and the Guild, and that's—"

"Hold on," Ashok protested, "I didn't know that."

"There's a lot you don't know, Ashok."

"You should have told me," he said. "You should."

"When you need to know something, Ashok, we'll tell you," Jaska said, "and you didn't need to know. Why would we? You've only worked for us for five bloody minutes."

"Sorry," Ashok mumbled, his head down.

"Okay, let's move on. Samira?"

"Like I was saying," Samira went on, "we're pretty sure there's a link between my dad's murder and the Guild. That means we need to know if you're caught up with them; otherwise we run the risk of blundering into something we shouldn't. Now, maybe you'd like to try again."

Ashok sagged in his seat. "Ah … I was hoping … Yes, I did meet them once on Klimath, then here to hand over the AIs. But all I'm going to tell you is this: They were only the go-betweens. I never did get to meet whoever was pulling their strings, and I don't know who they were. Might have been the Guild, might not have been. I don't know either way, and that's the truth."

"Okay," Samira said, deciding to let it go, persuaded by the look of defiance on Ashok's face that she would be wasting her time trying to get any more out of him. "We'll leave it at that. Our secret, Ashok, okay?"

"No, it's not okay. Have you been spying on me?"

"No. I'm trying to find out who was behind my father's murder, your name came up in passing, I asked the question, and that's what our contact came up with."

"You are spying! You damn well are!"

"Your name came up in conversation. I didn't plan it; it just happened. So get over it. All right?"

"No, it's not all right, Samira." Ashok glared at her. "You realize that talking about this, even mentioning Peng and N'dabele, puts me at risk?"

"I think we do," Jaska said, cutting in, "which is why we won't mention this to anyone. We need you, Ashok; you must see that. So why would we risk one of our key assets?"

"And we won't," Samira said. "I can promise you that. One thing you'll learn is that KSS is extremely good at keeping secrets."

"Because, Ashok, if we weren't, we'd all be dead," Jaska said, stabbing the desk with his forefinger. "Dead long ago."

Ashok nodded slowly. "Fine, I'll let it go, if only because I want KSS to survive every bit as much as you do. But do me a favor."

Samira nodded. "Okay."

"Word will get out that I'm working for you guys."

"It already has, Ashok," Jaska said.

"There you go. I understand why you'd want to know who killed your father—I would too if I was you—and you'll be a long time dead before those useless dimwits who pretend to be the Mendozan police ever tell you. But if that means making waves on Mendoza, then you've got to tell me what's going on. Who knows, I might even be able to help. After all," Ashok added with a twisted smile, "it seems I do have connections to the Mendozan criminal classes."

Samira and Jaska looked at each other; he nodded his agreement. "Fine," she said, turning back to Ashok. "We won't do anything without talking to you first."

"Thanks; I'd appreciate that. Now, if you don't mind, I've got an appointment with a simulator. I'll catch you later."

Samira waited until Ashok left before speaking. "This is getting interesting," she said, "very interesting."

"Well, yes, it is," Jaska said, his face creased into a worried frown. "It's also getting more dangerous: for Ashok, for you, and maybe even for me. We'll need to be careful."

"Let me have a think before we talk again. *Bitsa*'s postflight checks need doing, there was small power surge on Fusion Alfa I want to have a look at, and you need to get us our next job. Sitting around here won't pay the bills."

"True enough," Jaska said, levering himself to his feet with an effort. "True enough."

25

Like everyone else, Ashok had been staring at the holovid screen for a very long time, his lips squeezed down to thin bloodless lines.

"Here, here, and here," he said, his finger stabbing out, his words breaking the silence, "are the three new missile sites; they weren't there the last time around. Nasty, very nasty. I know the Zaiyati Freedom Movement is keen to do this mission, but I'm not sure I am. Do we want to do this?"

"Ricco's offering us good money, Ashok," Samira said. "Very good."

"Not if we don't live long enough to spend it," Ashok retorted.

"Jaska?"

"Seems the Zaiyat government's finally got off its ass to do something about Firebase Zulu." He got to his feet and went up to look at the screen. "Damn."

"Hmm," Samira said, "I'm no military expert, but Firebase Zulu looks important."

"It is," Jaska said. "It's critical, which is why it's so big. It anchors the ZFM's front line through the Kerath Mountains and supports this salient here—" His finger pinpointed a massive bulge. "—which is where the breakout from the mountains down onto the coastal plain will come from. And when the ZFM does break out, it's only a matter of time before it takes Foundation City, and then the war's over."

"So if they lose Firebase Zulu," Samira said, "they lose the salient, and then the entire Kerath front collapses. Am I right?"

"Yes." Jaska nodded. "The last time your dad and I escorted a resupply mission into Zulu, the government threw a bit of light stuff at us: nothing we couldn't handle. But even they learn, it seems. If those missile bases are for real, *Bitsa* won't last ten minutes, never mind the resupply ships."

"What about lander decoys? Would the ZFM pay?"

"I'll ask Ricco, but don't hold your breath. Anyway, we can't carry enough decoys to deal with missiles from three sites. One maybe, but not three."

"Jaska's right," Ashok said. "The KDF wouldn't mount a single-ship operation around these sites, and they don't have to worry about getting paid for the decoys they use."

"Do we know what missiles we're up against?" Samira asked.

"No, not yet," Jaska said. "I've got Brazzi working on that, but until then this—" He waved a hand at the low-definition satellite shot on the holovid screen. "—is all we've got."

"Mmm," Ashok said. "If I remember my intelligence briefings, the Zaiyat government gets all of its heavy weapons from Palekar. That means they'd be Dragon surface-to-air missiles. Mean sons of bitches: Mach 7, exoatmospheric, one-eighty-degree off-bore capability, command or autonomous guidance with radar, laser, infrared, and optronic sensors. Very hard to fool. You're right, Jaska. *Bitsa* wouldn't last ten minutes."

"Hold on a sec, Ashok," Samira said. "Let's not get carried away. They might be dummy sites. The Zaiyat government is broke; it doesn't even have the money to buy toilet paper, so how could it afford three missile installations?"

"Fair point," Jaska said, nodding, "but let's leave it at that. We can speculate until the cows come home. Why not wait and see what Brazzi comes up with. If he comes up empty-handed, then we'll have to think again. But I'll tell you this: You guys aren't going up against those sites unless we are absolutely certain they are dummies."

"Shit, no!" Ashok exclaimed. "We need to know one way or the other."

"Right, then. Let's talk about this afternoon's meeting with Ricco."

"I'm not even sure we want the job anymore," Samira said. "Much as I hate the Zaiyat government, much as I want the ZFM to succeed, I'm not going to die in a ditch for them. It's their fight, not mine."

"Afternoon, Jaska. Good to see you again."

"Pina, likewise. Take a seat, please. This is our new command pilot, Matti's daughter, Samira, and our new systems operator, Ashok Samarth."

The woman—tall, hard-faced, iron-gray hair cut in a fringe over tired brown eyes, a small red and gold "Free Zaiyat" badge in the lapel of her combat jacket—leaned forward. "Pina Ricco," she said, shaking hands with Samira and Ashok in turn.

"Before we get started, I think congratulations are in order, Pina," Jaska said. "We saw a report that one of your units took out the *Warlock*. That true?"

"Yes, it is," Ricco said with a smile. "The 27th Special Operations Group. It is—I'm sorry, it was a fine unit."

"Was?" Jaska looked puzzled.

"Yes. They were cut to shreds; only a handful of them made it back. But the *Warlock* was the last Zaiyat Navy warship still operational, so we think the casualties were worth it. Now the bastards don't own space anymore."

"What's happening to the hulk? Can the Zaiyatis fix it, get it operational again?"

"No; the *Warlock* was too badly damaged. The 27th killed most of the crew, blew every last auxiliary fusion reactor on-board, and crippled the main engines. She's not going any-where. Last report we had, the Zaiyatis were stripping the hulk of its weapons, though our people aren't sure they'll be any use."

"Still a great result, Pina."

"Yes, it was."

Jaska looked around the table. "Where shall we start?" he asked.

"With me," Pina Ricco said. "Jaska, let me come straight to the point. You and Matti—oh, Samira, forgive me. You must think me so rude. I was so sorry to hear about the loss of your father. He was a good friend of ours."

"As I hope to be, Pina," Samira said. "And thank you. We all miss him terribly."

"I'm sure. Anyway," Ricco said, turning her attention back to Jaska, "the movement knew you and Matti, Jaska. We trust-ed you both; you never let us down. I know we never have enough money to do all the things we want to do, but we never regretted a single cent we spent on KSS's services."

Samira tensed as she waited for the big "but." It was not long in coming.

"But … things have changed, Jaska. Sorry, Samira, but even though you are your father's daughter, that says nothing about your abilities. The regional committee isn't at all sure we can go forward with this. We're only here because I insisted."

Samira bit her lip—Jaska's instructions to her and Ashok had been short and to the point: no matter how strong the temptation, say nothing—leaving Jaska to take his time, as if considering every word Pina had said letter by letter.

"I understand," he said at last, "but let me make three points. First, you say you trust me?"

Ricco nodded. "The movement does."

"In that case, you need to trust me when I say KSS can do the job. The people might change, but KSS doesn't; I wouldn't sit be sitting here otherwise. If I say KSS can do the job, KSS can do the job. Second, I know every other operator in this sector of the Rogue Worlds. Orbital Military, Murchison Combat Systems, and KSS are the only ones who'll work for you. And why is that? Because your jobs are so damn risky, Pina, that's why. Problem for you is that Orbital's lander blew a fusion plant last month, so they can't help you. And Murchison's committed to a long-term contract on Prometheus-B and will be for months."

Lucky bastards, thought Samira.

"So it's KSS or nothing. Third and last, your mission brief is deficient." Ricco's eyes opened in shock as Jaska flicked a folder across the table; it slid to a stop only centimeters from where Ricco's hands rested on the table. "Willfully deficient."

"How's that, Jaska?" Ricco asked.

"Because it says nothing about the missile installations covering the airspace over Firebase Zulu. Three of them, in fact, and we find it hard to believe your intelligence people know nothing about them. To be honest, I'm pretty pissed with you guys. If our intel people could find them, then so could yours. So the issue's not what you want but whether we want the job or not, and right now, we don't."

Ricco blinked. "You don't? Why not?"

"Because I cannot say to the people I'm going to send in harm's way that they can trust you sons of bitches."

"Haven't lost your people skills, then, Jaska?" Ricco said, glaring.

"Don't fuck with me, Pina. This is business, those are the facts, and you know it. Now, either you stop messing us around and we start talking business, or we walk away. Your call."

Ricco's hands went up. "You are a complete bastard, Jaska, but I'd rather be screwed by you than anyone else, even flyboy here," she said, hooking a thumb at Ashok and winking. His skin darkened with embarrassment, and he looked at the ceiling. "Okay, let's talk business."

"Fine, but there's one thing you need to understand, Pina. Those missile installations are a huge problem for us. Unless we can find a way around them or you can prove they are just dummies, we can't do this mission, and we won't. I'm sorry, but that's the way it is."

"Fair enough," Ricco said after a moment's thought. "When we've agreed on commercial terms, let's talk about what we do about them, and I'm sorry, Jaska. I didn't know anything about any missile launchers."

"Fine. You have our proposal. Let's step through it."

"Let's."

. . .

"Phew," Samira said as Ricco's mobibot sped away, "that was pretty full on. What the hell got into you, Jaska?"

"Hemorrhoids," Ashok whispered.

"Watch it," Jaska growled. "I heard that. To answer your question, Samira, the ZFM hasn't changed in all the time I've known it. It always wants more for less, and we always refuse to give it. Your dad and I learned the hard way that it saves time to kick the ZFM in the balls right up front."

Samira and Ashok swapped glances. "Oh," she said. "No wonder you wanted to do all the talking. I would have been much more polite."

"Me too," Ashok said.

"Enough, children. Come on, we've got work to do if we're to be ready for this mission. I'm off to see Brazzi; we need to know whether these missile sites are a problem or not."

"I'll start the detailed mission planning," Samira said.

"Screw it," Ashok said, sour-faced. "Let me guess."

"Yup," Samira said. "Fusion Alfa's still not as stable as I'd like. Buq thinks it's a cooling problem, and—"

"And Buq would like a hand stripping down the primary coolant pump, am I right?" Ashok said, still sour-faced. "Gee, thanks."

"Don't mention it."

Samira lifted her beer to salute the sun, a ball of molten red fire quickly dropping below the western horizon. "Here's to another day gone," she said.

Ashok Samarth raised his beer in reply, the bottle sweating tiny pearls of moisture sucked out of the humid air. "I never want to see that damn pump again. Or Buq, come to that; the bloody woman is a hard taskmaster."

"She is, which is why I love her. And that pump's working properly again. Buq says you did well, Ashok. Damn thing's been screwing up for ages."

"My pleasure."

A long companionable silence followed, with Samira happy to lie back in the battered recliner to watch the night flush the spectacular reds and golds of a tropical sunset out of the sky. "You're a cagey bastard," she said eventually.

"Eh? Me, cagey?" Ashok said. "What the hell are you talking about?"

"You; I'm talking about you. We know a bit about you. Schools, your marriage and divorce, that you have a daughter you don't see anymore, your KDF time, your trial—"

"And my time in prison. Don't forget that."

"Don't worry, I wasn't going to. Where was I? Oh, yes. Your time in prison, and now here you are."

"Your point?"

"Friends and family. We know nothing about them."

"Yeah, pull the other one. What about your Mr. Brazzi? Isn't he supposed to be our intelligence whiz? He's already answered your questions, I'm sure."

"Yes, he is, and no, he hasn't. We could have asked him, but I wouldn't put him on to checking you out, not the family stuff anyway. Your grandfather told Jaska that you were the right stuff; that was enough for Jaska. They go back a very long way, and Jaska says he'd trust Charlie with his life. That was good enough for me."

"Yeah. Sorry; didn't mean to be so grumpy."

"Yes, you bloody well did. You don't like people trying to get to know the real Ashok Samarth."

Ashok put his hands up. "I surrender," he said. "It's true, I don't. My private life is just that: private. So stop being so damn nosy. If I want to tell you anything, I will."

"Hey, hey! Settle down, okay?" Samira said. "Just asking."

"Well don't."

"Even so, you're going to have to open up a bit. I need your help."

"Listen, Samira," Ashok said, struggling upright, "if you want something, why the hell don't you just ask?"

"Because you just clam up, that's why. But if that's how you want to play it, fine. We've got at least three weeks until the Zaiyat job kicks off."

"If it ever kicks off," Ashok muttered.

"And I want to use to the time to pay another visit to Mendoza. I thought you might be able to help me. Those guys you met, Peng and N'dabele—"

"Stop right there," Ashok snapped, his face twisted in anger. "That's what I've been talking about. All that stuff is off limits, you hear? Off limits! You talk to them, Samira, and I'm dead. You understand what I'm saying?"

"I'm not stupid, Ashok. Of course I'd never talk to them, not unless you said it was okay."

"Good! And I'm saying it's not okay."

"I think I'd worked that out. Now, get down off your high horse and tell me why, if that's okay with you."

"All right," Ashok said with a scowl. "Just after I was released on bail, they—"

"Who's they?"

"Nice try, Samira, but let's just leave it at 'they,' shall we? Anyway, they sent a message: If I told anyone about Peng and

N'dabele, that I'd passed the stolen AIs to them, it'd be the last thing I ever did. That's all. And you know what?"

"What?"

"To make sure I understood, the messenger stuck a shiv into my neck while his partner knelt on my chest. The shiv didn't go in far, but far enough to make me bleed like a stuck pig, enough to make sure I got the message. And believe me, I did."

Samira stretched out an arm to take Ashok's hand in hers. "And I do too. I promise; we'll never talk to Peng and N'dabele unless you say it's okay."

"Good."

"So here's my question: Did you meet anyone else from Mendoza who might be able to help me? Ashok, please," Samira said. "I need all the help I can get, and so far I haven't had a lot."

Ashok hung his head, hands clenching and unclenching. "There was someone: Samantha Tian," he said eventually, looking up. "She might be able to help you."

"Samantha Tian? Who's she?"

"Hard to say. A freelance criminal is probably the best way to describe her. I got the impression she'd do pretty much anything, legal or not, as long as the money matched the risk. Talk to her. She sounded very plugged in; she made a bit of a thing about knowing everyone on Mendoza."

"She was with Peng and N'dabele?"

"Yeah. First time we met. She was asking all the questions. Peng and N'dabele were just the grunts."

"Thanks for that, Ashok. She might be able to help me."

"Maybe, maybe not." Ashok shrugged. "You'll have to see, but Tian will make you pay either way."

"Thought she might. And before you nag me, I won't mention your name. By the way, if you think giving me Tian's name gets you off the hook, you're wrong. I need to know more about you, Ashok Samarth, and I will find out."

"You'll be waiting a long time, Samira. If there's one thing I'm good at, it's keeping my damn mouth shut."

"We'll see. Another beer?"

"First sensible thing you've said."

26

"Welcome to Mendoza City, Ms. Anders," the immigration avatar said once it had made up its mind that Samira really was who she claimed to be. "What is the purpose of your visit?"

"Vacation."

"And where are you staying?"

"I have a reservation at the Hotel Electra on Connaught and Nwosu."

"Thank you. Please proceed to the counter marked 'Immigration Control' to your left."

That doesn't sound too good, Samira thought. Everyone ahead of her in the queue had gone straight through to the baggage hall. An immigration agent waved her over as she approached the counter.

"Are you Ms. Anders?"

"Yes."

"Please come with me."

Samira followed him into a small windowless room occupied by a small table flanked by two chairs and overlooked by a pair of holocams behind plasglass windows. The place smelled stale and airless.

"Please take a seat. Someone will be along shortly."

"But why?" she demanded. "What's this all about?"

"Please bear with us, Ms. Anders. We won't keep you long." Then, without a backward glance, the man was gone, the door closing with a sharp metallic click behind him. Belatedly, Samira realized there was no handle on the inside of the door; she had been locked in.

What a bunch of pricks, she whispered under her breath, trying to quell a brief flutter of panic. *Come on, get a grip; you've done nothing wrong.*

To her relief, the immigration officer had been right; she was not kept long. Thirty minutes later, the door opened sharply, and in walked Detective Takahashi. Samira sat and stared, at a complete loss for words even as she told herself to stay focused, not to say anything that might compromise the Mendozan detective.

"Welcome back to Mendoza City, Ms. Anders," Takahashi said, all brisk and businesslike. "Lieutenant Okoro sends his regards."

"He does?" she said, wondering what the hell was going on. "That's nice. Please thank him for me."

"I will. Now, Ms. Anders, you told immigration you were here on vacation, but that's not correct, is it?"

"It is, in a way. This is my vacation time."

"Don't mess me around, Ms. Anders," Takahashi said, face grim, mouth tight and unsmiling. "Nobody from Klimath comes to Mendoza City on vacation. Why are you here?"

"Well, I, er … I was going to come to see you to see if there's been any progress, you know, on finding my dad's killers."

"Oh, really, Ms. Anders?" Takahashi said, his face making it clear what he thought of Samira's fumbling response. "And why would you do that? Lieutenant Okoro promised to keep you informed."

"He did, but I've heard nothing."

"That's because we have nothing to tell you. If we had, we would have been in touch. Lieutenant Okoro is a man who keeps his promises."

"So there'd be no point talking to you guys?"

"No. If you'd let us know in advance, we could have saved you a trip."

"I thought it might be better if I just dropped in. And I wanted to have a look around. See if I could find out anything that might help the case."

"Don't you think we would have done that already?"

"How would I know?" Samira shrugged her shoulders. "You're not making any progress, so what harm can it do?"

"More than you know, Ms. Anders, more than you know. You risk compromising our investigation by blundering around. You are not a police officer, so leave the policing to us. Is that understood?"

"Yes," Samira said, choking off the urge to tell Takahashi to bugger off. He's a friend, she reminded herself, which has to make this a piece of theater, presumably for the benefit of an unseen Lieutenant Okoro. "Understood."

"Good. One last word of warning. If you make any inquiries of any person regarding your father's death, you will be deported immediately."

"Don't worry, I won't. I'm here now, so I might as well do the tourist thing and then go home."

"Good. Enjoy your stay, Ms. Anders." Takahashi got to his feet and extended his arm across the desk. For an instant

Samira wondered what he was doing; then she realized he only wanted to shake hands.

"I will," she said, taking Takahashi's hand.

Only when she was safely in the mobibot and on her way into town did Samira open her hand to remove the small scrap of paper Takahashi had pressed into her palm. "In back, Henry's Bar, 18:30" was all it said.

Henry's Bar was packed, forcing Samira to fight her way through the throng to get to the back. There, in a small booth, Takahashi waited, slumped against the wall, a beer already in hand.

"Drink?" Takahashi asked, lifting his glass. Samira thought the man looked tired; all the bombast, all the vigor, all the aggression he had shown in the interview room at the Mendoza City spaceport had gone, leaving in its place a face drawn tight with fatigue and stress.

"Mendozan beer any good?" she asked.

"Matter of taste, I suppose, but I think so."

"Fine. I'll have what you're having," Samira said, punching buttons on the tabletop terminal.

When the beer arrived, Samira sank half of it in one go. "You're right. It is good," she said, wiping the foam from her upper lip.

"Sorry about all that bullshit at the spaceport."

"No problem," Samira said, waving a hand in dismissal. "Only took a few seconds to work it out."

Takahashi grinned, shaking his head. "Took you a bit longer than that," he said. "You looked shit-scared the whole time; Lieutenant Okoro thought so anyway, which made me happy. Anyway, thanks for not dropping me in the shit."

"Pleased I could help."

"Right," Takahashi said, finishing his beer and ordering two more, "let's get down to business. Okoro knows why you're here, but he thinks my little chat with you has persuaded you to pull your head in. He thinks you're just another empty-headed girl on some sort of crusade. But he's wrong, isn't he?"

"That I'm going to pull my head in or the crusade?"

"Both."

"Yes, he is. Dead wrong."

"Well, luckily for you, that's what Okoro thinks, and that's why you got your tourist visa. Otherwise you'd be on your way home by now."

"Oh."

"Hmm." Takahashi paused and leaned forward to look Samira full in the face, his eyes flicking left and right, up and down as if to record every last detail. "So," he continued, "let me see now … You're not here just to kick a few stones over, hoping something interesting pops out. So," he added, eyes narrowing, "yes, let me guess. I think you've come to see somebody."

Samira stared at the detective. He stared back, eyes unwavering, until Samira had to look away; any longer and he would have been looking into her soul.

"Oh, you're good, Jonah," she said. "I would hate to have you on my case; I don't think I'd stand a chance."

"No, you wouldn't. I don't like to say this, Samira, because you are a smart, determined woman, but you're also very young, naive, inexperienced, and way, way too trusting. Me? I'm the opposite of all those things: old, cynical, seen it all, and I rarely trust anyone. So no, up against me, you wouldn't stand a chance."

"Tell it like you see it, why don't you," Samira muttered. "And yes, I have a name."

"Tell me," the detective said in a voice that brooked no argument.

But for an instant Samira wavered. Tian and Ashok were linked; if Takahashi made the connection, so could others, and that might put Ashok's life at risk. But she decided she had to tell him; otherwise she was going nowhere. Takahashi had trusted her; she should trust him. "Tian, Samantha Tian. She lives down in—"

"Samantha Tian?" Takahashi sat back, shaking his head. "I know Tian," he said, "and she's bad, very bad, and she's very tight with the Guild."

"Oh!"

"'Oh' is right." Takahashi shook his head. "So what were you going to do, Samira? Let me guess: walk in, say hello, throw Tian some money, ask who killed your dad. Something like that?"

"Er, yeah," Samira said, humiliation painting the olive skin of her face a delicate pink, "pretty much."

"And when she said she didn't know?"

"Ask who I should talk to next, go and talk to them, and so on."

"That's one hell of a plan, Samira. Two points. First, that's a great way for us to find out what you're up to, and when we did, you'd be on the first shuttle out. Second, like I said, Tian's close to the Guild, and if they're behind your father's killing, Tian would almost certainly have told them you've been sniffing around."

"But what else was I supposed to do, Jonah?" Samira protested, face creased with concern. "A bunch of scumbags executed my dad, nobody has any idea who they are, and—worst of all—nobody except me seems to want to know. I can't leave it at that; sorry."

"Don't worry, you won't have to. If you were lucky, Tian would take your money and tell you nothing, which is a pity because she is a very connected woman. If you were unlucky and she was having a bad day, then who knows what might have happened. But she is a good place to start, I'll give you that. Not much goes on in this town she doesn't know about. Don't know how you got her name, but—"

"Stop right there! Promise me something, Jonah."

"Okay."

"Don't try to find out, please."

Takahashi nodded. "Okay, I won't," he said after a moment's thought. "I promise. So, however you got to her, Tian's a good start. We just need to make sure she doesn't screw you, which is where Mendoza's finest come in."

"If that means you coming along with me—"

"Hell, no. I'd be out of a job before the day was over. No. I'll pay her a visit just to make sure she knows to tell you what you need to know. I'll also make sure she understands that the Mendozan police department will take it very badly if she so much as breathes a word to anyone about your visit. It's the best I can do, Samira."

"You are a star, Jonah."

"No, I'm not," he said, shaking his head, a sad smile on his face. "I'm just a cop trying to live up to my oath of office. And understand this. Even with me leaning on her, Tian is a very dangerous woman. Get in, talk to her, and then get out—fast.

Don't tell her anything she doesn't need to know, and do not tell her where you're staying."

"Now you're frightening me," Samira whispered.

"Good; that's the idea. Your dad got on the wrong side of somebody powerful, somebody extremely dangerous, somebody who kills people who get in their way or crosses them or embarrasses them without a second thought. Assuming I can persuade Tian to cooperate, I'll leave a message at your hotel with the time and place for you to meet. If there's no message, sit tight until I contact you again. Okay?"

"Got it."

"See you, and this time it's your party, so pay the bill."

With that, Jonah was up and out of the booth, swallowed up by the crowd in a matter of seconds. Sinking the last of her beer, Samira flashed a cash card at the terminal and followed him out.

Five hours later, a persistent beeping dragged her up and out of a deep, dreamless sleep. "Bloody vidmail," Samira grumbled.

The vidmail was short and to the point: "Café Azocar, Kleinwort Street, 15:00 Thursday," and attached was a picture of a tall, stringy woman with lank blond hair falling straight to frame a face dominated by deep-set brown eyes over sharp cheekbones.

Samantha Tian would be a hard woman to miss, she thought, *and you're a good man, Jonah Takahashi, a very good man.*

Rolling over, she was asleep again in seconds.

27

Samira's heart sank as the mobibot dropped her off outside Café Azocar. The streets around her hotel were tired and run-down; Kleinwort Street was much worse: dirty, garbage-strewn, flanked by a shabby mix of shops, bars, and restaurants over which apartment blocks rose in cliffs that turned the street below into a shadow-cast strip of grubby ceramcrete busy with bots. The locals, as in every major system in the Rogue Worlds, were a mix of every ethnic type known to humankind sprinkled here and there with geneered cyborgs, their huge, heavily muscled frames the monstrous stuff of her worst nightmares.

She shivered despite the late-afternoon heat. This was not her sort of place, and the cyborgs scared her. Klimath did not allow them dirtside, and seeing so many of them up close took a lot of getting used to. *They're just people,* Samira told herself, *even if they are the size of small houses.* Taking a deep breath to steady her nerves, she pushed through the pedestrians and into Café Azocar. The place was almost empty, and she spotted Tian right away, sitting alone at a table on one side toward the back, nursing a half-full shot glass.

"Samantha?"

Tian looked up. "Are you a friend of mine?" she snapped.

"Er, no," Samira said, thrown by Tian's overt hostility.

"I didn't think so. You can damn well call me Ms. Tian, then."

"Right, sorry, Ms. Tian." Samira stood, dithering, so uncertain of herself that she did not know what to do next.

"Oh, for fuck's sake, sit down," Tian said, waving a hand at a chair. "So you're Samira Anders?" she asked as Samira sat down. "Seems you have friends in the Mendoza police, which is lucky for you, darling."

"Lucky? Why?"

"If your friend Takahashi hadn't leaned on me, this discussion wouldn't have lasted ten seconds."

"I only want to ask some questions, Ms. Tian, that's all."

"Pity, though," Tian said, her eyes flickering across Samira's body in a way that made her skin crawl. "If the filth weren't watching out for you, I could have made a lot of money out of you."

"Out of me?" Samira said, frowning. "I don't think so. I don't have any money. I'm not worth anything."

"Oh, but you are, more than you realize. I know some people who would love to get their hands on a prime piece of young Klimathian meat like you." Again Tian ran her eyes across Samira's body, her gaze so direct, so focused, it seemed to penetrate right through to Samira's skin. "And you wouldn't have been the first I've passed on to them," she continued. "Oh, no, not the first."

Samira's heart pounded as she realized just what she was dealing with. Tian was a dangerous woman, a woman who lived in a world she had seen only in trashvids. She had been naive and stupid to think Tian would want to help her just because she asked politely. If she had walked in here without

Takahashi's protection … The thought of what might have been made her stomach flip over. With an effort she forced herself to speak, even though her mouth was ash-dry with fear. "Ms. Tian, let me ask my questions, then I'll leave you alone. You'll never see me again, I promise."

"You can ask."

"I'll pay."

Tian sat back to get a better look at Samira. "You'll pay?" she said with a thin smile. "Why didn't you say so? Your ass-hole cop friend didn't tell me that."

"Here." Samira tapped a cash card on the table. "There's a thousand on this card. It's all I've got, and it's yours if you help me."

Tian's smile vanished as fast as it had come. "A thousand? Give me a break."

Afterward, Samira wondered where the sudden determination not to let Tian push her around anymore came from. "Don't mess with me, Tian," she snarled. "Not unless you want Detective Takahashi to pay you a visit. A thousand's more than enough, and you'll get it all if you answer my questions."

"Okay, okay," Tian said "Go on, ask your damn questions, pay me your money, then piss off. I've got better things to be doing than sitting here with you."

"My father was Matti Anders. He was killed here in Mendoza City."

"Matti Anders? Matti Anders? Wait … Oh, yeah. Matti Anders, a Klimathian. I saw that. It was splashed all over the newsvids. So?"

"Know anything that might help me understand why or who?"

"Nothing, and why would I? I had nothing to do with it." Tian leaned forward and dropped her voice almost to a whisper. "Listen to me. You seem like a decent kid, so let me give you some advice, good advice. Forget it. Go home. You shouldn't be asking questions like those, not around here, not if you want to get back in one piece."

"Okay, let me see," Samira said, angry now. "You know of my father's murder?"

"Said I did, didn't I?" Tian muttered, looking away, her face a sullen mask.

"And you know enough to tell me I shouldn't be asking?"

"I said that too."

"Which means you do know something. Come on, Tian." Again Samira tapped the cash card on the table. "There's a thousand here if you tell me what that something is."

Tian's eyes glanced at the card and then slid around the still nearly empty café, the tip of her tongue flickering across her lips. "Look, Anders. I can't. I wish I could, but I can't. It's more than my life's worth. Sorry, but there it is. Now go."

"No. I'm not going. You either tell me what you know or give me the name of someone who will. Or do I have to ask Takahashi to come down and ask you himself?"

Tian's eyes narrowed; with a start, Samira realized that the woman was afraid of her questions, afraid of Takahashi too. "I can give you a name," Tian said after a long pause. "Just a name, that's all. If I do that, will you go? I'm getting a really bad feeling about this."

"How do I know the name will be worth anything? You could be bullshitting me."

"You know why." Tian laughed, a short, sharp, bitter, and dismissive sound. "That damn cop would make my life a misery, that's why. Anyway, that's the best deal you're going to get, sister. Just promise me three things."

"What?"

"You'll never contact me again."

"Agreed."

"You'll tell that goat fucker Takahashi I cooperated."

"I will."

"And don't tell the guy I gave you his name. Okay?"

"Fine," Samira said impatiently. "Now, are you going to tell me or not?"

Tian took a deep breath in. "Caravacci, Jamie Caravacci," she said. "He usually hangs out in the Bar Creole on Jaffridi. Now give me my money and piss off. Oh, shit!" she hissed, her face all of a sudden turning the color of ash. "Oh, shit!"

"What?" Samira said, turning to see what had upset Tian.

Her heart raced at the sight of a cyborg squeezing his enormous frame—a huge mass of grotesquely overdeveloped muscle packed into skintight black jeans and T-shirt, blond hair cut to a short stubble—through a door at the back of the café, heading straight for the table at which the two women sat.

"Hello, Samantha," Blondie said in a gentle voice at odds with a body that screamed brutality and power. "Remember me?"

"How could I forget, you overgeneered lump of meat," Tian shot back, anger splashing two spots of color on ashen cheeks. "What do you want? I'm busy here."

"Not too busy to talk to me, Samantha. And be polite; otherwise I'll break your arm, okay?"

"Whatever," Tian muttered.

"So," Blondie said, looking at Samira from amber eyes pale as water running over sand, "you must be Samira Anders. Nice, very nice."

The man's face burned with barely controlled anger and aggression; terrified, Samira could only stare at him, unable to speak.

"She's a nobody," Tian said. "She was just leaving."

"Really?"

Something told Samira she had to get out fast. "Thanks for the drink, Samantha. See you around," she said, getting to her feet.

She'd barely moved before an enormous hand had wrapped itself around her throat, stopping her dead. "Not so fast," Blondie said, pushing her back into her seat. "Don't you know it's rude to leave without saying goodbye?"

Samira had never in her life been so frightened; the cyborg was so heavily muscled that he could tear her apart without even trying. "Sorry," was all she was able to say, rubbing her bruised neck, her voice a broken croak, the terror mounting as her frantic attempts to get her neuronics to talk to Takahashi went unrewarded.

"That's better. Now you sit there while I finish my business with Samantha, and then we're going to have a drink and a chat, but not in this shithole. I know a much better place, and I think," Blondie said, leering at her, "we might become friends."

"Fine," Samira whispered, jamming her hands under her thighs to stop them from trembling, her stomach a churning, fear-fed mess. "Whatever you want."

"Now, Samantha," the cyborg said, turning back to Tian, "you are one stupid bitch. You told Kemadi I was leaving to work for Johanssen over on the south side, didn't you?"

"No," Tian whispered.

"You damn well did. Mr. Kemadi wasn't pleased, not pleased at all. In fact, he tried to have me killed, so I had to … well, let's just say Mr. Kemadi won't be walking for a very long time. Jeez, how he screamed when I tore his leg off at the knee. Honestly, his security detail should be ashamed of themselves if I hadn't killed most of them to get to Kemadi."

Samira's stomach heaved.

Tian's face had gone from ash gray to dead white. "Honestly, I didn't say a word to Kemadi," she said, her voice quavering. "I swear it."

"You are a damn liar, Samantha Tian. Kemadi told me you did. And he told me how much he paid you for the information. That was just before I finished breaking his fingers, poor bastard," Blondie said with a chuckle.

"No, no. I swear. I didn't say a word."

"Stop wasting my time. Now, the question is this: Which leg would you like to keep? Left or right, I don't care. Your pick. Which is it to—"

Faster than Samira believed possible, Tian exploded out of her seat, hurling herself away from the cyborg, a laser pistol appearing as if by magic in her left hand. As she rolled away to get a clear line of fire, her first shot sliced through the cyborg's hand, the second his upper arm, the third his shoulder.

The fourth would have taken him in the head, but it came too late to save Samantha Tian. Fast as she was, the cyborg was faster; with a roar of pain and rage, he launched himself across the table into her, his enormous bulk crushing her to the floor, her screams cut off as two gigantic hands wrapped themselves around her neck and tore the life out of her. Her last action was a desperate failed attempt to bring her pistol up to the cyborg's head, only to send shot after shot snapping uselessly into the ceiling.

Samira knew she had only once chance to get out alive. If she waited, the cyborg—hundreds of kilos of incandescent rage—would kill her too, just for being there. Stumbling up out of her seat, she ran out of the café. Bursting out of the door, she turned and sprinted up the street, which was now deserted, until she found a mobibot. Without looking back, terrified that if she did, she would see the cyborg coming after her, she hurled herself inside, screaming at the mindless lump of metal to take her back to her hotel.

Slumping back as the mobibot sped away, she sat back, trembling as the adrenaline flooding her system began to leach away, her lips moving as she repeated over and over again the words "Jamie Caravacci, Bar Creole on Jaffridi, Jamie Caravacci, Bar Creole on Jaffridi."

Back in her hotel room, safe behind a locked door and protected by hotel security, Samira sat on the bed and shivered, fear flooding back as she relived Tian's brutal death. The fear was so intense, so tangible that it churned her stomach until she could not control herself anymore, a sudden spasm driving her in a headlong rush to end up on her knees, head down over the toilet, the contents of her stomach spewing in an uncontrollable stream into the bowl, spasm after spasm until, wracked by pain, her nausea finally began to subside and she could slide back and slump to the floor, tears of agony, tears of loneliness, tears of longing for all she had lost pouring down her face. Her chest was heaving as she sobbed out her distress, her cries bouncing unheard off the walls.

Finally, it was over, and she lay for a long time, motionless. Only when a soft beep announced the arrival of a message from Takahashi did she move.

The vidmail was succinct: "06:45, Mawson's Eatery, corner Redwood and Genadi."

28

When Samira had finished, Takahashi sat silently, stirring sugar into his coffee for a good minute. "You were damn lucky, Samira," he said at last.

"I know. I really thought Blondie was going to kill me too."

"He might have. Jacob Maariva is ... Sorry, Jacob Maariva *was* a bad piece of work."

"Was?" Samira asked.

"A tactical operations unit cornered him in a warehouse down by the river. Stupid bastard tried to shoot his way out. Can't say I'm sorry. Maariva has been implicated in at least twenty killings that we know of, and there'd have to be more. And Maariva wasn't just any old cyborg. He was one of Kemadi's best enforcers, and in return Kemadi always made sure we couldn't touch him. But it seems Maariva had just gone to work for a guy called Marcus Johanssen, who knows why. Money and women probably. Johanssen's second tier. His outfit doesn't have the Guild's clout, and that was all we needed. Without Kemadi to protect him, Maariva never stood a chance."

"None of that boring old 'innocent until proven guilty' stuff here on Mendoza, then?" Samira said.

"Hell, no!" Takahashi said with a derisive snort. "Money and power; that's what we're big on."

"I wondered why the police weren't interested in talking to me about what happened."

"Why would they be? Tian was dead, Maariva too, and my boss was really happy. As far as Lieutenant Okoro was concerned, you'd had a wasted trip, not to mention having the shit scared out of you."

"Okoro was happy?" Samira said, staring at Takahashi. "Why would he be happy because I had the shit scared out of me, Jonah? He's—"

Takahashi looked away.

"—a cop." Samira stopped, then shook her head as she worked it out. "Maariva knew my name ... Okoro tipped him off, didn't he? Didn't he, Jonah?" she snapped when he did not respond. "Maariva didn't come to talk to Tian; he came to talk to me. Luckily for me, he decided revenge came first."

"Looks that way."

"So why didn't you tell me, Jonah?"

"When Okoro found out I'd leaned on Tian for you, he locked me in the office and shut down all my comms. He's not pleased with me. I'm being transferred to a dump called Bagashwan as of tomorrow."

"Oh, Jonah," Samira said, "I'm sorry. If it hadn't been for me—"

"This is not about you, Samira. I did what was right, and to be honest, I'm glad to be out of this town. It's a cesspit full of people who think it's okay to live and work up to their necks in other people's shit. Well, I don't."

"What a clusterfuck," Samira said. "You've been screwed over, the Mendozan police are on to me, Tian's been killed, and Jamie Caravacci's probably a dead end. This trip's been a complete waste of time,"

"No, no, far from it. We've learned a lot."

"Like what?" Samira said, looking skeptical.

"We always knew Tian was close to the Mendozan Guild, just not how close. She knew how to keep a secret, that woman. But now, thanks to Maariva, we know Tian was working for Kemadi, and Kemadi was one of the Guild's senior guys. And there's something else: When I leaned on Tian, she admitted to knowing about your dad's death."

"Oh, come on, Jonah! So does half of Mendoza. Tian said it was splashed all over the newsvids."

"No, it wasn't. Do you know how many homicides there are in Mendoza City?"

"Let me guess. Lots?"

"More than any other city in the Rogue Planets, Samira. Your father's killing only appeared as a one-line listing in our daily crime summary. I've checked; none of the newsvids picked it up."

"Kemadi?" Samira breathed. "Kemadi told Tian?"

"Looks like it."

"So Kemadi's my man?"

"No, sorry, he's not. He was off-planet when your dad was murdered. But the fact that Kemadi knew about it means we can be sure the hit was organized by the Guild."

"So how does Maariva fit in to all this?"

"Maariva doesn't. He does odd jobs for Okoro, that's all. You'd have to say Maariva was the wrong man to send to lean on you."

"Because Okoro didn't know that Tian had double-crossed him?"

"Which he should have," Takahashi said, clearly relishing the moment. "Okoro really messed that one up. The Guild won't be happy with him, not one bit."

"So we're still no closer to knowing who actually killed my father?"

"Afraid not. The forensic evidence tells us there were five people at the murder scene: your father and his lawyer, the two cyborgs, and another man. No IDs on him or the cyborgs; sorry."

"So what about Caravacci?" Samira asked. "Why would Tian give me his name? How could she know I wouldn't tell Caravacci who sent me?"

"Yeah, I've been wondering about that. I think she was between a rock and a hard place. I'd made it pretty clear to her that she had to give you something, something worth having. So either she did that or I would make her life miserable. I could even get her killed if I wanted to, and she knew it."

"You said that to Tian?"

"I'm not proud of the fact," Takahashi said with a sigh, "but yes."

"So Tian offers up Caravacci to save her own skin."

"Exactly. And bear in mind she thought she'd still be around after you'd talked to Caravacci, so she had every incentive to give you someone worth talking to."

"You must have scared the shit out of her."

"I think I did."

"This Caravacci. Is he anybody?"

"No." Takahashi shook his head. "Just another lowlife. He has the usual string of arrests and convictions, all for minor stuff, though all of his jobs are Guild-related. I'll send you what I've got on him."

"Okay, so everything we have points to the Guild. We keep coming back to them."

"The Guild was responsible for your father's death. I'd bet my life on it."

"Kemadi, Tian, Caravacci." Samira frowned. "It's all a bit thin."

"It is, but it's all we've got." Takahashi paused. "Listen, Samira, I need to go. You going to be all right?"

"I'm learning, Jonah. And one thing's for sure. I'll be talking to Mr. Caravacci on my terms, not his."

"Forget Caravacci." Takahashi grimaced. "Forget this whole business. You've done well, but that's because I've been here to help you. With me banished to Bagashwan … Look, Samira, this is a dangerous city, and I won't be around to cover your ass. Promise me you'll leave things alone."

"No chance! I don't make promises I won't keep. I will find who killed my father, and I will make them pay for what they did. But you can trust me on one thing."

"Which is?"

"I'll do things properly. No more trusting to luck, no more walking into cafés alone, no more cosy chats with homicidal cyborgs. No, from here on out, I'll do things the right way, so you can relax. I'll be fine."

Takahashi looked unconvinced, but he nodded anyway. "I can't stop you, but I might still be able to help. Even in Bagashwan I'll have access to the crimint knowledge base, so if you need any background, comm me. I'll send you a number you can call when I get there. It'll be untraceable, so nobody will know we've been talking. But crimint accesses are logged and audited, so only ask if you really have to; otherwise I'm going to get busted, and if I do, it won't be some backwater they send me to."

"Emergencies only, understood."

"Right, then. I'd better go pack. Bagashwan, here I come. Take care, Samira."

With that, Takahashi was on his feet and gone. Samira stared at the man as he hurried out of the café to be swallowed up by the early morning crowd hustling its way to work. Suddenly, she felt very alone. Caravacci had to wait, she decided as she finished her coffee. When she'd told Takahashi she would be doing things properly, she had meant it. So she would check out, catch the shuttle off-planet, and get the evening starship home.

How she would tackle Caravacci, she had no idea. But she would work it out; that much she was sure of.

"Thank you, Ms. Anders," the immigration avatar said. "Please proceed to the counter marked 'Immigration Control.'"

"Whatever you want, you useless piece of crap," Samira snarled. She had had more than enough of Mendoza, and the closer she got to leaving, the more she wanted to leave.

"Verbal abuse of a public service avatar is a criminal offense, Ms. Anders, so please moderate your language. Proceed to the counter marked 'Immigration Control.'"

"Go screw yourself."

Leaving the avatar muttering threats behind her, Samira stalked over to the immigration desk. "I'm Ms. Anders," she said to the agent, "and all I want to do is get off this dump of a planet."

"If you want to get home, Ms. Anders, I suggest you be polite," the agent said, looking at her with an indifference that warned her to be very careful, "or I'll arrest you. And if I do, it'll be a while before you get off Mendoza; that much I can promise."

Samira stood silently until the agent, shaking his head, handed her a sheet of paper.

"What's this?"

"That, Ms. Anders, serves notice that you are a prohibited entrant. Once you leave Mendozan space, you may not return without a visa issued by a Mendozan embassy or consulate at least two weeks ahead of your intended visit. It's all there. Read it, then sign at the bottom."

Samira did not bother. Scrawling her signature across the densely printed text, she shoved it back at the agent. "I'll have a copy, if that's not too much trouble." *You asshole*, she added under her breath, though not quietly enough, it seemed, as the agent looked up sharply.

"Watch it, Ms. Anders," he said. "I've warned you once. Right, here's your copy. Agent N'gan will escort you to a holding cell until it's time for your shuttle, when he will escort you onboard. You'll be met at the transfer station and escorted onto the starship back to Klimath. Have a nice flight."

"Gee, thanks," she said. "And get off me," she barked at Agent N'gan, shaking his hand away as he tried to take her arm. "Believe me when I say I'm not going anywhere except off-planet."

29

"Okay, new business," Samira said, "and tell me we have some. Our cash flow is crap, so things are beginning to get very tight, and the bank's not happy about the pressure we've been putting on our line of credit. You all need to understand that we're in danger of losing KSS …"

She paused to look around the table, acutely aware that she was being less than honest. Jaska, Buq, Ashok—they would all think that her concern was for the business. Oh, she cared about KSS, of course, but only as a means to an end. And that end was finding her father's killers. With or without KSS, she would do that, but it did not take a genius to work out that it was going to be an awful lot easier with the help of the people around the table, KSS, and *Bitsa*.

"… and we don't have a lot of time left. Ashok?"

"Samira's right," Ashok said, grim-faced. "We've been going through the numbers. KSS is going to run out of cash inside three months unless we find ourselves a decent contract."

"Have you allowed for the strip-down and rebuild of *Bitsa*'s starboard main engine?" Buq asked.

"No," Ashok said, "we haven't."

"But it has to be done, Samira," Buq protested. "We can't go on postponing it."

"I know, I know," Samira said. She hated having to say no to Buq almost as much as she hated the thought of *Bitsa* not being a hundred percent. "But if we don't have the money, we don't have the money. Jaska, where are Pina Ricco and the Zaiyat job?"

"I just got a call from Brazzi," Jaska said. "He needs more time to see whether these missile sites exist."

Ashok frowned. "Ricco won't be happy about that."

Jaska shook his head. "No, no. Ricco's cool. She accepts that we need to know what defenses the Zaiyat government has covering the approaches to Firebase Zulu, so she's been in touch with the ZFM back on Zaiyat, asking for detailed intelligence on each of the three sites. She's undertaken to get back to us by the end of the month, and as proof of her bona fides, she's lodged a 10 percent deposit on the job, nonrefundable of course."

"Well, that's something, Jaska," Samira said with a relieved smile, working out in her head how much more breathing space that would give the business: some but not enough was the answer. "Though," she added, the smile gone, "that means we need another job to fill the gap. We can't afford to sit around scratching our asses until the Zaiyat job kicks off, if it ever does."

"I may have another job for us," Jaska said, "but the client still hasn't gotten back to me to confirm."

"Tell me it's a good one, Jaska," Ashok said.

Jaska nodded. "If we get it, yes, it is. Repeat business, an old client, a man we know well, a milk run."

"A milk run?" Samira snorted. "That's what you said about Calloway."

"I know, I know," Jaska said, putting his hands up.

"Who's the client?" Samira asked. "And more to the point, do you trust him?"

"The client is Martin Cheung, a retired businessman with a lot more money than sense, and yes, we can trust him."

"After Ms. Kohl," Samira said with a grimace, "I'm pleased to hear it. What's the mission?"

"Cheung likes to do field trips to obscure planets to collect exofauna. His current obsession is a place called Penrhyn-V, so much so that he's bought all the planetary development rights, not that they cost much. They've never been worth anything, anyway. Penrhyn-V is a place no sane person would go anywhere near."

Ashok sat up, eyes widening in alarm. "Hey!" he said. "A place no sane person would go anywhere near? That doesn't sound good. You said it would be a milk run."

"No sane person would go to Penrhyn-V, Ashok, because there's nothing worth seeing or doing there, and there's certainly no money to be made," Jaska said. "The place is a complete dud. So don't worry about it. It's safe enough. Nasty atmosphere, but the biggest animal Cheung has managed to find is the size of a bug. As long as he suits up properly and follows the decontamination procedures, the risk is minimal."

"And you've done this trip before?" Ashok did not look convinced.

"Yup. Matti and I last went there eighteen months ago; that was our third visit. It had its moments, but overall it was pretty straightforward. Weather and volcanic activity are the biggest problems, but they're manageable. You've flown it in the simulator, Samira. Remember?"

Samira screwed up her face as she tried to recall the mission; she'd flown every mission her Dad and Jaska had done, so she should remember. It came to her in a rush. "Got it," she said. "I do remember: crappy air and terrible weather. A pretty nasty place."

"You can say that again," Jaska said with a nod at the holovid screen. "Here's the planetary profile: It's a smallish planet, gravity 95 percent earth standard, and it has a hot A3 sun and two massive moons. Thanks to their gravitational influence, its planetary crust is highly unstable with endless earthquakes and thousands of volcanoes, almost all active and all spewing sulfur dioxide, which makes its atmosphere poisonous to people like us. To add to the fun, Penrhyn-V has an elliptical orbit around its sun, so it has bitterly cold winters and blisteringly hot summers. But it's not such a bad spot as long as you time it right."

"At least nobody would be shooting at us," Ashok said with a cheerful smile. "I'll take the crappy air and terrible weather, thanks very much."

"You've agreed on commercial terms?" Samira asked.

"Sure have," Jaska said, putting the contract summary up on the holovid screen, "and here they are. Okay, team, settle down," he went on, waving a rising chorus of disbelieving whistles into silence. "As you can see, the terms are good and KSS has done this mission before, which means there's no reason not to do it again."

"Provided Cheung says yes," Ashok said. "You think he will, Jaska?"

Jaska nodded. "I'm sure he will."

"Let's hope so," Samira said. "Right, next item, maintenance. Buq?"

"Okay, first, the starboard main engine. I think …"

• • •

Samira stood as the meeting broke up around her. "Jaska," she said, "you got a minute?"

"Sure. My office?"

Samira had to laugh. Jaska's office—complete with an elaborate sign proclaiming it to be the office of the "Chief Executive Officer, Klimath Security Services"—was a desk in a disused storeroom next to Buq's maintenance shop. Not that his ambitions were limited to a desk and a fancy sign: far from it. A reception area leading to a client meeting room and a small lounge along with a proper office were all in the cards, plans Samira wholeheartedly approved of. The disreputable look of KSS's current facilities was bad for business. The only problem was money; it would be a while before KSS could afford to do all the things Jaska wanted done.

"Your office will be fine," she said, grinning at him.

"Hey! Don't mock me, child," he said, face stern. "When I have the place fixed up, we won't have clients wondering what sort of half-assed outfit they're doing business with."

"Yeah, yeah."

Samira's cheerful mood did not last the short walk across to Jaska's office. By the time they sat down, her heart was pounding and her mouth was dry. *This*, she thought, *is going to go one of two ways: Either Jaska will kick me from one end of the base to the other, or he'll just laugh at me.*

What the hell, she said to herself. *Just ask and see what happens.*

"So what's on your mind, Samira?"

She took a deep breath to steady herself. "Promise me you'll hear me out, Jaska. No interruptions until I've finished. Then you can have your say."

"Not sure I like the sound of this," Jaska said, frowning.

"You going to hear me out or not?" Samira snapped.

"Hey, hey! Keep your hair on. I'll listen."

"Just before those assholes on Mendoza kicked me off-planet and told me never to come back, Takahashi and I talked about the man Samantha Tian told me about. Caravacci was his name, Jamie Caravacci."

Samira paused for an instant, glaring, as Jaska stifled a sigh.

"The problem is how to do that," she continued, "so I asked Brazzi to see if he could find anything more useful than the file on Caravacci that Takahashi sent me, and he came up with something interesting.

"It seems that our Mr. Caravacci has a nice little scam going: providing contract labor for Crummock Engineering's mines on an asteroid called Gorth-3312, which is, like all asteroids, a real dump and a hard place to find workers for. Caravacci's sales pitch is real simple: go work the mines for twelve months for good money plus a completion bonus for seeing out your contract or I'll blow holes in your husband's or wife's or kids' kneecaps or worse."

"Nice man," Jaska said, "with a great business model. Hell, he's a damn Mendozan; why am I not surprised?"

"Now, the good news," Samira said, ignoring Jaska's interjection, "is that Caravacci visits Gorth-3312 every month to make sure his people are behaving themselves, and that gives us the perfect opportunity to snatch him. We transit to Gorth-3312, lift Caravacci, take him somewhere quiet, ask him a few questions, dump him back, and then transit home. All over inside a week. Brazzi says Caravacci's next visit is due at the end of the month, so we could fit it in between the Cheung and Zaiyat jobs. So what do you think? Can we do it? Should we do it?"

Jaska stared at Samira and shook his head. "Klimath Security Services," he said carefully, "is a business, Samira. It supports you, it supports me, it supports Buq, and it supports Ashok, the poor bastard. He has no idea what he's let himself in for."

"That's where you're wrong, Jaska. He does, because I've spoken to him already, and know what he said?"

"You talked to him before you talked to me?" Jaska said, his voice rising to a half shout. "What were you thinking?"

"Stop shouting at me, Jaska, and settle down, please."

"Why the hell should I?" Jaska shouted. "You think this is some sort of game?"

"No, Jaska, I don't, and why would I?" Samira shot back, her voice rising to match his. "A few weeks ago we were dirtside on Calloway being shot at by scumbags; of course I know this isn't a game. But there's something you need to understand, and if you can't or won't, you can pack up your things and piss off, because I'll do what I have to do without you." Samira sat back, almost overwhelmed by frustration and anger. "Listen, Jaska," she went on when she'd recovered her equilibrium. "It's real simple. I need your support to find out who killed Dad. You going to help me or not?"

Jaska was quiet for a very long time; Samira sat and watched as he struggled to regain his self-control. It took what seemed like an age, but finally he spoke. "Of course I want to find out who killed your father," he said, his voice soft, so quiet that Samira had to lean forward to hear him. "Matti could be a total asshole sometimes, but we went through a lot together, and I did love him … in a way. And KSS is your business, so you can do what you like with it, I suppose."

"Yes, Jaska, I can. But not on my own. I need you. I need you to help me run KSS, but much more important I need you to help me track down the bastards who killed Dad," she said, getting to her feet to come around the desk, the tears flooding down her cheeks as she threw her arms around Jaska. "So help me, Jaska; please help me."

Jaska half turned, throwing his arms around Samira. Wordlessly, he held her.

Finally Samira pushed him away. "Can I take that as a yes?" she said, wiping tears from her eyes and cheeks.

"I think so," Jaska replied, wiping his face, "even if you are blackmailing me. Trust me, Samira. We'll find the people who killed your dad. We'll hunt them down and kill them like the dogs they are. I promise."

"Thank you, Jaska, thank you."

"Okay, enough of the touchy-feely stuff, Samira. Let's get serious. You talked to Ashok?"

"Yes, and I'm sorry I did before talking to you."

Jaska waved the apology away. "No, I'm the one who should be sorry. He listened to you, and I wouldn't. Come on, we'll do this together, okay?"

"Okay."

"Right. You said you talked to Ashok. Is he in?"

Samira nodded. "Yes, he is. He has a very straightforward view of things. He works for KSS, and provided KSS doesn't screw him, he'll do whatever KSS asks him to do … within reason."

Jaska chuckled. "That's always the catch with the hired help, Samira. You've got to be reasonable or they'll walk. So he's okay with snatching Caravacci?"

"He is. Ashok doesn't much like the Mendozans. Can't think why."

"That's all I need to know. So yes, the Caravacci operation is on. We'll need to make sure we don't let it screw up the Cheung and Zaiyat missions—they will be paying the bills, after all—but as long as we can fit it in, I don't see a problem."

"You're a star, Jaska. I'll get Brazzi started, then Ashok and I will work up a preliminary plan for the operation."

"Run it past me as soon as you can. I want to know exactly what's involved in this Caravacci business before you depart for Penrhyn-V with Mr. Cheung."

"Assuming we're going."

"Have faith."

"I've got plenty of faith," Samira said with a sigh. "It's money I'm short of."

"We'll get there, Samira; trust me."

"Hey!" Jaska shouted. "Get down here. We need to talk."

"Hold on, hold on," Samira said. "I've just got to get … this … crappy … sensor assembly … back … ah, right, done." She dropped her head out of *Bitsa*'s port wheel well, her face liberally daubed with grease and dirt. "What's up?"

"Just had a call from our Mr. Cheung. We're on. The bad news is he wants to leave Wednesday evening, so time's short."

"No kidding," Samira said. "Can you find Ashok while I go clean up? We need to do some planning."

"See you in five."

Wiping her hands, Samira watched Jaska walk over to where Ashok was stripping down yet another hydraulic pump. This was not how she'd ever imagined things: the never-ending struggle to keep *Bitsa* operational, arguing with suppliers, trying to keep the bank if not happy then at least not too grumpy, scraping together the money to pay bills, and—more important than anything—finding the customers they needed to stay afloat.

It was all a far cry from the buzz, the gut-churning mix of excitement and fear she'd felt flying live missions.

With a sigh, she set off after Jaska, wondering why she'd ever wanted to take over the business.

30

"Orbit nominal," the disembodied voice of Bitsa's AI said.

"Finally." Samira threw off her harness and removed her helmet. "Tell you what, Ashok. We will buy those new combat spacesuits. I'm sick of these bloody relics," she said, shoving the helmet onto the headrest of her seat rather more forcefully than was required. "Promise."

"Yeah, yeah," Ashok muttered. "If we have the cash, you should have said."

"Yes, I should. Right," Samira said, kicking and struggling her way out of her suit. "Let me go talk to Mr. Cheung. No doubt he's absolutely beside himself with excitement."

"Why?" Ashok said, scanning the holovid coming from *Bitsa's* external holocams. "This place is a real dump."

"It sure is," Samira murmured.

Wheeling slowly below the lander, Penrhyn-V was not a pretty sight, a ball of thick cloud under a gauzy high-altitude haze shot through with towering pillars of volcanic ash, their tops shredded into dusty plumes of dust and sulfur by the jet stream, a turbulent planet fast warming as it swung back toward its sun and summer approached.

"No, Ashok, you're wrong. It's not a dump." Samira shivered as she scanned the holovid. "It's a terrible place, we're thousands of light-years from civilization, and soon we're going be down on its surface, totally dependent on humanspace's oldest lander to get us all home safely. Milk run, my ass," she added.

Ashok nodded, his face somber. "No wonder the contract terms are so good," he said. "The money Cheung's paying us to indulge his hobby doesn't seem quite enough all of a sudden."

"You can say that again," Samira muttered. "I'd better go see what he's up to."

"Okay."

Samira dropped down the ladder to the cargo bay where Cheung had loaded what amounted to a one-man research station. "How's it looking, Mr. Cheung?" she said to the compact figure hunched over a holovid screen.

"Real good, Samira," Cheung said, looking up and brushing a mass of thick black hair out of eyes bright with excitement, "real good. I must congratulate you on our navigation; we dropped in-system precisely where I wanted to be, and I've already pinpointed the cluster of hot springs I've selected as my primary research site, so we should be able to go dirtside sooner than I expected."

"Sounds good to me."

"And me. The sooner we land, the more time I'll have to look for more of those sulfur-tolerant bacteria I discovered on my last visit."

"I want to have a good look at the weather. Assuming it's okay, we'll get on our way."

"I'm not sure about this, Ashok, not sure at all. I know Cheung is, but this storm system—" Samira stabbed her finger at an ugly blotch of crimson marking a tightly wound weather cell to the southwest of where Cheung wanted to land. "—is big enough to worry about. Are we sure we want to drop before it passes through?"

Ashok shook his head. "No, I'm not sure either. Problem is, if we wait, it'll be at least three days, maybe four, before it clears to the northwest."

"If we go dirtside now, we'll have less than a day before it hits us," Samira said with a worried frown. "I know the AI predicts it's only going to be a tropical depression, but that's just a guess, an educated guess, maybe, but still just a guess. We don't know enough about Penrhyn-V's weather to be sure it won't turn into a full-blown hurricane. I don't fancy being down there with one of those tearing up the joint around us."

"And the landing site is pretty low-lying; the sea's only ten klicks away. If we get a serious storm surge, the whole place is going to be underwater. Then we'll have no choice. We'd have to take off no matter how bad the weather was. Cheung won't go to the alternate site? No weather problems there."

"No, he won't," Samira said, shaking her head. "I've already asked."

"Well, in that case I think we should drop early. Maybe the storm won't be any worse than the weather model is predicting, in which case no problem. But if it does start to get worse, then we bail out to orbit."

"Cheung won't like that. We don't have the driver mass to do another reentry. If we bail out, we have to go home."

"Your call, Captain," Ashok said.

Samira sat back, fingers tapping out her concern on the well-worn arms of the command pilot's seat, all too aware that in the end it was her decision to go or wait and even more aware that making the wrong call might kill them all. She took a deep breath in, as deep as she could, then let the air out of her lungs in a long, slow hiss. It helped steady her, but only a little. "Your recommendation?" she asked, struggling not to let the responsibility crush her.

"Give Cheung the option of going now or waiting. If he insists on going, tell him we will lift off the minute the wind gets close to our takeoff limits, and if we do, that's the end of the trip. As long as he accepts that, we can go. Otherwise we'll wait until the storm cell passes through even though that will severely curtail his time on site."

Samira thought about it for a good while. Ashok was right, she decided eventually. Cheung was repeat business, and repeat business was very hard to come by; she needed KSS, and KSS needed Cheung, and that meant she had to give him as much as she could of what he had paid for: time dirtside on Penrhyn-V. The man was not a client she wanted to lose. Besides, if conditions got so bad that they had to abort to orbit, so be it. Cheung would not be able to work outside anyway in that case.

"Okay," she said, "I agree with you. Let me see … yes, we'll be at the reentry point in thirty-five minutes, so start prepping *Bitsa*. I'll go brief Cheung."

"Roger that," Ashok said, "but make absolutely sure he understands the provisos. We don't want to be having a pissing contest with him as a hurricane bears down on us."

"Don't worry, I will. And I'll record the discussion so there can be no argument."

"Sounds like a good idea to me."

• • •

"Contact … three greens. We're down. Welcome to Penrhyn-V, everybody," Ashok called out. "After-landing checklist."

"You take it, Ashok," Samira replied. "I'll check the site, make sure there's nothing out there bigger and uglier than us."

"Roger," Ashok replied as he started to shut the lander down, fingers flickering across the panels with well-practiced speed, calling out the checklist items in a soft monotone.

Sitting back, Samira breathed out a long sigh of relief. It had been a rough trip down, *Bitsa* punching into the frontal system ahead of the tropical depression, huge foamalloy wings at full stretch protesting as they absorbed the brutal, crunching power of endless rain-fueled updrafts. She switched the holovid screens to take their feeds from the lander's external cameras. What they showed was not a pretty sight; though the early morning sky to the east was a glorious riot of reds, yellows, and golds, it could not compensate for the dirty gray-black of the incoming storm to the southwest; huge clouds were piling on huge clouds as the front rolled toward them.

"Looks okay for the moment, Ashok," Samira said, scanning the area around the lander. "I can see the hot springs two hundred meters or so away at our ten o'clock. Apart from that, nothing much."

"Which is how I like it. Any nasties?"

"Nope, not a damn thing. I think we're good to go. Hold on a second … Mr. Cheung, the area's clear. We'll let things soak for another hour, and then we can start off-loading your gear."

"Don't think we need to wait that long, Samira," Cheung said with a frown. "There's nothing out there going to bother us."

"That's as may be, Mr. Cheung, but we did agree on the protocols before we left Klimath."

"Yes, yes, yes," Cheung said, scowling now. "We'll wait. I just hope that damn storm's not a bad one."

You and me both, thought Samira.

Dumping the last of Cheung's equipment boxes, Samira straightened up, wincing as overtaxed back muscles made their protests felt. Even with the help of *Bitsa*'s cargobots, it had been a long, hard slog, with box after box passed through the cargo lock before being coaxed across the broken ground to Cheung's laboratory, an overpressured plasfiber igloo positioned right alongside the hot springs and secured to the bedrock with explosive bolts.

"That's it, Mr. Cheung."

"Thanks," Cheung said, his voice muffled by the filters on his skinsuit. "I think I'm pretty well done here too."

"How's the igloo?"

"It's going to take more than a storm to shift it," Cheung said, standing back to admire his handiwork. "I'm going to set up my lab equipment and then start collecting samples."

"That's fine, Mr. Cheung. One of us will be keeping an eye on things at all times, so just let us know if you need a hand."

"I will, I will," Cheung said with a cheerful grin, looking around. "You know what? I love this place."

I'm glad you do, Samira said under her breath, *because if you weren't paying me to be here, Mr. bloody Cheung, Penrhyn-V is the last place in humanspace I'd want to be.* "Oh, one more thing," she said. "Your safety equipment. Where is it?"

"Ah, yes," Cheung said, looking around. "I think it's here somewhere."

"Mr. Cheung," Samira said with studied patience. "I know we all think there's nothing on Penrhyn-V that's going to give us any grief, but please, keep the harness on at all times. You might need that stunner, and if little green men do abduct you, we'll need the tracker to know where they take you. And please let us know if you want to leave the landing area for any reason."

With a dismissive snort, Cheung bent down and picked up his safety harness. "Whatever you want, Captain," he said, slipping it on, "whatever you want."

"Thanks, Mr. Cheung," Samira said.

"Bloody clients," she muttered as she made her way back to *Bitsa*. Just because they paid the bills …

Refreshed by a shower and a nap, Samira squeezed her way onto the flight deck. "How're things, Ashok?" she asked, slipping into her seat.

"Cheung's been busy; the bloody man hasn't stopped. I reckon he's been to and from those springs thirty times."

"As long as he's happy."

"He seems to be."

"What about the weather?"

"Not sure. Without orbital weathersats, it's hard to tell how the storm's developing. Here, have a look at the feed from *Bitsa*'s radar."

Samira studied the holovid for a long time. "Hmm," she said, staring at the chaotic mix of crimsons, reds, and yellows. "Looks to me like we might have more than a tropical depression on our hands. What's happening outside?"

"It's raining pretty heavily, and the wind's picked up a lot. It's looking ugly. I think we'll have to bail."

Samira thought for a moment, then nodded her agreement. "I agree. I'll go down and tell Cheung. We'll need to get his samples back onboard. Where is he?"

"Let me see … Yes, he locked himself into his lab twenty minutes ago along with yet another box of samples. I haven't seen him since."

"Okay. Wish me luck."

"You'll need it," Ashok said with a lopsided grin. "He won't be happy."

"No, he won't."

Dropping down to the cargo bay, Samira wriggled her way into her skinsuit. Checking to make sure that her filters were working properly and that she had no exposed skin, she locked out into a world gone mad. Struggling to keep her feet, she fought her way into a ferocious headwind, the rain painful even through the skinsuit.

Bloody hell, she said to herself as she locked into Cheung's igloo. *This does not look good.*

Five seconds later, things looked a lot worse. The igloo was empty, and Cheung's safety equipment harness lay discarded on the floor. "You stupid prick," Samira said, "where are you? Ashok, do you read me?"

"Go ahead, Samira."

"Cheung's not here, and he's dumped his tracker. Who knows where he is."

"Son of a bitch!"

"I'll start looking. Go back through the holovids. See if you can spot when he left and which way he was heading."

"Okay."

"On my way." Samira plunged back out into the storm; in the few minutes she had been sheltered in the igloo, it seemed to have gotten worse, the wind now so strong that it was shredding the rain into white streaks across the plasglass visor of her helmet. Methodically she started to quarter the ground around the hot springs, working her way outward until the scale of the problem she faced hit home. Two things were obvious now: Cheung was nowhere in the area she had searched, and the weather was deteriorating—fast.

"Ashok, Samira."

"Go ahead."

"Cheung's not anywhere close. You find anything on the holovids?"

"Nothing. The visibility's pretty bad and getting worse, so he could have slipped out without us seeing him, especially if he kept the igloo between him and the lander."

"Damn. How's the weather looking?"

"Bad. The AI's updated its forecast. Now it's saying things are going to get a lot worse. The AI reckons we'll be out of limits within a couple of hours."

"So what do we do? We told Cheung we'd bail out if the winds got too bad."

"I know.'

"Shit," Samira said, much more scared than she was prepared to admit. The speed with which the situation was getting out of hand was terrifying. She forced herself to sound calm, in control. "Here's how I see things. First, I don't think we can leave without Cheung even if he has deliberately screwed us over, which the devious son of a bitch has. Agreed?"

"I think that's right." Ashok nodded in reluctant agreement. "We can't go abandoning our clients in the middle of nowhere. Bad for business."

"Even if that's what the useless prick deserves." Samira took a deep breath to suppress a sudden rush of anger. "We've got to find Cheung. While I'm looking for him, you get explosive bolts into the ground around *Bitsa* and have the tethers ready. If I can't find him, I'll be back to help you tie her down."

"Go! I'll get started."

"Okay."

Samira looked around her. Where the hell was Cheung? She pulled up the radar images of the area around the landing site. Cheung had to have gone somewhere for a very good reason; he had not struck her as a man who did things without one. Here, she decided: a small cluster of hot springs a klick or so north of the lander; this was where he had gone, to the only place of any interest within walking distance.

"Ashok," she said as she set off, heart pounding at the thought of how far from help she was.

"Yes?"

"The hot springs north of us. I can't think of anywhere else he'd be interested in. I'm going to check them out."

"That fits, but hold on, Samira. That's a long way."

"Not much choice. Just get those bolts in; I have a horrible feeling we are going to have to ride this one out."

"All in hand. Just be quick."

"I will."

With the wind behind her left shoulder, Samira forced herself into a shambling half run across the rock-strewn ground. A lifetime later, the springs loomed up out of the murk, steam from their sulfur-laden waters stripped away by the wind. "I'm at the springs, Ashok. I can't see him anywhere."

"Damn!"

"I'll check the area around the springs. If there's no sign of Cheung, I'll come straight back."

"Roger. Do it fast."

"Okay."

Ten minutes later, Samira stopped for one last look around. Cheung was nowhere to be seen. "Come on, you useless piece of crap," she screamed into the storm. "Where the hell are you?"

The only answer came from the hissing roar of the storm. "Nothing here, Ashok," she said. "I'm on my—"

A blur, a gray streak, something long, almost a meter high, maybe more, slashed its way across the edge of her vision. Ripping her stunner from its holster, she snapped her head around; when she saw what had caught her eye, she wished she hadn't. The thing had stopped; it stared right at her from lizardlike amber eyes set in a massive scaly head that reared up a good two meters off the ground, its mouth agape to reveal twin rows of needle teeth. The thing's head went down, and for one awful moment she thought it was coming for her, but it just turned and vanished.

Samira stood motionless, fighting an urge to run and run and run until she reached the safety of the lander, terror, raw and uncontrolled, cramping her stomach so hard that the pain was almost unbearable, her heart racing out of control. "Ashok, there's something out here," she said, her voice catching in a throat dry as ash. "Something big with teeth, lots of teeth."

"What—Samira, get out of there—now!"

"But I haven't found Cheung yet."

"Screw Cheung. Back! Just do it, Samira, now!"

Samira did as she was told, breaking into a fear-fueled sprint, her heart pounding and lungs heaving as she forced her way into a wind now thick as water and white with shredded rain, expecting with every step to feel teeth slashing her back to ribbons. On and on she ran, eyes and stunner swinging in a frantic search for whatever the hell the gray thing was.

Moments later, a soft, yielding mass unseen in the murk grabbed her left foot, spinning her into an uncontrolled, crunching fall to ground that rammed the air out of her with an explosive whoosh. Badly winded, she could only roll onto her back as she struggled to drag the air back into her lungs. When she had recovered, she levered herself into a sitting position, only to recoil in horror when she found herself pushing on an unmoving body.

"Oh, shit," she hissed. "Ashok, you there?"

"Go ahead."

"I've found Cheung."

"How the hell did you manage that? I can't see more than a few meters on the holocams."

"I tripped over the asshole."

"Tell me he's okay."

Samira forced herself to check, her left hand working its way across Cheung's helmet, which was scarred and scratched but intact, until she found his filter ports. Was he breathing? Yes, she decided eventually, the man was alive. "I can't be sure, but he seems to be breathing, and his faceplate is okay though his helmet's taken one hell of a beating. Looks like one of those things had a go at him."

"Can you bring him in?"

"No, I don't think so. He's too big for me, and I need one hand free to look after myself. Whatever that damn thing was, it's still out there somewhere."

"I'm on my way. Sit tight."

"I will, and bring a machine pistol," she added as her fingers found a gash in Cheung's skinsuit. Its tattered material was encrusted with half-dried blood. "No, screw that. Bring two. Whatever I saw, it's big and nasty. I don't want it taking a piece of me."

"Will do."

Samira settled down to wait, stunner in hand, ready. She'd done all she could; now it was up to Ashok to pull her—and Cheung—out of the shit.

"How is he?" Samira said, lifting her head from her bunk, trying not to wince as pain from her badly bruised ribs burned through the painkillers loaded into her bloodstream.

"The medical AI says Cheung will be fine. The knock to his head is nothing too serious. The puncture wounds in his leg are pretty deep, though the damage is manageable, and there's no sign of any bacterial infection; I'd say the local bugs aren't interested in anything not saturated in sulfur. The medibot has cleaned and stitched him up; apart from a headache, Mr. Cheung will be fine."

"What happened to him?"

"He can't remember. My guess is he saw one of those things, panicked, ran for it, it had a go at him, and bang, down he went. He's just lucky that whatever bit him obviously didn't like the way he tastes."

"Well, even though he nearly got me killed, I'm glad he's going to be okay."

"I've got more good news. The AI's saying that eye of the storm has veered to the south, and *Bitsa's* come through unscathed. We were lucky, though. It could have been a lot worse, and even though *Bitsa* is one tough bird, she's not invulnerable."

Samira shivered at the thought. "I'm going to make sure Cheung understands that. We might have been stuck here."

"So much for Jaska's milk run,' Ashok said.

Samira grinned. "When we get back, I'm going to kick that man's ass, chief executive officer or not. And I might just kick Cheung's ass too. The son of a bitch deserves it, that's for sure."

"Join the queue, Samira. Okay, what's the plan, then?"

"Well, we're here, the storm's passing, Cheung's bloody igloo and all his samples have survived, so I'm pretty sure he'll want to be back at work tomorrow. I think we might as well let him get on with things."

"It's more than he deserves, much more."

"I know that, but he's the client," Samira said. "Anyway, I don't much care. All I want to do is sleep," she added, desperate to let her body to recover its equilibrium, to forget those terrible moments alone in the middle of nowhere, in a storm, surrounded by psychopathic gray streaks.

"You do that. I'll keep an eye on things."

"Thanks."

"Bloody Cheung," Ashok said with a moody scowl. "He'll be out there tomorrow morning as if nothing's happened. We'll need to keep an eye on him."

"With a machine pistol. I'm telling you this, Ashok: If Cheung goes wandering again, I'm going to shoot the shithead in the leg. And if I see one of those damn lizopards, I'm going to shoot it too. I don't care if they're new to science."

Ashok laughed. "Get some sleep."

31

"Unbelievable," Samira said, trying not to breathe too deeply—her ribs still protested furiously every time she forgot—as she watched the holovid screen. "That bloody man is carrying on as if nothing's happened."

"He is," Ashok replied. "Ecstatic is what he is," he added, waving his machine pistol in Cheung's direction.

"I reckon. I think we deserve a mission bonus."

"We sure do."

"And don't worry. I'm going to ask for one, a big one. We've earned it."

Ashok frowned. "Will he pay?"

"He will if he ever wants to fly with us again."

"Hey! Who says we want to fly with him?"

"We don't, though somehow I know we will. I think you'd better go give him a hand."

"Okay," Ashok said, switching circuits. "Hey, wait up, Mr. Cheung."

"How good is this?" Cheung called out. Despite his wounded leg, he was struggling to get the body of what had been officially christened the Penrhyn lizopard into a cold box. He gave up and lowered the beast—a four-legged juvenile with a scaly head, slitted amber eyes, and a body covered in a thin pelt of coarse yellow fur spotted with gray blotches, its mouth packed with a fearsome set of razor-sharp teeth set into a massively muscled jaw, its overdeveloped head anchored to a heavily boned frame by thick, corded neck muscles—back to the ground. "What a wonderful animal."

"Yes, it is … or was."

"That was a damn fine shot, Ashok," Cheung said. "That lizopard was fast."

"But not fast enough."

"Amazing," Cheung crowed, "absolutely amazing. Who'd have thought this planet would have a peak predator like this magnificent animal? I have to say that I had my doubts after Matti's death—terrible business that, terrible—but this trip has changed my mind. "You guys," he said, turning to Ashok, "are every bit as competent as Matti and Jaska were. It's been a privilege, Ashok, really it has."

"Thanks, Mr. Cheung, but we need to get a move on. Liftoff is scheduled for four hours, and we still have a lot of gear to load. Oh, yes, and I think I should let you know that we've picked up more lizopards moving this way. We suspect they're a lot more intelligent than they look; we're concerned they may have revenge on their mind."

Cheung's face went a chalky white behind his faceplate. "Shit," he whispered. "Look, there's nothing here I can't do without, so if you like, we can leave; we can leave right now. Help me put this lizopard in a cold box, then we can go."

"Just relax, Mr. Cheung, just relax," Ashok said, patting his machine pistol, his voice calm and untroubled. "We're watching things. We have time, so please. It would be a shame to leave anything behind after all we've been through. If they make a move on us, I think I can hold them off long enough for you to make it back to the lander."

"You sure?" Cheung said, so pitifully grateful that Samira had to put her head back and laugh, all the tension purged in an explosive release of emotion, the tears streaming down her cheeks. In the end, it was only the pain from her ribs that brought her back to reality.

She called Ashok on their private circuit. "Stop teasing the man," she gasped, "and get him, his fat useless ass, and all his damn samples back onboard soonest."

"Yeah, yeah."

"Oh, and by the way, there really is a large pack of lizopards circling to the west; just spotted them out seven hundred meters. I estimate twenty, maybe twenty-five. They don't look that interested, but you never know."

Ashok swung around sharply, lifting his machine pistol. "You're kidding me!"

"No, no, I'm not."

"Damn, we'd better get back."

"Oh, wait. Sorry, I got that wrong. It's just some rocks."

"You bitch," Ashok said, turning toward the lander and giving her the finger.

"Hey, hey! That's no way to treat your captain, Ashok. Just get your act together. I've had more than enough of this damned place."

"You and me both," Ashok replied with obvious feeling, "you and me both."

Happy that *Bitsa*'s vector through pinchspace was still as it should be, Samira handed control back to the AI and went back to rejoin Ashok in the lander's cramped crew room. As she pushed aside the curtains screening the door, she relieved to see that there was no sign of Cheung.

She'd had enough of their client. He just wanted to have a quick look at those springs, he had said in his own defense, to get some samples just in case they did have to leave early, he didn't know about the lizopards, blah, blah, blah. Samira had tuned out. All she'd wanted to do was tear Cheung's head off; if there was one thing she couldn't stand, it was people making feeble excuses for being deliberately stupid.

"What an asshole," she muttered, dropping into a seat across the table from Ashok.

"Who's an asshole?" He looked up at her, his face split wide by a huge grin. "Ah, let me guess. It can't be your fabulously competent systems operator you're referring to, and so it must be Mr. Cheung."

"No kidding. Where is he?"

"He's crashed out."

"Good. I've had more than enough of him."

"Me too. I think it's going to be a while before either of us forgives him."

"If we ever do. Selfish moron. Nearly got us all killed. He's got a lot to answer for. I had that same nightmare again last night." Samira shivered. "Lizopards coming out of the mist at me, one after another, never quite getting me. Scared the shit out me."

"I know. You woke me up, remember?"

"Yeah. Sorry about that. I must learn to scream quietly."

"Samira," Ashok said, reaching across the table to put his hand on hers, the warmth from his palm strangely comforting, "you sure you're okay? I can't imagine what it must have been like out there, all alone."

She shook her head, unable to reply as the horror of those awful moments came flooding back.

"Hey, hey," Ashok said, his voice soft, "things will be fine. You did well, you handled the situation, you found Cheung, and that's what really matters. Don't let it get to you."

"I'm trying, Ashok, I'm trying, but …"

"But what?"

"I'm wondering what ever made me promise to keep the business going. I'm so stupid sometimes. What the hell am I doing pretending to be a command pilot? I nearly had my ass shot off on Calloway, then I was nearly eaten by lizopards, which was a hundred times worse, I can tell you. Two missions, two close calls. What happens next?"

"You don't have to do this, you know. You can walk away. Nobody would think you'd done the wrong thing."

"But what would that make me?" Samira demanded. "A failure, that's what. No, I made that promise, and it's up to me to keep it. I owe my dad that much, so I'll just have to learn how to deal with people—and homicidal furry things—trying to kill me."

"That's not it, though, is it?"

Samira shook her head. "No," she said, "and you know why."

"Your dad's killers."

"Yes."

"You don't have to—"

"I do, Ashok," Samira hissed. "I damn well do have to find them, and I can't do that without KSS."

"Okay, okay, but look, maybe I can help. I've saved the routines the KDF has developed to handle postcombat stress. You have anything like that already?"

"No. I didn't even know there were such things. Would they help?"

"Oh, yes. Nothing but the best for the boys and girls of the Klimath Defense Force. I'll comm them to you."

"Thanks," Samira said, frustrated by Ashok's willingness to question her obsessive determination to find her father's killers but grateful to him for his obvious concern. Even though he had worked hard to keep his private feelings just that—private—she was beginning to sense there was a lot about Ashok she would enjoy getting to know if he ever allowed her to get close enough. "Right," she said, her spirits restored a little. "We have a small ritual here on *Bitsa* after every mission, and now's the time for it."

"Ritual? What ritual?"

"You'll see. That cupboard there, top left. Open it and get the bottle and two brandy glasses."

"Okay," Ashok said, doing as he was told, a puzzled look on his face.

"Now this, "Samira said, taking the bottle, opening it, and pouring two generous shots, "is 135-year-old Hennessey from Old Earth."

Ashok's eyes opened wide in surprise. "A hundred thirty-five years old?"

"Yup."

"You're kidding me. That stuff must be worth a fortune."

"I'm not kidding, and yes, it's worth a fortune. It's the real thing, one of a number of cases acquired from the president of Mooral by my grandfather under very dubious circumstances. So," she continued, raising her glass, "the toast is 'We made it back alive.' Cheers."

"We made it back alive," Ashok said, emptying his glass but only after a great deal of sniffing and sipping. "Now, that is seriously good cognac." He put the glass down on the table. "Oh, yes. Can't wait for the next mission; that stuff is like mother's milk."

"You don't have to wait, because there's one more toast," Samira said, pouring two more shots. "A new tradition that I've just started."

"This just gets better and better. What's the toast?"

"To my father," Samira said, raising her glass.

"To your father. I never knew you, Matti Anders," Ashok said, "but people say you were one hell of a good pilot, so here's to you."

"Thanks. Now, that's your lot, Ashok Samarth,' Samira said, replacing the cork and pushing the bottle across the table. "Put it back where it came from, please, and don't let me catch you sneaking a shot or two. Strictly postmission toasts only."

"Would I do that?" Ashok said, his face alive with mock outrage.

"Of course you would. You are a convicted criminal, after all."

"Gee, thanks."

With the bottle safely stowed, Ashok sat back down. "How're you feeling?" he asked.

"Tired. That was pretty bad."

"You can say that again."

"You know, I reckon I can fly the pants off most people—"

"Don't be so modest," Ashok said, wagging a finger.

"Oh, shut up, Ashok," Samira said. "And anyway, you know I'm right."

"Sadly, I think you are."

"As I was saying, I'm a damn good pilot, but down there, looking for Cheung, all alone in the middle of a storm, surrounded by those damn lizopards, I realized all of a sudden that my dad was right."

"How?"

"Simulators teach you nothing about the real world, and in the real world one thoughtless act of stupidity can get you killed, and I'm not talking about Cheung."

"I know that. Look, Samira, don't overcomplicate things. Just do what you said you'd do."

"Oh, I will, but keeping those promises means flying missions, and that means risking my life every time we fly, even on missions that everybody tells us are milk runs."

"For a moment back there I thought I was going to be shipping back two dead bodies."

"And I thought I was the neurotic one."

"Who wouldn't be neurotic? Not hard to imagine you lying dead out there on Penrhyn-V, your throat ripped out by an animal nobody even knew existed. Not hard at all."

"Gee, thanks. Should we be talking about this stuff?"

"Yes, Samira," Ashok said softly, "we should; no point bottling it up. When I came to get you and Cheung, I was shitting myself. I've never been so frightened in all my life. Stuck on that awful planet, our only way home an antique lander, the storm, those frigging lizopards." He shook his head. "I kept asking myself if it could get any worse. And then it did. Did I tell you about the pair of lizopards I saw? Right outside the lander, they were."

"Shit! No, you damn well didn't."

"It must have slipped my mind. I've never been so scared. I was shaking so badly, I missed the bastards. I needed a change of underwear when we got back."

"Ecchh! Too much detail, Ashok!"

"Sorry. But here's the thing. What we put ourselves through is so absurd. I risk my life because it's the only way I can keep flying. You do it because you made a promise you probably shouldn't have. Either way, I'm going through what you're going through. We're a team: We win together, we lose together, we suffer together."

Samira grinned. "I'm not sure that helps, but thanks anyway. I think I'll see if those postcombat routines are any good."

"Do it. They should help."

"So shut up and let me get on with it."

"Okay, okay."

Opening the routines, Samira settled back in her bunk and closed her eyes as an avatar appeared in her mind's eye: a man dressed in the high-necked midnight-blue uniform of a KDF officer. She liked him right away; his face was open and welcoming, the face of someone she could trust—no, *should* trust—a face dominated by wide-set brown eyes framed by laughter lines. The only odd note was the fact that the man was completely bald, his head smooth and round.

She decided to call him Mr. Potato Head.

Samira had to smile; bald or not, whoever had designed the avatar had worked hard to get it right, to make sure it pushed all the right buttons, and it did. Not that she cared; it was working, and to her surprise, she found she desperately wanted this man to help her. Even better, she knew he would.

"Welcome," the man said. "I'm here to help you manage the way you feel after combat. What you're going through is natural—some would say inevitable—after such a stressful experience. But we will work together; that way we will help you control the way you think about and react to what has happened. By working with me, your experiences and memories will be just that: things that happened in your past. They will no longer be things that influence your future, that affect your body, that control you."

"Way to go, Mr. Potato Head," Samira whispered.

"Instead you will control them. Now, first ..."

That night, the lizopards did not come back.

32

"I don't know what to say, guys," Jaska said, throwing a guilty glance at Samira. "We did three trips to Penrhyn-V, your dad and I, and the biggest things—the only things—we saw were the bacteria Cheung found."

"I think I've worked it out," Buq said. "None of your trips were in the late spring. Am I right?"

"Yes, that's right." Jaska nodded. "So?"

"I talked to Cheung. Even if he behaved like a complete jerk-off—"

"Which he did," Jaska growled.

"He knows a lot about exofauna. He reckons the lizopards hibernate all winter, then come out in spring to hunt and re-build their body mass. That's why you didn't see them."

"Um, makes sense, I guess," Jaska said. "Look, I'm sorry, Samira, I really am. You could have been killed."

Samira grinned at her uncle's obvious contrition. "The unknown unknowns?" she asked.

Jaska nodded. "The unknown unknowns."

"It was lucky you didn't go any later," Buq said. "Cheung thinks the lizopards might end up a lot bigger by the time winter sets in."

Samira winced at the thought of facing a giant lizopard. "Anyway," she said, "the mission's over, KSS got paid … Hey, we did get paid, didn't we, Jaska?"

"After what Cheung did, you're damn right we got paid," Jaska said. "And I got the mission bonus you wanted."

"You did?" Ashok said. "How the hell did you manage that?"

"Well, you shot the lizopard."

"I sure did. Pretty fancy bit of shooting, though I say it myself."

"So you've told us, Ashok," Samira said, "at least ten times."

"Never mind that," Jaska said. "I told Cheung the lizopard was KSS's property, not his, and if he wanted it, he'd have to buy it, which he did."

"Honestly, Jaska," Samira said, chuckling, "I wouldn't want to get between you and a buck."

"Lesson one, Samira, lesson one."

"Fair enough, and I'm glad Cheung agreed. We need the money, that's for sure. I don't know where it all goes. Anyway, Cheung's history, so can we talk about what we do next."

"Snatching Caravacci and then the Zaiyat run?"

"Yes. But first, where are we with Ricco?"

Jaska shook his head. "Still nothing back from her people on Zaiyat, but she's expecting a courier at the end of next week. That should tell us if those missile sites are for real."

"So we're right to go after Caravacci?"

Jaska looked at Ashok. "Your thoughts?"

"Technically, no problem. Gorth-3312 is a large asteroid, out on its own in Gorth deepspace. Crummock Engineering has its own security, of course, but Brazzi's brief says all they care about is looking after the plant and equipment. Apparently they have a lot of low-level sabotage. I don't think they give a monkey's ass for the poor bastards who work there."

"Pleased to hear it, "Jaska said. "But they must have hundreds of people, so—"

"Almost four hundred, working two shifts a day," Samira threw in.

"Jeez! That many?" Jaska said. "So how the hell do you find Caravacci? And when you find him, if you find him, then you have to get him out without anyone knowing he's been taken. We cannot have anyone knowing that KSS was involved. Caravacci has connections."

"Well, I think Brazzi's found us a way," Ashok said, "so here's how Samira and I see it. First …"

33

With the lightest of touches, Samira eased Bitsa down to the surface, letting the asteroid's tiny gravitational field pull the lander the last few meters dirtside.

"Contact ... three greens. Welcome to Gorth-3312," Ashok said. "After-landing checklist."

Samira threw off her straps and stood up, content to let Ashok shut the lander down. "Ashok, I'll go get suited up and get the sled prepped. You come down when you're ready."

"Roger that."

An hour later, Samira and Ashok stood outside the lander, *Bitsa*'s bulk visible in the nearly total darkness only as a shape cut out of the stars that hung in profligate confusion overhead. Samira shivered; Penrhyn-V had been an awful place, but this was much, much worse. Even with Ashok right alongside her, the loneliness gnawed at her soul.

"Ready?" Ashok said, bumping their helmets together so she could hear him, making her jump.

"Hope we look the part."

"Trust me, we do," Ashok said, patting the red and gold Crummock Engineering logos on his helmet and well-worn skinsuit. "Come on, time's a-wasting," he added, drifting his way onto the sled.

The sled was simple, almost primitive, the whole contraption a monument to Buq's engineering ingenuity: three seats atop a flat load bed, a single side-stick controller, fuel and oxidizer for the hypergolic thrusters in pressurized tanks, a small cluster of dimly lit instruments, and an inertial navigator.

Samira followed Ashok, strapped in, and connected her comm line. "You ready?"

"Let's do it."

"Lifting."

They moved off, neither saying anything as the sled flew a few meters above the asteroid's pockmarked rocky surface, the distance-to-run meter counting down the kilometers at a glacial pace, or so it seemed to Samira.

With three hundred meters to run, she broke the silence. "I see it," she said. "On the nose."

It was: The mine's accommodation module lay right ahead, a cruciform array of ceramcrete tubes half buried in trenches cut into the asteroid's surface, visible in the low-light display as pale gray smears against black rock. The airlock they wanted was impossible to miss thanks to its flashing amber lights.

"Brazzi better be right about the management," Ashok said.

"What? That they don't give a damn about what their workers get up to when they're off shift?"

"Yup. Otherwise we're in trouble."

"Well, here's hoping," Samira replied as she eased the sled onto the asteroid's surface. "Come on; let's go give Mr. Caravacci the worst night of his miserable life."

"Radio set to mine control?"

"Check."

"Okay, let's do it."

"Here's your backpack," Ashok said as they unstrapped and climbed off.

They moved off, Samira walking with the curious gait required of anyone on a microgravity object, leaning so far forward that her face was only centimeters off the dirt to push herself along with the toes. Finally, they came to an untidy, skidding halt outside the airlock. They touched helmets.

"You ready for this?" Ashok asked.

"As I'll ever be," Samira said, her heart pounding now.

"In we go, then," he said, slapping the airlock controls. Grudgingly, the airlock door opened. Intensely white light splashed out across the ground, the glare so bright that Samira was forced to half close her eyes as she followed Ashok, pulling the handle to the close position the instant she was inside; the artificial gravity cut in so fast that her knees buckled under the sudden weight.

"Airlock 2-Bravo, Control." The voice of the duty controller was shockingly loud in Samira's helmet, so loud, so unexpected, it made her jump. "I don't have any record of you guys locking out. What's happening? What's your authorization number? I don't see it on the system."

Ashok touched helmets again. "Stay cool, remember Brazzi's briefing, and we'll be fine, okay?"

Samira nodded as she flicked her radio to transmit. "Control, this is *srkkk* ... We locked out two hours ago to check the *srkkk srkkk* ... job number *srkkk* ... no problem. Took us a while ... *srkkk* ... but it's fixed now. Just a sticky microswitch, over."

"This is Control; you're breaking up. I don't have any record of you locking out."

"Sorry, you should have ... *srkkk* ... been giving us ... *srkkk* ... scheduled to pull it apart next week... *srkkk* ... over."

"Goddamn bullshit we have to put up with," the controller grumbled. "Get that damn radio of yours fixed. Control, out."

Samira glanced at Ashok; he grinned back at her. The man sounded thoroughly uninterested, just as Brazzi had predicted. Crummock Engineering had a hard-earned reputation for ruthless cost control; they never paid for good staff when marginally competent timeservers could do the job.

The instant the outer airlock door closed, air flooded into the airlock—Samira was working her jaws in a frantic effort to clear an ear reluctant to equalize—and then the inner door opened, allowing her and Ashok to step into a small compartment lined with lockers and racks of worn and patched skinsuits. It was an airlock prep room exactly like millions of other airlock prep rooms all across humanspace.

"I think we're in," Samira said, flipping her visor up, her nose wrinkling at the sour smell of the air. "This place stinks," she said. "Why the hell don't they service their ECUs?"

"Because environmental control units cost money to look after, Samira, and the people who run Crummock Engineering are a bunch of penny-pinching assholes. Come on," he said, reaching into his backpack and pulling out a blue Crummock Engineering shipsuit and cap. "Time to get changed, and I promise I won't peek."

"You'd better not," Samira said, strangely excited by the thought. Come on, she chided herself; concentrate.

She was soon out of the lightweight skinsuit and into her shipsuit and boots, the skinsuit safely tucked away on the rack among all the others, a Crummock Engineering cap pulled down low across her face, face mask in position. "I'm set," she said.

"Don't forget this," Ashok said, holding out machine pistol. "You might need it."

"Hope not," Samira said, feeling sick at the thought as she racked the bolt back. The KP-45 was a nasty piece of work. Short-barreled with a stubby suppressor and no stock, it had been designed for combat inside pressurized environments, its reduced muzzle velocity—to minimize the chances of compromising airtight integrity—more than compensated for by a heavy hollow-point round capable of tearing the guts out of anyone stupid enough to get in the way.

Ashok eased his head out of the door and looked left and then right. "Not a soul around," he said. "Come on, let's go."

Samira followed Ashok out of the airlock prep room and down a short cross-passage that opened into a long corridor, the spine of this accommodation block. Dimly lit by nightlights—it was well into the day shift's sleep period—it was interrupted every fifty meters by emergency doors, their frames marked with by yellow and black stripes, the words emergency door: do not loiter in red on the plasteel floor plates. Samira thought the air smelled even worse. They moved fast down the corridor, pausing only to check the side passages that accessed the miners' sleeping quarters.

"This is the one we want," Ashok hissed, turning into a passageway that if Brazzi's intelligence briefing was right would lead to where Caravacci was sleeping.

A small sign told her Brazzi had gotten it right. transient quarters, it said, pointing down a narrow corridor, its walls broken by a row of plasfiber doors. Ashok did not waste any time. Waving Samira into position behind him, he eased the first door open and stepped inside. "Empty," he said, moving on to the next room, his voice tight with stress.

By the time there were only two rooms left, Samira was beginning to worry. "Where are you, Caravacci, you useless piece of crap?" she muttered as Ashok eased his way into the second to last room. Seconds later, he reappeared. "I think we've got him. Check next door."

Samira did as she was told. Heart pounding, she peered into the last room. To her relief, it was empty. Closing the door carefully, she rejoined Ashok. "Empty," she whispered.

"Okay. Neuronics jammer?"

"On."

"Let's do it."

The pair slipped into Caravacci's room, which was dark except for a small night-light. The bed was a dark rumpled mass of bedclothes, the only sound the slow, steady breathing of a man deep in sleep, on his back, head to one side, one arm thrown out wide. Samira closed the door.

"Take this," Ashok whispered, handing her his machine pistol, "and keep him covered in case he gets away from me."

"Roger."

Ashok knelt beside the bed and, pausing only when Caravacci moved, eased one arm under the man's head, centimeter by careful centimeter. Then, in a single explosive movement, his free arm locked Caravacci in a choke hold, ripping him bodily out of the bed, thrashing and flailing in a frenzied attempt to break free, his feet drumming on the floor in futile protest.

"Settle down, Mr. Caravacci, and I'll let you go," Ashok whispered over and over until finally Caravacci got the message and lay still. "That's good," Ashok said, sitting him up.

"Now, I'm going to let you go. Make a sound and my colleague here will put a bullet in your knee. Make any more noise, the next one will be in your thigh. It's your call, Mr. Caravacci. You going to be quiet or have your knee blown to shit? What's it to be?"

"I'll be quiet," Caravacci croaked.

"Good man," Ashok said, releasing the choke hold.

Caravacci slumped sideways onto the floor, chest heaving. Ashok let him lie for a moment, then dragged him up and threw him into the battered chair, the only piece of furniture in the room apart from the bed. Pulling a handful of cable ties out of a pocket, he tied Caravacci's arms behind his back.

"What do you want?" Caravacci croaked.

"I thought I told you not to say anything, Mr. Caravacci. If I give the word, my colleague here will put a round in your knee. You understand that?"

Caravacci nodded, his face a mask of misery and terror.

"Good. Now, all we want is answers. We don't want lies, we don't want excuses, we don't want any bullshit. We just want answers, honest, truthful answers. Nod if you understand me, Mr. Caravacci."

Caravacci nodded.

"Good. And when you're answering our questions, remember this. Airlock 2-Bravo is not that far from here. You lie to me and I'll space you; that's a promise. You'll die the worst death a man can die: long, slow, and painful. Nod if you understand."

Again Caravacci nodded.

"Good. Now let's get down to it. I'll hand you over to my colleague. The sooner you answer her questions, the sooner

237

we'll be gone, the sooner this nightmare will be over. Nod if you understand."

Caravacci nodded as Samira stepped forward.

"Hello, Jamie," she said. "First question: Have you ever heard of a man called Matti Anders?"

Caravacci stiffened, his eyes casting left and right as if searching for a way out.

"Come on, Jamie; we know you know him. Answer the damn question or my friend here will take you for a walk."

"Yes," Caravacci said, his voice a grating rasp. "Yes, I knew about Anders."

"That's better. So you know he was killed."

"Yes."

"Who killed him?"

"Please, you can't ask me that," Caravacci said, looking up, shaking with fear. "They'll kill me. They will."

"Who? Who'll kill you?"

"The Guild. The Guild will kill me."

"So the Guild killed Anders. That what you're saying?'

"Yes, yes," Caravacci moaned.

"Okay, Jamie," Samira said, "the Guild did it. But who killed Anders? Tell us that and we're gone. Nobody will know we were even here talking to you."

Hope flared in Caravacci's eyes. "If I tell you, you'll go? You mean that?"

"Yes," Samira said, praying Caravacci believed her. She'd had enough of this already. "Tell us, and we'll go."

"Juri Saarinen," Caravacci whispered. "As far as I know, it was Juri Saarinen."

"Just him?"

"That's the word. He had two of those cyborg goons he was so fond of with him, but so far as I know, Saarinen pulled the trigger."

"The cyborgs, Jamie. I need names."

"Karla Banduna and Jacob Mueller. Last time I saw Karla, she was alive, but Jacob's no good to you; he's dead."

"Dead. You sure?"

"Yes, killed in a Guild operation on JuSen that went badly wrong." Caravacci managed a laugh. "It seems Armato didn't like what the Guild was up to."

"So who's Saarinen?"

"What?" Caravacci hissed. "You don't know who Juri Saarinen is? Who the hell are you anyway? I think you're full of shit."

Ashok's hands had wrapped themselves around Caravacci's throat before Samira even realized the man had moved. "Answer the lady's question," Ashok hissed, squeezing hard, "or I will space you. In fact—" Ashok let go and pulled out a knife, making as if to cut away the cable ties binding Caravacci's arms. "—I think I'll space you anyway. I'm tired of this, and I'm tired of you."

"No, no, no, please," Caravacci said, the words tripping over one another, his eyes darting frantically around the room as if its tired walls might tell him how to escape. "I'll answer, I will, please."

By now the fear radiating off Caravacci was almost palpable, the air thick with the smell of his sweat. "So who is Juri Saarinen?" Samira asked. "Come on, Jamie," she said, her voice gentle, dropping to her knees beside him. "Tell me what I need to know, and then we'll leave you alone. I promise."

Caravacci's eyes stared into Samira's, the eyes of a man certain he was about to be killed. "Okay," he said, licking his lips, his voice a broken croak. "Saarinen was the number three man in the Guild. He worked alongside Jaffar Terrini; Terrini was the Guild's chief of staff and the number two man after David Bevajec. Saarinen and Terrini hated each other; Bevajec liked it that way. But surely you knew that already," Caravacci added. "None of that's any secret."

It was to me, Samira thought. "Just checking, Jamie, that's all," she said. "Two more questions and then we're done, okay?"

"Fine."

"Why was Anders killed?"

"Because of the Armato job. The Guild didn't like what he'd done, so they figured he should pay."

"Last question. Why did Saarinen make the hit? Was it because of his part in the Armato business? To make amends? What?"

"Hell, no!" Caravacci spit. "Saarinen had nothing to do with the kidnapping. Jaffar Terrini planned that fiasco. David Bevajec told Saarinen to sort out the mess, so he did. He killed Terrini too. Bevajec was real happy, and now Saarinen's the Guild's number two man."

"I'm curious," Samira said. "How do you know all this?"

"Hey! You said two questions," Caravacci protested. "You've asked, and I've answered."

"So call me a liar, Jamie," Samira snapped. "Just damn well tell me. How do you know all this?"

Caravacci's shoulders slumped. "I was working with Saarinen's people on another project. I was with them for two, three months maybe. Those Guild guys always like to boast about the jobs they've done to let everyone know how tough and smart they are. So I listened. I'm a good listener; I got to hear a lot more than they realized. And that's all I know. A month after Anders was killed, Bevajec canned my project, and I left."

"All right, Jamie," Samira said. "I think we're done here, but before we go, I want you to think long and hard about something."

"What?"

"Whether what you've told us is the truth or not, because, if it isn't, we will hunt you down and we will kill you. And in case you're tempted to think we can't, think on this. If we can get to you here on this useless lump of rock in the middle of nowhere, believe me, we can get to you anywhere. You do understand that, don't you?"

"Yes, I do." Caravacci nodded, the fear plainly visible on his face. "I do, and yes, everything I've told you is the truth, on my honor."

"Honor?" Samira snorted with derision. "You are a cheap lowlife crook, Jamie Caravacci, a scumbag. You don't have any honor," she said, her voice dripping with scorn. "So anything you else want to tell us? Any answers you want to change?"

"No, no. I've been straight with you, honest."

"You better have, or you're a dead man, Jamie Caravacci." Samira paused to see if Caravacci had any more to say, but he stayed silent. "We're done here. It's time to go," she said, turning to Ashok, as sure as she could be that Caravacci had been telling the truth.

"I think so. Let's finish this."

Alarmed, Caravacci sat bolt upright, straining against the cable ties, his eyes wide. "You promised; you promised I'd be okay if I answered your questions. What are you going to do?"

"A lot less than you deserve, asswipe," Ashok said, stepping forward and ramming a gas gun into Caravacci's neck, a short *pfffft* marking the delivery of a powerful shot of mind wiper. "There, that should fry his neurons," Ashok said, stepping back as Caravacci first stiffened, eyes bulging as the drug took effect, before he slumped forward, unconscious. "He won't remember a damn thing in the morning, though he will have a shocking headache."

"He should count himself lucky he's still got a head," Samira said as Ashok cut away the cable ties and bundled Caravacci back into his bed. She took a last look around to make sure they had left nothing incriminating behind. "Place is clean. Let's get the hell out of here. Got everything?"

"Yes," Ashok said, cracking the door open and easing his head out. "Clear," he whispered, opening the door and slipping out.

Samira followed closely behind as Ashok moved to the main corridor leading back to Airlock 2-Bravo. Stopping short, he edged his head around the corner; Samira's heart jumped when he pulled back sharply. His hands told the story: two men, forty meters, wait.

They were coming their way, Samira realized, hearing the men's voices for the first time. Ashok put his mouth close to her ear. "Got to take them. Follow me on three. Just make sure you cover them. I'll do the rest."

The rest? The rest of what? Samira wanted to know. No, she decided, she did not want to know. Heart hammering, she gripped her gun tightly, worried that hands slick with sweat might slip.

Ashok raised his fist. A short pause—the men's voices were loud now—before a finger went up, then a second, then the third, and then he exploded out into the corridor, Samira right behind him.

The men were shockingly close, so close that Samira could smell their body odor, a rank mix of rock dust, sweat, and alcohol. "Down," Ashok rapped. "Down on your faces—now!"

For a moment the men stood there, mouths hanging open in shock, hands out as if to ward off the attack.

"Down," Ashok hissed, "or we'll shoot you both. Down! Down with your arms spread!"

The men got the message. Without a word, they flopped down to the deck, arms out wide, and Ashok was onto the first of them, waving Samira forward to cover the second, which she did by ramming the muzzle of her gun in the back of the man's neck, a neck creased with lines of ingrained dirt. "Don't move," she said to the man's prostrate form; he didn't.

In only seconds, Ashok had the gas gun out, and the two men lay unconscious. "Go!" he snapped.

That'll confuse the hell out of everyone, she thought as they raced on, thankful that Crummock Engineering's penny-pinching had denied the accommodation modules any holo-cam surveillance: two men, when last seen not that drunk, passed out on the floor.

The cross-corridor was clear, and they were in the prep room for Airlock 2-Bravo, Samira rushing to get out of her Crummock Engineering gear and back into her skinsuit. The seconds dragged by until her helmet sealed with a reassuring hiss and the welcome sight of a row of green status lights appeared in her heads-up display.

"My suit's green, Ashok."

"Check. Come on, you son of a bitch," he said, his voice tight with stress. "Come on ... Okay, I have all greens. Let's get out of here."

Samira followed Ashok into the airlock and punched the controls that closed the inner door and started the pumps evacuating the air. Come on, she urged, the situation made all the worse by their being so close now.

"2-Bravo, Control."

The voice, tinny in her helmet speakers, made her jump. "Go ahead, Control," she said, forcing her voice to sound calm, almost bored.

"What the hell are you guys up to now? I have no record of any authorization."

"Ah, roger *srkkk srkkk* ... 24D. You should have *srkkk srkkk* ... system. It's the same microswitch as last time. You sure you don't have it?"

"Goddamn it, guys. I told you to fix that radio. Say again your authorization number."

"Yeah, okay. It's BZ *srkkk srkkk* ... you got that?" Samira said, her eyes locked on an airlock pressure readout dropping with agonizing slowness, the status light over the outer door staying red as if to mock her burning desire to get away.

"No. Say again, and get those radios fixed or I'll come down to maintenance and shove them up your useless asses."

Samira glanced at Ashok, her guts churning. The man in control sounded seriously pissed. Would he force them to wait until he got his damn authorization number? Ashok shrugged his shoulders, seemingly unaffected by the drama.

"Hey, man, settle down," Samira said. "We don't run this joint. Talk to … *srkkk* … if … *srkkk* … problem."

"Just give me the damn authorization number."

"Roger. It's BZ4 … *srkkk* … over," she said as the air in the airlock turned to fog. Come on, come on, she urged the unseen pumps laboring to move the last of the air out. Faster, faster.

"This is hopeless," Control said. "You guys are a joke. You can't even fix your damn radio. Put your dickwad partner on."

"Er, sorry, Control. His radio is screwed … *srkkk* … waiting on spares, over."

"You're kidding me. He's got no radio? What the hell are you doing locking out?"

Shit, Samira thought. *He sounds sound like he's smelled a rat.* "He's got a radio," she said, trying to keep the fear out of her voice. "Of course he has… *srkkk* … on limited frequencies, that's all."

"You people really are a joke."

"Look, Control, I don't give a rat's ass what you think. Far as I'm concerned, you can shove … *srkkk* … fat butt. We work with what we're given. Now, you want … *srkkk* … abort until we sort this out? … *srkkk* … Not my time we're wasting … *srkkk* … so stop being such a fucking prick, Control."

That got Ashok's attention, his head snapping around to look at her. "What the hell?" he mouthed at her.

"Bluffing the bastard," she mouthed back.

"Okay, okay," Control said, all of a sudden losing interest. "You go on. But for fuck's sakes get that radio fixed … and make sure those tosswads pretending to run maintenance get those authorization numbers to Control before you lock out, not after. You got that?"

"Roger, underst ... *srkkk* ... We should be locking back in ... *srkkk* ... 2-Bravo, out."

With that, the status light switched to green, the outer airlock door opened, and Samira heaved an enormous sigh of relief. "Screw you, Crummock Engineering," she whispered as they plunged out into the darkness.

Ashok put his glass down on the table. "Aaghh," he whispered, "that stuff is sooooo good."

"It's horrible," Samira said, choking, her face screwed up in distaste, "but tradition is tradition, I suppose. Pity we can't use beer instead."

"No way. Traditions are important, and we shouldn't change them, especially when I'm drinking cognac worth a week's wages at management's expense. That stuff is fantastic. Never tasted anything like it."

"It's firewater, Ashok. Just because it's old and rare and horribly expensive doesn't make it fantastic."

"You are such a peasant," Ashok said with a happy grin. "You still have mud on your shoes. Where were you when they were teaching Consumerism 101?"

"Partying." Samira grinned back, enjoying the feeling of camaraderie that came from making it home alive and unhurt after doing something risky. For once, postmission jitters weren't bothering her. True, the mission had gone like clockwork, but it had had its moments—no, make that lifetimes—of nearly unbearable tension. Looking back on it, she realized that the pumps had drained the air out of Airlock 2-B in less than two minutes, just as they were designed to, even though it had felt like hours not knowing whether the asshole in Control would lose his temper and shut down the pumps.

She was not going to do that again, Samira vowed, not without proper fallbacks. Even though they cost a fortune, she was going to make sure they took photonic cutting charges with them the next time.

"Once again you did well, Samira. You're beginning to get good at this."

"Not sure about that."

"No, I mean it. And our man Caravacci coughed."

"You think he was telling the truth?"

"Yes." Ashok nodded. "Yes, I do. He told us things we hadn't asked for, and it all hung together."

"So Juri Saarinen's our man."

"Your man, Samira, your man. I know what you intend to do to the bastard, and I haven't said whether I want to have any part in that."

"I haven't asked you yet."

"No, but you will."

34

High on the hillside overlooking the base, on a bluff where the forest cut away to leave a small clearing, Samira sat beside the grave of her father, a simple headstone marking his last resting place.

"I like it here, Dad," she said. "I know you can't hear me, but I always feel good talking to you. It seems to help. Don't know why, but it does."

It was a beautiful day, the sky clear and the early morning sun not yet hot. For once the humidity that made living in Bellingen such a trial had gone, driven away by dry air coming across the mountains from the western deserts.

Below her the runway stretched into the distance. The cluster of ceramcrete buildings that had housed a complete lander wing until the base had been abandoned after the civil war was visible as dusty gray shapes cut out of the vegetation that carpeted the ground. Some of the buildings had already broken apart as trees forced their way through wails and roofs.

"Tell you what, Dad. That bloody jungle is on the move. It won't be long before it's takes over everything: the buildings, the roads, the taxiways, the shelters. It'll all go; there'll be no base left. Going to cost me a fortune, Dad, keeping the runway clear. Just hope we got the jobs to pay for the work.

"Anyway, I'm sure you don't want to listen to me complaining, so let me tell you the big news. We know who killed you. Juri Saarinen, that's who, the number two man in the Mendozan Guild."

Samira paused, struck yet again by how ridiculous it was that she should be sitting there talking to a man who no longer existed about killing a man who worked for one of the most powerful criminal organizations in humanspace.

"Which is all fine and dandy," she continued, "but what we do about it, I have no idea. Any ideas ... no? Oh, well, never mind. Something will come to me, I'm sure," Samira said, not at all convinced that it would.

She stared into the distance, across the base, out to where the ocean ran away to the horizon. "But any way we look at it," she continued, "it's going to be hard. Brazzi's tapped every information source he has to put together his report on the Guild. I've been through it, every last line, and I still can't see how to get to Saarinen."

She kicked her frustration into the dirt with her heel. "The Guild's a tough nut to crack, Dad. The Mendozan Navy keeps them safe from deepspace attack. The top guys live in compounds protected day and night by heavily armed guards. They travel in armored mobibots and shuttles, and everywhere they go they're escorted by cyborgs. The bastards look to be untouchable."

"But there has to be a way," she said, scrambling to her feet to stand for a moment looking down at her father's grave. "There has to be a way, I owe you that much. Look, I need to go now. Jaska says the Zaiyat job is going to happen, so I'd better be there when he gets back. I'll come see you again when we return, Dad. Wish us luck."

Turning away, she walked down the slope to her mobibot, leaving the wind to whistle softly though the grass, tumbling its way around the granite headstone and out into the void.

"No missiles, then?" Samira asked. "So you think things will be okay?"

"Looks that way," Jaska said. "Brazzi can find no evidence that Palekar has supplied any missile systems to the Zaiyatis in the last twelve months, none at all."

"If Palekar did supply any systems, would Brazzi know?"

"Yes." Jaska nodded. "He would. He has high-level access into the Palekarian weapons manufacturers."

"When was their last shipment?"

"Two years ago; Block 6 Dragon surface-to-air missiles. We know for certain those SAMs have been installed around Foundation City. We asked Ricco to confirm that, and she has. The holopix are in the mission brief, so there's no doubt about it."

"Hold on," Ashok said, his brow furrowed with concern. "That's fine, but what if somebody else supplied the missiles? Palekar's not the only system in humanspace with SAM systems to sell. What about N'dragan? They sell SAMs too, and so do Karpov-B and Altona. Not as good as Dragons, true, but good enough to keep the airspace over Firebase Zulu clear."

Samira waited while Jaska collected his thoughts; she felt for him. The business's Achilles' heel was and always would be poor intelligence. Even though Arturo Brazzi was as good as anyone could be, one man was no substitute for a decent intelligence organization able to sift through human, signals, and reconnaissance intelligence gathered over time and from multiple sources. As it was, Brazzi had worked wonders, but in the end his reach was limited, and it showed.

"That is a good point, Ashok, and I've already asked Brazzi what he thinks," Jaska said at last, picking his words with care. "He says it's unlikely the Zaiyatis have bought from anyone else."

"Reasons?"

"Two reasons. First, Brazzi has found no evidence of any weapons shipments from N'dranga, Karpov-B, and Altona to Zaiyat."

"But we don't have good access to any of those systems, so how can we be sure?"

"We can't, but Brazzi's talked to people who should know. They are confident that's the case."

"That's because they're not getting their asses shot off," Ashok whispered.

"Let it go, Ashok," Samira said. "Let's hear what Jaska has to say, then we can sit back and decide whether we do this or not. Okay?"

"Yeah, sorry. I'm just a bit wound up about this mission, that's all."

"You and me both. Jaska?"

"Thanks, Samira. There is a second reason, and to me it's the compelling one. Whenever the Zaiyatis have the money, they buy their high-end systems from Palekar; they always have. Yes, they could go elsewhere, but that would risk pissing off the Palekarians. After all, they are one of the few systems that refuse to let any morality get in the way of business. Remember the arms embargo?"

Ashok nodded.

"Well, I'll bet you the Zaiyatis do too. And which system was the only one to ignore it?"

"Let me guess," Ashok said. "Palekar?"

"You got it. Look, Zaiyat doesn't have many friends, and Brazzi doesn't think they'd risk alienating the few they do have."

There was a long pause before anyone responded.

"Sounds right to me," Samira said, all too aware that she would end up very dead if she and Ashok called this one wrong. "Ashok?"

"Yes," he said. "I agree."

"Buq, you look like you don't," Jaska said.

Buq shook her head. "No," she said. "I think Brazzi's called this one right. That means those sites are for show."

"Which is what Ricco's report concludes," Jaska said. "Her people believe all three sites are dummies. They found none of the things you would expect from operational SAM installations: radar transmissions, active datalinks, high-level security, lots of resupply activity. As you can see from the holopix they took, the launchers look exactly like the real thing, but all the evidence says they aren't."

"Okay, then," Ashok said. "That leaves us with two options. Either those sites are real, in which case there is a very high risk of *Bitsa* and the supply ships being hacked out of the sky during reentry, or they're an elaborate hoax, in which case we're safe and can ignore the sites."

"This smells wrong, somehow," Samira said.

"What do you mean?" Jaska asked.

"Why go to all that trouble if the sites don't stand up to scrutiny? What's the point? Why bother committing all those scarce resources if they don't stop Firebase Zulu from being resupplied from space? That's all that matters to the Zaiyatis, surely? I'm telling you, we're missing something here."

The long pause that followed told Samira she was not alone in her concerns.

Buq was the one who broke the silence. "Okay," she said, ticking the points off on her fingers. "They build these sites to look like full-on SAM installations. We have them checked out, and we're told they're dummies. The Zaiyatis must know we'd find that out. The last SAM systems the Palekarians sold them are still deployed around Foundation City. The Zaiyatis know we'd find that out too. So we go ahead with the resupply mission, and bang—" Samira winced as Buq smacked her hand down on the table. "—instead of Palekarian SAMs, the Zaiyatis hit us with something else, something capable of bringing down an assault lander and the supply ships it's escorting. The ZFM loses twice over: Firebase Zulu is starved of the supplies it needs and falls to the Zaiyati, and the ZFM loses all those precious supplies, supplies it will take time and money—neither of which they ever have enough of—to replace ... Oh, yes, and they also lose their resupply ships."

"So," Ashok said softly, "you're saying the sites are a double bluff?"

"That's what I'm saying." Buq's voice was firm. "Why else would they bother?"

"Hang on, folks," Jaska protested. "We're getting a bit paranoid here. Can someone please tell me because I can't see it: What's the problem?"

"The cheating scumbags," Samira said, breaking the quiet that followed, her voice soft. "Remember when Ricco was here that time, we talked about the *Warlock*?"

"Yes," Jaska said, his face creased into a puzzled frown. "They trashed it. It's no threat anymore. So?"

"Ricco said something else. She said the Zaiyatis were stripping the hulk of its weapons. I wonder—"

"If any of those weapons are hidden away in those dummy missile sites," cut in Ashok. "Sorry, Samira."

"No, no. You're thinking what I'm thinking."

"I do remember her saying that," Jaska said, a thoughtful look on his face. "Buq, you're the closest thing we have to an ordnance expert. Any ideas?"

"Hmm," Buq said, running her hands across her face. "Now, that's an interesting one. Let me think … Yes, the *Warlock* was once the *Imperator*, an N'dragan Empire-class light cruiser. The Zaiyatis bought it a good twenty years ago, and it was obsolete even then, but it was all they could afford. It carried the usual weapons—rail guns, antistarship missiles, offensive lasers—but you can forget all those; they're integrated into the fabric of the ship and use an enormous amount of power, so there's no way they could be redeployed. That leaves the ship's defensive weapons: missiles, lasers, and chain guns. Let me think … Missiles … no, their handling systems and launchers are integral. Lasers … no, mountings and power supplies would be the problem. Ah, now … yes, the chain guns. Now, they are a possibility."

"They sure are," Ashok said, grim-faced. "If my memory serves me right, Empire-class ships carry containerized ZDG-41 60-millimeter hypervelocity chain guns: Slide them in, connect up power and data, and away you go."

Buq nodded. "And they can be slid out just as easily as they went in."

"They're designed that way. Any problems, you just pull the container out and replace it."

"I've never heard of ZDG-41s," Samira said. "Are they a problem?"

"They sure are," Buq said. "The ZDG-41 is a gem of weapon system. Simple, easy to use, very high rate of fire. Very, very nasty."

"I've simmed every mission *Bitsa* has ever done," Samira said, "and I've never come across them."

"Shit, I'd hope not," Jaska said. "I wouldn't be here if we had. We always turned down any jobs that involved going up against warships, even small ones."

"Of course." Samira flushed, embarrassed. "Stupid me," she said, "but can those cannons work in air? They're obviously designed to work in hard vacuum, after all."

"What do you think?" Jaska said, looking at Buq.

"It'll take a bit of work to get them working dirtside, but I don't think that would bother the Zaiyatis too much. They need every weapon they can get their hands on, so they'd make them work. They have to."

"And guess what?" Ashok said. "I've checked the holopix Ricco's people took. Those containers might look like Dragon SAM launchers, but they are oversized; not by much, but enough to take a ZDG-41 container, and they're aligned to cover the airspace immediately over Firebase Zulu. Wind resistance and gravity means their accuracy will be crap, but that won't matter. They'll have the range, so all they need to do is pump enough rounds in the right direction, and if there's one thing the ZDG-41 is good at, it's getting rounds away. Bottom line? The chances of those resupply ships getting into Firebase Zulu safely are pretty close to zero."

"Damn it," Samira said. "Who'd have thought to measure the damn containers? I think we've just dodged a bullet."

"I think we have," Ashok said. "So what do we do? Ricco's not going to be happy."

"Oh, I think she is," Jaska said. "Very happy."

"Why the hell would she?" Samira demanded. "Those ZDG-41s have Firebase Zulu covered, and I know enough about ordnance to know that *Bitsa* is vulnerable to 60-mm cannon shells."

"All true, Samira," Jaska said, "and the more I think about it, the more I think we've stumbled onto something. But the good news is that the Zaiyatis are screwed because those guns will be firing effectively along fixed lines."

"Because they don't have the fire control systems to track a moving target?" Ashok asked.

"No, they don't," Jaska said. "Not dirtside. The fire control algorithms would be all wrong."

"Which means," Jaska continued, "that the target has to move into the line of fire, not the other way around."

"So if we stay out of their cones of fire, they're screwed," Samira said with a huge grin, excitement welling up in her.

Jaska shook his head. "Slow down, Samira. Let me talk to Brazzi. We need to be sure on this. We need to confirm that the *Warlock* is missing its ZDG-41s."

"We do, though I bet you next month's profit they will be."

"What, five dollars?" Jaska said with a sniff. "Come on, Samira. Get serious."

35

"Let me introduce Captains Rasmussen, T'chengiz, and Fuaalini," Pina Ricco said, ushering in three spacers, their well-worn blue shipsuits unadorned except for small red and gold "Free Zaiyat" badges, out of the airlock and into Bitsa's cargo bay.

"Samira Anders," Samira said, shaking hands in turn, "and this is my systems operator, Ashok Samarth."

"Good to meet you, Samira, Ashok," Rasmussen, the oldest of the three, said. She looked tired, her face drawn and tinged with the gray of fatigue. But Samira could not help noticing her eyes: a deep green and, like the eyes of other two, burning bright and restless.

These are not washed-up supply ship skippers, Samira thought. *These are people who believe in what they are doing.* "Please," she said, waving them into seats set around a crude table. "You know Jaska, I think."

"More than a bit. Hello, Jaska," Rasmussen said. "It's been too long."

"Yes, it has," Jaska said, "but KSS is back."

"So it seems, and rejuvenated, I'd have to say," Rasmussen said with a smile, looking right at Samira, who flushed. Why did everyone feel compelled to comment on how young she looked? "But before we start, Samira, we'd just like to say, all of us—" She waved a hand across her fellow captains. "—how sorry we were to hear about the death of your father. He was a good friend of the ZFM. Considering he had no stake in what happens on Zaiyat, he always did more than we ever paid him for."

"Thank you, Captain," Samira said, ignoring a soft cough of protest from Pina Ricco. *No prizes for guessing who pays the bills,* she thought. "We miss him."

"I know you do. Now, Jaska, Ricco tells us that you've caught those Zaiyati scum out?"

"As far as we know, yes. Have a look at the holovid screen. It sums up the threat environment we expect to face."

Jaska paused as the screen blossomed into an ugly mass of red lines running out from the three supposed missile sites to intersect in a thick, impenetrable mass over Firebase Zulu. The three supply ship captains winced. Samira didn't; she had already done all the wincing she needed to do.

"Now," Jaska continued, "this presentation reflects the intelligence we have received confirming that these sites—" His finger stabbed out. "—do not house surface-to-air missile because if they do, we're all screwed. But we don't think they do."

"Otherwise you wouldn't be talking to us," Rasmussen said, "good friends of the ZFM or not."

"Exactly," Jaska said, laughing along with everyone else. "We believe they contain ZDG-41 chain guns," he continued when the laughter had died away, "and this is where they came from." A sequence of holopix flashed up on the holovid screen. "The *Warlock*. If you look closely, you'll see that all the chain gun stations are empty."

Rasmussen and the rest sat stunned into silence, their mouths open.

"Damn," Ricco whispered softly, "we didn't know. I'm sorry, Jaska; we should have. Your sources are obviously better than ours. We did wonder why the Zaiyat government didn't release any holopix of *Warlock*, and now we know."

"Don't worry about it," Jaska said, dismissing her concerns with a wave of his hand.

"And you can do the mission?"

"Well, we can, though this does complicate things. Samira? Can you run through the ops plan, please?"

"Sure," Samira said. "The first phase of the operation looks like this. You'll see …"

Suited up and strapped into the command pilot's seat while Ashok ran through the prejump checklist, Samira watched the ZFM shuttle pull away from *Bitsa*, accelerating hard.

"Stand by, Samira," Ashok said, throwing off his straps. "There's a small anomaly on Fusion Alfa. Jaska and I'll go take a look."

"That damn coolant pump," Samira muttered. She unlatched her helmet, lifted it off, and hung in on the back of her seat, relieved to be free of its awkward mass. Stripping off her cap, she shook her hair free, running her fingers through its sweaty tangles.

"What the hell are you doing here, Samira?" she whispered. Any excitement she might have felt knowing the Zaiyat operation was going to happen had evaporated long ago. Now, thinking about what they were being asked to do, all she wanted to do was throw up. Putting her head back, she forced herself to relax while she waited for Ashok to return. It was a long wait.

"Hey," Ashok said, dropping back into his seat at last, "you okay? You look a bit pale."

"No, no, I'm fine," Samira said, her voice shaky. "How's that pump?"

"Seems to be an unstable pressure sensor. Jaska says we've had the problem before."

"Let me guess. Crappy spares from that dickwad Kaitana?"

"Almost certainly. Jaska's going to get Buq to have a chat with him when we get back."

"I'll tell her to take a baseball bat with her," Samira said, sour-faced. "I think it's time to remind the old crook we're not here to be screwed."

"We probably should, not that I care right now. All I care about is getting home."

"Me too. Okay, let's do that checklist again."

Ashok sighed. "You might only be a fresh-faced young maiden—"

"Watch it, spacer," Samira growled, for some inexplicable reason suddenly cheered by Ashok's irreverence.

"—but underneath that flawless veneer, you're a hard woman."

"Oh, please! Get on with it, Ashok."

"Aye, aye skipper," Ashok said, throwing a salute at her. "Right, prejump checklist. Pinchspace matrix generator ..."

36

"You are a star, Detective Jonah Takahashi," Samira whispered, "an absolute star. Jaska, are you free?" she called.

"Yes."

"Takahashi's come through for us."

"Get in here."

Once in Jaska's office, Samira put Takahashi's vidmail up on the holovid screen; in silence she and Jaska read through it. It took a while; it was a long message.

"Well, I'll be damned," Jaska said. "You said he'd come through for us."

"He has," Samira replied, shaking her head in silent admiration. "Looks to me like he's given us everything the Mendozan police have on Juri Saarinen."

"Right down to his shoe size," Jaska said, paging through the vidmail. "I tell you what, though: Saarinen takes his security seriously."

"He sure does," Samira said, "but everyone makes mistakes."

"Especially thugs like Saarinen. The man's been a Guild apparatchik for what, seventeen years?"

"That'd be right."

"That long inside the Guild would corrupt anyone. He'll be like all the rest of them—brutal, arrogant, drunk on power—and people like that always make mistakes. We've just got to find the right mistake, and when we do, we'll have him."

"Come on, then, Jaska; let's start looking."

"Okay."

Two long hours later, Samira thought she had it. "Hey, Jaska, check this out. What do you think?'

"Hmm," Jaska said. "You know what? I think you might be on to something."

"Can Brazzi check this out for us?"

"After all the money we pay him? He damn well better. Let me call him now."

Samira sat back to let Jaska make the call, happy to enjoy the feeling that she might at last be getting close.

"Right," Jaska said. "Brazzi's on it. He'll get back to us as soon as he's checked it out."

"Good. Now, what do we—"

"Samira, Jaska," Ashok said, shoving his head around the door. "Ricco's here. Final briefing. Come on."

The briefing over, Samira and Ashok watched Jaska walk Ricco back to her mobibot.

"You okay, Samira?" Ashok asked.

"Think so. Shit! What am I saying? No, I don't think I am okay, Ashok. I have a really bad feeling about this one. I don't know why. Truth is I'm scared shitless. Look!" Samira held out her hands; the fingers trembled.

"You think you've got problems?" Ashok laughed. "Well, have a look at these puppies," he said, holding out his hands.

"Oh," Samira said, embarrassed to see that Ashok's hands shook every bit as badly as hers, worse even. "You too?"

"Haven't slept properly for days." He pulled his hands back and shoved them into the pockets of his shipsuit. "That's the only reason I want to get this bloody job done, so I can get shit-faced and crash out."

Samira grinned at him. "But," she said, her facing hardening, "in all seriousness, there are far too many things that can go wrong for any of us to feel comfortable. We can still say no."

"We can; I know that." Ashok sighed. "But this is what we do, isn't it?"

"It is. Though at times like this I wonder why."

Ashok said nothing—he just nodded—and they waited in silence for Jaska to return.

37

"Zebra, this is Boxcar." Ricco's voice was unmistakable.

"Zebra," Samira replied, wiping hands slippery with sweat on the sleeves of her shipsuit, trying to ignore the thumping of her heart.

"Jericho has confirmed that Phase 1 is under way. Will execute Phase 2 at time 05:45."

"Roger that. Execute Phase 2 at 05:45. Zebra, out."

"About time," Ashok said. "This wait's killing me."

"Hope those poor buggers aren't getting chopped up," Samira said, grim-faced.

"You know they are. It's going to be murder getting into those lander bases."

"One thing the Zaiyatis don't seem to be short of is razor wire."

"Or land mines."

"Or antipersonnel lasers. It'll be a bloodbath. I just wish they weren't sending so many good people to their deaths."

"Necessary sacrifice, I'm afraid," Ashok said. "Anyway, better them getting chopped up than us. And the ZFM knows how to run a decent diversion, which is all I really care about."

"I suppose." Samira rubbed eyes gritty with worry. "You've got to wonder how long their bloody war's going to drag on."

"Well, it's been thirty years so far, so who knows? Jaska says it'll end only when the Zaiyatis finally run out of money."

"It can't be long now. As it is, they're fighting hand to hand. Precious few landers, no missile batteries, no armor, and as for artillery, you can forget that too. Rifles, grenades, machine guns, and shoulder-launched SAMs—that's all they've got left. It'll be machetes and sticks soon."

"How crazy is that?" Ashok said. "The rest of humanspace is gliding through pinchspace in starships, and those poor bastards are down in the mud, clawing each other's eyes out. But remember this. Much as we want the ZFM to destroy the Zaiyat government, it's their problem, not ours."

"You're right. Come on," Samira said, her pulse going up a gear, if that were possible; it had been hammering away ever since Ricco had confirmed that the mission was on. "We're jumping soon. Checklist?"

"Okay, let's do it. Pinchspace matrix generator …"

The familiar routine over, *Bitsa* was ready. Samira wasn't sure she was. She glanced across at Ashok; he sat in his seat, head back, eyes closed, waiting while the minutes ticked away second by plodding second. If the thought of what might be waiting bothered him, it did not show. Samira shook her head; even after all the hours they had spent together, she did not understand the man. She sighed. The only thing that mattered was that Ashok did what he was paid to do.

She checked the countdown timer. "Reentry in two minutes," she said. "Helmets on, faceplates down, and final checks."

Ashok nodded, reaching back for his helmet. Grabbing her own, Samira wrestled it over her head and onto the neck ring;

it sealed with a reassuring hiss, and a few seconds later a reassuring row of green lights on her heads-up display confirmed that she had a good suit.

"Suit's green," she said.

"Suit's green," Ashok replied. "All systems nominal, threat board remains green; we're good for reentry."

"Roger that, here we go," Samira said at last, pushing the throttles forward onto the stops.

With the main engines at full power, its frame rattling and banging, *Bitsa* decelerated with savage force, the speed decaying frighteningly fast.

"Now," Samira whispered, turning *Bitsa* back nose-on to bludgeon a path into Zaiyat's upper atmosphere, the mission pushed to the back of her mind for an instant as she reveled in the raw excitement of a max-g reentry that saw the lander's armored bulk plummeting dirtside. The fireball that enveloped the lander splashed the last of the predawn darkness that lay over Firebase Zulu with flickering daubs of yellow, red, and gold.

And still there was no response from the Zaiyatis.

"Where the hell are they?" Samira said; this was too easy, and it should not have been.

"Sitting there, stone broke," Ashok said. "Maybe the sons of bitches can't afford search radars anymore. I don't—" The screech of the radar intercept alarm cut Ashok short. "Damn," he muttered, shutting the alarm off. "Red 20, radar intercept, JJG-45 mobile search radar … antiradiation missiles away, infrared flares to auto. Hold vector."

"Roger, hold vector," Samira replied, wondering where the Zaiyat government had dug up a JJG-45. Long obsolete, it was still more than good enough to track a 750-ton lump of radar-reflective ceramsteel dropping out of orbit. But she was taking a chance—a big chance—holding vector in the hope of encouraging the Zaiyatis to keep their search radar transmitting long enough for *Bitsa*'s missiles to take them out.

"ARMs have target lock ... emitter position confirmed ... radar's shut down, but up yours, boys, too late," Ashok hissed. "Missiles on target ... now ... radar destroyed ... We're clear, no missiles inbound."

"Nice one, Ashok," Samira said, wondering why the Zaiyatis had bothered lighting them up if they weren't going to try to hack them out of the sky. "Taking manual control. She forced herself to relax her grip on the side stick. "I have control, AI assist is off. Confirm break left."

"Confirm break left on my mark. Stand by ... in three ..."

Her skin crawling as she imagined what it would feel like to be hit by hypersonic cannon fire, Samira held the lander on vector.

"... three, two, one, break!"

With the lander barely a few hundred meters above the fixed lines of fire running in from the three dummy missile sites, Samira threw the lander onto its port side, pulling the nose around into a hard plunging turn that took *Bitsa* away from the death zone over Firebase Zulu.

"Damn," Ashok muttered. "I really thought they'd have a go at us. Would be nice to know those cannons aren't a figment of Brazzi's imagination."

"Focus, Ashok."

"Sorry. Okay, targets confirmed and set, threat board still green, cannons to auto, cluster bombs armed, and release set to auto. She's all yours."

"Roger," Samira said, her body filling with fierce elation. She was sure, absolutely sure, they had picked the threat correctly, and now she was going to make the Zaiyatis pay. She flew *Bitsa* down until the ground was so close that it was just a green-brown blur streaking past under the lander's nose, the aft-facing cameras browned out by the massive duct cloud ripped into the air by the lander's passage.

"Approaching initial point … at IP now, turning in," she said, standing the lander on its starboard wing for its attack run.

"Roger. Threat board's still green. Target's on the nose."

"Got it visual," Samira said.

"Optronics have target acquisition. Stand by."

Then *Bitsa*'s cannons opened up, and streams of hypervelocity cannon shells ripped into the missile site, scouring every square meter until the Zaiyatis' elaborately constructed fiction disappeared beneath a roiling cloud of dust punctuated with the blinding flashes of fusion plants losing containment.

"Cluster bombs away."

"Roger," Samira said, the slight tremor when *Bitsa* unloaded a pattern of cluster bombs on the hapless missile site passing almost unnoticed as she reefed the lander around. "One down, two—"

The unmistakable wailing of a missile launch alarm overlaid by the AI's urgent call to break left cut her off short. Samira rolled the lander onto its port side and smashed the throttles back onto the stops. Shifting all the power *Bitsa*'s fusion plants could produce into the belly thrusters, she forced the lander into a violent skidding slide, the air behind it filled with flares dropping searingly bright dirtside, trailing plumes of white smoke. Samira held *Bitsa* on its side for only for an instant; shifting power back to the main engines, she rolled the lander level and dropped the nose in a frantic run to safety.

"Samisen surface-to-airs," Ashok hissed. "Bastards. Where the hell did they get them from?"

Four of the incoming Samisen missiles allowed themselves to be seduced into a fruitless chase after the flares, but the rest ignored the distraction, their optronics locked on to the lander's unmistakable bulk and the enormous infrared signature from its main engines. They were closing fast, but not fast enough to stop *Bitsa*'s close-in defensive lasers from hacking them out of the air, first one, then another and another and another.

"We're clear," Ashok said as the last missile died, its warhead exploding in a futile flash, and the threat board reverted to all green. "They fired too early. We were lucky."

"Yeah," Samira said, wondering how the hell he could sound so damn calm. "Next target," she added, marveling at how calm she too sounded even as her heart, driven by adrenaline-fueled excitement, tried to batter its way out of her chest, her breathing short, shallow, and rapid. She tried not to think about the Samisens that had to be waiting for them.

"Roger," Ashok said. "Target confirmed."

Taking a deep breath in an attempt to settle her body down, Samira flew *Bitsa* in a long, arcing turn, and the second missile base disintegrated under a hailstorm of cannon shells and cluster bombs. Scattered ground fire climbed up in response, tracers slow at first to close before accelerating at a frightening rate and then whipping past, the few rounds to hit the lander brushed aside with contemptuous ease by *Bitsa*'s ceramsteel armor. Then the missiles came, first one, then another, then more, ignoring the flares, forcing Samira to throw

Bitsa off track to give her defensive lasers a few more precious seconds to react.

You should have waited, she thought when the last missile exploded in a savage blast of light, a few wayward pieces from the warhead smacking into the lander's armor.

"Next target," she said, easing *Bitsa* away from the smoking wreckage of the missile base.

"Roger," Ashok replied. "Target confirmed."

Samira settled *Bitsa* down to make the run in.

"Target on the nose. Optronics locked on. Let's do it and get the hell out of here."

An instant later, *Bitsa*'s cannons opened up, the lander juddering as hundreds of cannon shells ripped into the missile site, the ground erupting into boiling clouds of dust and smoke. Samira was shocked to see the people she was shooting at for the first time: tiny figures, black anonymous shapes running for their lives, arms flailing when the cannon shells took them, pitching them to the ground. The whole scene was over in a heartbeat; first one, then another fusion plant lost containment. *Bitsa*'s frame shuddered as the shock waves smashed into the hull, one explosion so close under the port side that the foamalloy wing snapped upward, rolling the lander onto its side before Samira managed to regain control.

"Holy shit," she called out as the missile site erupted in a second storm of dust and smoke, the entire area battered into submission as a carpet of thousands of bomblets exploded, a lethal storm of shrapnel that tore people and equipment apart with an indiscriminate, mindless ferocity. "Okay, we're done," she said to Ashok, pushing the lander's nose down. "Tell the supply shi—"

Once again she was cut short; the missile alarms were shockingly loud. "Break right, break right," the AI called. Without hesitation Samira did as she was told, rolling the lander and shifting power to the belly thrusters to throw the lander off track, with yet more flares spewing out in a spectacular display of aerial pyrotechnics. But this time, the Zaiyatis had waited until the encounter geometry was in their favor. The small shoulder-launched missiles with their infrared and optronic seekers, lethally fast and highly maneuverable, burst from the ground in brilliant flashes of propellant as *Bitsa* roared past the missile base. *Bitsa's* flares distracted some, and its lasers did their best with the rest, slashing missile after missile out of the sky.

But their best was not enough: Two missiles survived, and, only microseconds apart, the Samisens smashed home.

The first came from below and behind, its onboard optronics processor hunting out the weaknesses in *Bitsa's* huge mass, the missile slipping past defensive lasers preoccupied with keeping the salvo away from *Bitsa's* vulnerable main engine nozzles. And then the warhead fired, punching a slug of metal into the starboard belly thruster, its molten mass penetrating the complex array that controlled the thruster's attitude, shredding the thruster nozzle, hydraulic lines, power cables, and data feeds with a ferocity that left the thruster bay inside its armored shell a gutted wreck, bleeding hydraulic fluid in thin streams that were torn away by the slipstream into tattered skeins of white mist.

The second missile was even luckier. With millimeter accuracy, the optronics found the gap between the frame securing the crew access hatch and the hatch itself, and the missile's warhead fired its slug. The incandescently hot molten metal blasted its way in, and the slug's kinetic energy dumped into the lander's ceramsteel armor, spalling metal shards off the lander's inner walls.

The crew capsule saved Samira and Ashok, its armored skin just thick enough to stop the storm of metal that transformed the passageway leading to the crew capsule into a lethal hell. But one shard that had been formed by chance into a compact ball spalled a tiny piece of metal off the inside of the crew capsule.

"Oh," Samira whispered as the fragment slashed its way into her combat spacesuit, into her right thigh and out again, to waste the last of its energy on a storage bin. Strangely, for a moment she felt nothing except the impact, but then the pain started, a faint buzzing tingle that exploded into a searing agony that burned its way up into her body, and with it the shock, her chest tightening and heart racing as she struggled to keep control.

"Ashok," she grunted through teeth gritted tight to stop herself from screaming. "Ashok, I'm hit."

Ashok's helmeted head swung around. "Where? You okay?"

"No, I'm not okay," she muttered as her suit's AI took over, pumping woundfoam in to stop the bleeding even as it flooded her system with a cocktail of drugs that left her pain-free and light-headed. "Hold on. My AI says it's nothing too serious, so I guess I'll live. Let's get out of here, and then I'll get the medibot to have a look."

"Fine," Ashok said, sounding unconvinced. "Just let me know before you fall over, okay?"

"Yeah, yeah," Samira said, light-headed as the drugs took over, the lander wallowing away from the missile site. Alongside her, Ashok and the AI struggled to isolate the lander's compromised systems while Samira steadied *Bitsa* into a slow climb, leaving behind her three pillars of smoke climbing into the sky, the early morning sun painting them in yellows and reds. "Ashok, how are we doing?" she said, her throat dust-dry, the pain in her thigh burning through the painkillers, radiating upward until it threatened to consume her entire body.

"Stand by … okay, but we're damaged. Starboard thruster's out, but the compartment armor contained the blast, and we've isolated all the systems. We'll be fine, Samira."

"I'm going to call the supply ships in, okay?"

"Yup. Do it."

"Okay. Dakota, this is Zebra."

"Go ahead, Zebra."

"Missile sites suppressed," Samira said, forcing the words out past pain-clenched teeth. "You're clear to drop. We've taken two missiles and have one casualty, not serious, but we are still operational. We will orbit to suppress any ground fire until you've landed. Over."

"Roger. Stand by … the supply ships are on their way in."

"Roger. Zebra, out."

And make it quick, Samira thought, *please make it quick.*

"Samira! Hey, wake up. Talk to me."

"Uurgghh … water," Samira grunted, forcing the words out past a tongue seemingly glued to the roof of her mouth. "Get me some water. My mouth feels like a bloody yak has crapped in it."

"Aha! Welcome back," Ashok said, putting a beaker to her dry and cracked lips, "and I'm glad to see you haven't lost your sense of humor. Here you are."

"More," she said.

"Coming up."

"That's better," she said when the beaker was empty, lifting her head to look around, for a moment unable to understand why she was on a stretcher in *Bitsa*'s cargo bay. Then the memories came flooding back; piloting *Bitsa* back into orbit was the last thing she could remember. "Where are we?"

"We're in pinchspace on—"

"What?" Samira said, struggling to sit upright and failing miserably. "We're in pinchspace?"

"We sure are. Our job's done, the resupply ships got through untouched, the client's happy, and we're on our way home. You're a bit beaten up, but the medibot says you'll be fine."

"Oh. What about *Bitsa*?"

"The starboard belly thruster is history—" Samira winced, and not because of the sudden stabbing pain from her thigh; KSS was about to make old man Kaitana very happy. "—and we have a lot of damage to the starboard crew access hatch, plus damage to the passageway and crew capsule, but nothing too serious. Buq's going to be a busy girl; that's for sure."

"And Ricco's going to be seriously out of pocket."

"She sure is." Ashok grinned. "We dumped a shitload of ordnance on those damn Zaiyatis, so what with all of that plus the cost of repairing *Bitsa* … But guess what."

"What?"

"I gave her a heads-up we'd be sending the account to end all accounts, and she said that's no problem. She says getting those three resupply ships into Firebase Zulu should allow the ZFM to break through the Zaiyati lines, and if they do …"

"Then it might all be over," Samira said, closing her eyes as shock washed over her. "No wonder she's not fussed about the money. Though I'll believe it when I see it."

"Me too."

"I don't think I can stay awake, Ashok," she said, "but you've forgotten something."

Ashok frowned, then shook his head. "Don't think so."

"Tradition, Ashok, tradition."

"Tradition? What, the gazillion-dollar-brandy tradition? You've got to be kidding, Samira."

"No, I'm not," she said, her voice determined. "Get the damn bottle, two glasses ... and a straw. I won't have anyone saying I abandoned tradition just because of a flesh wound."

"Flesh wound? It's a bit more than that," Ashok muttered, rolling his eyes, "but if you insist."

"I do insist, so go! And get a move on before I pass out."

38

Ashok and Jaska watched the mobibot taking Samira to the hospital disappear down the road before turning away and walking back to the operations room. Inside, Ashok took a beer from the fridge and dropped into one of the battered armchairs, happy to be out of the late afternoon heat.

Jaska followed suit, and for a while nothing was said.

"You did well," Jaska said eventually. "I've only had a quick look at the datalogs, but I can't see anything I'd have done differently. Just a pity you ran into a bunch of Zaiyatis with Samisens and the balls to wait until *Bitsa* was at its most vulnerable."

Ashok nodded, getting to his feet to fetch another beer. "Nasty little fuckers," he said, sitting back down.

"The Samisens or the Zaiyatis?" Jaska said with a smile.

"Both. Any news from Ricco?"

Jaska shook his head. "Nothing she hasn't already told you."

"You agree with her?"

"That this is the beginning of the end for the Zaiyatis?"

"Yes."

Jaska pondered the question for a while. "Yes, I do," he said, his face wearing a thoughtful frown. "That resupply operation was a disaster for them, and the diversionary attacks too. The ZFM lost a lot of people, but they've screwed the Zaiyatis over big-time. Those bastards don't have any landers left, not one. Unbelievable."

"Yeah," Ashok said, grim-faced. "Those swarm attacks do the job, but what a cost."

"Hard to believe so many people are prepared to throw their lives away like that."

"It is."

Silence returned, broken only when Buq appeared. "Hey," was all she said as she grabbed a beer and slumped into a chair, wiping a hand black with dirt and grease across a face beaded with sweat.

"Well?" Ashok said.

"Not well at all," Buq said. "You've got at least a month off, flyboy. *Bitsa* needs a lot of work. By the way, it was a damn good thing you didn't need to eject."

Ashok sat bolt upright. "What? Why?"

"More than one fragment from that missile got into the flight deck. The one that hit Samira you know about, but there was a second; it took out the escape capsule attitude controllers. If you'd had to eject, the capsule would never have stabilized. It would have …"

"Goddamn!" Ashok slumped back in his seat. "There was nothing on the status boards."

"That's another defect; sorry."

"I should be used to things not working by now." Ashok grimaced. "I'm just glad we didn't know."

"Yeah," Buq said, struggling out of her seat to lob her beer bottle into the recycler. "Anyway, that's it for me. See y'all tomorrow, and don't be late. We have a shitload of work to do."

"I'll be here," Ashok said without much enthusiasm.

Jaska followed Buq's example. He paused in the doorway. "I'm going to see Samira. You want to come?"

"Tell her I'm sorry. I'm screwed. I'll drop in before work tomorrow."

"Okey-doke."

39

"Hey, you awake?"

Samira's eyes flickered open. "Oh, hi, Ashok," she whispered.

"How're you doing, kid?"

"Oh, not too bad," she said, sliding herself upright with an effort as Ashok pulled up a chair. "The doctors say I'll be out of the hospital inside a week and fully fit in a month."

"I'm glad to hear it, because you look like a sack of shit."

"Thanks, Ashok. That's just what I need. Let me know who your motivational technique instructors are. I'll hunt the sons of bitches down and break their legs."

"You'll be fine." Ashok laughed. "Unlike me, you have youth on your side."

"Unlike you, you decrepit old fossil."

"Hey!"

"Can we talk business?" Samira said after an awkward silence.

"Sure, if you're up to it."

"I need your help again."

"Oh." Ashok sat back. "Right," he said, "let me guess. Your dad's killer?"

"Yup. I got Saarinen's crimint file just before we left for Zaiyat. I think there's a way to get to him."

"Damn." Ashok rubbed his eyes. "Look, Samira. I would help, but if that means going back to Mendoza, then sorry, I can't. There are people there I'd rather not … Well, let's just say I don't think going back is a good idea, not for me, anyway. Sorry. Gorth-3312's one thing; Mendoza's quite different."

"Look, I know that. Anyway, I'm a proscribed person, remember? I can't go back."

"Oh, yeah." Ashok put his hands up as if surrendering. "I'm not sure what it is about you, Samira Anders, but I do find it very hard to say no to you. And don't flutter your bloody eyelashes at me."

"It usually works." Samira grinned at him, the smile chasing the fatigue from her face. "You're a good man, Ashok Samarth, even if I still don't have the faintest idea what goes on behind that handsome face of yours."

"Oh, stop it." A faint pink wash colored Ashok's cheeks. "You know everything you need to know, Samira. The rest is my business."

"I know; I'm just teasing." What the hell is he concealing? Samira wondered for the umpteenth time. "Sorry," she added. "Now, let me comm you the report. I've tagged the important bit; you'll see what I mean."

Five minutes later, Ashok reopened his eyes. "I do see what you mean," he said. "Saarinen's daughter. That's the chink in his armor."

"I think so. Amazing, really. When Saarinen's back on Mendoza, it would take an entire battalion of Klimath's finest to get through his security, and even then it would be touch and go. But when he goes to Prasad to visit his daughter, he slips in and out in a soft-skinned starshuttle. Hard to believe a man like that could be so stupid."

"But true," Samira said. "He must think he's invulnerable. He's light-years away from Mendoza on a planet that's almost uninhabited and that nobody cares about, so why not slip in and out? Nobody on Mendoza's going to touch him."

"And we all know what happens to people who piss off the Guild," Ashok said, his voice tight all of a sudden.

Samira looked at him intently. *What's behind that remark?* she asked herself. *There's something there, so why won't you talk to me, Ashok Samarth?*

"Yeah," she said, keeping her voice neutral, unemotional. "So," she continued, "the problem is timing. Saarinen's not that stupid. Takahashi says he varies the dates of his trips; They can be two weeks apart or six. I've looked carefully: There's no pattern, none at all."

"Can't Takahashi help?"

"No, I don't think so. I've asked, but he's gone quiet. I haven't heard anything since he sent me the report on Saarinen."

"That doesn't sound good."

"No. Truth is, I'm a bit worried, though I probably don't need to be. We use a cutout, so he never replies right away."

"Which means he can't help us."

"And he probably can't anyway. He's thousands of klicks from Mendoza City. How could he know when Saarinen leaves for Prasad?"

"You're right; that won't work." Ashok sighed.

"Damn," Samira whispered, her head falling back onto her pillow.

"Hey, hold on!" Ashok said. "We can't find out when he leaves Mendoza, right?"

"Right."

"But we know he goes to Prasad on average once a month, right?"

"Yes. So?"

"So we wait for him to come to us."

"In Prasad nearspace? What about the locals?"

"Forget the locals," Ashok said with a dismissive flick of the hand. "Prasad is a failed system. The economy's totally screwed, and there's been massive depopulation. The place is pretty much a bust. Their pissant navy has been laid up for the best part of a decade. They can't even run antipiracy patrols anymore—the Rasovians do that for them when they can be bothered, which isn't very often—and their planetary defense forces are nonexistent. So we can pretty much do what we like."

"Pleased to hear it. But we can't hang around, orbiting Prasad and waiting for Saarinen to turn up. Somebody will get around to asking us just what the hell we're doing, surely."

"They will."

"Come on, Ashok," Samira said, sounding tired. "I don't know you as well as I should, but I do know when you've got the solution to a problem."

"I think I do. Takahashi says Saarinen uses a Planetary Dynamics starshuttle, the FG-665. It's one of the Guild's and seems to be Saarinen's personal transport. It's very fast, but it's small and carries limited driver mass. It can't do Mendoza to Prasad, drop dirtside, return to orbit, and make it back to Mendoza without remassing, and the only place it can do that is Vrijac-7."

"Oh, hell, I get it now," Samira said, groaning. "Let me guess. We jump to Vrijac-7, then sit and wait until a Planetary Dynamics FG-665 turns up to remass. If it departs on vector for Prasad, we follow it and blow the lander and Saarinen to hell when they drop into Prasad nearspace. Am I right?"

"No, not quite. We don't hit Saarinen the first time. We need to know where he goes dirtside. And we need to get Brazzi to find out as much as he can before we take Saarinen out. Otherwise we're just asking for trouble. When we know all that, we do it all over again, only this time we don't follow, we—"

"Go on ahead and ambush him," Samira interrupted, eyes bright with sudden excitement.

"Yup."

"That sounds like the bones of a plan to me, Ashok, even if hanging around Vrijac-7 for weeks on end doesn't exactly fill me with joy."

"Not much option, I'm afraid. Anyway, leave it to me. I'll talk to Jaska—"

"No, Ashok," Samira said. "Let me talk to him first. It's my job to get him onside."

"You sure?"

"I'm sure. I'll talk to Jaska. Once he's bought in, we'll get into the detailed planning."

"Fine. We've got plenty of time. Buq says it'll be a while before *Bitsa*'s fully operational." Ashok took Samira's hand and squeezed it gently. "We'll do this, Samira; we'll do this."

"I hope so. Now piss off. I'm zonked."

"See ya."

Samira watched Ashok through half-closed eyes as he left her room. The more she worked with him, the more she liked and trusted the man. But she knew full well that the person she worked with was not the real Ashok.

She sighed.

Who the hell was the real Ashok? She had no idea; even Brazzi had not been able to uncover any more than was on the public record. Something bad must have happened to Ashok along the way, something he would not talk about. Ashamed, maybe? Embarrassed? Guilty? Whatever it was, he was doing a great job of concealing it.

Dad had always said flying with someone you did not know was a good way to get killed, and she was about to do just that. She was beginning think that her father's reluctance to let her sit in the systems operator's seat had more to do with his complete faith in Jaska than in any lack of faith in her.

Not that I deserve any faith, she thought, trying to forget what a total dipstick she'd once been. She sighed. She still missed him terribly; she just wished he could see her now. He would have been proud of her.

None of which changed the fact that she was stuck with Ashok. All her instincts told her that he would turn out okay; she could only hope that she'd find out the truth about the man sooner rather than later.

40

"After-flight checklist complete," Ashok called out, "and I think we can safely say that Bitsa is back, which means it's beer time!"

"Can't come soon enough," Samira muttered, climbing out of her seat, wincing as her leg reminded her to do it slowly. "I'd forgotten how uncomfortable this damn suit is."

"Keep telling you to buy new ones," Ashok said. "And don't tell me we don't have the cash. I know Ricco just paid her bill."

Samira paused, one leg half free of the combat spacesuit but refusing to move, still gripped tight by some unseen force lurking somewhere deep inside its awkward, uncooperative bulk. "You know what, Ashok?"

"What?"

"We will. We damn well will. I cannot … wear … this—" Reluctantly, the suit conceded defeat and allowed her foot to come free. "—piece of crap anymore, and I won't."

"Halleluiah," Ashok declared. "About time."

"I'll tell Jaska to do it."

"He'll try to talk you out of it. 'If those suits were good enough for me,'" he added in a passable imitation of Jaska's voice, "'they should be good enough for you.'"

"Don't worry." Samira laughed. "It'll happen. Owner's perks, Ashok, owner's perks. Right, I'm going to talk to Buq. I want to see how she explains away that power surge in Fusion Bravo."

"Let me know what she says."

Samira walked aft and dropped down the ladder into the cargo bay, bracing herself for the heat and humidity of a late Bellingen morning as she slapped the airlock door switches to open. Outside on the apron, Buq and Jaska stood waiting, both squinting, the sun hammering down out of a cloudless sky.

"How was the old girl?" Jaska asked.

"Good, real good, apart from that power surge on Fusion B. That had us worried for a bit."

Buq grimaced. "Yeah, me too." She stopped to look at Jaska before turning back to Samira. "The problem's with one of the magnetic flux controllers."

"Goddamn it!" Samira said.

"Hey!" Buq protested. "It's not that big a deal. I'll have the old controller out and replaced before the close of business tomorrow. I've checked with Kaitana. He has one in stock; we'll have it this afternoon. So give me a break, okay?"

"Oh, shit. Sorry, Buq. I didn't mean it that way. It's Ashok."

"Ashok? What's he got to do with anything?"

"I just promised him new combat spacesuits, but if we've got to pay that money-grubbing parasite Kaitana for a new controller ..." Her voice trailed away. *Why do you never learn?* she berated herself, upset at the thought of letting Ashok down. *Don't promise what you can't deliver.*

"Don't worry about that right now. We'll talk about suits later," Jaska said. "Come with me. I've got something for you."

"It'd better be good," Samira muttered as she followed Jaska across the apron to his office, happy to be getting out of the sun. Once in the office, Jaska waved a hand at two large boxes stacked on the floor. "What are these?" she asked, looking at them, confused; they were huge, well over two meters high and at least a meter deep.

"These, Samira Anders, are the best combat spacesuits your money can buy. Erikksen Mark Vs."

"Oh, wow!" Samira exclaimed, stunned. "Erikksen Mark Vs? You're right; they are the best." She looked at Jaska. "But why? Every time I've mentioned new suits, you've bitten my head off before giving me a long lecture on cash flow management. These," she added, waving a hand at the two boxes, "are seriously expensive. And now Buq needs a new controller. Are you sure about this, Jaska? Because I'm not."

Jaska exploded; head back and mouth open, he roared with laughter, eyes streaming.

Samira looked at him, mouth open wide in astonishment. "What's the joke, Jaska?"

"Oh, Samira," Jaska gasped, struggling to get himself back under control. "I don't think you have any idea just how much you've changed, and to hear you worrying about cash flow … well, it's priceless."

"Humph," Samira grunted, her face set in a frown of disapproval. "I'm happy I make you laugh, Jaska, but answer the damn question! Where's the money coming from?"

"Jeez, you're like your dad; you know that? He wasn't big on being made fun of."

Samira glared at him. "Jaska!" she barked.

"Sorry. Look, first of all, you were damn lucky that missile didn't kill you. If you'd had a better suit, your leg might only have been bruised, not sliced open. And Buq and I agree: Much as we have to watch the pennies, keeping you alive is more important."

"Okay," Samira said, somewhat mollified. "But that still leaves us the problem of paying for these."

"Ah, well. Good point. Ricco called while you were out putting *Bitsa* through her paces."

"Ricco? What does she want? And what's she got to do with new suits?"

"Everything, Samira, everything."

"If it's another job escorting supply ships into Zaiyat, then I'm not sure we want to that again."

"Ricco says the Zaiyat government is about to collapse."

"She does?"

"She does. Thanks to the breakout from Firebase Zulu, the government has had to fall back to protect its flanks. Not that it's done them any good; Liberationist units reached Foundation City yesterday, and the whole place is falling apart. I think she's right, and so does Brazzi. He's says it's only a matter of days before it's all over."

"That's not good for us, surely?" Samira frowned. "No more jobs, I mean."

"The opposite, at least in the near term. When the Zaiyat government sues for peace—and Ricco says they will before this week is out—she wants us to ferry the Liberationist delegation dirtside to negotiate the surrender."

"And let me guess. Ricco doesn't want some disaffected asshole blowing their shuttle out of the air?"

"Correct. But it gets better. Ricco's offered us a regular contract to shuttle VIPs to and from Zaiyat."

"Commercial terms?"

"Fixed retainer plus fee per flight and consumables."

"I'll be ... Well, I guess that's what happens when you look after your clients."

"It is."

"One small problem, though."

"I'm ahead of you, Samira," Jaska said, putting his hand up. "I haven't forgotten our Mr. Saarinen. I've already told Ricco we have two commitments. As long as we coordinate things, I don't think there'll be any problems. Not that I'm happy about you going after the bloody man," he added, "even if he did kill your dad."

"No ifs about it, Jaska. Saarinen did, and he has to pay for that. Look, I know how you feel, but I made a promise when Dad was killed, and it's a promise I'm going to keep, just like I've held to my promise to keep the business going. I've said I won't let it screw up KSS, and I won't, so can we move on, please?"

Jaska nodded with a scowl that was hastily suppressed.

Samira stepped around his desk to put her arms around him. For a moment, Jaska stood unyielding before he relented and put his around her.

"Oh, Jaska," Samira whispered, squeezing him hard, "what would I do without you?"

"Not much," he replied, "but it'll need more than a bit of sweet talk and a hug to win me over. And you're still a monster," he added, the catch in his voice fleeting but unmistakable. "My little monster."

Samira's eyes filled with tears. That had been Jaska's baby name for her; he hadn't used it in years. "Yes, I am," she said, trying not to choke up. With an effort, she broke the embrace. "Come on, we've got work to do. I don't pay the chief executive officer to stand around being sentimental, even if I do love him to death, which I do."

Jaska sighed. "Why did I ever allow your father to talk me into being his systems operator?"

41

"Where the hell is the bloody man?" Samira said, trying to rub the tiredness out of her eyes.

Ashok said something under his breath in reply; Samira didn't need to know what he'd said. His body language screamed frustration at her, at Saarinen, at everything. It had been a long wait.

"Sorry, Ashok."

"Don't sweat it. I'm sick of this place too. Hanging around half a million klicks off a lump of iron drifting in the middle of nowhere is not my idea of fun."

"Nor mine," Samira said, sitting up as the threat plot reported yet another freighter dropping out of pinchspace to start its run into Vrijac-7 to replenish bunkers. "We're running out of time. If Saarinen doesn't show soon, we're going to have to come back and do this all over again. We can't afford to piss Ricco off."

"I know that. Jaska made sure I did."

"Me too," Samira said with a grin. "Let me see … 'I'll tear you a new one if you're not back in time for the next Zaiyat run.' I think that's what he said."

"And he will," Ashok said, returning the grin. "Okay, we have the beacon ID on the new arrival. Let me see now … Yes, it's the mership *Annapurna*, Jedachi registration, five days out from Ergo en route to Navelle with general cargo and passengers, all of which means it's not our man, sadly."

Samira flicked a glance at Ashok; he looked as bored as he sounded. "Roger that," she said. "You sure we haven't missed him?' she asked for the umpteenth time.

"I'm sure," Ashok said with a sigh. "Even if the beacon is broadcasting a false ID, the radars on Saarinen's lander are unmistakable. If he drops into normalspace, we'll spot him. The chances of two Planetary Dynamics FG-665 landers visiting Vrijac-7 are minute, so relax. If we don't get him this time, we'll just keep coming back until we do."

"Right, enough of this," Samira said. "I'm going below."

"I'll be down in five. I want to run some diagnostics first."

"Okay."

"And promise me you'll get some sleep. A zombie's no good to anyone, and a zombie is what you're beginning to look like."

"Don't worry, I will."

Ashok's only response was a snort of disbelief.

The intercept alarm jolted Samira awake, dragging her out of a dreamless sleep. "Yes?" she said to the AI, forcing her eyes open.

"We have a ship inbound, beacon identity AG-0417-KM. Radar intercepts and optronics scans confirm it is a Planetary Dynamics FG-665."

"About bloody time," Samira muttered. "Ashok," she called as she slipped out of her bunk and scrambled into her shipsuit. "Ashok, move your ass; we're on."

"What's up?" Ashok said, sticking his head out from between the plasfiber curtains that shielded his bunk.

"It's our man. Come on."

"About time. But are you sure?"

"The AI is."

Five minutes later, Samira looked across at Ashok. "That's him. No doubt about it."

"No, none."

"Right, let's go. He'll be jumping in a few hours, and I want to be in Prasad nearspace when he arrives."

"You don't want to wait to make sure?"

"Nope. If he's our man, we'll see him again. If he's not ..."

"You're the boss."

Samira did not respond, her attention focused on setting up the pinchspace jump even as the AI sent *Bitsa* accelerating on vector for Prasad.

"Okay," Ashok continued, "prejump checks."

"That's got to be him!" Samira could not contain her excitement when a bright flash of ultraviolet announced a new arrival in Prasad nearspace, followed seconds later by a beacon squawking its registration number. Holding her breath, she waited until *Bitsa*'s AI confirmed the new arrival's identity. "And it is," she said.

"Yup," Ashok said, fingers flickering across control panels. "Target is designated Tango-1, optronics have acquisition, tracking is good. Okay, let's see where he goes."

Without another word being said, Samira and Ashok watched as every sensor *Bitsa* possessed tracked Saarinen's starshuttle while it decelerated in-system. "Tango-1 has commenced reentry," the AI said at last.

"We have Tango-1 visual," Ashok said when one of the tiny optical drones *Bitsa* had pushed into low-earth orbit around

Prasad picked up the starshuttle's black shape, plummeting dirtside at the head of a flaming plume of smoke and fire. "Stand by vector … I don't think there's any doubt," he said, bringing up a geosat image of Prasad's surface overlaid with Tango-1's predicted vector. "Unless he's planning to crash into the jungle, I'd say that's where he's going."

Ashok zoomed the holovid in until the screen filled with a small cluster of buildings set in a clearing cut out of towering rain forest and flanked by a river; the morning sun struck splinters of mirrored glass off the water as it wound its way through an ocean of green-gray forest that broke against the Shaanxi Mountains, huge walls of rock and towering peaks that ran away for hundreds of kilometers in both directions.

Across the river from the compound lay a single runway, a long ceramcrete slash cut out of the jungle, its precise shape at odds with the luxuriant chaos all around. At one end was a pair of small hangars and what looked like a meet-and-greet shed, with six utility fliers sitting on the apron in two tidy rows out front.

"No doubt about it," Samira said with a nod. "There's nowhere else to go."

"What a place," Ashok said. "Beautiful, but who the hell would want to come here?"

"Juri Saarinen, that's who. And come on; it's stunning."

"Give me a break, Samira. What's there to do? Shoot the local wildlife; that's all."

"Not my idea of fun, Ashok. Very few leopards are dumb enough to let themselves be shot, and they're extremely dangerous. They lose people all the time."

"I read that. Two guys were torn apart by a pack a few months ago. I suppose the risk is part of the attraction. You'd think they'd be more careful. Not my sort of place at all."

"You only say that because you're a soft city boy."

Ashok snorted, a soft grunt of derision. "And what are you, party girl?"

"Focus, Ashok, focus."

"Sorry."

Samira watched intently as the starshuttle, now safely through Prasad's upper atmosphere, slowed for landing, tracked every meter of the way by *Bitsa*'s drones. "That's it," she said as the starshuttle pitched nose up and dropped onto the runway, small puffs of white smoke bursting out when the tires bit. "It's down, and that's enough for me. Okay, let's recover those drones and get the hell out of here."

"Fine by me," Ashok said. "Zaiyat, here we come."

"You sure know how to spoil things, Ashok. I wouldn't mind if we never went anywhere near the place again." Samira shivered. "All those damn SAMs. They give me the creeps."

42

"Welcome back, Samira," Ashok said as Samira emerged from the battered all-terrain vehicle into the steaming heart of a Zaiyati morning, the olive skin of her face gray and slick with sweat. "How was it?"

"Awful." Samira took a long pull from her water bottle in a futile attempt to wash the acrid taste of smoke out of her mouth. "What the hell was I thinking?" she said. "You made the right call, Ashok. I should never have said yes to Ricco's damn city tour."

"It was that bad?"

"Worse than bad. I've never seen anything like it. Foundation City is a ruin: smashed buildings, wrecked bots, roadblocks, bridges blown, overpasses brought down, debris and ash everywhere. And the bodies, Ashok; everywhere dead bodies that should have been buried a week ago."

"Thought I recognized the smell even out here."

"You can, though it's a hundred times worse in town. What with that and the smoke, the air's damn near unbreathable. Tell you what, though: The Zaiyatis didn't stop fighting until the ZFM blew every last one of their heads off."

"Why would they go on like that? Surely they must have known they couldn't win."

"You'd have thought so." She paused, looking across the perimeter wire toward Foundation City, its position marked by ugly gray pillars of smoke. "Strange to think," she continued, "that Zaiyat was once a rich planet, richer than Klimath even. Now the place is just a wasteland."

Ashok shook his head. "Not a wasteland," he said. "It's a graveyard, Samira, one big graveyard stuffed with millions of corpses. And Ricco says the ZFM is the winner." He shook his head again. "That woman's lost the plot."

"They all lost the plot, Ashok, years ago. Tell you what: I'll be happy when we're done here. I like the money, but it's still a dangerous place. Too dangerous. All those deserters."

"All those missiles, you mean. I thought the Zaiyat government was too broke to buy missiles."

"Only the big ones. The small ones, no problem. Got lots of those."

"What a waste," Ashok said with a despairing shake of his head. "Makes you realize just how stupid humans can be when they put their minds to it."

Samira nodded. "We good to go?" she asked.

"Oh, yeah. Trust me, we are good to go … if and when Ricco ever turns up."

"I'll do the meet and greet then."

"Fine. I'll be on the flight deck"

Depressed by the unremitting horror of it all, Samira sat down in the shade thrown by *Bitsa*'s huge wing, resigned to a long wait.

An hour later, she looked up as a mobibot with an escort of two armored vehicles was waved through the cordon of Liberationist troops that protected what was left of Foundation City's spaceport. She commed Ashok. "Visitors," she said.

"Please tell me they're Ricco and her team."

"Looks like it."

"About time. Why is that woman incapable of being on time?"

"That's President-Designate Ricco to you, Ashok, so if she wants to be late, that's fine by us. After all, she is paying handsomely for the privilege. And yes, it's definitely her, so get started on the prelaunch checklist."

"Will do."

The armored personnel carrier pulled up alongside *Bitsa*, its ATV escorts spilling heavily armed troops into a protective ring around Ricco before she made her way over.

"Samira," Ricco said.

"Madam President. Welcome back."

"Thanks." Ricco shook her head. "I can't get used to the Madam President thing and don't much like it either. Are we ready to go?"

"We are, so if you'd like to make your way onboard?"

"Thanks," Ricco said. The woman looked and sounded exhausted, her voice hoarse and scratchy. "I can't wait. I haven't slept since we landed. Lead on."

Five minutes later, Ricco and her team had found their seats and Samira was in hers. "Welcome aboard, everyone," she said, fingers flicking across control panels to bring *Bitsa's* fusion plants online. "This is your captain from the flight deck. We will be taxiing for takeoff shortly. Please make sure you are all well strapped in and your suits are showing all greens. We have intelligence reports of hostiles north and west of us, so we'll be doing a hard right turn as soon as we're airborne to stay clear of them. All being well, that should give us a clear vector into orbit. As soon as we're out of the missile danger zone, I'll get back to you with an updated arrival time. Thank you." She turned to Ashok. "All set?"

"We are."

"Let's do it."

Samira sat back and took a deep breath. "Right," she said, "let's get the hell out of this place. Foundation Control, this is Gipsy Four, two crew and twenty-six pax, outbound for Orbital Transfer Station Golf, flight plan Red 43 Alfa."

"Roger that, Gipsy Four. You are clear to take off. Follow taxiway Bravo 2 onto Runway 70 Left; flight plan Red 43 Alfa is approved."

"Gipsy Four cleared for takeoff, roger," Samira responded. *Bitsa*'s frame trembled as first one and then the second fusion plant came up to power. "Taxiing now."

"Roger, Gipsy Four. Have a safe flight. This is Foundation Control, out."

Samira nudged the throttles forward, and slowly, reluctantly *Bitsa* began to move. *I know how you feel*, she thought, wondering how many crazies armed with surface-to-air missiles were out there waiting for them. Pushing that thought away, she punched the main engines to emergency power the instant *Bitsa* was lined up, sending the lander screaming down the runway.

"Come on, you scum suckers," Samira muttered, lifting the nose before hauling *Bitsa* around into a hard banking turn the moment the wheels lifted off. "Where the hell are you?"

She and Ashok had little faith in the ZFM's intelligence reports. They'd had missiles fired at them every trip in and every trip out so far, and for all their evasive routing, she was damn sure there were more to come.

"Maybe they'll leave us alone this time," Ashok said, his eyes locked on the threat plot.

"I bloody well hope—"

The missile launch alarm cut Samira off. Instinct took over, her hand shoving the side-stick controller hard over even before the AI barked instructions at her to break right, slamming *Bitsa* over onto her side in a sickening fall to ground, spewing flares. The belly thrusters kicked in a microsecond later to ram the lander bodily sideways as *Bitsa*'s defensive lasers engaged the incoming missiles, hacking them one by one out of the sky.

It was all over in less than a minute, the attack by long-obsolete Sandworm shoulder-launched missiles too poorly coordinated to cause *Bitsa*'s defenses any problems.

"Threat board is green," Ashok called, "and … we're now clear of the Sandworm threat envelope."

"Roger that," Samira said, only now aware of the adrenaline flooding her body. "I'll give the self-loading cargo the good news. Hello, folks; this is your captain. As you would have noticed, we attracted the interest of some of the locals. They fired seventeen surface-to-air missiles at us, none coming even close. We're out of range now, so we're expecting a smooth ride into orbit. We'll be berthing on the orbital transfer station in a bit under half an hour. I'll call you when we're on final approach. Thank you."

Samira swore softly under her breath when she finished the update, hoping her passengers had not noticed the tremors in her voice. "How many is that we've dodged now, Ashok?"

"Not sure. I stopped counting when we passed a hundred."

"Not a good feeling knowing there's some bastard out there trying to kill us." She forced herself to concentrate on the job at hand. "Have you passed the coordinates to Foundation Control, Ashok?" she asked.

"I have. They've sent quick-reaction units to make sure those dumb shitheads don't ever fire any more missiles."

"Amen to that," Samira said. "Okay, we're at Mach 5 passing through thirty thousand meters … retracting wings … and now we're a spaceship again." She breathed out, the relief impossible to ignore as *Bitsa* accelerated into orbit. It would take exoatmospheric SAMs to reach them, and the Zaiyatis had run out of those long ago. "OTS-Golf, this is Gipsy Four."

"Go ahead, Gipsy Four."

"Inbound, request docking clearance."

"Clear to dock, Gipsy Four, Bay 13. Welcome back."

"Pleased to be back. Gipsy Four, out."

Nerves still jangling, Samira passed control over to *Bitsa*'s AI and settled back to watch it fly the approach. One thing she knew: She would never get used to being shot at. She also knew that each attack chipped away at her emotional reserves, the reserves that allowed her to gamble her life, to accept that she might not survive, that she might die a terrible death trapped in *Bitsa* as it plummeted dirtside in a blazing shower of tangled wreckage.

She wondered how much longer she could go on doing what she was doing. *You are a total moron*, she said to herself. *I knew the answer before I even asked the question: I will keep doing this until Juri Saarinen is dead.*

"You know what, Samira?" Ricco said, pausing as she left *Bitsa*.

"What, Madam President?"

"I am going to call you Captain Anders from here on out. Seems only fair, don't you think? You call me 'President,' I call you 'Captain.'"

Samira's cheeks reddened. "There's really no need, Madam President."

"Oh, but there is, Captain Anders. I do this because I have a whole planet at stake. You do it because you are a professional; it's what you do. How, I have no idea. The first time they shot missiles at us was bad enough, and it doesn't get any easier. So thank you for getting us here safely."

"Our pleasure, Madam President," Samira said, bobbing her head as Ricco turned to disembark. *If only you knew,* she thought as she watched Ricco stride away down the access tube.

43

"Ricco's people say they have sanitized the area around Foundation City," Jaska said, "so our contract is reverting to an on-call arrangement. I've said we need a minimum of one week's notice because of other commitments." He frowned. "Not that we have any commitments right now," he added.

"Damn," Samira said, half disappointed, half relieved. "We were making good money. I'd even stopped worrying about how we'd pay our bills."

"Can't say I'm too sorry," Ashok said. "I never want to see Foundation City ever again."

"Me neither," Samira added with some feeling. "Anyway, Jaska, I think that means we can deal with Mr. Saarinen now, don't you? *Bitsa*'s good to go, we have the time, and he is due to make a visit sometime in the next two weeks."

Jaska looked at Samira, his eyes locking onto hers. "If I thought I could change your mind, I'd say no. But—" He put a hand up to forestall Samira's response. "—I know I'd be wasting my time, so I won't try. Ashok? You sure you want to do this?"

Ashok frowned. "No, not really. But I know Samira's made a promise she feels she has to keep. Got to say there are a few people I'd like to—" He stopped abruptly. "Never mind that," he said. "Let's just say I'm in and leave it at that."

"Thanks, Ashok," Samira whispered.

"Fine," Jaska growled, clearly unhappy, "if that's the way it is. Right, then." Suck it up, Samira wanted to say; suck it up. Wisely, she said nothing. "We need to make sure we've planned this right, and Brazzi's come up with some additional intel we need to consider. First …"

44

"If Brazzi's man is right, we should see Saarinen any second now! I'll bet my ass that's him," Samira said as the threat board reported the ultraviolet flare of a ship dropping out of pinchspace. "I'm impressed. Seems like Brazzi's man is on the ball."

"Should be, the money you're paying him," Ashok muttered.

"It's worth it, every cent."

"New arrival is Mendozan starshuttle, registration number … AG-0417-KM," *Bitsa*'s AI said.

"And about time. Start counting the hours, Juri Saarinen, you son of a bitch," Samira murmured, the blood roaring in her ears, "because that's all you have left."

"Let's go," Ashok said. "We'll catch the bastard when he gets to Prasad."

"That we will."

"Can't be long now."

Samira hoped Ashok was right; the tension was unbearable. "No," she said, her voice soft, eyes locked on the screen taking its feed from one of the holocam-fitted drones orbiting at a safe distance from the hunting lodge where, if Brazzi's latest intelligence was correct, Juri Saarinen's daughter, Sahar, was working as a trainee guide.

"Nothing yet," she said, eyes raking the screen for the track of a starshuttle on reentry, looking for the telltale red-gold slash across the morning sky, a huge blue bowl thrown over the small jungle clearing into which Samira had landed *Bitsa* five lifetimes earlier. "Goddamn you, Juri Saarinen, where the hell are you? Sensors showing anything?"

Ashok shook his head. "A few shuttles, all civilian. This place really is stuffed. And nothing even remotely like an FG-665. They're way too pricey for this dump. So how long do we wait?"

"Does it matter?" Samira snapped. "We wait for as long as it takes. We wait until the prick turns up, all right?"

"Hey! Don't take it out on me," Ashok shot back, glaring at her. "I'm just the hired help, remember?"

"Sorry. It's just … you know."

"I know. Waiting's the worst part."

"No, no, it's not that. I'll wait forever if I have to."

Ashok's face creased into a puzzled frown. "What, then?"

"I'm not sure this is right anymore."

"What is this, Samira?" Ashok pushed his head back against the worn headrest of his seat, hands balled into fists so tightly that the knuckles were white against his skin. "Now is not the time for second thoughts."

Samira laughed. "Is that what you think, that I'm having second thoughts? Hell, no. We're going to do this even if we have to sit here for a month—" Ashok winced. "—or even longer. No, it's not that."

"Samira!"

"Sorry. No, it's guilt, good old-fashioned guilt. If everything goes to plan, I'm going to look a man in the eye, and then I'm going to kill him in cold blood."

"Hey! How's that a problem? That's what he did to your father, remember? And we would not be here if the Mendozan police had done their job."

"I know all that. But it's wrong, Ashok, morally wrong, and I know it. I think you know it too. And where does it stop? This is a vendetta, Ashok, and vendettas can run for decades, centuries even. What's next? Saarinen's daughter coming after me?"

Ashok turned away. "Deal with it," he said so softly Samira could barely hear him over the hiss of the flight deck air-conditioning. "Either we do this because you believe it is the right thing for you to do or we don't. I don't care either way; just don't lay all this shit on me, please. I have enough trouble with my own—" He stopped abruptly.

"What trouble, Ashok? Tell me!"

"My business, my responsibility, Samira, not yours. Now, we doing this or not?"

"Yes, we are," she said, her voice firm.

"Good, because if you weren't going to kill the son of a bitch, I was going to, if only to stop your endless bitching."

"Bastard!"

What are you hiding, Ashok Samarth? Samira wondered as he turned away to check his screens. What?

"Anything?" Ashok asked as he squeezed past Samira to drop into his seat.

"You'd be the first to know," Samira said, her voice sour with fatigue and disappointment.

307

"I'll take that as a no, then, shall I?"

"I would. Get any sleep?"

"Sure did. Go on, Samira; time you hit the rack. You look exhausted. I'll keep an eye on things. Go, now!" he added when Samira did not move. "When he turns up, we need you rested, and anyway, sitting there staring at the screens is not going to make him get here any faster."

"When he gets here? You still think he's coming?"

"Yes, I do. Why else would anyone stop off at Vrijac-7? Something's held him up, that's all. Now go, before I put a tranquilizer dart into you."

"I will, I will."

Even though it was hard to see in the mist, the lizopard was a big one, a gray shape that came and went, its huge scaly head turning to look at her from narrow slit eyes, pale yellow and intense before it vanished back into the mist.

Samira knew it would be back; it always came back. And it did, the head appearing out of the mist, at first nothing more than a dark gray patch, barely discernible, its shape emerging as it moved closer and closer until she could see right into its eyes. The irises opened wide until no more yellow remained, a black hole that pulled her forward no matter hard she tried to resist, until she was close enough to count the razor-sharp teeth in a mouth opening wider and wider. Then she was falling into the void, tumbling down and down into the darken—

With an explosive jerk, she awoke, eyes staring out into the half darkness, a sweaty mess tangled in the sheets. "Damn it," she whispered. "Why now?"

Samira had thought she'd put the lizopards behind her. She lay there for a while before checking the time. With a start, she realized that Ashok had left her to sleep for the best part of six hours.

She called him. "You bastard," she said. "You should have called me."

"And good morning to you, Captain Anders, sir."

"I do so hate a smartass. I'm going to shower, then I'll be up to take over."

"No rush. Nothing's happened here apart from a couple of fliers taking clients out to slaughter a few more dappled leopards."

"Go, leopards," Samira said. "With a bit of luck they'll eat the fat pigs for lunch."

"We live in hope. Those animals are no pushovers, that's for sure."

Ten minutes later, Samira eased herself into her seat. Ashok wasted no time, starting the handover before she had time to stow her coffee mug in its holder.

"So apart from those fliers, nothing's moving. Right, I'm off. I need a feed and a shower, then I'll turn in. Call me in four."

"I'll call you in six."

"You are too good to me, Captain Anders."

"Piss off."

The electronic intercept alarm jolted Samira upright in her seat.

"Pinchspace drop," the AI said. "Stand by identification … New arrival is Mendozan starshuttle AG-0417-KM. Identity confirmed by radar intercepts."

"Roger. Designate intercept as primary target, Tango-1. Ashok!" Samira barked.

"Waddyawant?" he mumbled, his voice thick with sleep. "What's up?"

"Get your fat ass up here, flyboy. Saarinen's arrived."

"About bloody time too," he said, all traces of sleep gone from his voice. "I'm on my way."

Barely two minutes later, Ashok tumbled into his seat, his hair still tousled from sleep, though his eyes were bright with anticipation. "Let's see," he said, scanning the screens. "No, I don't think there's any doubt about it. That's our man."

"No doubt at all. Right, then, I'm off. I'll do this as fast as I can, but remember, if I can't make it back for whatever reason, then you go. The AI will get you and *Bitsa* home. No heroics, okay? This is not your fight."

"Yes, Captain Anders, sir," Ashok said, throwing her a mock salute. "Understood."

With a disapproving snort, Samira made her way aft and down into the cargo bay, where she grabbed her pack and assault rifle before slapping the airlock switch to open and made her way outside. Filling her lungs with hot and humid jungle air, air rich with the smell of slowly rotting vegetation, she dropped to the ground, a solid compact shape in combat overalls under a lightweight tactical vest, and made her way across to her tiny one-man flier.

"Comms check," she said, jamming her backpack into the flier's stowage bin.

"Fives," Ashok replied.

"Fives also. Out."

She clipped her assault rifle into its quick-release clips and climbed in. She settled herself into the cramped cockpit, strapped in, and went online to the flier's AI, a final check to make sure the data and holovid feeds from *Bitsa* and her drones were stable.

"Okay, Ashok. Everything's good at this end. Confirm you're seeing my data feeds."

"Confirmed. I have you and the flier online."

"Right, let's do it."

Fingers flying across panels, she brought fired up the flier's microfusion plant. With a silent prayer that all would go according to plan, she ran a final check to make sure she had not forgotten anything, then closed and latched the plasglass canopy.

"Launching," she radioed.

"Roger. Be careful, Samira."

"I will."

Nudging the throttle forward, she eased the flier carefully into the air, the tiny aircraft balanced atop a pillar of super-heated steam that blasted earth and plants outward.

"Airborne," Samira said, putting the flier's nose down once she had cleared the jungle canopy. Banking sharply right, she let the flier accelerate hard, the jungle below blurring into a stream of random shades of green. "Update, Ashok."

"Roger. Tango-1 is inbound, decelerating, vector nominal for reentry for a landing at the lodge. Estimate time to touch-down four hours fifteen."

"Roger that." Everything Ashok had told her she already knew thanks to the data feeds updating her holovid screens, but she needed to hear it to know that Ashok was on the ball, something no screen could tell her. More important, it told her she was not doing this alone and hadn't missed anything. "Flight time to my lay-up point four zero minutes."

"Roger," Ashok replied. "Four zero minutes."

Samira forced herself to relax even though every fiber in her body screamed at her to go faster. Nobody knew how long Juri Saarinen would be at the lodge. It could be days; it could be hours. More likely the latter, Ashok had concluded, and Samira agreed; he could not imagine a man that senior in any organization, criminal or not, being away from business for long.

She eased the flier into a shallow climb, following a small valley cut into the mountains that screened *Bitsa's* landing site. The aircraft was alive and responsive under her hand as she threw it left and right, the turns increasingly tight as the valley sides steepened into slopes of shattered rock before steepening again into walls of rock that narrowed the valley into a slab-sided canyon. She increased power and put the flier into a steep climb as the canyon gave way to a long boulder-strewn slope flanked by precipitous walls of granite that soared away into the sky far overhead.

"Approaching Zhao's Pass," Samira said.

"Roger," Ashok replied. "Tango-1 is on vector."

"Confirm I'll be screened from Tango-1?"

"Confirmed. He's still well to the east, behind the Shaanxis. You've got forty minutes before he has the lodge visual, so make sure you're down and tucked away before that."

"Don't worry, I will be."

The flier shot over the pass and into clear air, with Samira throttling back to keep it close to the ground as it tumbled away below her. Ahead lay the hunting lodge, and her heart skipped a beat at the thought of what she had come so far to do.

• • •

An hour later, Samira stepped back to inspect her handiwork.

That'll do, she said to herself, looking at what would appear, even on a determined examination, to be a tangled mass of vegetation set on the downstream side of a small island. Satisfied that the flier was safe, she settled her pack on her back and her helmet on her head and picked up her rifle.

"I'm moving," she whispered into her mike.

"Roger."

"How's the target?"

"Will commence reentry as scheduled, so get going. And watch out for the leopards."

Samira shivered; dappled leopards were ambush predators, and they hunted in packs, large packs. This was their jungle; they had evolved here over tens of millions of years.

They belonged here. She did not.

"Thanks, Ashok," she said, burying the unwanted image of a dappled leopard erupting out of cover and coming right at her. With a quick check to make sure the area was clear, she set off across the stream. "Moving," she said, "so get that drone overhead. I don't want any surprises."

"It's waiting for you, twenty meters past the stream."

Samira searched for the microdrone, but she could neither see nor hear it. "I'll take your word for it," she murmured, splashing across the stream and into the jungle, the canopy closing in overhead to plunge her into a world of green gloom and clinging vegetation.

That drone's useless, she thought. *It wouldn't see a battalion of heavy armor camped out across my line of advance; this jungle's too damn thick.*

• • •

Samira squirmed the final few meters on her belly. Chest heaving from the effort of forcing a path through the jungle, she paused for a minute to recover, then eased the undergrowth aside, and there it was. In front of her ran the road to the lodge; beyond it lay the runway, a strip of ceramcrete shimmering in the heat of the morning sun. Off to her right, at the northern end of the runway, sat the small reception building, with three open-topped mobibots waiting along with what had to be the ground crew.

"I'm in position," she whispered.

"Roger. Perfect timing. Tango-1 will be landing. Stand by … now!"

The starshuttle, flaps fully extended and wheels down, burst into view and thumped down onto the runway, the back blast from its engines tearing the air apart as the pilot selected reverse thrust and pushed the engines to full power, the noise so loud that Samira had to drop her head into her arms to protect her ears.

Lifting her head as the starshuttle decelerated down the runway, she shifted her attention back to the people at reception. She stiffened; a woman had emerged from the reception building and was walking toward the cluster of mobibots. She lifted her rifle to her shoulder and powered up the optical sight, pushing it to maximum zoom. The image wavered for an instant, then steadied.

"Sahar Saarinen," she hissed, "as I live and breathe."

She double-checked the file picture Brazzi had supplied. It was pretty close, though it had obviously been taken long before Sahar had turned rebellious, thought Samira. Your dad must love the new look: face masked by elaborate nanocrystal tattoos; the ice-blond hair cut brutally short; heavy black eye makeup; lip, eyebrow, and ear studs; and the purple-black lip-stick popular with Mendozan kids.

This is very bizarre, Samira thought, feeling like an old woman all of a sudden.

"Ashok," she said, "I have eyes on Tango-1's daughter."

"Roger ... Yes, that's Sahar Saarinen."

Samira waited, mouth dry and heart hammering, while the starshuttle made its way back up the runway. With a final burst of power, the starshuttle turned off the runway and made its way onto the apron; turning sharply to face back the way it had just come, it stopped, the silence almost oppressive when the engines shut down. There was a flurry of activity: The door opened, steps were put in place, and the ground crew got busy off-loading bags into the luggagebot.

And then there he was.

Juri Saarinen—there was no doubt it was him—stepped out and stopped for a moment, blinking in the sunlight, before making his way down the steps and across to where his daughter waited. Saarinen was a tall man with heavy jowls, olive skin, short black hair, blue-gray eyes, and a goatee beard, dressed in a shipsuit immaculately tailored to flatter a thickset, overweight, frame.

"Tango-1 acquired," she whispered as Saarinen bundled his daughter into an awkward embrace, Sahar twisting her head away as Juri tried to kiss her on the cheek. *Oh, yes, I've got you now, you murdering cocksucker*, Samira thought. "Oh, shit," she said. "Ashok, we have a problem."

"Tell me."

"Saarinen's bodyguard. Takahashi's report said he normally has two cyborgs for close protection. Well, he was wrong; he's brought four of them with him."

"Damn. Wonder why."

"Don't know. I'm no expert, but they all look very relaxed. Saarinen came out first; the cyborgs followed. Don't think that's standard operating procedure."

"No, it's not. They must feel safe here."

"Don't think much of their threat assessment. Hold on … yes!" Samira exclaimed. "One of the cyborgs is Karla Banduna."

"All good things come to those sit and wait, Samira."

"I suppose. But those additional cyborgs change things, Ashok, and not for the better. Much as I want to take Saarinen and Banduna out, I'd rather not die in the process. If I hit him on his way to the lodge as planned, I can take Banduna and maybe one of the cyborgs if he's close. But there's no way I can take the other two. I've seen cyborgs move; they're fast, Ashok, faster than any human I've ever seen. They'd cut me down before I got five hundred meters."

"So where does that leave us?"

"I'm aborting, Ashok," she said, her voice bitter with defeat.

"You sure?"

"I'm sure, Ashok. Much as I want Saarinen dead, I want to stay alive more."

"Your call."

"Yes, it is. We need to rethink things."

"We do. Leave it to me; I'll see what I can come up with."

"Okay."

With a sigh of angry frustration, Samira trained her optical sight back onto the lander door, where two shipsuited figures were coming down the steps, the first waiting at the foot of the steps as the second walked across the apron to a gray cubicle about three meters high and equally wide. The starshuttle crew, Samira decided as the second man opened the cubicle. Pulling out a thick black cable, he dragged it back across the ceramcrete and connected it. Moments later, a third figure appeared, also shipsuited; as he closed the door behind him, the three figures made their way across to the mobibots.

Somebody must have said something funny, because the group erupted in laughter, Saarinen's head going back as the crosshairs of Samira's optical sight locked onto his open mouth. For one terrible moment, she knew she was about to pull the trigger and blow the man's head off. Then the will to live reasserted itself, and she eased her finger away.

"You are a lucky man, Juri Saarinen," she breathed as the group—Saarinen, his daughter, the four bodyguards, and three crew—climbed into the mobibots and took off.

The three vehicles had set off and were close now, the three mobibots trailed by a luggagebot stacked high with bags. When they passed her, they were so close that she could hear Saarinen's voice as he talked to his daughter.

"… . so your trackers have found a new leopard pack, out to the west. That's great news, Sahar. I think this time I might see if …" was all she could make out before the mobibots were passed and gone.

You think this time you might see if what? Samira wondered. She swore softly. Was hunting dappled leopards his thing? Had he come to bag one? Or was he just here to catch up with Sahar?

She called up Ashok. "You see what the crew was doing?" she asked.

"The ground power cable?"

"Yup. Saarinen's not planning to leave any time soon, is he?"

"I think you're right."

"How's the starshuttle's infrared signature look?"

"Dropping fast," Ashok said. "If I were a betting man, I'd say they've shut down the fusion plants. I think they're here until tomorrow at least."

"That fits. I heard Saarinen talking about a new pack of dappled leopards they've found. Then he said, 'Maybe this time I might see if,' but that's all I heard. What do you reckon?"

"Can't be sure, but I figure Saarinen will be here for two nights."

"That doesn't give us much time."

"It doesn't. Assuming you hit Saarinen at the lodge, we have the first night to reconnoiter and tomorrow to plan; then we execute on the second night … Oh, shit. Sorry, Samira, but you know what I mean."

"Don't sweat it, Ashok." She paused for a moment. "Things are not going well, are they?"

"Not so far, but we have time."

"Maybe, maybe not. Tell you what, it's … let me see … yes, it's four hours to sundown, and I think it's pretty clear our man will go hunting tomorrow. Agreed?"

"Agreed."

"Which gives us a full day and two nights to play with, yes?"

Ashok thought about that for a moment. "Yes," he conceded, "almost certainly."

"So this is what I suggest. I'll pull back. There's a small creek just north of the runway, and I should be able to find somewhere safe to lay up for the night. Apparently those leopards aren't too keen on crossing running water."

"As far as we know, that's right."

"Good. Between now and sunset, we'll see if the drones can identify a time and place to hit Saarinen at the lodge. If there is, I take him down, and then we're out of here. If not …" Samira's voice trailed off. She had been so close to Saarinen that the thought of failure was hard to bear.

"Sounds like a plan, and let's worry about a fallback if we have to."

"Fine. Right, I'm moving. Keep one drone ahead of me and task the rest to cover the lodge."

"Roger that."

With a leaden heart, Samira squirmed backward until she was well clear of the runway perimeter, any confidence she was going to be able to kill Saarinen fast disappearing. After taking a careful look around to make sure no carnivores were waiting to tear her apart, she climbed slowly to her feet and, settling her pack on her back, set off.

Samira lay with her back against a small rock, safely tucked away out of sight in a cluster of boulders set in the middle of a small stream, the afternoon sunlight splashing daubs of gold across the trees. It was breathtakingly beautiful, so beautiful that she forgot for a moment where she was.

Ashok pulled her back to reality. "Update, Samira," he said.

"Go ahead."

"No movement outside the lodge. Our man's shown himself a few times, but nobody's going anywhere. All the lodge mobibots have been parked for the night."

"That's that, then."

"You okay?"

"Yeah, think so. This seems as safe a place as any." Samira paused. "Not that I can see this miserable stream stopping any dappled leopard worth its salt."

"Maybe not, but hopefully the drone will pick them up before they get to the island. You'll get warning."

"Why does that not reassure me, Ashok? Oh, wait, I know why. It's because dappled leopards hunt in big packs, and they make those damn lizopards look like slugs. Somehow I don't think an assault rifle's going to hold even a small one off."

"You'll be fine, Samira. Stay under cover and you'll be fine."

"I wish. Any ideas on how we can take Saarinen?"

"I'm beginning to think there's no way of hitting him at the lodge."

"I was thinking the same." Samira pulled up the holovid feed from one of the drones. "I can see him now," she said, looking at Saarinen as he lounged on the deck of his suite, drink in hand, talking animatedly to some of the houseguests, his daughter off to one side with one of the cyborgs.

After a good twenty minutes, she shook her head in despair. "There's no way, Ashok. One access stair, two cyborgs patrolling all the time, all that lighting, the staff moving around, and no cover around the lodge for hundreds of meters. No, it can't be done," she added, her voice thick with defeat.

"I think you're right."

"Damn it," Samira said softly. "So what do we do now?"

"I think there's another way to take Saarinen."

"You do?" Samira said, sitting bolt upright. "How?"

"Watch this."

Five minutes later, her heart in her mouth, Samira splashed her way off the island and onto the riverbank. Moving fast, she set off toward her flier, praying hard she would make it before darkness fell.

45

Samira woke as dawn broke.

I hate this place, she said to herself as she rolled out of her sleeping bag to put on her boots, wincing when muscles overused in the previous day's forced marches made their displeasure known. Boots on, she stood up, stretching the kinks out her back, and looked around.

"Oh, no, I don't," she whispered, entranced by the sight of the river, a sinuous black strip stippled with tiny flecks of pink and gold, tangled skeins of mist lifting slowly into the air, rising away between gray-green walls of trees. It was a magical sight, a moment out of time, and Samira felt privileged just to be there. "This is some pl—"

Then a hand gripped her heart and squeezed hard. "Oh, shiiiiiiit," she hissed, reaching out to pick up her rifle before backing up one centimeter at a time, praying harder than she had ever prayed that she could make it to the dubious safety of her flier before the dappled leopard drinking downstream from the little island decided it was time for breakfast.

"Ashok, I'm in trouble," she whispered. "Big trouble."

"What's up?"

"Dappled leopard, a big one. Bastard's close."

"Has it seen you? Can you pull back?"

"No and yes."

"Do it!"

"Don't worry, I am."

Terrified though she was, she could not drag her eyes away from the animal; she had never seen anything like it. It had none of the lizopard's alien menace; it was a magnificent sight: a good three meters long with a thick, stubby tail, its body pale gray mottled with darker patches, crouched down, its head bobbing as it lapped, heavily muscled hindquarters bunched over its back legs, its attention seemingly focused on the business of drinking.

It was a spectacular animal. Why would anybody want to kill one just for the hell of it?

With a rush of relief, she felt her left hand touch chromaflage netting, and still the leopard had not noticed her. Sliding underneath, she found the plasfiber skin of the flier. Holding her breath, she eased her way onto the skid, up onto the step, and into the cockpit, sealing the canopy down with a soft hiss.

The noise broke the leopard's concentration. Lazily, it lifted its head and turned to look at her, enormous eyes staring right through the chromaflage from a face dominated by massive cheekbones and a wide slash of a mouth over huge jaws.

The damn thing doesn't look anything like a leopard, Samira thought in passing. *It's got no proper nose or ears for a start.*

Then she started to worry how strong plasglass really was. Would it keep out an animal as big as the one she was looking at? With a start, she realized that she was no longer looking at a single dappled leopard. A second had arrived, then another and another, until the riverbank was thick with gray shapes drinking.

"I'm in the flier, Ashok," she said, "but things are not getting better."

"I know. The drone's spotted the pack. If they move toward you, I'm going to drop the drone in front of them. It might scare them off."

"You think so?"

"Best I can do; sorry."

"Should work," Samira said, almost certain that it wouldn't.

Every instinct told her that she should get the hell out; these animals were big, and there were enough of them to batter their way into the flier if they wanted to. And even if they couldn't, the flier would never take to the air again.

Still the first leopard stared at her as if it was deciding whether to bother.

Go! Go now, her body screamed at her. Go now or you will die.

But something kept her from powering up the flier. Somehow, the leopard did not seem … She struggled to find the right word. It was interested in her, yes, but not that interested. With sudden clarity, Samira realized that these animals were no threat to her. Why that should be when she was only kilometers from a lodge full of people dedicated to slaughtering them, she had no idea. But she was sure; captivated by the combination of alien beauty and raw primal power, she continued watching.

After an eternity, the leopard turned away; dropping its magnificent head, it started to drink again. Five minutes later, the pack slipped down the bank and into the river, stepping their way unconcerned though the water to the opposite bank, where they disappeared.

"So much for the 'dappled leopards hate water' school of thought," she said, breathing in and letting it go in a rush of relief. "Glad I didn't know that last night. Anyway, I think that's that, Ashok."

"That was quite something."

"You should have been here."

"No, thanks. I like plenty of ceramsteel armor between me and my dappled leopards. Want me to airdrop clean underwear?"

"No need." Samira laughed. "Can't say why, but I knew they weren't going to bother me. Okay, enough of the tourist thing. Where are we up to?"

"Well, the good news is there's been no sign of Saarinen's pilots; the starshuttle's fusion plants are cold, so they are hours away from leaving. A pair of fliers went out before first light, and they're on their way back now. If they've found a pack, I'd say your man's going hunting today."

"Bastard. Hope the leopards tear his guts out."

"Focus, Samira, focus."

"Sorry. Any idea where the pack might be?"

"No; the scouts stayed high and circled a lot. Could be anywhere, but they did stay west of the lodge the whole time."

Samira thought for a moment. "Okay," she said, "let's assume they've found a pack, in which case Saarinen is going hunting and we're on."

"Maybe. We ne—"

"Wait up, Ashok. What's with the 'maybe'? I thought we'd agreed on the plan."

"Well, yes, we did, but I've been doing a lot of thinking."

"And what?" Samira demanded.

"And it's way too dangerous. You'll only get one go at this, that's all, one go, which wouldn't be so bad if your chances of success were good. but they're not. In fact, any way I look at it, your chances of pulling this off are pretty poor."

"Why's that? I'll have the advantage of surprise."

"Yes, you will, but what if Saarinen or one of his crew spots you? And they will be looking, Samira … not for you but for leopards. And when they do see you, Saarinen will come after you. The problem is you'll have nowhere to run, and it's only a matter of time before he cuts you down. He's got the numbers, he's got the guns, he's got backup. I'm telling you, Samira, this is crazy. A one-shot operation with no support and no fallback? That's amateur stuff. We aborted yesterday because the risk to you was too high. Guess what? It's not any better with today's plan."

"That's not what you said last night," Samira said, her voice all ice.

"I know, and I'm sorry about that. I … I just got a bit caught up, I guess. I didn't stand back, and I should have. I wish I had."

"Goddamn it, Ashok! It's a bit bloody late for second thoughts, don't you think?"

"It is, and I'm sorry about that. But you need to know how I feel about this."

"Hmm," Samira said. She did not say anything more for a long time. "Look," she said eventually, "you're right. You usually are. But we don't have a plan C, do we?"

"I know we discounted using *Bitsa*; maybe we should rethink that."

"No," Samira said, her voice firm. "That was the right call. *Bitsa* is massive overkill. It's Saarinen I've come all this way for, nobody else."

"Banduna; you've forgotten Banduna."

"No, I haven't. I'll take that bitch down if I can, but she wasn't the one who pulled the trigger. No, Saarinen's the one who really matters."

"So it's plan B or go home?"

"Yeah, I think so."

"I don't like it, Samira. I really don't like it."

"So I gather. Tell you what. Let me think on it. I'll call you back."

"Okay."

With a sigh, Samira walked to the stream's edge and sat down on a water-worn boulder. She did not need to think about it; her mind was made up, and nothing Ashok might say was going to change that even though everything he had said was right. But so what? Deep down, she knew that the job had to be done now; she would not be coming back to Prasad. As for the risks, nothing would change them. She just had to make sure she did not blow it. She got up and walked back to the flier.

"Ashok?"

"Go ahead, Samira."

"Had a think about things. You're absolutely right, but I'm going ahead with it anyway."

"Why am I not surprised?" Ashok sighed. "Okay, you're the one taking all the risks, and it's your call, so I think that's the end of the discussion. The mission's on."

"It is. Now, are the drones in position?"

"They are."

"Good. Any more thoughts on timing?"

"No. Like I said, this is a luxury lodge. Nobody's leaving until they've had a decent breakfast."

"I could do with a decent breakfast," Samira muttered.

"What?"

"Oh, nothing. I'll be at Alert 5 from 08:00."

"That should work. The bad guys have no infrared surveillance capability, so the fact that your fusion plant is online won't matter."

"Fine." Samira took the time to run through the plan in her head. "I think that's it," she continued. "Are we missing anything?"

"No, don't think so. Just remember to ditch the canopy."

"Don't worry, I won't forget."

Time dragged by, the morning sun hot and getting hotter by the minute, the air thick and humid as heat dragged moisture out of the ground. Samira sat, willing herself to be still, doing her best to ignore the worst attack of premission nerves she had ever experienced.

"Come on, come on," she whispered, her eyes scanning the holovid feed from the drone Ashok had in place to monitor activity around the lodge. The place was quiet, with only the lodge staff and two of Saarinen's cyborgs moving around.

It was two long tedious hours before anything changed.

"Heads up, Samira," Ashok said at last. "Something's happening."

The holovid told the story. Long-barreled hunting rifle in hand, Saarinen was walking down the stairs to meet Sahar. Followed by Banduna, machine pistol held tight across her enormous chest, and a second cyborg also carrying a machine pistol, father and daughter made their way from the lodge to a waiting mobibot.

"I've got Saarinen, Banduna ... and the daughter and a second cyborg as well," Samira said. "I see one hunting rifle, two machine pistols. The daughter's not carrying."

"Stand by ... No, she's not."

"That's good. Let's hope that means she's not going with them. Anyone else, Ashok?"

"No, that's it. Looks like one of the cyborgs will do the flying."

The mobibot was soon on their way, the drone tracking it away from the lodge and on toward the reception building, where two of the ground crew waited.

"They're prepping a single flier, Samira," he said. He paused as the mobibots pulled up and everyone climbed out. "Oh, wait ... Yes, the daughter's going with them."

"Shit!" Samira swore; she did not want Sahar Saarinen complicating things. "This might not be so easy," she said. "How the hell am I going to take out Saarinen without killing the daughter? I don't give a shit about the cyborgs. They've signed their own death warrants by working for Saarinen. But Sahar?"

"I can't help you, Samira. It's up to you. If it's too risky, if you want to call it off ..."

"We've been through all that, Ashok," she hissed, "and my answer's the same. I'll see how we go; if I can do the job without hurting Sahar, I will. If not, I won't, okay?"

"Fine by me. I'm bringing *Bitsa* to Alert 5, so when you want to go, we can go."

"Roger that," Samira said, her confidence fading fast, all too aware that things were getting away from her.

A single flier up against two cyborgs and a man who had made killing his business?

It was crazy.

Yes, Samira Anders, she said under her breath, *it is crazy, but it has to be done.*

"Target is airborne. Stand by to launch."

"Vector?"

"Two seven zero, speed 200. They're staying low. They'll be past you in five minutes."

"Roger." Working fast, Samira stripped and stowed the chromaflage concealing the flier, then detached the canopy, burying everything under a mound of brush. Breathing hard, the sweat trickling from under her helmet and down her back, she climbed back into the cockpit, fingers dancing across the screens in a final check that all was well.

"I'm ready to launch," she said. "All systems nominal."

"Canopy?"

"Gone."

"Roger ... and when you launch, make sure you stay well back. You can't afford to let them see you."

Samira did not bother to reply; she had no intention of letting anyone in Saarinen's lander see her until it was too late for them.

"Target's coming up on closest point of approach ... Stand by ... Okay, you're clear. Good hunting."

"Thanks ... launching now." Advancing the throttle, Samira lifted the flier into the air, dropping the nose to keep it close to the river, letting the speed build, driving the aircraft hard, twisting and turning between the towering ranks of trees that flanked the river.

"I'm airborne."

"Target now at Red 20, range opening."

"Roger," Samira replied.

She eased the flier up and away from the river, flying close to the jungle canopy, the trees a green blur streaking past below as she pushed the throttle onto the stops. Her heart pounded hard and then harder still when she spotted the small speck racing ahead of her. "Target in sight," she said, banking the flier gently to port to tuck in on Saarinen's tail. "Confirm who's sitting where."

"Pilot's starboard side. Saarinen's alongside him up front with Sahar behind. Banduna's on the starboard side behind the pilot. The doors are off, so you'll be able to see them clearly."

"Roger, got it."

Samira flew on in silence, the gap closing meter by agonizing meter until finally she was close enough to see every last detail of the hull above and ahead of her, the two craft rock-steady in the still morning air.

"I'm going in," she said, struck by the absurdity of what she was about to do, wondering if anyone had ever done anything as crazy as this before.

"Good luck."

"Thanks."

I'll need more than luck to pull this off, Samira thought, drifting the flier out from behind Saarinen, then nudging the throttle forward fractionally to start climbing up alongside them. Satisfied that the flier was going where it should, she handed control over to the AI. Reaching back, she unclipped her machine pistol, an ice-cold focus flushing all the nervousness out of her body.

Centimeters at a time, the flier gained on Saarinen, and then there he was, only meters from her, oblivious, his body buffeted by the slipstream, hunting rifle cradled in his lap, obviously talking, head turned inboard. Just stay that way, Samira prayed, bringing her gun up to her shoulder. The instant Saarinen's head filled her optical sight, she took a deep breath and squeezed the trigger.

She was a fraction of a second too late.

Even before the first round left her gun, Saarinen's flier had banked toward her, causing her salvo to track not through Saarinen's head but across the flier's instrument panel, a blizzard of splinters exploding outward as bullets ripped it apart.

"Goddamn it," Samira shouted as the AI, reacting faster than any human could, rolled the flier away and down in a savage, gut-wrenching turn, only just fast enough to allow Saarinen's flier to slide overhead, so close that its bulk filled Samira's windscreen before disappearing overhead.

"You son of a bitch!" she screamed, heart racing with the terrible suddenness of it all, hoping that her first shot had been a good one. "Ashok, I've blown it," she said, forcing her voice back under control. "Where are they?"

"Target now heading 220, descending. It's going down."

Head swinging from side to side, Samira searched frantically for Saarinen. "Got him," she said when she spotted the flier losing altitude, trailing smoke.

"Stay with him!" Ashok snapped. "You have to finish this, and fast. They'll be screaming for backup."

"I know. Let me know when they're on their way."

Taking control back from the AI, Samira had pushed the throttles forward to catch up; she was closing fast on the stricken craft when, without warning, it staggered, wallowing through the air as the pilot struggled to regain control, its engine spewing a hypersonic plume of steam in a frantic attempt to lose speed and stay airborne at the same time. For a moment the flier steadied, and the nose came up as the pilot flared before landing. Samira thought the flier would make it, but then it half rolled to one side and rolled back; the engine cut out, and it smashed into the forest canopy, slashing a path for thirty or so meters through the treetops, slowing as it went before it disappeared, swallowed in a sea of green, a single lazy thread of smoke marking the crash site.

"Ashok, Saarinen is down."

"Let it go, Samira. Job's done."

The blood was roaring in Samira's ears, her whole being consumed by the urge to kill. "No it's damn well not," she hissed. "Not until I see the man dead."

"Your call."

"It is. Any movement at the lodge?"

"Plenty. Two mobibots are on their way, and the ground crew is prepping the fliers. I'd say you've got twenty minutes before they are over the crash site, maybe less. Time to abort, Samira. You can't head off two fliers."

Screw you, Ashok, Samira said under her breath. "I'm setting down," she said. "I need to finish this. Keep feeding me their ETA. Out."

Spotting a rocky clearing close to the crash site, she decelerated savagely and dropped the flier into a bone-crunching landing, all finesse lost in the desperate rush to get the aircraft down. Leaving the fusion plant online, she jumped out of the cockpit, moving as fast as the jungle would allow, changing magazines as she went.

It took only minutes to reach the Saarinen's flier. It was an ugly sight, a crumpled, broken ruin, upright with the starboard side facing her but tilted forward with its nose buried in a tangled mess of vegetation. The undercarriage had been smashed up into the fuselage, and acrid, eye-watering smoke from the fusion plant and engine was filling the air. Samira, gun raised, inched her way closer, eyes scanning the wreckage for signs of life.

Nothing moved; looking in, Samira swore softly. The portside seats were empty; Sahar and Juri Saarinen had managed to get out.

The pilot and Karla Banduna had not. They both were slumped over, hanging in their safety straps, heads forward, eyes half closed, their faces bloody wrecks. Banduna's lips were moving in a feeble plea for help.

Samira ignored the pilot; she did not care whether he lived or died. Banduna was another matter. Stepping forward, she put her gun to the cyborg's head. "This is for my father," she whispered. Closing her eyes, she pulled the trigger, trying not to think what the bullets would do to the half-conscious cyborg.

Without looking back, she stepped away and edged around the wreck to check the port side, hoping, praying that she would see Juri Saarinen's body on the ground.

It wasn't; Sahar and Juri had gone. Samira swung around, telling herself they could not have gotten far.

"Update." Ashok's voice broke her concentration. "Backup is airborne. They'll be at the crash site in fifteen."

"Roger. Now, where are you, Saarinen?" she murmured, edging away from the crashed flier, her eyes scanning the bushes for any sign of movement. "Where are—"

A pistol shot rang out, tearing its way through the under-growth and past her right ear, then another, this one punching hard into her right shoulder, so hard that she stumbled back, tripping and then falling. Rolling onto her stomach, Samira fired a sustained burst into the bushes, a wavering, uncertain effort thanks to a right arm that was suddenly wooden and uncooperative. But uncertain or not, the burst was rewarded with a scream that dribbled away into soft, sobbing moans.

That's Saarinen, she thought. *It has to be.*

"Shiiiit!" she hissed as she forced herself to crawl toward the sound, the effort driving waves of searingly hot pain out from her shoulder, across her chest, and down her arm. It was almost more than she could bear; she had to stop, heart pound-ing and chest heaving, her head pressed into the dirt while she fought to regain control. When the pain eased a touch, she forced herself to move on through the undergrowth, squirm-ing on her belly in an awkward half crawl, half wriggle, her right arm dragging uselessly beside her.

Only thirty meters from the wrecked flier, she found Saarinen. She had guessed right; the moans were his. Propped against the scarred trunk of a tree amid a chaotic mess of bul-let-shredded greenery, Saarinen lay with his legs out, his up-per body and face a blood-splashed ruin, a pistol close to an outstretched hand, his face screwed up with pain. And to one side, crouching next to her father, was Sahar, her face white underneath the blood oozing from a long gash that ran down from her left temple across her left cheek, eyes staring wide in shock, ice-blond stubble blackened by dirt and leaf mold, makeup and blood smeared into a gory mess.

"Hands," Samira barked. "Get your damn hands up where I can see them, Sahar, and keep them there—now!" she barked, firing a single round over the girl's head when she hesitated.

Shaking, wide-eyed with fear, Sahar Saarinen did as she was told.

"Thought you could get away from me?" Samira said, never once taking her gun off Saarinen while she struggled to her feet. "So wrong, Juri Saarinen," she continued, trying not to sway as the shock set in, "so say goodbye to your daughter, because I'm here to—hey!" Samira snapped as Sahar Saarinen started to edge away. "Don't move or I'll blow your head off, okay?"

Sahar froze. "Who are you?" she whispered. "Why—"

"I don't care who you are," Juri Saarinen spit, staring up at Samira. "You'll pay for this, you—" He stopped abruptly, tilting his head to one side, eyes narrowing. "Wait one second. I thought you looked familiar. I don't believe it … Samira Anders," he said, his voice soft, "and don't waste my time pretending you're not."

Samira swore under her breath. In the space of a few minutes, everything had gone to shit, her carefully crafted plan to kill Saarinen quickly and without leaving the Guild with any clues to the killers' identity collapsing around her. *I should have worn a damn ski mask*, she thought, wondering how the hell Saarinen knew who she was.

"Yes, I'm Samira Anders," she said, as there didn't seem much point in pretending otherwise, "and I'm here to make you pay for killing my father, Matti Anders. Remember him?"

"Ah, yes," Saarinen said softly. "Of course I remember, but Matti Anders, your father?" He shook his head and laughed, a terrible parody of a laugh that degenerated into a racking cough that forced blood from the corner of his mouth. "Matti Anders wasn't your father," Saarinen went on. "I am your father, you poor, stupid girl."

The words were so unexpected, Samira could not make any sense of them. She stared, shocked into silence by the awful conviction in the man's voice. "You ... my father?" she said at last, shaking her head emphatically. "No way. You can't be."

"Oh, but I can," Juri Saarinen said, the effort foaming his lips with fresh blood. "Your mother, was her name Farnaz Anders?"

"How the hell do you know that?" Samira whispered, the assumptions that underpinned her entire life threatening to crumble around her.

"Because I loved your mother with all my heart, Samira, she loved me, and we both loved you. Having to leave you behind broke both our hearts."

"Why are you saying this?" Samira shouted. "I don't believe any of it, not a damn word."

"You should, Samira, because it's the truth. Matti was a brutal pig, and yes, I killed him even though he was my brother." A long, choking cough forced Juri Saarinen to stop. "Now," he went on, wiping the blood from his lips with the back of his hand, "it looks like you've killed me. Fair enough, I guess, but what about Sahar? She's your sister; you going to kill her too?"

"You lying sack of shit," Samira hissed, reeling as she fought to come to terms with what Saarinen was telling her. He's lying, she told herself; he had to be lying to escape what was coming to him. "I don't care what you say, so save your breath," she said, pushing away the awful possibility that he might be telling the truth. "You killed my father, so I'm going to kill you."

"Wait, wait; we can sort someth—"

"Too late, Saarinen, too late." Taking a step back, she shot him, a single shot right in the bloody mess that was his face, punching his head back against the tree. His eyes stared back at her as he died: wide, surprised, accusing eyes that Samira knew with a terrible certainty she would never forget.

Samira turned her gun to cover Sahar. "I've got no beef with you," she said. "I'm glad you're okay. I'll make sure your people know where you are."

"Fuck you, Samira Anders," Sahar Saarinen spit. "If you think this is over, trust me, it's not."

"We'll see," Samira said. She pulled back until screened by the undergrowth, then turned and started back to her flier in a shambling, staggering run, almost defeated by the effort it took to stay upright and keep moving.

"Ashok, the job's done," she said, her voice husky as shock began to shut her body down. "I've been hit, but I'll be okay … I think. I'm on my way back to the flier. I'll be airborne in two. What's my best vector out of here?"

"Northwest and stay low. With a bit of luck they may not see you. But move it."

"How long?"

"They'll be at the crash site in seven minutes. Looks like they're firewalling those fliers."

"Shit! Okay … I'm at the flier now. I'll call you when I'm airborne."

Wincing as the pain from her damaged shoulder punished her efforts, Samira crawled into the cockpit. Wedging her gun between her legs, she rammed the throttle to emergency power and grabbed the side-stick controller, lifting the flier into the air before dropping the nose, keeping it close to the jungle canopy.

Handing the flier back to the AI, she fumbled in the warm, sticky mess that was her shoulder until she found the sleeve of her combat overalls; gritting her teeth, she ripped it away in a single, sharp heave that drove white-hot barbs of agony into her chest and down her arm. Sobbing, she opened the flier's medikit and pulled out woundfoam dispenser, stifling a scream as the lurid green froth bit into the wound. A trauma pack followed onto her damaged shoulder, the pain and shock-induced dizziness starting to fade as the pack took control of the wound, her neuronics pumping drugbots into her system.

"Okay, Ashok. I'm on my way," she said, her voice shaking, relieved to feel the drugbots working their magic.

"I've got you. Hostiles are at Green 110, speed 300, range thirty klicks and opening."

"Three hundred? Are they that fast?"

"Yes, but the good news is that they are tracking direct to the crash site."

"I hope they keep going."

"Yeah. You okay? You don't sound so good."

"I'll be fine. I've got woundfoam and a trauma pack on my shoulder; the pain's manageable, and the shock is under control. Get *Bitsa* to Alert 1. We'll break for orbit as soon as I'm back onboard."

"*Bitsa* is already at Alert 1 ... Oh, hold on, Samira ... Shit, one of the fliers has come hard right. Looks like they've spotted you."

"Damn it. Help me here, Ashok. What's the plan?"

"Firewall the engine. I'll think of something."

"I already firewalled the engine."

"Okay. We need time, so come left. That'll put the hostile on your tail and give me enough time to get to you."

"Coming left," Samira said. "Hey, wait. What do you mean you'll come and get me?"

"What I say. They'll follow you until you run out of driver mass, and I'm sure they'll have called for more backup, so there's no chance of you getting away. The state you're in, you couldn't hold off one flier, let alone a posse, so I'm coming to get you."

For a moment, Samira thought of arguing with Ashok—getting away was her problem, and it wasn't his fight; besides, he couldn't fly a lander to save his ass—but sheer exhaustion got the better of her. "Whatever you say," she mumbled. "No heroics, though."

"No heroics."

Samira slumped back in her seat; despite all the drugbots, she felt exhausted. Ashok had said he'd come and get her, and that would have to do. Closing her eyes, she settled back to wait.

Ashok's voice made her start. "Sorry, Ashok, I missed that. Say again."

"I'm airborne and inbound to intercept the hostile on your tail."

"What's the plan?"

"Hack the bastard out of the air, pick you up, and then piss off."

"Nice plan."

"I thought so."

"What do I do?"

"Just keep clear."

"Okay."

Concentrate! she said to herself as she stepped through the holovid feeds from the drones still circling overhead until the hostile on her tail appeared on the screen. *You will die if you don't.*

"Oh, shit," she murmured, dismayed to see how close the flier was. Ashok would have to get a move on; it would not be long before it was close enough to shoot her down. Reluctantly, she took manual control; if it came to a dogfight, she'd do a better job of staying out of trouble than the flier's AI ever would.

As long as I stay awake, that is, she thought, watching the holovid feed as it tracked the hostile flier close in. *Damn*, she murmured under her breath, flicking the screen over to the flier's rear-facing camera, *they are getting awfully close*. She could see the men hanging out of the doors, guns in hand. Another minute and they would be in range, she realized.

"Ashok, I'm going to have to take evasive action," she said, pulling her gun out from between her legs and laying it in her lap. She put her right arm, by now numb and almost useless, across the gun to keep it in place. "The bastards are right on my tail."

"I know," Ashok said, his voice taut with stress, "but it's taking me a bit longer than I expected. I'm having trouble getting *Bitsa* to fly the way I want it to."

"Take your time," Samira said even though she wanted to scream at Ashok to hurry up. "I'll dodge them until you get here."

"Do that. Out."

Eyes locked on the holovid screen, Samira watched the incoming flier close the gap. "Any second," she muttered, "any second ... now!"

With that she pulled the flier's nose skyward; the massive g force clawed at her ruined shoulder, forcing her to scream in pain. Desperately she hung on until the flier reached the vertical before pushing the nose down. Samira had kept her eyes locked on the hostiles; slow to react, the pilot had banked to starboard, the crew hanging out on both sides, their heads swinging every which way as they searched for her. She followed them around, tightening her turn until her nose led the enemy flier.

"Got you now," she whispered.

Saarinen's men spotted her too late; Samira plunged unseen out of the sun under full power, her flier slashing across their bows, her gun held one-handed out of the cockpit, spraying rounds in all directions as she hammered past.

Whether she hit the flier, she had no idea. She did not much care anymore. Leaving it behind her, she turned away and ran, praying that Ashok would arrive soon. The hostiles would not make the same mistakes the next time. If Ashok did not save her ass and soon, she was dead.

Ashok did arrive soon.

"I have the target in sight," he said. "Sorry I'm a bit late."

"About fucking time," Samira said through pain-gritted teeth. "I can't do this shit much longer."

"You don't have to. Stand by to break left ... cannons to auto ... target acquired, break now! "Ashok said. "Engaging ... and that's that, I think."

"That is that," Samira said, watching the shattered wreckage of the hostile flier as it fell to earth, the fragments blasted apart when its fusion plant exploded in a searing white flash, *Bitsa*'s massive bulk rocketing past, the debris brushed aside with contempt.

"Okay, Samira," Ashok said, "I want you dirtside, now! I've sent your AI the LZ coordinates. Sit back and let it do the work."

"Just come and get me," Samira said, handing control back to the flier's AI.

"We're right behind you."

"Good," Samira whispered, any relief she might have felt evaporating as Juri Saarinen's words came flooding back. "I'll be waiting."

46

Buq bustled into Jaska's office, clearly pleased to be dragged away from the tedious if necessary business of making sure the small army of repairbots she needed to keep Bitsa operational were working properly. "You called?" she said.

"Yeah, I did, Buq. Have a look at this. It's just in from *Bitsa.*"

"Samira's mission report?"

"No, it's from Ashok," Jaska said, grim-faced. "It's not what we expected."

"Oh? I thought things had gone well, apart from Samira taking a round in the shoulder, that is."

"That's what I thought, but it seems there's a lot more we weren't told. Here," Jaska said, waving a hand at the holovid screen. "Check it out."

"Holy shit," Buq whispered when Ashok's face appeared on the wall-mounted holovid screen. The man looked terrible, his face gaunt and haggard. It was not the face of a man returning in triumph after a successful mission. "What the hell happened to him?"

"You'll see."

Five minutes later, the screen went blank. Buq turned to Jaska, her face taut with shock. "I didn't see that coming," she whispered.

"Me neither," Jaska said, gray-faced. "Samira finds out that Matti wasn't her dad and kills her natural father … all at the same time. Never mind the shoulder wound; it's no wonder she's almost catatonic."

"Yeah," Buq said. "And now we know what happened to Farnaz."

"Poor Farnaz," Jaska said, his face grim. "Samira needed her mother. Shit, I've spent so long trying to forget what Matti did to Farnaz."

"When she told Matti he wasn't Samira's father and Juri was or the umpteen other times he took to her with his fists?"

"All of them."

"I've tried, but I've never been able to forget."

"Who could? When Farnaz told Matti, that was the worst day of my life. That poor woman; how Matti didn't kill her I'll never know."

"He would have if Juri hadn't gotten her away."

"I'm so stupid," Jaska said, shaking his head. "It never occurred to me that Juri Saarinen and Juri Anders were the same person."

"Be fair, Jaska. Why would it?"

"You're right. Farnaz obviously recovered well enough to have a second daughter."

"Yeah. Poor Samira; she deserves better than this."

"She does. And we missed something else, Buq."

"We did?"

"Yeah. Remember the one and only time Juri got in trouble, when he was in high school?"

"Ah, yes, vaguely."

"Well, that was David Bevajec; he and Juri were friends, though Bevajec always called the shots." Jaska sighed. "No wonder Juri ended up working for the Guild. Bevajec vouched for him."

"I'll be damned. I always thought Juri and Farnaz had gone to Argentia, not Mendoza."

"Can't remember what I thought, it's all so long ago. Jeez, I'm getting old, too old for this shit."

"You and me both," Buq said.

The pair sat wordlessly for a long time before Buq broke the silence. "Ashok's answered another question," she said.

"What?" Jaska asked.

"Samira thought, I thought—hell, everyone thought the reason Saarinen killed Matti was payback for Matti's part in freeing the Armato girl."

"Of course it—" Jaska stopped himself dead. "Oh, wait a minute. It had nothing to do with the Armato business, did it?"

"No, I don't think so. Juri spotted an opportunity to pay Matti back, so he took it. Revenge; that's what it was. The Armato fiasco was just the pretext."

"All those years he waited," Jaska said, putting his head into his hands. "Unbelievable. What a bloody mess. And there's one more thing," he added, lifting his head. "Sahar Saarinen was there when Samira killed her father."

"She was," Buq said, nodding, "which means the Guild will know. They'll come after Samira, Jaska."

"They will. They have to. They can't afford to ignore this. We've got a fight on our hands, Buqisi Karua."

"We do."

• • •

Jaska and Buq waited on the apron while *Bitsa* taxied in. Ashok was the first off. "How is she?" Jaska asked him.

"Not good. She's hardly spoken. Not surprising, really."

"Damn. How's her shoulder?"

"Not too bad. She was damn lucky it missed the shoulder joint. The medibot has fixed it all up, and it's healing well; she'll be stiff and sore for a while, but that's all."

"That's something, I suppose."

"It is," Ashok said, rubbing red-rimmed eyes. "Anyway, I've had all I can take of Klimath Security Services, so if you don't mind, I'm going down to Carpenter's Bar, where I'm going to get blind, stinking drunk. Feel free to join me."

"Damn," Jaska said as Ashok walked away. "Oh, no," he whispered when Samira appeared, her wounded shoulder heavily strapped and her arm in a sling. She looked like she had aged ten years. "Samira. Glad you're back."

"No more lies, Jaska," Samira hissed, putting her face right up against his. "Saarinen said he was my father. He knew Mom's name. How could he know that? Was he my real father or not?"

"Ah …"

"Here's the deal, Jaska. Answer my questions or I'll tear your fucking head off your fucking neck and shove it down your fucking throat. Your choice."

"Tell her, Jaska," Buq said.

Samira rounded on her. "Thank you, Buq," she snarled. "I'm so glad to hear you were in on the secret too. What a shame I wasn't," she added, her voice dripping acid, "so do me a favor and piss off while I talk to this lying turd. Right, Jaska," she continued once a grim-faced Buq had left. "Your answer?"

Jaska shook his head, his eyes casting around for a way to escape. There was none. "Yes," he said so softly that he was barely audible. "Yes, Juri Saarinen is … was your father. Your dad … Matti, I mean … he wasn't your real father. His brother was—"

"Hold it!" Samira shook her head, confused. "Brother? What are you talking about?"

"Juri was your dad's brother."

"You are kidding me!"

"No, I'm not. Matti refused to let anyone mention Juri."

"You don't say," Samira snapped. "Otherwise I'd have known about him, wouldn't I?"

"Yes, you would. Look," Jaska said, his voice pleading, "what can I say, Samira?"

"And you knew all along?" Samira glared at Jaska. "So when Dad was beating the crap out of me, you knew? When Dad told me what I could and could not do with my life, you knew? All along, you knew he wasn't my real father, and you never told me? You, of all people, Jaska. I trusted you!"

"Samira, it was never that simple. Anyway," Jaska added, "it was not my business. I wasn't your father."

"Neither was Matti Anders, it seems," Samira said. "I think you'd better tell me how things got so totally screwed up."

"Your father made me promise I never would, but I guess things have changed."

"I guess they have," Samira said, the anger gone all of a sudden, leaving only a terrible emptiness. "So what happened, Uncle Jaska?"

Jaska took a while to answer. "When the anger took over," he said at last, "your father was the most dangerous man I've ever met: hair-trigger temper, big, strong, fast, and never worried about consequences. All he ever wanted to do was make people hurt, really hurt, for whatever they'd done."

"Saarinen said he was a brutal pig. Was he right?"

"Yes, he was. Before he met your mother, he killed a man on Chungking. I never found out why, but whatever happened, it was bad enough to make him understand that he couldn't go on beating everyone who upset him half to death … or worse."

Samira stared at Jaska, her eyes opening wide with horror. "Chungking wasn't the first?" she said.

"No, but it was the last. He had himself committed to some clinic specializing in psychopathic disorders; they fitted drug implants to help him keep control. That seemed to work; he still had a temper, but it was nowhere as bad."

"So what happened, with Mom and Juri, I mean?"

Jaska's face twisted, the pain all too obvious. "It was terrible," he said. "Not long after you were born, Matti found out that your mother had been seeing Juri behind his back. There was an argument, a bad one, it got out of hand, and your mother let it slip that Juri was the one she really loved and she'd had you to prove it. I still wonder why she said what she said; maybe she wanted to hurt him. I don't know."

"So Dad lost it?"

"He did, and badly. He almost killed her." Jaska's head dropped. "When I found your mother, I thought he had."

"Then what happened?"

"Juri knew he had to get you and your mother away from Matti, and he would have except Matti came home early, just as they were leaving. Matti ran Juri's mobibot off the road. He was ripping the doors off to get at them when I turned up. He would have killed them both if I hadn't been there to stop him." Jaska stopped, his hand going to his cheek. "Needless to say, that was one fight I didn't win," he went on. "The bastard smashed my face, but Juri and your mother got away, though they ended up in the hospital as well."

"But what about me? Why didn't they take me too?"

"You were trapped in the wreckage of the bot; they couldn't get you out and fight off Matti at the same time. Like I said, they'd have both ended up dead."

"And they never tried to get me back? Isn't that why we have the police?" Samira said with a bitter scowl. "Or were the useless shitheads too busy locking up people like me?"

"Those were bad times, really bad times. The civil war had another eighteen months to run, and the police existed in name only, so it wasn't hard for Matti to convince Juri and your mother that he would kill them both if they didn't leave Klimath. And if he had, who'd have cared? They were burying fifty people a day just in Bellingen; two more bodies wouldn't even have been noticed. Anyway, they believed him—I know I did—and so they fled."

"I still can't understand why my own mom left me," Samira said. "I wanted a mom, I needed a mom, so how the hell could she do that to me?"

"She never wanted to, but she didn't have much of a choice."

Samira looked hard at Jaska, long enough to make him look away. "There's more, isn't there?" she said.

"I didn't want to tell you this, but …" Jaska stopped to take a deep breath before continuing. "A week later, Matti got drunk, really drunk, and when he did that, he was almost uncontrollable. He went looking for your mom and Juri; he was going to kill them, and nothing and nobody was going to talk him out of it. I tried, though. I tried to stop him, but he had a gun and I didn't. The only thing that saved them was a rebel attack on Bellingen, a big one, the biggest they'd ever mounted. Matti was lucky to get out alive; by the time the attack was over, he was sober, and they had gone."

"You told them to go, didn't you?"

Jaska's face was gray with misery. "I had to," he said. "I managed to get a comm through to Juri at the hospital. I told him it was only a matter of time before Matti got drunk again, and when he did …" His voice trailed off.

"You really think he'd have killed her?" Samira asked.

"Yes. I did then, and I still do."

"But I still don't—"

Jaska's hand reached out to take Samira's. "It's history," he said gently. "It's over. Please let it go."

Samira let the silence drag on and on before speaking. "So what happened next?" she said finally.

"We never heard from them again, and until you got to him on Prasad, we had no idea where they'd ended up."

"So all that stuff about Mom dying when I was a baby was bullshit?"

Jaska nodded. "I'm afraid it was," he said.

"It's like something out of a trashvid, a bad one." Samira shook her head. "But you know what? I've seen Dad lose it so badly I thought he was going to kill me. So do I think he could have beaten Mom almost to death? Yes, I do. And if I can believe that, then I guess the rest is not so hard."

"It's not. Matti loved your mom in his own way, but not as much as she loved Juri."

"So why did she marry Dad?"

"She married Matti because he was the flashy one. He was pushy, he kept asking, he refused to take no for an answer. And he could be a real charmer, you know. Poor old Juri just could not compete. He was very different: quiet, shy even, never looked for a fight though he'd never walk away from one. Anyway, it was only after Matti and Farnaz were married that your mother knew the terrible mistake she'd made."

"Dad's temper, you mean?"

"Yes. Poor Farnaz; she did her best to calm things down, but Matti was … well, Matti was Matti. A year after the marriage, the arguments started, mostly about money, and then Matti started to use his fists on her. It was horrible, Samira; you have no idea. That marriage was a farce; it was doomed the instant they took their vows. And when Matti found out about Farnaz and Juri—I thought he'd killed her, I really did— she was months in the hospital …" Jaska's voice trailed off into silence. "And the rest you know," he said. Samira thought he looked terrible; he had aged ten years in ten minutes, his face haggard and drawn.

"Not so fast, Jaska," Samira said, hardening her heart. This had to be sorted out. "Start again from the beginning. I want it all, every last detail, everything you can remember. And don't look at me like that, Uncle. I've been lied to all my life, and you're going to put that right, here and now. And when you've done that, I'm going to find Ashok, and when I do, I'm going to get shitfaced with him."

"Must I?" Jaska sighed, the heartfelt sigh of a man in pain.

"Now, Jaska!"

"So that's the whole, grubby story, Ashok," Samira said, "and who's the dipshit? Me, that's who. I killed my own father,

I nearly killed my sister, and I've pissed off the Guild so much they're probably already on their way to kill me … and you while they're at it. So here's to an early death," she said, lifting her beer.

"Live hard, die young," Ashok replied, raising his beer in reply. "Wait! What am I saying? Fuck the Guild. I'm too young to die."

"Me too."

"So what the hell are we going to do, Samira? After all we've been through, we can't just sit back and let those Guild assholes walk all over us."

"No, we can't, and we won't."

"So what are we going to do?"

"No idea. Something, I guess, but I'm too smashed even to think about it. In fact, I'm so smashed, my arm doesn't even hurt anymore. So are we staying here or what?"

"Let me see," Ashok said. "I think what, don't you?

"I thought you'd never ask," Samira replied.

47

Ignoring a pounding headache, Samira opened her eyes warily, wincing as her headache kicked up a gear—Why the hell hadn't she taken a detox tab to kill the alcohol when she'd had the chance? she wondered—then wincing some more as her shoulder reminded her that it was far from fixed. She lifted her head a fraction and looked around, confused, unable to work out just where she was. Everything was alien: the bed, the room, the way the light slipped past the curtains, the smell, the sounds filtering into a place she had no recollection of.

So where the hell was she? Leaving the bar was the last thing she could recall, leaving the bar with—

Oh, no, she thought. *I left the bar with Ashok* ... and then she remembered the rest of the evening.

"Damn, damn, damn," she groaned, turning her head to look at Ashok's sleeping form. "I am an idiot." Much as she liked the man, how could she have been so stupid? Cradling her arm, she eased her way out of the bed and started to get dressed.

"Hey, you," a sleepy voice mumbled just as Samira eased her jacket on over a stiff and sore arm and turned to leave.

"Morning, Ashok," Samira said. "Sorry, got to go."

"Must you?"

"Yes, I must." She turned to look at him. "Sorry I was … you know, a bit tired."

"Don't apologize, Samira. You've been through a lot."

"Yeah, but maybe it wasn't the best idea, coming here."

"Not sure that's right." Ashok grinned at her, sleepy eyes dancing in amusement as he patted the bed. "I can't persuade you to stay?"

"No! No, you can't, so don't try. I'm off; I'll see you back at the base."

"Okay, okay. I'll see you there. We've got to get our shit together. Like you said, those assholes from the Guild will be coming after us, and we—"

"They're coming after me, Ashok, not us. Just me. This is my fight, not yours."

"Wrong, Captain Anders, sir."

"Cut it out, Ashok. That joke's wearing a bit thin."

"The Guild is KSS business," Ashok continued, ignoring Samira's interruption, "which makes this KSS's fight. And since I am a KSS employee, that makes it my fight as well, though it would be nice if I heard you say it."

"Well, I won't," Samira said with an emphatic shake of the head. "Anyway, I've caused enough trouble for everyone. The Guild is my problem, and I'll deal with it. I'm not going to allow you or Jaska or Buq to get hurt, okay?"

"That's total bullshit," Ashok snapped, sitting up. "Give me a break, Samira. I know all about the …" He paused to recover his self-control. "Listen to me. The Guild is more dangerous than you can ever imagine, and things are going to get very dirty very quickly, and if you think I'm just going to sit back while they blow you away, then think again. I'm already involved, for fuck's sake. I was there on Prasad, remember? I can't get uninvolved."

Samira sat back down on the edge of the bed. "What do you know all about, Ashok?" she said, her voice soft. "The Guild? Come on, tell me."

"No, I can't." Ashok stared at her for a second. "But I will tell you this, Samira, since you seem to have worked it out already. I know a lot about the Guild, and I know a lot about their scum-sucking friends here on Klimath, none of which I can tell you."

"Why?"

"Because I'd be signing my own death warrant and the death warrants of some people I really care about. Even if they don't know that," he added in an undertone. "But what I can do is fight them when they come after you, and I will, whether you like it or not."

"That doesn't make sense, Ashok. If the Guild finds out you're helping me, surely they'll kill you too."

"Maybe, but I don't think so. It's the people here on Klimath who are my problem, and that includes the police, I'm sorry to say. Look, that's enough, okay?"

"Okay." She leaned forward to plant a gentle kiss on Ashok's lips, fighting an overwhelming urge to get back in the bed, to be held the way he had held her, to let the world take care of itself. "Now that I think about it," she said, pulling away and standing up, "I'm pretty sure it was a good idea."

"A good idea?" Ashok asked with a puzzled frown on his face.

"Last night, silly."

"Oh … Yes, it was a good idea, Samira, a very good idea."

"Yes, it was. I'll see you later."

"I'm part of this, Samira," Ashok called to her back as she walked out, "I'm part of what happens next, so get used to it."

Samira's only response was the wave of a hand, and then she was gone.

"I think I'm beginning to fall for you, Samira Anders," Ashok whispered as his door banged shut.

48

"She wants to do what?" Jaska exclaimed, his eyes wide with surprise.

"Sahar Saarinen wants a face-to-face meeting," Samira said, "and I'm going to say yes."

"Face to face? You're kidding! It's a trap, Samira. It has to be."

"Maybe, maybe not."

"But why?"

"She won't say."

"This makes no sense, Samira. What's wrong with a ho-lovid conference? That way she can say whatever she's got to say and there's no risk to you."

"All true, Jaska, but she's specifically ruled that out. We either meet face to face or there's no meeting."

"Samira! It's a trap."

"I don't think so."

"How can you know that?' Jaska sat back and threw his hands up in frustration. "You killed her father, and Sahar Saarinen watched you do it. The last thing she wants is a quiet chat. She's either a saint or she wants you dead."

"Yeah, yeah," Samira said, sighing, "and you don't believe in saints. I know; you've told me."

"She wants to kill you, Samira. She said so. Come on! Don't be dumb."

"Jaska! You can keep banging that drum, and it won't change anything. I'm going to agree to meet, and that's that. Yes, she might try and blow my head off, but that's a risk I'm willing to take. Okay?"

"No, it's not okay." Jaska said, his lips set in a stubborn line. "I don't understand why she'd do this. It doesn't make sense. Come on, help me here, Ashok."

"You're wrong, Jaska," Ashok said. "It makes perfect sense."

"How?" Jaska demanded. "Tell me how."

"Simple," Ashok said, his voice emphatic. "If Samira agrees to meet Sahar, the Guild will know exactly where she'll be and when, and if the Guild knows, then so will their hit team. It is a trap. It has to be. Nothing else makes sense."

The silence that followed was long, broken at last by a long, heartfelt sigh from Samira. "I'm sorry, folks," she said, "but I'm going to agree to meet Sahar. Hey, hey, hey!" she shouted over the storm of protest. "One at a time."

Buq got in first. "You mean it?" she asked.

"Yes," Samira said, "I do. How can I not?"

Jaska, Buq, and Ashok stared at Samira. She glared back, her face an implacable mask. Jaska sighed. "What have I done to deserve this?" He looked across at Buq. "Are you thinking what I'm thinking?" he asked.

"Don't ask," Buq growled, sour-faced.

"Ashok?"

"Well," he said, "if you're thinking we'd be wasting our time trying to talk the most stubborn woman I've ever met—"

"Hey, I'm still here, you know," Samira protested.

"—out of meeting Sahar," Ashok continued, ignoring Samira, "even if it's the dumbest thing I've ever heard of, then yes, I am."

"That's exactly what I'm thinking." Jaska shook his head. "Okay, Samira, fine. But why?"

"Because it's the last thing she'd do if the Guild was coming after me, that's why. It's too obvious, much too obvious. This is not what she would do if she was after me; no way."

"Bullshit, Samira," Ashok retorted. "Ever heard of a double bluff? Well, you have now. Sahar's the bait, and you've just swallowed it."

There was another very long silence. "Damn it, Samira," Jaska said at last, his voice soft, "what Ashok says could be true, but I think you may have a point. If the Guild were planning to kill you, this is not the way they'd do it. They're straightforward people; they'd put together a hit team, send them in, and wham! All over. This—" He waved his hands in frustration. "—this is just too bizarre to be anything other than what Sahar says it is."

"Thank you, Jaska. Can we stop arguing about whether the meeting's going to happen—which it is—and start working out how to do it instead?"

"All right, then," Ashok said. "If we go along with this, what's she suggesting?"

"Bellingen, Monday at 09:00," Samira said. "She'll be coming in on the maglev from Morgannen."

"Bellingen? That won't be easy." Jaska looked at Buq and Ashok; they both nodded. "We need to work out how Samira and Sahar can meet without Samira getting killed. That'll take a lot of planning."

"And more bodies," Ashok said. He thought for a moment. "I'll talk to my grandfather," he went on. "Charlie would be up for it, I reckon."

"And I can talk to my buddy Bedar," Buq said.

"Which gives us five altogether," Jaska said, "not including Samira, of course. That should be okay as long as Samira—"

"Hey!" Samira said. "I'm in this too, you know, so stop talking about me like I was somewhere else."

"Sorry," Jaska said. "Okay, if the meeting goes ahead, we have to assume it's a trap and plan accordingly. Agreed?"

Heads nodded as one.

"Good. Anyone got the faintest idea how we can do that?"

"Yes," Ashok said. "I think we need to ...

49

"The maglev is approaching," Ashok said. "Positions, everyone. Samira, all set?"

"All set," Samira replied, mouth dry with tension, heart hammering as she tried to bury the very real possibility that she might have only minutes left to live. It was an outcome the laser pistol in her pocket had little chance of preventing.

With Charlie Samarth as bodyguard, Samira had been stationed well away from Bellingen Station with strict instructions to stay put. They had waited while the minutes dragged past, Samira trying hard not to hop from foot to foot, consumed by impatience, her nerves jangling, the lightweight body armor Jaska had forced her wear hot and uncomfortable. Charlie, in contrast, stood quite still, face impassive, head swinging from side to side in a never-ending search for anything out of the ordinary.

"Maglev's arrived," Buq radioed.

"I think I've got her," Ashok said after what felt like a lifetime. "Stand by … Yes, it's her."

"Has she brought any backup?" Samira asked.

"Wait one," Ashok replied. "No," he said a few seconds later. "Brazzi says the surveillance AI hasn't spotted anyone; looks like she's following instructions. Okay, she's out of the station

… Right, we've boxed her in. Still no sign of any backup … Good; she's turned south onto McKinsey. Okay, Samira, stay where you are. We want her past Kerwan before we contact her."

"Roger," Samira said, trying not to sigh out loud, wishing that everyone would stop treating her like a complete idiot even if meeting Sahar was something only an idiot would do.

"She's across Kerwan," Ashok said at last. "You can't miss her: short white-blond hair under a black beret, heavy make-up, black top and jeans, Time to make contact, Bedar."

"Roger. I've got her; stand by." There was a long pause. "Okay," Bedar said eventually, "she's agreed to come with me into Bedalski's Patisserie so I can check she's clean."

"Roger that," Ashok replied. "Samira, don't move."

"Oh, please," Samira replied. "Don't worry, I won't."

"Saarinen's good," Bedar said five anxious minutes later. "I've done a complete body scan: no weapons, no trackers, no comm units, I've masked her neuronics, the blindfold's on, and she's now dressed like my mother. We're in a mobibot now on our way to the meeting place."

"Thanks Bedar. Okay, Samira, Charlie, let's do it. The rest of the team is covering your approach, and Brazzi's confirmed the AI still hasn't picked up anyone suspicious."

"Good," Samira said. "We're on our way now."

"Stay close, Samira," Charlie said, "and remember, if the shit hits the fan, let me deal with it. You just get off the street, find some cover, and stay down. Okay?"

"Okay," Samira said as they set off, trying not to feel so guilty, praying that nothing happened to Charlie or anyone else.

Ten minutes later, Samira walked into Peroni's Café, and there she was. "Hi, Sahar," she said.

Sahar looked up. "Hello, Samira," she said, her face impassive under the heavy makeup. "I wondered when you'd turn up."

For a moment, Samira could only stand there, heart pounding. "I'm here now," she said.

"Glad to see your tame goon isn't pointing a gun in my face," Sahar said, waving a hand at Charlie.

I'd feel a lot happier if he was, Samira thought, taking a seat. With her back safely against the wall, she sat opposite Sahar in silence until the coffees turned up. Bedar and Charlie were at the next table to keep an eye on things, with the rest of the team outside watching the street.

"I'm not sure what to say to you, Sahar," Samira said, "though I have discovered two things: I've been lied to all my life, and I know a lot more about my family than I did. I wish I'd known the truth a long time ago. Things might have turned out differently."

"They probably would have," Sahar replied.

"They would, trust me."

"This all a bit awkward, sitting opposite the woman who killed my father—and hers—drinking coffee." Sahar smiled, a bleak smile that came and went in an instant, a finger stroking the faint scar still visible cutting through the elaborate spread of nanocrystal tattoos on her left cheek. "How weird is that?"

"Very," Samira said, "but what's done is done. Why did you want to meet? Last thing you said was that you wanted to kill me."

Sahar sipped her coffee before responding. Putting the cup down, she leaned forward, piercing blue eyes rimmed with thick smears of black makeup—her eyes were the same color as her own, Samira realized—staring into Samira's face. "Yes, I did," she said. "After you killed Dad, all I thought of was killing you."

"Really?" Samira murmured. "What a surprise."

"And I still think about killing you, just not all the time."

"Listen, Sahar," Samira said, shooting a glance at Bedar and Charlie. "Nobody wanted me to be here with you, so start convincing me I haven't screwed up or I'm leaving."

"Sorry." Sahar took a deep breath, letting it out in a long sigh. "I made a mistake. It took me a while, a long while, before I realized that you weren't the person I should be blaming."

"But I killed your father!" Samira sat back, eyebrows arched in surprise. "Who else is to blame? That makes no sense, Sahar."

"Let me explain."

"No. Start by telling me who you do blame."

"Ah, right, I blame my dad," Sahar said in a matter-of-fact voice.

"Wha …" Samira's mouth sagged open. "You blame your dad?" She shook her head, bewildered. "Why would you blame him?"

"He was not the man you think he was."

"I know exactly what he was. Juri Saarinen might have been your father, but he was also a Guildsman, a crook, and a killer. Come on, Sahar, get to the point; I'm not going to sit here all day while you go around in circles."

"I will get to the point." Sahar paused for an instant as if to marshal her arguments. "Quite early on," she continued, "I realized that it didn't matter what I said to my father, what I thought, what I really wanted to do with my life, because none of it really interested him. That bothered me a lot, so I decided I had to understand why, and to do that I had to understand him. Problem was, when I did work him out, I discovered he was a bad man, a very bad man."

"I know that."

"Yeah, well, he was so bad, I couldn't stay with him anymore. Dad was totally pissed when I said I wanted to leave, but I left anyway. He dragged me back, I ran away again, and around and around we went until he sent me to live with one of Mom's cousins on Prasad. That was when I was seventeen, and I celebrated by getting my new look," she added, lifting her beret and running her hand across her ice-blond stubble. "Dad was so angry when he saw it … Anyway, understanding him meant understanding the Guild, and the day I understood what the Guild was all about, I despised everything it stood for. The corruption, the brutality, the endless killings, the families destroyed, the way it turned Mendoza into a criminal state. The people who run the Guild don't give a shit about any of that. Power and money, that's all they care about, and heaven help you if you get their way. I hate them."

"And so you hated him? Your dad, I mean."

"I ended up hating him, yes, though I never stopped loving him in a funny sort of way, which was why I asked him over and over to quit the Guild, to leave Mendoza, to start again somewhere new, but he always said no. You see, he loved the power the Guild gave him. They say power is a drug, and they're right. It is a drug, and he was addicted to it."

"No wonder he killed my father," Samira said. "He must have had plenty of practice."

"Actually, no. He was what the Guild calls a clean-hands."

"A clean-hands?"

"Yes. Someone who leaves the dirty work to others. Dad used cyborgs or contract killers for all the nasty stuff; believe me, there was a lot of it, and us kids got hear all about it. Guildsmen like to tell everyone how tough and smart they are; the bastards have turned boasting into an art form."

"Nice."

"Only if you've got the morals of a sewer rat, Samira, and don't mind swimming in shit, which my dad did. He never pulled the trigger, planted the bomb, broke the leg, raped the wife, or threatened the kids. He gave the orders, and that makes him every bit as guilty as the person who pulls the trigger, more guilty in fact."

"Hold on one second, Sahar. This doesn't make sense. You say you hate him, but I watched you when your father arrived at the lodge. You let him hug you. I saw you."

"Only because I had to. Trust me, I hated him, but I loved him too. To begin with, he was a warm, caring father. He loved me, he listened to me, and most of all, he made me feel like I was the most important thing in the world." Sahar laughed, a sharp, bitter laugh, brittle as glass. "I got that so wrong," she continued. "As I got older, he changed until it was obvious the Guild was all he really cared about. But I went along with things until I couldn't stand the hypocrisy anymore; that's why I left. But even then I ignored the truth. After I came to Prasad, I never let him talk about the Guild; I just pretended he did something else. So life went on, one long charade," she added, her face twisting into an ugly scowl.

"Maybe so," Samira said, "but I killed him." She shook her head, perplexed. "And what are you going to do to me in return? Nothing! It's all a bit hard to believe. What the hell are you? Some sort of saint?"

"Me a saint?" Sahar laughed. "Hell, no!"

"So shouldn't you be trying to kill me? Is that how you Mendozans do business?"

"Yes, it is, but I don't need to. The Guild will do that for me."

"Is that why we're here?" Samira hissed. She took a deep breath to clear her mind; it did nothing to steady her uneasiness. "I don't like this, Sahar. I'm going. I'm not sure this is a safe place for me to be."

"Oh, relax, Samira! The Guild is a huge organization, and even whacking a no-account Klimathian like you takes time to organize. Trust me, you're fine, especially with the crack team you've got around you." Sahar waved at Bedar and Charlie. "Where the hell did you dig them up? Aren't they all a bit old for a close protection detail?"

"Try them, Sahar, just try them. And there's more of them outside in case you're wondering."

"Thought there'd be. I must say I'm impressed, though. Your team seems to have its shit together. Hi, guys," she called. "Doing a great job."

"Can we stick to the point, please?"

"Sorry."

"So you sort of loved your father even though you hated him and all that, but you said one thing that doesn't make sense. You said your dad was a clean-hands man."

"Yes, he was, always had been. Deep down he was squeamish, I think."

"But he killed my father with a single shot to the head. I've seen the police report."

"He killed Matti Anders because he needed to."

Samira frowned. "He needed to?"

"Let me explain. You've heard of David Bevajec?"

"The man who runs the Guild?"

"He does, and Bevajec is the most evil man this side of Old Earth," Sahar said, grim-faced. "He's no clean-hands man. He likes to kill with his bare hands, though these days he saves himself for the special jobs."

"Special jobs?"

"Yeah. Young women; the younger, the better. I've lost count of how many. It's no secret that Bevajec is a psychopath, and since he became the boss …" Sahar's voice trailed off into silence for a moment. "Even the gutless pigs who pretend to be the Mendozan government couldn't ignore the way Bevajec's men were kidnapping women to order right off the streets, so now he's started to get them from Kerrick and M'duna."

All of a sudden Samira understood what Sahar was telling her. "Shit," she whispered. "I'm on Bevajec's shopping list, aren't I? He wants me."

"He certainly does," Sahar said, "and worse than you can imagine."

Badly shaken, Samira tried not to think about what that meant. She took a deep breath to steady her nerves. "We're getting off the subject," she went on. "Now, your father killed mine because he needed to; that's how you put it. Needed to: What the hell does that mean?"

"The Armato kidnapping was a huge deal for the Guild. Everyone assumed it was just about the ransom, but they were dead wrong. No, it was much more than that. It was a strategic play: The Guild wanted to hit Armato hard, to humiliate him, to show everyone the Armatos weren't invulnerable, that they could be beaten, that the Guild was not to be messed with by the Armatos or anyone else."

"Let me guess," Samira said. "Because the Armatos were taking too much interest in Mendoza?"

"That's right. The Guild had to stop Armato or risk losing everything. And so, when it all went wrong, it was a disaster for the Guild. It made them look weak; what was worse, it made Bevajec look weak. He knew he had to fix things, and quickly; otherwise the Guild's investors would throw him to the wolves. So to cover his ass, Bevajec put all the blame for the screwup on his chief of staff, Jaffar Terrini. Then he made my father an offer he could not refuse: kill Terrini, kill Matti Anders, and he could have the Terrini's job as chief of staff."

"But why did Bevajec want my father killed? Matti was just a gun for hire, surely."

"That was personal. During the Armato operation, your father took out two shuttles, right?"

"Yes, he did."

"Bevajec's oldest son, Jason, was onboard one of them. Bevajec didn't get enough of Jason's body back to fill this coffee cup. Bevajec was understandably upset—he was grooming the boy to take over—and he's the sort of man who believes in payback."

"Not good."

"You said it. You swim in dangerous waters, Samira."

"So why didn't your father say no?"

"Say no to David Bevajec?" Sahar smiled and shook her head. "Not a chance. Bevajec would have had my father killed. But why would he say no? He craved power, and power was what Bevajec was offering him. The Guild's chief of staff is one of the most powerful men on Mendoza. My father was never going to say no, and Bevajec knew it."

"And we know what happened next."

"Yup; my father killed Terrini, and two days later he killed Matti."

Samira sat for a moment, unable to comprehend how such evil could exist. "We all thought it was a just a matter of revenge. It seems we got that wrong."

"You sure did."

"I don't know what to think anymore," Samira said, playing with her cup. "I'm sitting here, pretending to drink coffee with the sister I never knew I had, and even though I killed her father—who was my father as well, it turns out—she isn't going to kill me because her father was a murderous asshole. Meanwhile, the man I'd always called Dad turns out not to be my father; instead, he's the man who half killed my mother, the mother I never knew, hurting her so badly that she was dead a few years later, before trying to kill her a week later. Oh, yes, I almost forgot: On top of all that, a psychopath with a preference for young women is coming after me. How am I doing so far?"

"That's a really neat summary," Sahar said with a fleeting smile. "Well done; you've been paying attention."

"Piss off, Sahar. I'm not in the mood."

"Okay, just one more thing. Did I look familiar the first time you saw me?"

"Ah, sort of, but … no, not really. I just had this feeling that I'd seen you before even though I hadn't."

"Wrong, Samira. You have seen me before, thousands of times."

"No," Samira said with a dismissive flick of her head. "No, I haven't. Maybe you looked familiar because we're sisters, but that's all. But trust me, I'd never seen you until I came to Prasad."

"Yes you had: every time you looked in the mirror."

"What the hell?"

"I'm not just your sister, I'm your clone, an exact copy."

"You're kidding me!" Samira hissed. "How the hell could that happen?"

"Having to leave you behind nearly tore Mom apart; she blamed herself for not being braver, for letting Dad talk her out of taking Matti on, for not trying to take you back. Dad said she was never the same again mentally or physically, knowing that she'd never see you again. So he settled on what he thought would be the next best thing. He had your full DNA profile on record; cloning is just a matter of simple bio-engineering, and so here I am."

"You're joking."

"I'm not. The only difference between you and me is that you're naturally born, while I was pseudo-wombed. Matti hurt her so badly that she couldn't have children; she had no choice. But apart from that and the fact that I'm a year younger than you, we're identical."

"I … I don't believe it," Samira said, wide-eyed.

Sahar laughed. "I'm not surprised." She reached into a pocket to pull out a holopic. She pushed it across the table. "This has been edited for me," she said. "It shows how I would look with your hair, without the makeup and studs and all the other shit. Tell me who you see, Samira."

Samira looked at it, and her heart lurched as the ground fell away from underneath her. She was looking at herself.

"And if that doesn't do it," Sahar said, "then here's the proof. Know what this is?"

Samira looked at the slim black box Sahar slid across the table. "Sure. It's a memory vault."

"It is a memory vault: my memory vault. Fancy a peek at the real me?"

"No, not really."

"I don't care. Go on, get into it."

"How can I do that? It's keyed to your DNA, not mine … Ah, right, sorry."

"Do it," Sahar said when Samira hesitated, her fingers over the vault, trembling. "Do it now."

"Okay." Samira took the box; inserting a finger into the access port, she waited for it to confirm her identity. It took a while, but finally the vault connected with her neuronics implants.

Then, with an overwhelming rush, she could see, taste, touch, hear, and smell all that Sahar had experienced for the five minutes after she had boarded the maglev for Bellingen, her mind engulfed by a chaotic, tangled riot of senses, thoughts, and emotions. "Holy shit," she said, pulling her finger away after only a few seconds, unable to cope with the raw power of another human's psyche, "I've never done that before. That's scary."

"We're clones, Samira. Believe me now?"

"I think I have to."

"You're me, and I'm you. So tell me, how could I kill myself?"

Stunned, Samira sat there for a good few minutes. "Well," she said softly at last, "I guess I'm going to have to trust you after all since it's me I'm looking at."

"You should trust me even though I will never forgive you for what you've done, never. I might have hated my father, but he was still my dad. You need to understand that."

Samira's head dropped. "I do," she said, "but when the Mendozan police refused to do anything, I wasn't left with too many options." She looked up, cheeks flushing with sudden anger. "So what the hell did you expect me to do?" she hissed. "Your father killed my father, so I killed him. That's a pretty fair exchange, I reckon, and I don't give a flying fuck why your dad did what he did. The fact is he could always have refused. He didn't have to do what Bevajec wanted."

"Hey!" Sahar protested. "I understand all that. The good news is this: Much as I hate you for what you've done, I hate David Bevajec more—much more. He's the reason my dad's dead, he's the reason the man you thought was your father is dead, he's the reason we're sitting here, he's the reason I haven't blown your damn fool head off, and he's the reason why I'm not going to let the Guild blow your head off either."

"I'm pleased to hear it."

"Look, Samira," Sahar said, her voice soft, conciliatory, "that's enough history. We need to move on. We need to work out what we're going to do about Bevajec."

"Bevajec?"

"Yes. You killed Juri Saarinen, the Guild's newly promoted chief of staff and number two man. You've embarrassed Bevajec. You've made the Guild look like a bunch of piss-weak amateurs again. Bevajec is coming to get you, and there's nothing we can do to stop him. Don't tell me you're just going to sit there waiting for Bevajec and his team of thugs to turn up?"

"No, of course we're not. We know the Guild wants me dead."

"Well, you'd better work out how to deal with him and fast unless you're happy to have David Bevajec arrange your dying, which he will. You have to kill him, because if you don't, he'll kill you."

"Wait! That's easy to say, but this is the Guild we're talking about. After what's happened, Bevajec's going to have more security than ever. How am I ever going to get close enough to take him out?"

"You don't need to."

"Who, then?" Samira face creased into a puzzled frown. "Who's going to kill Bevajec?"

"You will."

"Me? But … Sahar! Stop going around in circles. I'm having enough trouble keeping up as it is."

"Right now, Bevajec's putting a hit team together. The plan is to take you out here on Klimath, though when—"

"Whoa! How do you know that?"

"How?" Sahar shrugged her shoulders. "Bevajec told me."

"He told you?"

"Yup, he did. Bevajec thinks I want revenge, and since he feels so guilty about the whole business—well, to the extent a man like him feels guilty about anything—he's made a point of keeping me aware of his plans."

"So a hit team's going to come for me; big deal. I told you we'd already worked that out."

"I'm sure you had, but what I can do, what I will do, is give you all the details—who, when, where, and how—the moment Bevajec tells me. And I'll make sure he does. I do a very good grief-stricken daughter."

"So I'm to sit and wait, am I? What am I, the bait?"

"I said you were smart. Yes, you're the bait, and yes, we—I want you to wait."

"Why? Let the police deal with it. It's their job, after all, and they're not as useless as the Mendozan cops."

"Did I just say you were smart?" Sahar said, rolling her eyes. "What the hell was I thinking? You Klimathians are such dumbasses. The Guild—"

"We might be sisters, but that won't stop me from belting the crap out of you, Sahar Saarinen."

"That'll never happen. It'd be a draw, you idiot; we're clones, remember? What was I saying? Oh, yes, the Guild. It has big plans for Klimath."

"Why Klimath? It isn't the richest system around."

"It's richer than Mendoza, and it's halfway to New Guangzhou, and that is one of the richest systems around. Besides, like Dad, Bevajec was born and grew up here; he has a soft spot for the place. He's convinced the Guild they should take over Klimath, so that's what the Guild's going to do. Not even the threat from the Armatos is enough to stop them. The bad news is that they're already here working away, even though you guys don't seem to have realized that yet."

With a start, Samira remembered what Ashok had let slip about who was threatening him: "It's the people here on Klimath who are the problem, and that includes the police."

Damn, she thought, *all of a sudden the pieces are beginning to fall into place.*

"All right," she said, "so I shouldn't talk to the police. That leaves me sitting back, waiting for Bevajec's hit team. Now, why would I do that?"

"Two reasons. First, they're going to come after you wherever you try to hide; better to take them head on, on your ground and on your terms. And second, because Bevajec is coming for you himself. He wants to take care of you his way."

"His way?" Samira whispered, very afraid all of a sudden as the threat started to crystallize in her mind. "He said that?"

"Yes, he did, and a lot more, though I'll spare you the details. They were pretty gruesome."

"I don't want to know," Samira said with a shiver.

"Trust me, you don't. Anyway, when Bevajec comes to you, that's your best chance to take him down. If the man's dumb enough to stick his head in the noose, then—" Sahar's hand closed into a fist and snapped up.

"Which all makes sense," Samira said, "but I'll need to talk to the team. I'd be taking a big chance, though. If you don't get Bevajec's plans to me or this is all some sort of elaborate hoax, I'm a sitting duck."

"That's true, so you're just going to have to trust me. Not that you have much choice; like I said, they're coming after you no matter what any of us do."

"Okay. What's next?"

"I need to start steering Bevajec in the right direction. Where's the best place for you to stand and fight?"

"Mmm." Samira thought for a while, wondering if she should tell Sahar. "Our base," she said finally, deciding that half trusting the woman wasn't an option; either she did or she didn't. "I can't think of anywhere better. Lots of old bunkers to hide in, all our weapons and ammunition are stored there, we have a razor-wire perimeter with intruder alarms and holocams, and there's our lander if we need to get out of there."

"That makes sense. I'll make sure he buys that. Now, it's important that Bevajec believe you don't expect an attack. They'll put surveillance on you before long—I'll let you know what they're up to as soon as I can—so you need to act normally, though I wouldn't sleep at home."

"Let me think … Yeah, we can arrange to have a major problem with *Bitsa*. That's the obvious reason for keeping us all on base. Our lander's always breaking down."

"Fine. I'll send you the address of a blind mailbox so we can talk, and we'll, ah … I'll keep you posted on what Bevajec's planning."

"Sounds good," Samira said, wondering why she was putting herself in the hands of someone who had—notwithstanding how persuasive her arguments had been—every reason to want her dead.

"Right, I think that's it," Sahar said. "I need to get the maglev back to Morgannen. I'm supposed to be visiting with one of Mom's aunts, and I shouldn't be away too long in case Bevajec finds out I've been moonlighting, and we don't want that. Good luck, Samira."

"Yeah," Samira said, still stunned by the ease and speed with which Sahar had turned her whole world upside down. "I'm going to need it."

"Any questions, just message me."

"Will do," Samira said, getting to her feet. "I'll leave first. I want you to wait five minutes, and then you can go."

Sahar shook her head. "You still don't trust me, do you, Samira?"

"Just do it."

An hour later, they were all safely back in Jaska's office.

"Did everybody hear what Sahar and I talked about?" Samira said, looking around. Heads nodded, faces still sporting looks of stunned disbelief. "That was something else, eh?"

"You can say that again," Jaska muttered.

"Quick question before I forget," Samira said. "Did I imagine it, or did she start to say 'we,' then change it to 'I' a couple of times?"

"Funny you should ask," Ashok said. "I noticed that."

"You think it means something?" Jaska asked.

"Yes," Ashok replied, his face hard and unsmiling. "Yes, I do. I have this terrible feeling we've blundered into somebody else's game. Problem is, we don't know the rules, who the players are, what side we should be on … We don't know a damn thing. But I'd bet my life it's a big game with a lot at stake, the sort of game where the losers get killed."

"Well, we only know one thing for sure," Buq said, "which is that Sahar wants us to wait for a Guild hit team to turn up so we can nail Bevajec." She paused, her face troubled. "It's all too easy. Are we being bluffed?"

"If she gets Bevajec's plans to us, then no, probably not," Samira said, looking at each of them in turn. "Surely that's the acid test."

"No, it's not," Ashok retorted. "The acid test is whether or not what she sends us proves accurate, and we won't know that until it's too late to pull out."

"You're right, Ashok." Samira's face was troubled. "Can we … do we trust her?"

"I think so," Jaska said after a long pause. "Ashok?"

"I believe her," Ashok said. "Logic says I shouldn't, but I do. So yes."

"And me." Buq nodded.

"Bedar, Charlie. What do you think?"

"Trust her but plan for the double cross," Charlie Samarth said, "just in case."

"My thoughts exactly," Bedar said.

"Trust her but plan for the double cross," Samira said, nodding. "I like that."

"Okay, this is what I suggest," Jaska said. "We wait for Sahar to send us Bevajec's plans. Until then, our priority is protecting Samira just in case Sahar is double-crossing us. When we get Bevajec's plans, we have a decision to make: either bail out because we think she's double-crossed us or stay and fight."

Everyone nodded.

"One last thing," Samira said, looking at each of the team in turn. "I'd just like to say thanks to you all. It means more than you know not being alone in this."

50

A soft series of beeps jerked Samira awake.

"At last," she breathed as she read and reread the message. Scrambling out of her bunk, she dressed hurriedly and climbed the stairs from the old bunker's lower level—Jaska had insisted that she sleep there, arguing that even the Guild would have trouble reaching her through double armored doors and five meters of ceramcrete—to where Ashok sat surrounded by holovid screens, taking video and data from cameras and intruder alarms, backed up with information from *Bitsa*'s suite of sensors.

"Hi, Samira," Ashok said, rubbing tired eyes. "What got you out of bed?"

"We're on," Samira said, putting the message up on one of the screens. "Sahar's come through for us. Here, have a look."

Ashok read Sahar's message in silence. It took him a while; it was comprehensive and very detailed. He whistled softly when he finished. "Bloody hell," he said. "This is either the best damn intelligence ever or the most elaborate con of all time."

"I don't think it's a con, Ashok. No con would be this detailed, this intricate."

"I agree. It's an oporder the military would be proud of. They're taking this business seriously."

"If you're Bevajec, that's a good thing, surely?" Samira asked with a puzzled frown.

"No, it's not. He's overplanned the operation. Look here: task after task, all timed to the minute. This plan is too rigid, too inflexible. Here's an example: Tell me where there's any allowance for the fact that *Bitsa* might actually be a problem for him."

"Nowhere," Samira replied after another look.

"Exactly," Ashok said. "He's assumed it won't be and planned the operation accordingly. This is good, really good … well, for us anyway. Not so good for Bevajec."

"Is the plan really that bad?" Samira asked. "I'm having trouble seeing past the fact that it's me he's coming after."

"No. It's not all bad. It stays focused on the main game. But I can see two flaws. The plan might be simple, but it's too obvious: flankers left and right, the main attack right down the middle. Second, Bevajec has assumed everything will happen just as he's planned it. This is not an operation order, Samira; it's a script, and Bevajec's the director."

"Isn't that what he is?"

"No, because things never run according to plan. You have to allow for things to go wrong, and Bevajec hasn't. The only uncertainty he's planned for is where you'll be when the attack goes down, Samira. Apart from that, there are no fallbacks, no alternatives, no delegation of command. Bevajec is the only person allowed to change the plan. His plan has zero flexibility. It's nuts."

"It's … it is very precise."

"Precise? It's choreographed to the nth degree, which tells you a lot about Bevajec. He's scared of losing this, so he's over-compensated by dictating exactly what will happen minute by minute. And when things start to go wrong—which they will, because we'll make sure they do—he's screwed because he's the only one who can give orders. The rest of his team are there to do as they are told. Hey, you know what, Samira?"

"What?"

"I think we're going to kick his ass."

"Hmm," Samira said, not looking at all convinced. "I wish."

"And I'm bloody glad we knew about it beforehand," Ashok continued. "If we hadn't … I tell you what: That Sahar's certainly delivered."

"Whoa, Ashok! Hold on just a moment. She's only delivered if what she's given us is accurate. Don't forget she might be setting us up."

"I haven't forgotten. Don't worry; just in case she is screwing with us, we're going to make sure we put as much effort into our fallback planning as we do into responding to this."

"Pleased to hear it, though everything she's given us so far has been dead right. What are those Guild dumbfucks up to tonight?"

"Hold on … Right, here we are," Ashok said when one of the screens turned a ghostly speckled green. "Let me see," he said as he scanned the low-light image. "Three of them are asleep … There, that's them behind the guy on watch," he added, pointing to a huddle of sleeping-bagged bodies.

"What the hell is he up to?" Samira leaned forward to get a better look at the image. "Is that snoring?"

"I think it is," Ashok said, turning up the volume until the room filed with the soft buzz of a man soundly asleep. "He seems to have decided to take a quick nap. So much for the Guild's professional killers."

"And their holocams?"

"Hold on ... there you go," Ashok said as screens split into multiple panes, each from a remote holocam, the center pane displaying a high-definition image of *Bitsa*, its massive bulk sitting on an island of blazing light set amid a sea of darkness, the familiar figure of Buq bustling around the apron. Ostensibly, she was working on a litany of defects a kilometer long, a catalog of problems discussed at great length by Buq and Jaska right in front of one of the Guild's covert holocams.

Samira shook her head. After much persuasion—most of it financial in nature—Brazzi had sent his best intercept technician along to put taps on all the tightbeam lasers feeding information from the holocams, movement sensors, remote microphones, and radio scanners back to the Guild's surveillance team. "Piece of cake" had been her only comment on leaving; that people with such skills even existed amazed Samira.

"I'll go tell Jaska," Samira said.

"No, don't. We've got plenty of time. Let him sleep. He's finding this hard."

"You're right." Samira nodded, the nagging guilt at what she was putting everyone through impossible to ignore. "You want a brew?"

"Please."

Returning with two mugs, the air rich with the glorious aroma of fresh coffee, she put them on the desk and sat down beside Ashok. "How're you going?" she asked.

"Okay. Bit tired. It's good we know when Bevajec's going to make his move. Makes the waiting easier somehow."

"I'll be glad when this is over, though I can't help feeling we're being played. Sahar's up to something. I just wish I knew what it was."

"I suspect we'll find out once this is over." Ashok yawned. "My money's on her being part of a plot to bring down the Guild."

"You reckon?"

"Nothing else makes sense."

51

"Thanks, Jaska," Samira said, making her way up to the make-shift podium. "Before we wrap up, I'd like say thanks to you all for agreeing to help."

She paused to look at the three new faces: Meraani and Lifueng, friends of Charlie Samarth, and Bedar's sister, Efia. Samira liked them, not least because nothing seemed to faze them, most likely because they had all had been long-serving members of the KDF. But she could not help thinking that it would have been good if they had been three or four decades younger.

"I cannot tell you how much I appreciate your support—"

"Only because Jaska hasn't told you how much he's paying us," a voice said amid laughter.

"—and no matter how much I've had to pay for it"—more laughter—"it's worth it. Now," she continued, "that the rest of the bad guys have arrived on schedule, I think we've done the briefing thing to death, and so, if there no more questions … Anybody? … No? Good. One last point. Watch out for the double cross. None of us think it's going to happen, but you never know, so remember the abort plan.

"Okay, the equipment for each of you is down the back. When you've checked it, food's down a level. We start moving out in an hour, so take your time. Jaska, anything else?"

"No, that's it."

"Okay, folks, let's give those Guild scum the shock of their lives. Good luck and good hunting."

Samira stepped down from the podium as the briefing broke up in noisy disarray, making her way to where Ashok was on watch, his eyes glued to the screens. "Where's Bevajec?" she asked.

"Son of a bitch is still at base camp."

"Total Guildsmen?"

"All up, thirty-two, just like Sahar said."

"Jeez, that woman's good." Samira smiled.

"She is. And Bevajec's following his script to the letter."

"If she's right, how long before they move out?"

"Let me see … Okay, Bevajec's recon teams will be in position a hundred meters outside the wire, waiting to guide the flankers in any minute now. They're due to cut their way through in a bit over two hours; the main assault party will follow them an hour after that."

"Claymores in place?"

"Yes, they are, Samira, so relax. It's going down just the way Sahar said it would."

"I hope so. Okay, Ashok. I'll go mingle, though it's the last thing I want to do. Make sure you keep track of Bevajec. I don't want to lose sight of him."

"I won't. Off you go."

One by one, they slipped into the night through a missing panel in an old storeroom backing onto the scrubby bush that was slowly reclaiming the base, chromaflaged blurs making their way into position along routes carefully charted to avoid Bevajec's holocams.

"Samira," Jaska radioed thirty long minutes later, "you're good to go."

"Thanks, Jaska." Samira started to push open the maintenance shop door, then paused and turned to Ashok. "I think this is when I find out if trusting Sahar was the biggest mistake of my life," she said, "so wish me luck."

"You can trust her," Ashok said, folding her into his arms. "You'll be fine."

"I hope so," she mumbled into his shoulder, her arms around his back, squeezing hard. "You keep your damn head down, Ashok Samarth," she said softly, pushing him away, her hand going to her face to wipe away the tears in her eyes.

"I will. I'm too pretty to die young. Now go!"

"I'm going, I'm going," Samira said, even though it was the last thing she wanted to do. "You ready?" she asked Buq.

"Ready." Buq nodded. "I'm right behind you."

Her skin crawling at the thought that David Bevajec would almost certainly be watching her every step, maybe even through the night sight of a rifle, she took a deep breath and stepped into the full glare of the floodlights rigged around *Bitsa*.

Come on, girl, she thought, forcing herself to walk across the apron to where Buq was waiting, *have faith. Sahar's been right so far.*

"Hang in there," Buq whispered when she got close. "Samira," she went on, raising her voice, "this piece of shit isn't going to fix itself. I want the weight off that port undercarriage so we can see why it's not retracting properly."

"Let's get her up, then," Samira called out, making her way across to the hydraulic lift, forcing her voice to sound relaxed, untroubled, the voice of a person with nothing more exciting than a late night and hard work to look forward to. It took only a minute to get the lift moving, but not before making sure the assault rifle was where it was supposed be, in a box clipped to the side of the lift along with a combat helmet and body armor.

Just in case, Jaska had said; just in case.

Jaska's voice broke into Samira's thoughts, making her jump. "All stations," he said. "Fifteen minutes. Charlie and Meraani have confirmed that the hostile flankers are in position, one group behind the crash rescue building, the other behind the operations center. Bevajec knows that Samira's on the apron, so we should see the assault group coming through the wire soon. Samira, Buq, get that lift cleared away."

Samira walked over to the lower crew access door. "Buq," she called out, sticking her head inside. "Damn thing's still not right. What do you want me to do? Okay, will do." She walked back to *Bitsa*. "Confirm undercarriage is down and locked. Roger … I'm disengaging the lift now."

Trying not to look too rushed, Samira worked fast to remove the lift that had taken *Bitsa*'s weight off the undercarriage. Then she stayed with it as the lift trundled its way away from the lander to the edge of the pool of light thrown by the floods even though it took every gram of willpower and courage she possessed to do so. Looking out, all she could see was darkness broken by the faint ghostly shapes of old buildings, and who knew what they concealed.

If Sahar was right, they were empty. But was she right?

Heart pounding, Samira waited as the edge lifted the last few meters; then, with a final check to make sure it would not foul *Bitsa* when it taxied, she walked back into the light, step by agonizing step.

"All stations, Jaska. Eight minutes. Samira, get back to the crew access hatch. But slowly."

"On my way," she replied, hoping the rush of relief flooding her system did not show. She had spent a lifetime out there on the apron, more often than not alone while Buq was busy inside *Bitsa*, lowering and raising the undercarriage in an impressive display of pointless activity.

Buq appeared at the hatch. "I think that's as good as that damn undercarriage is going to get," she called out, raising her voice. "I want to have a look at the auxiliary power intercoolers. Get them online while I fetch the test equipment."

"Yes, boss," Samira said, throwing Buq a mock salute.

"Watch it," Buq growled. She dropped onto the apron to walk slowly back to the maintenance shop while Samira climbed into *Bitsa*, leaving the access hatch wide open behind her.

Once she was inside, Samira's self-control vanished; she sprinted through *Bitsa*'s cargo bay before climbing up the ladder to the flight deck, fingers dancing across the system panels even before she dropped into her seat. "Jaska, this is Samira," she said, breathing heavily, adjusting her headset. "I'm in position. Auxiliary power is online. I have hydraulics. I've overridden the ground interlocks; the cannons are good to go."

"Roger, Samira. They'll fire wherever you point them, so try not to shoot the undercarriage off. Jaska, out."

Heart pounding, Samira sat and waited as the seconds ticked away, her eyes flicking across the screens.

"All stations, Jaska. The assault group is through the wire. It's now moving down the main access road toward the apron. We have the support group with Bevajec plus one Guildsman fifty meters behind them. Samira, stand by jammers. Lifueng, report when you have Bevajec visual. Jaska out."

Samira waited, barely able to breathe.

"All stations, Lifueng. Assault group is passing me now … They've stopped behind the office … They're moving again. Samira, you'll see them any second now."

"Roger." The breath hissed through her clenched teeth as the first of the assault group appeared, wavering blurs she could see only because she knew where to look. One by one, they drifted into sight, spreading out to work their way through the ground equipment spread out along the front of the storage building, wary, heads and guns swinging, two of the men dropping to the ground to set up what Bevajec's op order said would be light antiarmor missiles; their dial-a-yield warheads would be useless against *Bitsa*'s ceramsteel skin, but they'd be more than enough to blow the hatch she had left open off its hinges.

"All stations, this is Samira. I have the assault group visual."

"Samira, Lifueng. Support group has stopped. Have Bevajec visual!; I'll take him when you open fire."

"Roger."

"All stations, Jaska. On my mark, engage targets. Stand by … in three, two, one, now!"

Samira flicked *Bitsa*'s suite of jammers to transmit even as she slewed the cannons hard left, her thumb mashing the fire button to send shells ripping through the ground equipment sheltering the hapless assault group before they knew what was happening. The buildings behind were disintegrating in a blizzard of ceramcrete splinters. Her focus was so intense that she was barely aware of the heavy cracking thuds as the claymores set up around the flankers were fired, the screaming of the wounded filling the air.

Shame about your office, Jaska, she said under her breath as she gave the slumped Guildsmen—what was left of them—another salvo, walking the cannon shells from one side to the other and back again before slewing right to send a long burst of suppressing fire across the apron toward what was left of the Guildsmen tasked with securing the eastern perimeter. Their return fire wandered haphazardly through the air, the occasional round smacking into *Bitsa* with a metallic *whang*.

Then they too fell silent, and Samira lifted her thumb.

"Assault group is down; no movement; flankers are pulling back, I think," Samira said, aware for the first time of the fierce crackling of small arms fire underscored by the insistent hammering of heavy machine guns. "Buq, Ashok. You're clear to move."

"Roger," Ashok replied, "Moving."

"All stations, Lifueng. Bevajec is down; he won't be getting up again. Support group mostly destroyed; survivors are pulling back."

Yes, Samira thought exultantly. She watched Buq and Ashok emerge from the maintenance shop, hustling along close to the wall, rifles in hand. Dropping to their stomachs, they crawled behind the cover of one of the bunkers that flanked the base's extensive taxiways.

"Buq and Ashok in position," Ashok said.

Samira allowed herself a sigh of relief. Buq and Ashok now were protecting her exposed flanks. Contrary to popular belief, all landers were vulnerable while on the ground: get in close, and a simple demolition charge would blow a way in.

"Samira, this is Jaska. Charlie and I are pushing the Guildsmen toward you. Take them out as they go past." Jaska was breathing heavily. Samira knew why; the audio from the security holocams covering his sector racketed with the hammering of his machine gun. Without a loader, he would be working damn hard.

"Samira, roger."

"Ashok, copy?" Samira asked.

"Copy. We'll fire when you do, Samira."

"Roger," she said as the first hostile appeared, running hard across the apron. Torn between self-preservation and duty, he paused only briefly to fire his rifle at his pursuers before taking off again. Then came the rest. "Now!" Samira called, pushing the fire button, instinctively bracing herself for the appalling racket as the cannons unloaded. But nothing happened. "Jam, jam, jam. Go for it, Ashok."

Cursing under her breath, Samira wasted precious seconds confirming that the cannons had jammed, that there was nothing she could do to fix them, and that she'd be more use out on the apron. Galvanized into action, she bolted aft and down the ladder. Grabbing a rifle and helmet, she dropped onto the ceramcrete and scuttled as fast as she could toward the only cover at hand: *Bitsa*'s nose wheel assembly. Trying not to think how useless her cover would be if anyone started firing at her in earnest, she squirmed into position and joined Ashok and Buq as they poured rounds into the fleeing Guildsmen who were being flushed into the open by yet more claymores. Only one responded, turning to send a volley of fire in her direction, the rounds banging off *Bitsa*'s undercarriage and armor like demented hornets before Samira dropped the man in his tracks. The rest ignored her; with nowhere to hide, all they cared about was escaping from the hail of machine gun fire that flayed the air around them, the unlucky ones plucked out of step and thrown to the ground, arms and legs flailing, the air now thick with the screams of the wounded and dying.

"All stations, Jaska. I'm moving … ah, I … mov—"

"Say again, Jaska … Jaska?" Samira's heart pounded. "Jaska, do you copy?"

There was no answer. *Please, no,* she thought. *Please, no, not you too, Jaska.* She forced herself to focus; the attack was not over, not until the last Guildsman was dead or hotfooting it into the hills. "All stations, Jaska's down. I have command. Lifueng, when the last hostiles are past you, take Meraani, Bedar, and Efia and keep the bastards moving."

"Lifueng, roger."

"Charlie. Soon as you can, check Jaska for me. I'm calling the paramedics in now."

"Will do."

The instant the last Guildsman disappeared from the apron and into the night, Samira broke cover, waving Ashok and Buq toward her. "Can you secure the area? Get me a head count. We need to account for all thirty-two attackers. I'm going to see how Jaska's doing."

"Okay." Ashok nodded. "Let's go, Buq."

"Lifueng, Samira. Sitrep."

"Six Guildsmen heading north." There was a sustained crackle of rifle fire. "No, make that four heading north. We're in pursuit."

"Roger."

Samira ran on, going around the bunker, skidding to a halt when she saw Charlie on his knees bent over a huddled mass on the apron, its arm thrown out wide as if stretching for the black shape of the machine gun just out of its reach. "Oh, no," she whispered, please, no." She switched frequencies. "Medic One, where are you? We need you, now."

"We've turned onto the runway. One minute … Confirm the area is secure?" The woman sounded nervous.

Not that Samira cared. "Goddamn it," she barked, "yes, it is secure. We have a man down, so move it!" She broke into a run. "Charlie, how is he?" she called.

Charlie leaned back, his hands pressing a trauma pack onto Jaska's stomach, high up, just below his ribs; the pack was already a bloody mess. Saying nothing, he shook his head.

Samira crouched down on her knees beside Jaska, taking an outstretched hand in hers. "Hey, Jaska," she said softly, "what the hell do you think you're doing?"

"I'm so cold." Jaska's eyes opened for a few seconds, then closed again. "So cold."

"You hang in there, Jaska. The medics are on the way."

"Tell the buggers … they're too late. I think this is it for me."

"No, Jaska, no. Stay with me. Please, Jaska, stay with me."

"Sorry … can't … so cold."

How Jaska did it, Samira had no idea, but even as death approached, he somehow lifted a hand up to her face, running icy fingers down her cheek in a strangely gentle caress. "I'll miss you," he murmured. "From the day you were born, I've loved you … You know that, don't you?"

His words shattered her heart into a million razor-edged pieces, each one slashing lines of guilt deep into her soul. "Yes, Jaska, I do," she said. "I've always known that."

"I know." Jaska opened his eyes and looked right at her, a faint smile washing the pain from his face for an instant. "You've done well, Samira. I'm so proud of you … so proud." He smiled for a moment longer, then his eyes closed and his head slipped back with an awful finality.

"Stand back, please," a brusque voice demanded.

Samira started; she had not noticed the paramedics arriving. She let go of Jaska's hand and stood up.

"Goddamn it, Charlie, why?" she demanded, tears running down her cheeks. "Why?"

52

"Ms. Anders, thanks for coming in again."

"Did I have a choice, Lieutenant Levallois?"

"No, you didn't. This way, please."

Once they were seated in one of the interview rooms, Levallois took his time before saying anything. Is he gathering his thoughts or just trying to piss me off? Samira wondered.

"I must say, Ms. Anders," Levallois said at last, "this case has been a first for the Bellingen police department."

"How's that?"

"It's the first time we've been called to a crime scene to find what ... twenty-eight dead and four wounded. That's impressive. I'm not surprised the holovid news has been all over you."

"I'm sick of them," Samira said. "They've been calling it the Battle of Bellingen Base."

"We heard KNN paid you a lot of money for their exclusive."

"They did. So what?"

"That money is forfeit if we charge you and you're convicted. You do know that, don't you, Ms. Anders?"

Samira snorted derisively. "What, convicted for defending myself against a bunch of murderous thugs? Never going to happen."

Levallois nodded. "We'll see."

"It was self-defense, Lieutenant, and you know it. And like I said the last time, we were lucky, Lieutenant."

"We don't think luck had anything to do with it, Ms. Anders. Let me see … Yes, five of you just happened to be at KSS's base when David Bevajec and thirty-one Mendozan Guildsmen came looking to … Sorry, remind me. Just what were they coming to do?"

"If I've told you once, I've told you a thousand times: They came to kill me because of KSS's role in breaking up the Armato kidnapping, though I can't be sure about that. We piss a lot of people off in our business, Lieutenant, so take your pick. If you want to know for sure, then ask one of the lucky bastards we left alive."

"Oh, don't worry; we have. Unfortunately, they aren't talking."

"That's not my problem."

"No, I suppose not. Though we're not surprised; we didn't expect them to talk. They're professionals, and professionals never do. But you? We expect you to talk, Ms. Anders, and when you don't, it makes us ask why."

"Look. We've been through this over and over again. I don't know about you, but I have better things to do. I've told you how it happened, I've told you why I think it happened, and that's all there is to it."

The police officer shook his head. "You expect me to accept that, Ms. Anders?"

Samira rubbed eyes still red with grief, fatigue, and stress, all the color from her face washed out by the harsh white of the interview room's lights. "Yes, Lieutenant Levallois," she said, "I do."

"Five of you fought off thirty-two heavily armed attackers, killing twenty-eight and wounding four while suffering one killed and none wounded? Come on, give me a break. That sounds like cold-blooded murder to me."

"Don't forget my lander's 30-mm cannons."

"We haven't. Come on, what are you not telling me?"

Samira shrugged her shoulders. "Nothing."

"That's not true, is it, Ms. Anders?"

"I'm sorry, Lieutenant, but it is."

"I'll tell you this," Levallois said. "If I send a full forensic team back up to your base to spend a week tearing the place apart, I know we'll find plenty of evidence that there were at least … let me see, ten of you altogether, I'd say."

"Look, Lieutenant. How many times do I have to say this? Those guys came all the way from Mendoza to kill me, we fought them off, they lost, and we won. It's not my fault that they made the mistake of underestimating us. If you want to make more of what happened, then go for it. Those bastards killed the last member of my family three days ago, so you'll forgive me if I don't give a shit what you want to do."

"Hey, settle down, all right? I'm not the enemy here."

"Really?" Samira looked hard at Levallois. "And how do I know that?"

"That I'm not the enemy?" he said with a frown of indignation. "The uniform I'm wearing: Isn't that enough?"

"Ever ask yourself why we didn't call you when Bevajec's people attacked us?"

"No. Too busy?"

"We were busy, but that's not the reason." Samira shook her head. "Wake up, Lieutenant. We didn't call you because we don't trust you, not anymore."

"I think that'll do, Ms. Anders," Levallois said, sitting back in his seat, glaring at her. "You've said more than enough."

"Fine. Can we finish this, then? Or are you just going to keep asking the same damn questions over and over again?"

"I'm done with the questions." Levallois stood up. "I'll be back in a minute," he said.

"Why can't I go?" Samira demanded.

"Because I say you can't."

"What a jerk," Samira muttered as the man turned and left.

Levallois returned ten minutes later.

"About time," Samira said.

The man ignored her. "Right," he said, sitting back down. "We've had a look at everything, and it seems pretty straight-forward to us. This is how we see it: David Bevajec and his criminal associates attacked you, you defended yourself with weapons KSS is licensed to hold, the bad guys screwed it up, and they lost. In our view, you exercised reasonable force in defending yourselves, and so we will be recommending to the prosecutor's office that no charges be laid against you or your people. Have I missed anything?"

"No, Lieutenant Levallois, I don't think you have."

"Good, because my boss thinks committing any more resources to this case would be a waste of taxpayers' money, and I agree. You'll receive formal confirmation of what I've just told you once the prosecutor's office has signed off. Oh, yes, one more thing: I'll be releasing the crime scene today. Now piss off before I succumb to my instincts and change my mind."

"Thank you, Lieutenant Levallois."

"Come on, I'll see you out."

Samira and Levallois walked in silence out onto the street. There was an awkward pause for a few moments before Levallois spoke.

"I can't say you or your people have been very cooperative, Ms. Anders, but thank you anyway. Knowing the Guild, I'd be very careful for the next few months. I can't imagine they'd be too happy with what's happened."

"No, I'm sure they're not. And don't worry; we will be careful."

"Good. One last thing: It's not smart to say you don't trust us, not when we're talking about the Guild. You were lucky it was me you were talking to."

Samira looked hard at Levallois. "I hope so," she said.

"Goodbye, Ms. Anders." And with that, Levallois turned and disappeared back into the police station.

Samira watched him go, wondering if she should go with her instincts, instincts that told her that Levallois was a man she might be able to trust, a man who might be a useful ally. Maybe she should call him up in a few weeks, when things settled down.

If they settled down, she reminded herself as she flagged down a mobibot, because Levallois had been right. The Guild was not finished with her; of that she could be certain.

53

"Sahar," Samira said, waving the young woman into a seat, one of the few things to survive the deluge of cannon fire that had destroyed Jaska's office.

"Jeez, you trashed this place big-time," Sahar said, looking around the wreckage. "And you look terrible, Samira."

"You're too kind. But you are right; I feel terrible. It's been a rough couple of weeks."

"I suppose it has. I was sorry to hear about your uncle. I'm told he was a good man."

"He was. One of the best."

"I'm sure." There was a brief silence. "Right, can we get down to business?" Sahar continued, her voice brisk. "I'm sorry to rush you, but I don't have a lot of time."

"Be my guest; it's your meeting."

"Right, then. First, nice job nailing Bevajec and his team. You did well."

"Thanks to you. Nothing will ever make up for what's happened, but I suppose it's justice in a strange, warped way."

"Yes, it is," Sahar said. "Second, the people I work for would like to make you an offer."

"The people you work for? What people?"

"Um, well ... let's just call them the Organization."

"I don't care want you call them, Sahar. And who says I want an offer? Bevajec's dead, end of story."

"The Organization doesn't think the Guild will see it that way."

"No kidding," Samira said. "Why am I not surprised?"

"Trust me, it won't. There's no way the Guild's going to forget you, though it'll take them a while to decide what to do next. They are struggling to contain the fallout from Bevajec's death, but give them a few months and it will be business as normal. And when it is, the Guild will be coming after you."

"I was afraid of that."

"You should be, and that means you can't walk away. The day you went after my dad, you started something you cannot stop. And you can't run away either; humanspace is too small for you to hide, and the Guild will find you eventually."

"All right, all right, I get it," Samira said a touch peevishly. "You've made your point, so make your offer."

"There's much more at stake here than Bevajec. He was a product of the Guild. He worked for it from the day he left Klimath. The Guild nurtured him, protected him, and trained him to think the way the Guild thinks, to do things the Guild way. And he's not alone; if the Guild can produce one Bevajec, it will produce another."

"I get it," Samira said. "The Bevajecs might die, but the Guild goes on. Am I right?"

"You are. Bevajec is not the enemy; the Guild is. I've hated it for as long as I can remember."

"So you've said."

"And after everything that's happened, I hate it even more. It has to be destroyed, and that's why we wanted this meeting. We need people like you."

"No problem," Samira said, throwing her hands out wide. "Hell, that's what KSS and its clapped-out old lander are here for. You pay, we do. When do we start?"

"Come on, Samira, please. This is serious."

"Sorry," Samira said. "But who is this 'we' you keep talking about?"

"People who think it's time to change things on Mendoza, to put an end to the Guild, to put a stop to their plans for Klimath. One of our people thinks you'd be an asset."

"Who? Who thinks that?"

"No names, sorry."

Samira's eyes widened. "Detec—" she started to say before common sense stopped her.

"Who?"

"Nothing, nothing. Go on."

"The source says you're young and impulsive but have guts, are good under pressure, and can be trusted. With training, we think you can become the sort of person we need."

"Shit, you're serious." Samira sat back in her seat. "I thought I'd had my share of surprises for this month."

"We are serious, so here's the deal. Join us to free Mendoza, to stop the Guild's move on Klimath, to put an end to the criminal organization that killed your father, killed my father, killed Jaska." Sahar stood up. "That's my offer. I've said all I need to say at this stage, so I'll leave it with you. When you've had a chance to think about it, just let me know. A simple yes or no will do. But soon."

"Can you give me a week? I can't make this decision on my own."

"I know you can't," Sahar said. "Goodbye, Samira."

Samira watched Sahar's mobibot pull away. She did not need a week; she had made up her mind the moment Sahar made the invitation. But first she needed to talk to Ashok. She commed him. "Where are you?" she asked.

"Hi, Samira. I'm at my place."

"Any plans for this evening?"

"Not really."

"Good. There's something I need to talk to you about."

"All right. How about Carpenter's Bar at six?"

"I'll see you there."

"Okay, bye."

Barely a second later, Samira had another comm. "Oh, hi, Nat." Her best friend sounded very excited.

"Hi, Samira. How do you fancy going to a party tonight? It'll be a good one, so say yes, pleeeeease."

Samira's heart sank. Much as she needed to talk to Ashok, she had been neglecting her best friend. "Sure, Nat," she said, doing her best to sound enthusiastic. "Just tell me where and when."

"Meet me outside KNN at half past eight. We're going from there to Ruffino's."

"Wow," Samira said. "Ruffino's? I hope you're not paying."

"Hell, no. The boss is, thank goodness. You know that project we were working on?"

"The supersecret one?"

"Stop right there! Whatever you think you know, don't say it; it's not safe."

"Okay, okay," Samira said, wondering why Nat was being so paranoid. Nat had never said exactly what she was involved in but had revealed enough for Samira to know that it was about Mendozan organized crime moving into Klimath. She'd made Samira swear that she would never, ever tell another soul. And Samira hadn't.

"Anyway," Nat went on, "we've just finished, the program goes on the air next week, and we're going to celebrate and have the prelaunch function at the same time. It's so exciting, Samira. You've got to be there."

"Don't worry, I'll be there. Oh, can I bring Ashok?"

"Sure. You can crash at my place afterward if you like. I assume you'll be sharing a bed."

"No way, Nat," Samira said firmly. "Ashok can sleep on the floor."

"Right," Nat drawled in her best "I do not believe a word you're saying" tone of voice. "I've gotta go. See you later."

When Samira finished, Ashok sat silent for a while, not saying anything, one hand fiddling with his beer. "I was right," he said finally. "I said Sahar was part of a plot to bring down the Guild."

"You did," Samira replied.

"She used us. You do know that, don't you?"

"Yes, I do. We were her best chance of removing Bevajec, and I don't blame her for taking it. I would have."

"Even though it meant losing Jaska?"

"It breaks my heart knowing he's gone, Ashok, but it's not Sahar's fault that he was killed. It was Bevajec's, and he's paid for what he did. So now it's time to move on, don't you think?"

"You can be a coldhearted bitch, Samira."

"Yes, I can. And I have reason. The Guild has taken away the two people who mattered most to me, and even though we've killed Bevajec, the Guild still goes on. And while it does, everything we value is at risk."

"So Sahar keeps saying," Ashok said with a soft sigh of disapproval. "For all we know, what she wanted was to eliminate Bevajec, and she didn't much care how—or who—did the job. Everything else she's said could be a smoke screen to keep us from seeing what she's really up to." He paused for a moment before continuing. "Has it occurred to you that we might be pawns?" he said. "Pawns in a plot designed to put Sahar and her faction in control of the Guild by removing Bevajec?"

"What the hell are you saying?" Samira demanded. "Sahar's some sort of puppet master? Get real, Ashok."

"Hey! It's a possibility, Samira. Surely you see that."

"No, I don't. Sahar is only a kid. She's not the puppet master, she's the puppet. Someone else is pulling the strings."

"You might be right." Ashok nodded. "In fact, I think you are right, but it doesn't make me wrong. Sahar could well be part of a Guild power struggle."

"Is that what you think?"

"I wonder sometimes, but no, I don't. I'm sure she's used us, but if that's the price of keeping you out of Bevajec's hands, then it was a price worth paying. And why try to recruit us? We're tainted, and badly, so we're no use to her if she is part of some internal power play. No, I think she's on the level."

"And so do I, Ashok, I really do. But if she's the puppet, who are the puppet masters?"

"And do we want to throw our hand in with them when we don't know who they are? For crying out loud, one minute we're a small lander-for-hire business, the next we're part of a conspiracy to bring down the Guild."

"Not just the Guild. The Mendozan government as well."

"Not to mention whoever the Guild is using here in Klimath to help them get their foot in the door."

"Ah! Including the police maybe?"

Ashok grimaced. "You know perfectly well the Klimath police are part of the problem."

"Yeah, I do, the way Levallois reacted. And how much longer are you going to pretend what happened to you never happened?"

"You don't know what happened, Samira."

"I know that. And why? Because you won't bloody well tell me, that's why."

"No, I won't. It's my business, not yours. End of story."

"Wrong. It's not end of story. In fact, I think it's just the beginning."

"Look," Ashok said, starting to his feet. "I'm not going to sit here listening to you go on. I'm just not."

"Sit down, Ashok," Samira snapped, her voice crackling with sudden anger. "Sit down and shut up. I'm sick of this."

"Okay, okay," Ashok conceded, putting his hands in the air, "but only because it's you and you asked so nicely."

"Look," Samira said. "I'm sorry I lost it. Just hear me out; then if you want to go, you can. I won't stop you."

"Two minutes," Ashok growled. "That's all."

"Okay. Here's what I think." She took a deep breath. "You were an honest, law-abiding, ambitious KDF officer, minding your own business, when along comes an offer, an offer you can't refuse. I can't be sure, but I think the offer was delivered by one of Klimath's finest, and it involved threats of extreme violence to someone close to you. Exactly who was being threatened, I have no idea, but it had to be somebody you loved enough to make you steal gazillions of dollars worth of KDF equipment for … guess who? The Mendozan Guild, that's who. You stole those AIs, you got caught, they—whoever the hell they are—said keep your mouth shut or the loved one gets it, so you kept your mouth shut, did your time, and then you ended up working for a raggedy-assed outfit called KSS. So am I right?"

Ashok nodded. "Yeah, pretty much," he said reluctantly.

"Right, then. That gives you two choices. Either you let things slide, even if that lets the slimeballs who wrecked your life get away with it, not to mention letting the Guild destroy Klimath the way they've destroyed Mendoza, or you fight back."

"What is this, Samira?" Ashok said, eyes blazing with anger "It's all black and white for you, isn't it? Well, let me tell you, it's not that easy."

"But why?"

"Because it's my daughter they're going to kill!" Ashok cried. "My daughter. She's five years old. She's so cute, it breaks my heart every time I think of her, and there are people out there who say they're going to kill her if I step one centimeter out of line. And you know what?' he said, his voice razor-edged. "I believe them. I believe they'd kill my only daughter. Do you have any idea how it feels to be up against people like that?"

Numbed by the raw power of Ashok's agony, Samira could only shake her head.

"No, I didn't think so," Ashok said, gently now, though his voice was still choked with anger. "I didn't think so. And you know what's even worse?"

"No, what?"

"I didn't know who approached me, so I went to the police. That was a big mistake. A day later, Asha disappeared, only for an hour but that was enough. Everybody thought she had just wandered off, but I knew. So I did what they wanted me to, and you would have too."

There was an awful silence; it dragged on and on. Then Ashok spoke. "I'm not allowed to see her anymore," he said. "I'm a convicted criminal, you see. I might corrupt her. That's what they said, I might corrupt her, and that bastard family court judge agreed."

"They don't know? The families, I mean."

"No. Nobody does. My family doesn't, my wife's family doesn't, my friends don't. They just think I'm a greedy opportunist who was too dumb to stay out of jail. From the day I was found guilty, the only one who'd ever talk to me was my grandfather, and I never told him."

"Oh, Ashok," Samira said softly, "what a mess."

"You said it. So you see, I wasn't being cute with you or anything. I'm screwed, and that's a fact. I can't help you; I'm sorry. I won't risk Asha's life. Not for you, not for Sahar, not even if helping meant the end of every last criminal corporation in humanspace. I'm sorry, but that's the way it is. Now, are we done?"

"No, we're not, Ashok."

"For crying out loud, Samira, enough."

"No. We need to fix this."

"Why?" Ashok demanded. "Just keep your damn mouth shut and things will be fine."

"No, they won't. Don't you see? If we do nothing, the Guild will have this place by the balls inside five years. Is that the world you want Asha to grow up in? Corrupt, brutal, violent? Run by men like Bevajec, by men who get their kicks killing young women, women like me, like the woman Asha will become?"

"That's not fair," Ashok protested.

"No, it's not fair. But that's what's at stake here. If people like you can't be persuaded to get up off their asses, then the Guild takes over. If that happens, we're all screwed."

"You're right, but I can't be part of this. I can't."

"You can if we make Asha's safety a condition of our working with Sahar's people."

"How's that ever going to happen? Listen, Samira. This is the Guild we're talking about. Look what it took to fight them off this time, and even then we lost Jaska. We can't protect Asha."

"You might be right. But we shouldn't we talk to Sahar's people, see what they have to say?"

"You go ahead," Ashok said. "Just leave me out of it. You'll be fine; you don't need me."

"That's where you're wrong, flyboy."

"How?"

"I do need you, Ashok. I've gotten used to you; I don't want to do this on my own. I want you alongside me."

"Jeez, Samira, you make it hard for me, you really do. But what you're asking me to do is too much. I'm sorry."

Samira sat back and let the wave of disappointment wash over her. "Shit," she whispered. She had been so sure Ashok would join her in taking on the Guild. "Well, if that's your answer, that's your answer. I know when to give up."

"I'm not sure you do," Ashok said, "but you'd only be wasting your time trying to change my mind. I've said no, and I mean it."

"Yeah, yeah. I hear you." She paused for a moment before continuing. "Okay, fair enough. I don't know about you, but

I've had just about as much of Carpenter's Bar as I can take. How does a party in Morgannen sound?"

"Morgannen? You're kidding. Even if we catch the next maglev, we wouldn't be there until after eight."

"Good; that means we'll just make it, and Nat says we can crash at her place afterward."

"Whoa. What's the party all about?"

"A big bash KNN's putting on to celebrate finishing a project. Nat's invited us, and we'll be going to Ruffino's. Say you'll come. I don't want to go on my own."

"And I'm guessing you won't take no for an answer; am I right?"

"You are."

Ashok sighed. "Fine," he said, getting to his feet. "Let's go."

"Good man," Samira said, putting a hand on his shoulder as he forced a way through the crowd.

"Better be a damn good party is all I can say. It's a bloody long way to go for a free meal. Or are you just trying to seduce me … again?"

"Shhh!" Samira hissed. "Not so loud. Anyway, that was a one-time thing; it won't happen again. Besides, Nat's promised me her spare bed, so you will be on the floor."

"What? You're kidding! No party's worth that. I'm way too old to be sleeping on other people's floors."

"You're a miserable bugger, Ashok Samarth. Don't worry; it'll be a great party. Since when did a bunch of journalists put on a bad one?"

"I don't know," Ashok replied, sour-faced. "I've never met one I've liked enough to drink with."

• • •

Ashok and Samira turned into the landscaped plaza that fronted Klimath Network News's offices, a lush, well-lit oasis amid the ceramcrete buildings that made up Morgannen's city center. Here and there couples, families, and a few singles were making their way home after work.

"There she is," Samira said, walking over to Nat, a slight figure sitting on a low stone wall with her back against the massive bulk of one of the plaza's signature sculptures. "Hey, Nat," she called, "get your drinking boots on, girl, because—"

The world turned a searing white; a microsecond later, a giant hand smashed her onto her back, the air filled with a roaring hiss that faded away until she heard nothing but the ringing in her ears. She lay looking up into the night sky, wondering why one eye wouldn't open, why one side of her face was numb, why her body refused to do what it was told to.

Slowly, feeling returned to her face, and with it came pain and the screeching of alarms and sirens. Shakily she forced a hand to her cheek; pulling it back, she was shocked to see so much blood. "Oh, no, please no," she said, struggling to sit up, ignoring the protests from her abused body. "Ashok, Ashok!" she shouted at the body sprawled at her feet. "Ashok, get up. We've got to help Nat. Ashok!"

"Goddamn it," Ashok mumbled, lifting his head. "Everything hurts." He pushed himself upright, shaking his head. "You okay?"

"Cuts and bruises, I think," Samira said, trembling with shock and fear. "Come on, help me up. We've got to find Nat."

Samira took Ashok's hand, and together they climbed unsteadily to their feet. "Oh, no," Samira whispered when she saw the full the extent of the damage. The plaza was a blast-shattered ruin—the scattered dusty bundles were bodies,

Samira realized with a start—and beyond the plaza the lower floors of the KNN building were a gaping black hole spewing dust and smoke shot through with scarlet shards of flame, the remnant walls flickering blue and red as emergency response bots flooded in.

"Come on; Nat was over there," Ashok said.

Ignoring the pain, Samira followed Ashok as he limped unsteadily toward the shattered stump of the sculpture. "That's her," she said. "There, just by that rubble."

"We need a response bot, Samira. Nat's going to be in a bad way. Get one of them here, Samira, and make it fast. I'll see how she is."

Heart pounding, Samira did as she was told. "A bot is on its way," she said. "How is she?"

Ashok looked up from where he knelt beside Nat's bloody and broken body. "She's alive, just. But she's in a very bad way. We need that bot now."

"It's coming."

The two minutes it took for the bot to turn up lasted a lifetime, the bulky machine brushing her aside as it went to work on Nat. Five minutes after that, Nat's body had been bundled into a crashbag, limp and unresponsive, and the bot was taking her to the nearest hospital. "Natalie Qaaliba is stable," the bot's AI reported as it rolled away. "Please contact the Morgannen crisis management center for status reports."

"Thanks," Samira said, utterly crushed by the brutal indifference of it all.

"Our turn now, Samira," Ashok said. "They've set up a casualty station for the walking wounded over there. I think we need to get you looked at. You look like a madman's had a go at you."

"I just hope Nat's going to be okay."

"Let's get you fixed up, then we'll get to wherever they've taken her. Have you contacted her folks?"

"No; I'll do it now. Damn, they're offline. I've left a message."

"Come on," Ashok said taking her by the arm. "You've done all you can for the moment. It's your turn ... Oh, no ... Oh, please no," he whispered, stopping in his tracks.

"What is it?"

"It's ... ah, shit ... sorry, it's nothing," Ashok said, pointing with a shaky hand at a tiny shape with its arm outstretched, the hand open wide in a last appeal for help. "For a moment I was so sure that was Asha. Stupid of me."

"But who'd do this, Ashok?" Samira said, the tears pouring down her cheeks. "Who'd do this to a child? Who'd ..." Her voice trailed off. "Oh, no," she whispered. "Oh, no."

With an awful certainty, she knew just who had ordered this atrocity and why.

The jagged slash across Samira's scalp had been cleaned and stitched; now, with a clean bill of health from the casualty station, she sat beside Ashok in one of Morgannen General's waiting rooms, a room filled with the friends and relatives of the casualties from what was being called the KNN bombing.

"Samira Anders?" a voice asked.

Samira looked up. "Yes?"

"Marty, Marty Jensen. I'm one of the crisis support team. You're a friend of Nat's?"

"Yes, yes, I am. How is she? Tell me how she is."

"She's out of surgery and in a regen tank. Her condition is critical, so it's still too early to say whether she'll make it. We'll have a better idea how she's doing by the morning."

Samira tried to speak but could not, her throat choked tight; she just nodded.

"We've been in touch with Nat's parents," the man continued. "They are out-system and won't be here until tomorrow, so I think you should go home. There's nothing more you can do here, and both of you have been badly shaken up. Get some sleep, and we'll see you tomorrow. Hopefully we'll have good news for you then."

"Thanks, Marty," Ashok said. "We'll be back first thing. Come on, Samira."

And without a word, Samira let Ashok lead her away.

Samira had spoken barely a word since they'd checked in; she lay folded in Ashok's arms for a long time. "I know who did it," she said, breaking the long silence.

"You said you did. I didn't want to ask."

"It was the Guild."

"You can't be serious, Samira." Ashok pushed her back so he could see her face. "The Guild? How the hell can you know that? This is Klimath, not Mendoza."

"I know; that's what makes it worse. I can't be sure—Nat never said very much—but she did say she was part of a KNN team working on an exposé of the crime syndicates trying to move into Klimath."

"One them being the Guild?"

"For sure. I think the KNN guys must have found out more than the Guild wanted people to know."

"That's a bit of stretch."

"A bit of a stretch?" Samira snarled. "For crying out loud, Ashok, what's the matter with you?"

"Hey, take it easy. I'm one of the good guys, remember?"

"Sorry. It's very hard to …" She took a deep breath, letting it go in a long, soft hiss. "It's too much of a coincidence," she went on, "and I do not believe in coincidences as obvious as this one. Sahar says the Guild's moving into Klimath, and Nat said that KNN was investigating Mendozan organized crime syndicates doing just that. And when it comes to crime syndicates, which one is the biggest, the most aggressive, the most brutal?"

"The Guild."

"Exactly. I'm telling you, Ashok, this was the Guild's work."

"So the bombing's a message, an attempt to stop the program going on the air?"

"I can't prove it, but yes, I think so. I need to talk to the police. They have to know—"

"No!" Ashok snapped. "No, I don't think that'll be a good idea," he continued, his tone soft now. "If you're right, then this is way beyond them, and besides, we don't know who to trust."

Samira pulled away. "So what, then?" she demanded. "What are we going to do? Sit on our asses? Let the Guild turn Klimath into another Mendoza? Stand back while they blow innocent families apart? I know Klimath's no paradise, but for all its faults it's a decent place; it deserves better. We can't stand back, Ashok; we can't. We have to do something."

"Not now. This is not the time."

"So when is the time?" Samira shouted.

"Let's get through the next few days, then we can talk about things. I'm sorry, but this is not the time."

"This is the time, Ashok," Samira yelled. "I'm bloody sick of this; you can stick your damn head up your ass if you like, but the Guild's never going to go away. Never!"

"That's not fair. We will talk, just not now, okay?"

"Screw you!"

The insistent beep announcing the arrival of a new comm dragged Samira out of a nightmare-ridden sleep.

"What the hell," she grumbled. "Oh, no," she whispered when she saw where it had come from. "Ashok, Ashok," she said, shaking him awake. "It's the hospital. They want us in, now!"

"But it's the middle of the night. Why would … Oh, shit. Let's go."

Ten frantic minutes later, Samira and Ashok were at the hospital waiting for Marty Jensen. When the man arrived, he seemed to have aged ten years, his face gaunt and drawn.

"Come with me," he said. "It's been a bad night. We're not used to this sort of thing. In here," he added, waving them into a small room with armchairs and a small coffee table. "Please take a seat."

"Oh, no," Samira whispered as she sat down, almost overwhelmed by a terrible feeling of dread. "Please, no."

"Forgive me, Samira, but I'll come straight to the point. Nat died half an hour ago. The doctors and medibots did their best, but her body could not cope with her injuries. I'm so sorry."

Samira sat, the tears flooding down her cheeks, unstoppable, Ashok's hand crushed in hers. "Thank you, Marty," she said finally, her voice choked by the effort it cost her to stay in control. "We'll be fine. You've got a lot going on, I'm sure."

"Yeah, I do." Marty Jensen rubbed bloodshot eyes. "It's been terrible. This is the eighth time I've had to do this tonight, and I don't think it will be the last. Now, is there anything I can do to help?"

"No, Marty," Samira whispered. "Nothing."

"You sure? It's what we're here for."

"No, I'll be fine."

"Just call me if you need to, any time, okay?"

Samira nodded.

"Right, then." Marty got to his feet. "We're expecting Nat's parents about nine in the morning. Can you be here?"

"We'll be here," Ashok said.

54

"It makes you think about things," Samira said, running her hands through the grass that carpeted the ground, "being up here with Dad and Jaska."

"It does," Ashok said, dropping to the ground beside her. "Your father picked a beautiful place."

Samira nodded. Ashok was right; it was a beautiful place, all the more so because it was such a perfect day, the horizon a razor's edge slashed across the flawless blue of a cloudless sky, the early morning sun already hot on her face. She took Ashok's hand and, squeezing it hard, lay back, staring up into the sky. "I'm sorry, you know, for what I said the other night. I was a … I was a bit …" Samira's voice trailed off.

Ashok leaned over to look Samira full in the face. "Forget it," he murmured, and then he kissed her on the lips, a gentle, fleeting kiss. Before Samira had a chance to respond, he had rolled away onto his back.

"You've had time to think about things?" Samira said, breaking the long silence that followed.

"Yes, I have."

"So what do you think?"

"I think we're in the shit; that's what I think."

Samira grimaced. "Oh, yeah," she said, "right up to our necks, Ashok. What the hell are we going to do?"

"The smart thing to do would be to run as fast and as far as we can."

"Sahar says the Guild would find us. She said humanspace is too small for us to hide."

"I'm not sure about that," Ashok said, shaking his head. "The Guild's got enough to worry about, Karlos Armato for one. Why would they care about us? We're small fry."

"You know and I know that the Guildsmen are a vindictive bunch, Ashok, and we've just killed their top man, not to mention a shitload of their men. We're not small fry anymore; we're a serious embarrassment. They have to hunt us down. If they don't, they'll look weak, and that just makes things all the easier for Armato."

"Maybe, but that doesn't mean they'll find us. I don't care what Sahar says. Humanspace is huge, and there are tens of thousands of places we could hide, millions if you include orbital habitats, asteroids, and all the other places people live out their crappy, meaningless lives." The bitterness in Ashok's voice was obvious.

"True," Samira said, "but I hate the idea of spending the rest of my life looking over my shoulder, wondering if the person I'm looking at is a Guild assassin. What sort of life would that be?"

"An unhappy one, Samira."

"That's what I'm afraid of." She rolled over, pushing herself up on an elbow to look into Ashok's face. "We really don't have much choice, do we?" she said.

"No," Ashok replied, "I don't think we do. I don't want to spend the rest of my life running away."

"Me neither. But are you sure? If we stand and fight, there's no going back. You know that?"

"Yeah, I do. It scares me death to say it, but it's us or the Guild."

"Us or the Guild." Samira shook her head. "You should be scared to death, Ashok; I am. You and me, up against an organization run by people the likes of Juri Saarinen and David Bevajec. We might have killed those two, but that still leaves thousands more of the bastards. It's madness."

"Of course it's madness."

"It is, but only if we take on the Guild by ourselves, Ashok. And Sahar says we don't have to do this on our own."

"If she's to be believed. And who is the 'we' she keeps talking about, Samira? I know she came through for you, but I wish we knew more about the people behind her."

"We never will, never. Clandestine Organizations 101, remember? Whoever they are, they'll operate in cells."

"So we either trust her or we don't. Is that it?"

"No. We either trust her or we start running and pray that the Guild never finds us."

Ashok sighed. "You're right," he said, "but …"

"But what?"

"If it was just me, I wouldn't hesitate, you know that, but what about Asha? I can't just abandon her; I can't."

"I wouldn't ask you to, and we won't. We'll talk to Sahar, see what she says."

"I'm not sure she can help, not when we're up against the Guild. That poor little scrap killed outside the KNN building; that could have been Asha. Kerriann Jedani was her name; did you know that? She was six, that's all, six years old. Her only crime was being in the wrong place at the wrong time. What sort of sick bastards would do that?"

"What are you saying?"

"I'm fucked whatever I do; I'm completely fucked. You were right. If people like me won't stand up to the Guild, then Klimath's screwed. If we run, you and I are screwed. But if I stand up to the Guild, then Asha's screwed, and I have no right to do that."

Samira thought for a while. "We're not in this alone, you know," she said at last. She paused to think some more. "Okay," she went on. "Here's the only thing that works: We'll say yes to Sahar, but only if there's a way to protect Asha."

"Mmm." Ashok frowned. "I don't know about that. It has to be guaranteed, Samira."

"Yes, it does."

"When I say guaranteed, I mean a hundred percent. Not ninety-nine, one hundred. Can they do that?"

"I don't know," Samira said with a sigh. "Maybe they can."

"I'm not going to risk Asha's life, not for you, not for Klimath, not for anything."

"All we can do is ask. If you're not satisfied with what Sahar says, then we'll run and keep on running. There's got to be a chance Karlos Armato will destroy the Guild before it catches up with us."

"It's possible, I guess."

"Oh, it's possible," Samira replied, forcing a confidence she did not feel into her voice. "There's only one outfit worse than the Mendozan Guild, and that's Armato Industries. Takahashi said Karlos Armato was planning to go after the Guild."

"Great life strategy," Ashok said. "Keep running in the hope that the criminal psychopaths trying to hunt us down are killed off by another bunch of criminal psychopaths."

"That's the way it is."

Ashok took a deep breath in before letting it out in a long, soft hiss. "Okay, then," he said softly. "We'll ask Sahar and see what she says."

"It's deal," Samira said with a fleeting, uncertain frown as the enormity of the decision facing Ashok hit home, the long shadow thrown by the Mendozan Guild weighing heavy on her mind.

"Yes, it is," Ashok whispered.

For an instant it was all too much, and a wave of fear swamped Samira, raw and unchecked, fueled by the vastness of the task that lay ahead of them. Then, as quickly as it had come, it went, leaving her heart pounding at the walls of her chest. She leaned over and buried her face in Ashok's neck, the air sweet with the sun-warmed smell of him, his arms wrapping themselves tightly across her shoulders.

The Guild was just going to have to wait for another day.

ABOUT
THE AUTHOR

Graham Sharp Paul was born in Sri Lanka. He has an honors degree in archaeology and anthropology from Cambridge University and an MBA from Macquarie University. He joined the Royal Navy in 1972; he qualified as a minewarfare and clearance diving officer in 1977 and reached the rank of lieutenant commander before transferring to the Royal Australian Navy in 1983. Graham left the RAN in 1987. After working on a range of business development and corporate finance projects, he retired in 2003. Vendetta is Graham's sixth book. He lives in Sydney with his wife, Vicki, has three sons and two granddaughters.

Printed in Great Britain
by Amazon.co.uk, Ltd.,
Marston Gate.